AS VICTORY REIGNS, TREACHERY THRIVES

RENNO—Born among white men, the mighty Iroquois chief now lies seemingly on his death bed, struggling against the onslaught of the Big Sleep.

JA-GONH—Renno's proud and daring son, he must now follow the path of his valiant father, and unite two warring worlds in peace.

AH-WEN-GA—Beloved of Ja-gonh, her passionate beauty holds an impossible lure for the French monarch, but her indomitable spirit will fight to the death for her nation.

LADY ARLENE—Shrewd and ambitious former mistress to King Louis XV, she will teach her savage captive the ways of the courtesans of France.

GRAY FOX—Huron agent of the French, his evil plans only strengthen the swiftness and fervor of Iroquois retaliation.

DEBORAH—The first great love of the mighty Renno, she now sits at his sickbed, using her special healing powers to bring the great chief back to the living land of the Seneca.

The White Indian Series
Ask your bookseller for the books you have missed

WHITE INDIAN—Book I
THE RENEGADE—Book II
WAR CHIEF—Book III
THE SACHEM—Book IV
RENNO—Book V
TOMAHAWK—Book VI
WAR CRY—Book VII
AMBUSH—Book VIII
SENECA—Book IX

The White Indian Series
Book VI

TOMAHAWK

Donald Clayton Porter

 Created by the producers of
**Wagons West, Children of the Lion,
Saga of the Southwest,** and
The Kent Family Chronicles Series.
Executive Producer: Lyle Kenyon Engel

BANTAM BOOKS
TORONTO • NEW YORK • LONDON • SYDNEY • AUCKLAND

TOMAHAWK

A Bantam Book / published by arrangement with
Book Creations, Inc.

PRINTING HISTORY
Bantam edition / June 1982

2nd printing	*....... June 1982*	*4th printing*	*........ June 1983*
3rd printing	*........ July 1982*	*5th printing*	*... December 1984*

Produced by Book Creations, Inc.
Chairman of the Board: Lyle Kenyon Engel

ISBN 0-553-25039-6

Published simultaneously in the United States and Canada

Bantam Books are published by Bantam Books, Inc. Its trademark,
consisting of the words "Bantam Books" and the portrayal of a
rooster, is Registered in U.S. Patent and Trademark Office and in
other countries. Marca Registrada. Bantam Books, Inc., 666 Fifth
Avenue, New York, New York 10103.

PRINTED IN THE UNITED STATES OF AMERICA

H   14 13 12 11 10 9 8 7 6 5

TOMAHAWK

Chapter I

R enno, the white Indian adopted by the Seneca when he was an infant, dreaded each winter and the bone-chilling cold that swept across the land from the lakes that lay to the north and west. The chill seeped into his very marrow, and he was tired of fighting the elements, tired of the constant battle for survival in the raw wilderness of North America. Though this winter, his sixtieth, was coming to an end, he felt the full exhaustion of the struggle against it, and his sleep each night, as this night, was very deep and dream-filled.

In his dream, he found himself standing in a forest glade, and the season was no longer winter. It was summer now. The grass was deep and green and lush, the bushes were heavy with ripe berries, and the trees overhead were in full leaf.

Suddenly, Renno sensed rather than saw or heard someone approaching soundlessly through the forest. He knew instantly that his father, Ghonka, the late chief of chiefs, the Great Sachem of the entire Iroquois League, was appearing before him.

Ghonka, wearing the feathered headdress and buffalo robe decorated with dyed porcupine quills that were the symbols of his exalted rank that Renno himself had inherited when he had succeeded to the post of Great Sachem, came forward slowly. Inexplicably, he looked years younger than he had on the last day of his life before he had been murdered by the treacherous Huron half-breed, Gray Fox.

Renno looked hard at his father and was astonished. Although he could see Ghonka clearly, at the same time he found himself looking through a transparent face and figure. The trees in full leaf were plainly visible behind him. Renno knew that the spirit of his father had returned from the land of their ancestors to greet him.

"I bring greetings to Renno, my son, from the land that lies beyond the great river."

"Is it my father's wish that I join him there?" Renno asked.

Ghonka chuckled, and the sound echoed and reechoed through the vaulted forest. "When your time comes, you too will cross the great river. But that time is not yet upon us. It has not been easy for me to arrange this visit. So heed my words that I speak, my son."

"I heed them, my father," Renno replied, and bowed his head.

"You soon will face a crisis in your life," Ghonka said. "It is a crisis that will threaten your very existence."

"What must I do to overcome this crisis?" Renno demanded anxiously.

"Have faith in the Seneca, faith in the ancient ways of our people, and faith in one who knows little of our people and our ways."

Renno was bewildered by the contradiction in his fa-

2

ther's statement. It was well-known that spirits who returned from the afterlife were very touchy and imperious and, when examined too closely, were inclined to vanish.

"Ja-gonh, my grandson and your son, faces a crisis also—one that is far removed from the problem that will beset you. Do not interfere with him. Make no attempt to intervene for the sake of his salvation. He must solve his problem in his own way. Only in this way can he overcome the forces of evil arrayed against him and fulfill the destiny that the manitous have ordained for him!"

Renno absorbed all that was said to him, hoping he would remember it clearly when he awakened.

"To you, to your mother, and to your wife, I wish many days of peace." Ghonka raised his left arm high above his head in the traditional signal of the Seneca greeting and farewell. Then his image faded slowly from sight; only the trees remained. Then a cold wind blew and the forest itself disappeared.

Renno's dream had come to an end.

Major Henri de Bienville, the powerful director of French intelligence in the New World, stood pensively at a window at his headquarters in the Citadel, the great Quebec fort of stone and wood that stood at the top of a peak overlooking the majestic St. Lawrence River. He sighed deeply, and when he spoke, his voice sounded preoccupied.

"If I were an Indian," he said to his companion, "I would be just superstitious enough to be convinced that the spirit of Ghonka is protecting his Seneca and their allies in the Iroquois League. I would have no other explanation for it."

Gray Fox, a Huron brave who was the husky, half-breed son of the late Colonel Alain de Gramont, nodded slowly, his dark eyes stormy. "I am afraid you speak the truth, Frenchman," he said. "I thought our troubles were ended when I killed Ghonka with my own hands. But his son, Renno, the white Indian, who succeeded him as the Great

3

Sachem of the Iroquois, has performed miracles just as Ghonka performed them, and the son of Renno, Ja-gonh, is a fighting man of great skill."

"It's true that between them they destroyed our seemingly foolproof plans," Major de Bienville agreed. "I could have sworn that our Indian allies would defeat the Iroquois and the forces of the English colonists. But Renno and Ja-gonh turned the tide on us, just as Ghonka defeated us so often in the past."

Gray Fox laughed without humor. "I wonder if it would do any good if I were to go back down to the land of the Seneca and assassinate Renno."

"I would urge you to do just that if I thought it would be effective," Major de Bienville told him. "But unfortunately, it would turn out to be just another blunder. You have become quite an expert at blundering, Gray Fox."

The half-breed bristled. "You are annoyed because instead of becoming the primary force in North America, France is only slightly better than a second-rate power. But I refuse to accept the full blame for it. In fact, you're far more responsible than I am."

De Bienville wrenched his gaze from the river and turned, one hand on the hilt of his sword. "So I am responsible now, am I?" he demanded. "It strikes me that you go too far!"

Gray Fox reached for the bone-handled knife in his belt, and for a moment it seemed certain that a violent scene would develop, but Major de Bienville made a supreme effort and regained his self-control. "Enough!" he said. "If we fight, certain catastrophe lies ahead for both of us. We must work together now and in the future. Our careers are at a crossroads and we need to sustain one another, not cut each other down."

Gray Fox gradually subsided, too, and after his temper cooled, he extended a brawny hand. The major shook it, and they grinned a trifle sourly at each other. "We require the support of King Louis XV and of his prime minister, Cardinal André Fleury," de Bienville said. "With their help, we will have unlimited financial backing and can

4

rebuild for our next major attempt to dislodge the English colonists and disrupt their alliance with the Iroquois. But make no mistake about it, without the unstinting support of the King and the Cardinal, our careers are in ruins.''

"You exaggerate slightly," Gray Fox suggested.

De Bienville shook his head emphatically. "That, my ignorant friend, is where you are totally mistaken. I have spent years at the court at Versailles and I know what I am talking about. If we can point to solid accomplishments, if we can get rid of the English colonies and replace them with our own, we will become men of great importance at the court. On the other hand, if we fail, or if we do nothing, we will become as nothing. I will be transferred from the New World and will be given a minor post on the frontier in Lorraine. You will become just another Huron half-breed. No one will care what becomes of either of us, and we will have no future.''

Gray Fox retreated into his Indian shell, and his face became expressionless. Filled with hate for Renno and Ja-gonh especially, among all the Seneca, he was dedicated to humbling them, and to making the Huron—tribe of his mother—supreme in the New World. In addition, he craved the power and prestige that large battles would bring him. "I am willing to do whatever is necessary," he said in a slow, even voice, "but I cannot operate blindfolded. What manner of men are King Louis and Cardinal Fleury?"

De Bienville saw that he had taken too much for granted. His companion might be extremely forceful in the wilderness of North America, but he knew nothing of the key personalities of Europe and their peculiarities. "The King," he said, "is much like his great-grandfather, Louis XIV. Certainly he has inherited his great-grandfather's great vision that France can become the greatest and most powerful nation in Europe, and therefore, the greatest on earth.''

When Henri de Bienville spoke with earnest sincerity, as he was now doing, he was an impressive figure. Tall, lean, and swarthy, his complexion obviously Mediterranean and his features aquiline and Gallic, he spoke with the confidence of one who ranked directly below the governor-general of New France in importance. His powers were virtually unlimited, sufficiently great for him to countermand the orders of the general commanding the army of New France if he chose to do so. His dark eyes burned and his voice had a ring of authority.

Gray Fox leaned forward in his straight-backed chair and a sheen appeared in his dark eyes. "What are his *weaknesses*?" he demanded.

De Bienville was impressed in spite of himself. The half-breed was clearly capable of great shrewdness. "I wouldn't say that His Majesty has any real weaknesses as such," he said, "but he is known for one soft spot in his character. He is unable to resist the bewitchment of beautiful women."

Gray Fox nodded sagely. His own father had told him in detail how Louis XIV had been led into many ventures by his impetuous mistresses.

"He demands variety in women—and his demands are insatiable," de Bienville continued. "He is never satisfied and he loves to experiment. It would not surprise me if once he had conquered the world, he became a Muslim so he could enjoy a whole harem."

Gray Fox smiled politely.

The major did not waste time explaining his joke. "As for Cardinal Fleury," he said, "he is totally unlike either of his great predecessors. Cardinal Richelieu was a man among men. He loved power, lovely ladies, good food, fine clothes, and jewels. Cardinal Mazarin was a family man. He had five nieces, and he devoted his private life to providing them with suitable dowries and marrying them to rich and powerful suitors."

"What of the present prime minister?" Gray Fox prompted.

Major de Bienville shrugged. "Cardinal Fleury," he said, "has two great passions—the Church, and France. As the nation's Primate he does his duty to the Church. As for the rest, the state is embodied in the person of Louis XV. What Louis wants is what the Cardinal wants. He shares Louis's vision of greatness, and he goes a step beyond his master. To him, France already is great and the King can do no wrong. Fleury may be wise in dealing with other men, but he does not think of Louis XV as an ordinary mortal."

"He is not overly fond of drink perhaps?" Gray Fox suggested.

The major shook his head. "He has no vices, no weaknesses. He wants whatever it is that will further the cause of King Louis."

There was a tap at the door, and an extraordinary young woman entered without waiting for an invitation. Lady Arlene d'Amarante—a ravishingly beautiful redhead and the cousin of the powerful Duc de Guise—was, according to those who knew her, the coolest, shrewdest, most ambitious woman in all of France. A former mistress of Louis XV, she was visiting the New World to ascertain its assets for herself. In that role she deemed it expedient to be engaged in a liaison with Henri de Bienville. Certainly, she was the only woman in New France who could be a match for the ruthless and immoral attitudes of the two men who were engaging in such an earnest conversation. Opening her cloak and striking a pose in her snug-fitting, full-skirted gown of heavy white silk, she allowed the pair to ogle her for a time. "There is a faint hint of spring in the air today," she said. "I think the Canadian winter is about to end, so you two should be rejoicing instead of sitting here brooding."

Henri de Bienville knew her sufficiently well to cut through the artifice and reply brusquely. "We're discussing His Majesty and Cardinal Fleury," he said, "because we're hoping to gain sufficient favor with them to obtain their personal support for campaigns in the New World."

Arlene was intrigued immediately. "Why so much interest in the New World?" she demanded.

The major gestured impatiently. "France," he said, "is engaged in a long-term campaign against the English and the Spaniards to see which of them gains control of North America. He who becomes the master of this continent, with all of its natural riches, inevitably will be the master

7

of Europe. The kings of England and their ministers know it. The King of Spain knows it and so does his *Cortes*. And France must never be allowed to forget it. I intend to remind her of her glory, her destiny."

Arlene became thoughtful as she perched on the edge of his desk. "If you can win all of this continent for France," she said, "you will become a great and powerful man yourself, Henri."

"That is my intention," he replied.

"I was like so many others in France in my unconcern with the New World, until my curiosity overcame me and I journeyed there," she said. "What I have seen for myself convinces me that you do not exaggerate."

"That brings us back to our original discussion," de Bienville said crisply. "How do we win the favor of Louis XV and the prime minister?"

Arlene tapped slowly on the desk top with long fingernails whose color matched that of the large ruby ring that graced one finger. "I don't know how this can be achieved," she said, "but I see an opportunity to win fresh favor for myself at Versailles. A woman in my position, when she is wise, perpetuates her hold on Louis by sensing when he is growing tired of her and naming her successor. I neglected to do this, and consequently I have lost all influence, of course. I see a chance—perhaps—to recoup my losses."

She was speaking of matters beyond Gray Fox's comprehension, but the major listened with care to every word.

"You'll win the interest, the affection, and above all the gratitude of Louis by providing him with a new mistress," she said flatly. "A woman who will excite him and who challenges him. You will find, when he is satisfied, Cardinal Fleury is satisfied. His Eminence has an amazing ability to close his eyes to any wrongdoing on the part of the King, and he automatically approves of everything Louis does."

"So all we need to do," de Bienville said with a hopeless laugh, "is to find a fascinating, bewitching young woman—someone as lovely and as charming as you, Arlene, and I suppose we will search for her in the limitless forests of North America." He gestured toward the heavily wooded area on the far side of the St. Lawrence.

She smiled sympathetically. "It is a rather tall order, I am afraid," she admitted, "but I tell you the truth. Any other means you might use to attract the King's attention are far more likely to fail."

Gray Fox folded his arms across his chest and was lost in thought. "There is an Indian girl," he said finally, "who would be right as a gift for King Louis."

De Bienville and Arlene glanced at each other, and she nodded slowly. The idea was perfect! Knowing Louis intimately, she realized at once that the Huron's notion was inspired. The King enjoyed collecting women, so the erotic appeal of an Indian girl who would be unique in his experience and unavailable to anyone else in Europe would be overwhelming.

"Her name," Gray Fox said forcefully, "is Ah-wen-ga. She is a Seneca."

The major raised an eyebrow. "We were just discussing the Seneca a few minutes ago, you and I," he said. "I am slightly astonished to find that you—despising the Seneca as you do—would think that a woman from the tribe of Ghonka and Renno and Ja-gonh could be beautiful."

"She is very beautiful," the half-breed assured him solemnly. "She is the elder daughter of Sun-ai-yee, the sachem of the Seneca."

Arlene knew nothing about the relationship of the Indian nations and looked questioningly at Henri de Bienville as he began to chuckle.

He shook his head. "I still find it difficult to believe, Gray Fox," he said, "that a Huron would recommend a girl of the Seneca for this purpose."

Gray Fox did not lose his dignity or his aplomb. "She was abducted by Gray Fox," he said, "and unfortunately, she was rescued by Ja-gonh, who tricked Gray Fox and his Huron, but you must accept what I tell you as the truth. There is no Indian maiden in all of North America who is as lovely as Ah-wen-ga. Her face looks like it was chiseled out of stone." He turned his gaze to Arlene and inspected

9

her slowly, looking at her from head to toe. "Her body," he added, "has as much appeal to a warrior as does your body."

His bluntness amused her, but de Bienville was not yet satisfied. "You claim she is a great beauty, and for the moment I will take your word for it," he said. "But is she civilized?"

"She is a Seneca in all things," Gray Fox replied flatly.

Henri de Bienville turned to Arlene with a sigh. "I am afraid that whatever merits the girl might have, she'll be completely unsuitable for our purposes. She is a savage in all her ways. She has no sophistication, no knowledge of clothes, no knowledge of manners, and so on."

Arlene did not react pessimistically. "If she's bright," she said, "she can be taught how to dress and use cosmetics and can learn which knife and fork to use."

"She's very bright," Gray Fox declared.

"In that case," Arlene said, "I would be delighted to act as her instructor, and while I am at it, I can also teach her a few of Louis's secrets so that she'll be certain to please him in bed."

Henri de Bienville weakened in his resolve, but there were aspects of the idea that he still found unappealing. "Will this Ah-wen-ga go along with our plan?"

Gray Fox reluctantly admitted that initially he felt certain the girl would violently resist any attempt to train her to be the mistress of Louis XV. "However," he added, "I believe that in time, as she realizes how much she has to gain, she will not only accept the scheme, but will become an enthusiastic participant."

Arlene agreed heartily. "It stands to reason that when she sees how well-off she could be, she would be very foolish not to cooperate. I can't imagine any woman being less than totally cooperative in such a venture."

"Very well," the major said. "I still entertain grave doubts but I am willing to try, because if we are successful, the results will be so fantastic. So tell me, what is to be the first step?"

"First," Gray Fox said, speaking almost casually, "I

will abduct her." He spoke with certainty, allowing no hint of possible failure to enter his mind.

Arlene d'Amarante nodded in still greater enthusiasm. "Good," she said. "Then the three of us will sail to France with her. Not only will you win favor with Louis XV, but my own influence at court will be restored. I am so pleased that I decided to pay this visit to the New World!"

Night had just fallen, and in the main town of the Seneca, located beside a large lake set deep in the unending forest of what would someday become part of upper New York State, a peaceful quiet prevailed. Warriors who had been absent from the town on hunting and fishing expeditions had returned before sundown with their trophies of the day. The women had left the fields, where soon would be planted the season's vegetables. Now the high palisade gates were closed, and in the forests, sentries guarded against those who might steal on the town at night.

The hour of the evening meal was approaching, and everywhere there was a buzz of conversation. In the lodges, especially those of the junior warriors and those of the teenage maidens, the chatter was loud and incessant, before everyone settled down—in keeping with Seneca custom—to a subdued and decorous meal, virtually devoid of conversation.

The leaders of the Seneca dined at their own lodges. At the dwelling of Renno, the Great Sachem of all the Iroquois, there was a special excitement in the air, for this was to be an unusual meal.

Ena, Renno's adoptive mother and the widow of the great Ghonka, was noted for many accomplishments, among them her preparation of a savory venison stew that was said to be unique. This very day, her grandson, Ja-gonh, and her younger son, El-i-chi, had returned from a hunting trip with two splendid specimens of deer. Now the animals had been butchered and the meal had been prepared, with Betsy, Renno's wife, supervising.

11

The venison had simmered for hours on a low fire, and a secret blend of herbs and plant roots from the forest had been added to it. About an hour before, generous quantities of corn, squash, and beans, the three principal vegetables of Indian fare, also had been added. Now the time of testing had arrived.

Renno, a feathered bonnet of his high rank upon his blond-gray hair, the buffalo robe of the Great Sachem around his shoulders, was served first, and as was customary, he took the first mouthful. He scooped up a goodly quantity onto his wooden spoon, and after tasting it, a slow grin spread over his face.

Then Ena, trying not to be too critical, tasted it and nodded in approval, her white hair bobbing up and down. Her granddaughter, Goo-ga-ro-no, also tasted the dish.

Goo-ga-ro-no had recently returned home after running away with a Frenchman who had taken her to Quebec and had abandoned her. Because she was white by race, she had thought of herself as English or French and had despised the Seneca and all their ways. Now, however, she felt that all that was Seneca was good; all that was not Seneca was bad. Her face expressionless, she folded her hands in her lap.

El-i-chi, wearing the feathers of a Seneca war chief, helped himself to a large gourd of the stew, tasted it, and chuckled aloud.

At last it was the turn of Ja-gonh, whose hair was as light as his parents', his eyes as deep a shade of blue, and his skin as tanned. On either side of his scalp lock, he had daubed the green and yellow paint of a senior warrior of the nation, and he was at ease, his posture naturally erect. He tasted the stew, and after looking at Renno for permission to speak, he turned to his mother. Betsy, like her husband, was white. The daughter of a prominent Virginia citizen and militia head, she had astonished her family by adopting the manners of the Seneca and becoming one of them after her marriage. Renno was a true Seneca in every sense of the word because he had been adopted practically at birth by Ghonka and Ena after a Seneca raid on a frontier town. He had known no other parents and no other home. Betsy, however, had come from a civilized community, and her adaptation to the ways of the Seneca was a little short of miraculous.

Ja-gonh inclined his head respectfully and then spoke in a deep solemn voice. "Ja-gonh, son of Renno," he said, "rejoices over the stew that Betsy, his mother, has made. He has won a wager made with his esteemed uncle, El-i-chi, and another with his sister, Goo-ga-ro-no. They were foolish enough to wager that the stew would be inferior to that made by Ena, the grandmother of Ja-gonh. The stew is identical, and I defy anyone present to say that it is inferior to that which is cooked by Ena herself."

Only Goo-ga-ro-no, being a woman, knew the secret of the similarity of tonight's delicious dish to the venison stews prepared by Ena. It was obvious to her that her grandmother had given her mother the recipe. This was perhaps the highest compliment one woman of the Seneca could pay to another. A recipe was passed from mother-in-law to daughter-in-law only when the older woman completely approved of the younger, and it was then promptly committed to memory. Betsy accepted the praise gracefully, inclining her head for a moment; then she looked across the open pit where the fire was located, and her eyes met her mother-in-law's.

There was no need for words between them. Ena knew that Betsy was expressing her gratitude and was overjoyed because her acceptance by the Seneca was so complete.

The talk surged, and Renno continued to eat in complacent silence. His manners were totally those of Ghonka, his father. He spoke only when he had something of significance to say, and then everyone fell silent. The Great Sachem never spoke lightly or in vain.

So when he cleared his throat after he had emptied his gourd, El-i-chi looked around the circle, quickly instructing members of the family to be still. A silence fell on the group. Renno's face was wooden but a twinkle in his eyes

13

betrayed him as he handed his bowl to his wife. "I believe I will eat more," he said. "Hunting today has given me a sharp appetite."

Betsy smiled happily as she refilled his gourd, and their hands touched when she gave it to him. Both prolonged that touch. They had been married for more than thirty years, yet their love was as fresh as it had been when they had first married.

The atmosphere was relaxed and they enjoyed themselves thoroughly. If the sister of Renno and El-i-chi, Ba-lin-ta, and her husband, Walter, who had come to the land of the Seneca from Fort Springfield, had been present, their joy would have been complete.

Only Ja-gonh was neither happy nor at ease. His mother sensed his restlessness, and so did his grandmother. Neither knew the cause, but aware of Ja-gonh's forthright personality, they knew he could not keep his thoughts to himself.

So the mood of those who had dined in the family circle of the Great Sachem changed abruptly when Ja-gonh, observing that his father had finished his stew, said suddenly, "My father, I wish to have words with you on a matter of grave importance that is close to my heart."

"Speak," Renno said as he put aside his gourd, the meal having been completed.

"As I sit here," Ja-gonh said, "I am aware of the presence of the manitous who watch over us and guide us. I am aware, also, of the presence of Ghonka, my grandfather, the Sachem of Sachems. He dwells now in the land of our ancestors and he, too, keeps watch over us. Ghonka is sad, and the manitous share his sorrow." Renno nodded thoughtfully.

Ja-gonh, feeling compelled to bring the entire problem into the open, squared his shoulders and braced himself before continuing.

"When Ghonka was killed in cold blood by a merciless foe," he said, "Ja-gonh swore to avenge his death. Ja-gonh took an oath to find and kill the murderer of his beloved grandfather. Many moons passed before the identity

14

of the murderer was fully known. Now, however, we know he was killed by Gray Fox of the Huron. Gray Fox is at liberty, and lives as he pleases in safety. Ja-gonh sits with his parents before a warm fire and eats a venison stew prepared by his mother. This is not right."

Ena interrupted him and spoke solemnly; it was right and just for her to intervene because she was Ghonka's widow and, therefore, was better able to speak on behalf of his spirit than was anyone else in the circle.

"Ja-gonh speaks the truth," she said. "He did indeed take such an oath while the dead body of his grandfather was still warm. Ghonka rejoiced, knowing that justice would be done. Now his spirit grows restless because his killer has not yet been punished."

"It was my destiny," Ja-gonh declared, "to come to the aid of my people in their recent war with the Indian allies of the French. Now that the war has been won, I can rest no longer. Now I must find Gray Fox. I must follow him, if need be, to the far ends of the earth. When I find him, I must kill him, and only then will the spirit of Ghonka truly rest in peace."

It was Renno's place to approve or disapprove, and he did not hesitate. "The grandson of Ghonka," he declared, "speaks words that come from his heart. He must not be denied the right to obtain vengeance for which all of us long." He rose slowly to his feet, placing the buffalo robe of high office more firmly around his shoulders.

Betsy braced herself for the inevitable.

Renno raised his right arm and faced his son, his palm outstretched. "Go, Ja-gonh, son of Renno," he declared. "May the manitous watch over you. May the hawk that is the special intermediary for the men of our family, between us and the manitous, lead you to Gray Fox. May you cut out his heart, his lungs, and his liver. May you condemn his soul to rot for all time in the land of the damned. May you succeed in your enterprise, and may you come back to us in safety."

Ja-gonh bowed his head as his father spoke, and when Renno was done, he picked up the bow and arrow that

15

rested on the ground beside him. He looked briefly at his grandmother, then at his mother and sister, and finally at his uncle and his father, but he addressed none of them.

Indians were wise beyond measure, Goo-ga-ro-no told herself, to conceal their feelings in times of crisis and emotional stress. Her mother and grandmother would weep if there was a prolonged farewell, and Ja-gonh might be so moved that he would behave in a less than manly manner. It was best that he folded his arms across his chest, bowed stiffly to Renno, and left the family circle.

Even Betsy did not follow him with her eyes, although she had no way of knowing when—or whether—she would see him again in this world.

A certain standard of conduct was expected of the Great Sachem, even within the confines of his immediate family. Renno put aside his empty bowl and inclined his head slightly toward his wife. "It would please me," he said, "to eat some berries sweetened with the sap of the maple tree."

Betsy nodded to her daughter, and Goo-ga-ro-no hastened to fetch their dessert. All of them ate tranquilly; no stranger looking in on them would have guessed that they were under great emotional strain.

After they finished the meal, they went about their separate business, and Renno quietly went into the house and withdrew to the chamber where he and Betsy slept. With no one present to see him, it was no longer necessary for him to maintain a facade, and he wearily removed his elaborate feather headdress, and, shrugging out of his buffalo-skin cloak, he hung it on a wall peg. Then he stretched out on the bed.

It was strange, but every muscle, every bone, every sinew in his body ached. He had enjoyed the robust good health of the physically blessed for more than sixty summers, and never before had he been so tired. Never before had he been forced to expend so much energy keeping up a front so that no one would guess that he was ailing.

It was difficult for him to admit to himself that he was ill. What bothered him most was that he had no idea of the nature of the illness that plagued him. But he had no intention of mentioning the sickness to Betsy, who would force him to consult the white man's physicians, or to Ena, who would insist that the principal medicine man of the Seneca visit him and minister to him.

He was determined to fight his ailment by himself. Under no circumstances would he give in to it; that was the correct Seneca attitude, especially so for the son of Ghonka.

Sun-ai-yee habitually fell asleep in a corner of his lodge after eating the evening meal, but it was his privilege as sachem of the nation and his right as an aged war chief to do as he pleased. He hated to admit that he was very old, and his wife, Talking Quail, knew better than to remind him of it.

His elder daughter, Ah-wen-ga, took great pains to foster and keep alive the illusion that Sun-ai-yee was still in the prime of life. Certainly, it could not be denied that he had only recently beaten back the Huron and the other foes of the Seneca when Gray Fox had besieged the town. Sun-ai-yee had won one of his more notable victories, and the entire nation recognized his prowess.

His younger daughter, White Deer, was not impressed. Now in her early teens, she took nothing seriously except the attentions of several junior warriors whom she fancied. She, unlike her mother and sister, who moved quietly about the house in order that they not awaken Sun-ai-yee, spoke up loudly when she informed her mother that she intended to go to the far side of the town that evening.

Talking Quail shook her head. "We have no need for water from the well," she said, "and I have enough stones to wash our clothes tomorrow."

White Deer was prepared to argue the point and began to protest.

Ah-wen-ga knew that her sister was just seeking an excuse to spend a short time flirting with boys, and she glared at her. Before she had had an opportunity to whisper a sharp remonstrance, however, a tall figure loomed in the entrance to the house.

Even before Ah-wen-ga turned to see who was there, she sensed the presence of Ja-gonh.

Ja-gonh was instantly aware of her proximity, too. It was miraculous to him—something that defied reason, as the acts of the manitous defied reason—that he and Ah-wen-ga should feel about each other as they did.

As members of their families well knew, they had long been attracted to each other. As only they themselves were aware, after he had rescued her from Gray Fox, who had abducted her, they had slept together. What he found amazing was that their intimacies had merely whetted their appetites. Their thirst for each other was unquenched and unquenchable, and they had the sense to know that it was dangerous to see too much of each other before they were married.

They had discussed marriage, but postponed it by unspoken agreement. First things came first, and there had been too many immediate problems to solve.

Ja-gonh caught a glimpse of Sun-ai-yee napping in a far corner of the room, his back propped against the wall, so he did not speak, but instead raised a hand in a greeting to the mother of the girl he loved. Talking Quail, a native of a small tribe near the Mississippi, believed—unlike the Seneca—in expressing her feelings freely at all times. She beamed at Ja-gonh, making no secret of her liking for him. The truth of the matter was that she was hoping, desperately but privately, that the romance between them would flourish. Ah-wen-ga was the daughter of the sachem of the Seneca, after all, so she could rise still higher to the very top of the Indian society's ladder only if she became the wife of Ja-gonh, the son and grandson of the leader of all of the Iroquois.

Ah-wen-ga realized, as she looked at the young warrior, that he was about to depart from the town of the Seneca on a long journey. He was clad in a loincloth and shirt of buckskin, on his feet he wore moccasins of tough buffalo hide, and his head on either side of his scalp lock had been

18

freshly shaved. War paint was smeared on his face and torso, so she knew, too, that he was leaving on no ordinary mission.

Over his shoulder he carried a bow and a quiver of arrows, and from his belt were suspended his tomahawk and knife. He was capable of wielding all of these weapons with deadly accuracy, and Ah-wen-ga realized that he felt compelled to carry only Indian weapons on his mission. His grandfather had been the finest of the Seneca, the leader of the nation for more than a quarter of a century, and it would have dishonored his spirit to kill his murderer with any weapons other than the traditional ones of the Seneca.

Sun-ai-yee opened his eyes, blinked, and instantly was wide-awake. He, too, regarded Ja-gonh's choice of weapons as significant, and he immediately guessed the reason he was carrying them. "Ja-gonh," he said, "goes into the wilderness to seek and kill the Huron who murdered the Great Sachem, Ghonka."

Ja-gonh nodded but did not speak.

"May your mission succeed," Sun-ai-yee continued, struggling to his feet and exchanging a clasp of wrists with the younger man. "May your foe and the foe of all the Seneca suffer ten thousand deaths."

Talking Quail, who followed her own impulsive traditions, ignored the taboos of the Seneca and said, "May you suffer no harm, Ja-gonh, and return in health and in safety."

Sun-ai-yee and his elder daughter exchanged a rapid, annoyed glance. It was impossible for either of them to silence Talking Quail, so Ah-wen-ga did the next best thing and swiftly guided the visitor outside the building. The night was cool, and there was the hint of wood smoke from many supper fires still lingering in the night air. But the young couple were aware only of each other. Inevitably, when they were together, everything else faded from their mutual consciousness.

Ja-gonh stood very still and feasted his eyes on Ah-wen-ga. She recognized his admiration, and blossomed, looking

19

radiant. He spoke softly. "It grieves me to leave you," he said, "but it is a greater grief to know that my vow has not been fulfilled."

Ah-wen-ga knew what was expected of her and reacted accordingly, with simple courage. "It is right that you go and avenge the death of your grandfather," she told him.

He continued to look at her intently, as though memorizing every detail of her features. "I do not know," he said, "how long I shall be absent. If the manitous are good to me, I will return very soon. If they have lost patience with me, my quest may take much longer."

"You will go to the land of the Huron?"

He nodded. "I will seek the half-breed who is called Gray Fox in the town of the Huron that lies near the city that the French call Quebec. That is where Gray Fox makes his home, and I hope I will find him there. If I do, I shall make short work of him, and I shall return soon. If he is not there, however, I have no way of knowing how long it will be before you and I meet again."

She took a deep breath. "However long it may be, I will be here waiting for you."

"It is my wish," he said, "to ask you a question."

Ah-wen-ga nodded and folded her arms across her breasts. "Ask," she replied, "and I shall answer."

To Ja-gonh's surprise, he felt his heart pounding as beads of perspiration stood on his forehead. In spite of his relative youth, he had already acquired a reputation for phenomenal courage. It was said that he could face any enemy, be it a wild animal or a score of heavily armed Indians, without flinching. Now, however, he was so frightened that he had to gather his wits and steady himself before he could speak again. "When I return," he said, "it is the greatest desire of my life to marry you. Ponder well on this while I am absent and give me your answer when I return."

Ah-wen-ga was not surprised and remained seemingly cool and serene. "There is no need for me to ponder the question any further," she said. "I have thought about it long and hard, to the exclusion of all else since we returned to the land of the Seneca, and I know in my mind and in my heart that there is nothing I want as much as I want to become the wife of Ja-gonh."

He was so elated that he actually smiled.

The chemistry that drew them together whenever they were near each other worked its usual magic and they felt an irresistible pull. They started toward each other, and then, with one accord, they stopped. They had no need for words; both knew that they had to exercise supreme self-control now, at this juncture, or it soon would be too late. Once they touched, the magnet that tugged at both of them would become too powerful to resist.

Ja-gonh took a half-step backward. His fists clenched.

Ah-wen-ga stood erect and averted her gaze. There was silence between them, and then the danger was past. They recognized it simultaneously, and she smiled as she bowed her head. "I will pray that the manitous send a wise and ferocious hawk to guide you in your mission and to return you safely to me."

"When I return to the land of the Seneca," he said, "I shall speak with Sun-ai-yee and ask him for the hand of his daughter in marriage. You may tell him to expect such a visit."

"I will tell him," Ah-wen-ga replied, her voice filled with pleasure. Their betrothal had become official as a result of his few simple words.

There was no more to be said, and like all Seneca, they knew better than to prolong their farewell. Ja-gonh raised his arm in salute and then withdrew.

Ah-wen-ga followed him a short distance so she could watch his departure. He walked with the sturdy, graceful stride of a senior warrior, and once outside the gate, he broke into the famous Seneca trot, a slow running pace that, like all men of the tribe, he could maintain for many hours. He swept past the fields, soon to be planted with corn and other vegetables, and without a backward glance, he plunged into the deep sea of trees at the far end of the fields.

Ah-wen-ga watched him with seeming impassiveness.

She knew that his mission was dangerous in the extreme, and she recognized the possibility that she might never see him again, but she did not dwell on the pessimistic. He was Ja-gonh, whom she loved, so she was confident the manitous would offer him their protection and would return him safely to her. Turning on her heel, she reentered the small house of her parents.

Talking Quail looked at her anxiously, ready to ask a score of questions, but Ah-wen-ga swept past her and went directly to her father. "When Ja-gonh returns from his mission," she said, "he will ask Sun-ai-yee for the right to marry me."

Talking Quail could not hide her joy, and clasped her hands together.

But the grizzled old warrior knew what was expected of him, and played his role to the hilt. "I will give thought to this matter," he announced, "and I will decide whether he who wishes to marry my daughter is worthy of her."

White Deer almost destroyed the solemnity of the moment by giggling. Her father and her older sister glared at her. Then Ah-wen-ga immediately retired to her bed, for she was so filled with emotion that she knew she could not speak even to her mother or sister.

Ja-gonh, his pace unvarying as he made his way through the deep woods, had to admit to himself that in spite of the seriousness of the mission that took him away from home, he was enjoying himself. Like his father, he was at home in Boston and Fort Springfield and Norfolk. But there was no place in the world he loved as he loved the trackless wilderness. This was his real home, his real love. Others might think that he was traveling through uninhabited territory, but that was not so. Everywhere he saw signs of animals: a pair of deer had passed this way less than an hour earlier, a bear had paused to gather wild honey from a hive, and there were signs invisible to the neophyte that indicated raccoon, opossums, and rabbit had also been in the vicinity recently. He recognized the many varieties of birds that lighted on the upper branches of towering trees

22

to rest, and he knew instinctively, whenever he passed within the shooting distance of an arrow, the location of a Seneca sentry. He exchanged no greeting with the sentries because that was not his nation's way. He had his work to do, the sentries had theirs, and there was no need for an exchange between them.

Neither then nor at any later time did he know how close he came to a headlong encounter in the forest with Gray Fox and the small band of Huron that the half-breed had taken with him for the purpose of abducting Ah-wen-ga.

The northbound Ja-gonh and the southbound Gray Fox passed within a scant mile and a half of each other. Had they been closer, events of the coming months would have been far different, but it was not their destiny to meet. The manitous apparently had other thoughts in mind, other plans that they wished fulfilled.

Gray Fox, traveling far more cautiously because of his desire to avoid Seneca sentry patrols, was quite pleased with himself. In fact, he could freely admit what he could never tell Major Henri de Bienville or his French mistress. Far more was at stake than kidnapping and training the young woman who would win the favor of King Louis XV for the plotters.

Gray Fox conceded to himself that just as he had hated Ghonka, whom he had killed in cold blood, so he despised Renno, his father's implacable foe, and Ja-gonh, who had thwarted his efforts repeatedly in the past. Gray Fox expected that Ja-gonh and Ah-wen-ga had reached a mutual understanding, and if they were not formally betrothed, surely they soon would be and, left to their own devices, undoubtedly would be married by the end of the summer. It gave Gray Fox a deep feeling of gratification to know that he was going to spoil those plans. His revenge against Ja-gonh was only partial, to be sure, and would not be complete until they finally met in a showdown duel to the death, but in the meantime, he realized he would be causing great unhappiness for Ja-gonh, and for that much he was thankful. Beyond that, he could look forward to the rewards of power, wealth, and prestige. Vengeance would be sweet indeed, but the material gains would be even more lasting.

The task that awaited him was simple, and he was not concerned about bringing it off successfully. His mind dwelled instead on the anguish that Ja-gonh would feel when he realized that the woman he intended to wed had vanished once again.

Chapter II

It was said by the aged seers of both tribes that the Seneca and Huron had been one people in the far distant past. Certainly the similarities between the two nations were striking. They spoke the same language, they had almost identical customs, and they even worshiped the same manitous.

So it would have been a simple matter for Ja-gonh to change his war paint and to pose as a Huron brave when he arrived at their main town, located on the banks of the St. Lawrence River about two or three hours by boat from the French town of Quebec. But he recalled all too vividly the complication that had ensued when he had adopted such a disguise on his first visit to the town. It was better, he decided, far better, to present himself openly as a senior warrior of the Seneca. His nation was now at peace with the Huron, and despite their recent conflicts, his life would not be endangered. In fact, the bold maneuver he contemplated was so startling that it might have beneficial effects.

He made no particular attempts to conceal himself in the forest as he approached the town of the Huron, and when he heard drums throbbing, he could easily guess the message they were sending: a strange warrior of the Seneca was abroad in Huron territory and was drawing ever nearer the town.

He found a canoe tied to a stake on the south bank of the mighty St. Lawrence River, and, borrowing it, he crossed the river in broad daylight. The thumping of drums became more insistent as he paddled across the river.

A larger-than-usual detail of warriors guarded the palisade of the town, and it was not accidental that a war chief emerged and greeted the intruder as he stepped ashore. "I come in peace," Ja-gonh said, presenting the war chief with a strip of leather to which a number of shells had been sewn.

The war chief inspected the wampum, was satisfied with it and, grunting his acceptance, thrust it into his belt.

"Take me to the sachem of the Huron," Ja-gonh declared.

Within a few minutes, he was admitted to the presence of a middle-aged Indian with a chiseled face and bright, beady eyes that peered at him beneath heavy lids.

"You are welcome in peace," the chief of the sentry detail said, and led him before the sachem of the tribe.

Ja-gonh faced the older man unflinchingly. "I am Ja-gonh," he said, "son of Renno, the Great Sachem of all the Iroquois. I seek him whose mother was a Huron and who is known here as Gray Fox." He was prepared, if need be, to explain his reason for his search. No Huron, he felt certain, would dishonor his nation and himself by trying to intervene in a personal blood feud, but the chief shook his head and sounded genuinely regretful as he said, "Gray Fox is not here. He left this place on private business several days ago."

Ja-gonh made no attempt to hide his disappointment. "Where may I find him?" he wanted to know.

The Huron leader shrugged. "He absented himself on personal business, not the business of the Huron nation. I cannot tell you where he has gone, nor can I tell you when he will return."

"Might he be found in the city of the French?"

The Huron pondered the question and tried to answer it honestly. "It's possible," he said, "but I think not. It is more likely that he is gone out of the land of the Huron. He and his companions took parched corn and jerked venison for many days of travel."

Ja-gonh knew intuitively that the man was telling the truth, and he realized simultaneously that his search for his enemy would not be a simple matter. He accepted the invitation of the Huron chief to spend the night in the town because he wanted to respond to the gesture of goodwill with a similar gesture of his own. Perhaps he would meet someone at the evening meal who could give him some clue as to Gray Fox's whereabouts. There was no way of determining where the half-breed had gone or what business had taken him from his home. So it would be a waste of time to search the limitless forests for him.

Ja-gonh could only pray that the manitous would send a hawk to guide him to his foe or would reveal Gray Fox's whereabouts to him in a dream. Otherwise he could not in all honor and dignity marry Ah-wen-ga, since he had to first kill the murderer of his grandfather.

Gray Fox and the two Huron braves he had hired to assist him in his venture were taking no unnecessary risks. Shortly before they reached the land of the Seneca, they stopped beside a stream, washed off their war paint, and replaced it with the green and yellow paint of the Seneca. Now, if they were seen or apprehended, they would be taken for a local hunting party. Even so, they avoided sentry outposts, using all of their skills to remain undetected. Their complete success in this effort was due, at least in part, to good fortune, as Gray Fox well knew.

In any event, he was on the alert when he and his companions approached the main town of the Seneca. If necessary, he was prepared to go into the town itself to perform his mission, but he preferred to accomplish it in the fields outside the town, if that was at all possible. Again fortune smiled upon him. From his place of concealment in the forest, he peered out at the women who were at work in the fields, and taking his time, refusing to become flustered, he examined them one by one, until, at last, he saw Ah-wen-ga.

Having abducted her previously, he had spent a number of days in her company, so he could hardly mistake her identity. Peering at her critically, he had to admit that he admired the taste of Ja-gonh. The young woman was truly a ripe beauty, and after she received appropriate training, King Louis should be very grateful to the donors of such a splendid gift.

He pointed her out to his companions; they took careful note of her, too.

Now the major problem that confronted him was that of how to separate Ah-wen-ga from the other women of the town without arousing their suspicions or causing them to raise an alarm. He thought of many schemes and one by one rejected all of them.

As always, as he well knew, a simple scheme had far more chance of success than did a complicated one. He crept a little closer into the underbrush at the very edge of the forest, and there he waited patiently. His vigil was rewarded when Ah-wen-ga approached, turning over the soil of the cornfield with a wooden hoe. Soon she paused in her labors, no doubt intending to rest for a short time and chat with her friends.

Using a voice that almost resembled that of an old woman, he spoke her name just loudly enough for her to hear.

She raised her head in surprise.

"Ah-wen-ga!" he called again, disguising his voice once more.

She appeared slightly puzzled, but did not seem to be alarmed or upset.

Gray Fox called her a third time.

Her curiosity clearly was aroused, and it was apparent she was not anticipating foul play of any kind. She wandered slowly toward the edge of the forest, the half-smile on her face indicating that she thought perhaps someone was playing a joke on her.

Gray Fox tensed as he waited, scarcely breathing.

When Ah-wen-ga came within reach, his arms shot out. With one hand he caught her firmly by an arm, and the other he clapped hard over her mouth.

Realizing her mistake instantly, Ah-wen-ga began to struggle.

But it was too late. One slender woman, no matter how courageous and resourceful she might be, was no match for three burly warriors. Making scarcely any sound, they placed a gag securely in her mouth, and at the same time bound her ankles and tied her wrists firmly behind her.

Then, with one of his companions in the lead and the other bringing up the rear, Gray Fox picked up his captive and threw her across his shoulders as he would a deer carcass. They started off at a rapid trot, moving deeper and deeper into the forest.

Ah-wen-ga was both terrified and disgusted with herself. Having been abducted previously, she was all too painfully familiar with the routines of her captors, and she knew better than to struggle. Her bonds were secure, and she would wait until she was untied before she tried to break away from them. In the meantime, she craned her neck at her tormentors, and her blood ran cold when she recognized Gray Fox. This was the very

Huron half-breed who had kidnapped her previously and was the object of Ja-gonh's search. She had no idea why he had chosen to abduct her again, but she was determined that he would not get away with his scheme, whatever it might be.

The Huron did not halt until they were out of earshot of the women working in the field. Then Gray Fox stopped and cut the bonds that held Ah-wen-ga's ankles secure. "You will walk now," he told her, and hauled her to her feet. Her hands were still tied, and she still had the gag in her mouth, but she instantly broke into a run and headed back in the direction from which they had come. Gray Fox was prepared for just such a maneuver, however, and, catching up with her, gave her a mighty cuff across the face that caused her to stagger and drop to her knees. "Play tricks on me and I'll make you sorry you're alive!" he told her.

She looked at him with loathing, and as she again tried to escape, he reached out, caught her, and retied her ankles with a new length of leather thong. "If you refuse to cooperate," he said, "we shall be forced to keep you trussed like a doe." He picked her up and swung her across his shoulders again.

The Huron who constituted the advance guard stiffened and halted. Gray Fox followed the direction of his companion's intent gaze and saw that in the forest, just beyond the small clearing in which they stood with their captive, they were being observed by a Seneca sentry.

No-da-vo, a young senior warrior of the Seneca, was in charge of the sector through which the Huron were passing with their captive. He could easily discern that they wore the war paint of the Seneca, and resembled Seneca in their dress as well. He assumed that they were carrying the carcass of a deer, and was startled when he saw that their "prize" was a young woman.

"Who are you?" he demanded. "Identify yourselves."

Gray Fox replied swiftly and glibly, "My friends and I were out hunting," he said. "My sister followed us. She hurt her ankle so badly when she tripped on a hidden root that the pain has almost deprived her of her reason. I was obliged to restrain her and carry her." Not waiting for a reply, he signaled to his companions, and all three moved on, pushing ahead into the deep forest.

No-da-vo was bewildered because his question was answered by someone whom he did not recognize, yet who was speaking the tongue of the Seneca without a trace of an unfamiliar accent. Although the circumstances seemed suspicious, he had no reason to doubt the authenticity of the story he had been told. Nevertheless, he had been taught that as a sentinel he should take nothing for granted, and his experience in war had proved the value of such advice. So as the group moved away, he peered hard at the "sister" of the man who had replied to him, and he was horrified when he suddenly recognized Ah-wen-ga. Furthermore, he realized that she was gagged. He was tempted to fire an arrow to halt the flight of the trio, but recognized the futility of a lone sentry trying to stop three armed men.

So he picked up his small drum, which he had placed on the ground nearby, and quickly sent a message to all other sentries, alerting them to the flight and to the fact that the trio, ostensibly fellow Seneca, had made Ah-wen-ga their prisoner.

Ah-wen-ga heard the message and was heartened. Perhaps a group of sentries could apprehend her captors in time.

Gray Fox also heard the throbbing of the drum, and although he could not understand the message, because it was being sent in a Seneca code, he knew that the other sentinels in the forest were being summoned to help. Feeling certain that the sentry who had seen them would follow them from a distance as well, he ordered his companions to increase their pace swiftly, and even though he was burdened by Ah-wen-ga's weight, he took the lead himself. He followed an erratic course, and realizing that he and his companions were leaving footprints, he removed his moccasins when he came to the bank of a small, cold, swift-running stream. Although he could not maintain much speed, he nevertheless waded in ankle-deep water, following the stream as it led toward the north.

His companions did the same, and although their technique was crude, they nevertheless left no trail.

No-da-vo, who was indeed following them at a distance and was able to hear their footsteps, realized that they were slipping away from him. When they entered the creek, he sent another message on his drum. Ah-wen-ga, hearing it, began to lose heart. It appeared that the sentinels would be obliged to give up their chase.

For all his faults, Gray Fox was not lacking in strength, cunning, or courage. The stream led in approximately the right direction. So he stayed in the water and continued to plod through it for several miles, even though the chill numbed his feet and ankles.

A trained Seneca warrior could have carried such a burden as Ah-wen-ga for three or four days and nights and seldom paused. Gray Fox and his companions were not Seneca, to be sure, but they proved that the Huron were also a nation with a deservedly fearsome reputation. They did not slacken their pace all through the long night and were still moving rapidly when daylight came.

The forest thinned, and they emerged into a hilly section interspersed with meadows where waist-high grass grew. Gray Fox called a temporary halt at the crest of a high hill and satisfied himself that he had lost the Seneca sentry who had been following them.

His analysis was correct. In the late hours of the night, No-da-vo had been forced to give up the chase.

Only now was Gray Fox willing to relax slightly in his strict vigil. Ah-wen-ga's bonds were removed and when her captors ate jerked beef and parched corn, washed down with cold brook water, they offered a similar meal to her.

Under no illusions, Ah-wen-ga knew she had to keep up her strength, and so she ate. The men did not address her, so she didn't speak to them, either. But her hopes of escape were fading rapidly. As much as she despised Gray Fox, she had to admit he knew his business well.

Wherever he was taking her and for whatever the reason, he had eluded his pursuers and appeared to be on the verge of success.

Ja-gonh was disgruntled as he approached the Seneca town on his return home from the land of the Huron. His journey had been made in vain. He had learned nothing useful at the evening meal at the Huron village, and he was no closer to fulfilling his vow than when he set out. On the way home, he had even detoured three times from his normal route, when sudden bursts of intuition seemed to suggest one place or another where Gray Fox might have decided to go. In so doing, he had added at least four days to his homeward trek—all to no avail.

Though he paid scarcely any attention to the throbbing of the sentries' drums that told of his return, he should have known that something out of the ordinary had happened. When he emerged from the forest, Goo-ga-ro-no stopped her work in the fields instantly and joined him, accompanying him to their parents' dwelling. There Betsy and Renno—pale beneath his tan as his undiagnosed illness persisted—awaited him. One look at their grim faces told him that something had gone amiss.

Ja-gonh listened without comment as his father told him of Ah-wen-ga's abduction and No-da-vo's near-apprehension of her kidnappers.

When his father had finished his recital, Ja-gonh had to use all of his willpower to maintain a facade of calm. "Where is No-da-vo?" he asked. "I would speak with him."

Renno had anticipated the request, and No-da-vo, who had been waiting to confer with him, soon appeared.

"If you will," Ja-gonh said, "describe for me the principal abductor, the man who was carrying Ah-wen-ga, as they fled." The other young warrior, long his close friend and one who knew how he felt about Ah-wen-ga, spoke slowly and carefully, describing Gray Fox in precise detail. He added a vow personally to do all he could to help in avenging the abduction.

Ja-gonh listened carefully and then nodded. "It is as I thought," he said. "While I went to the land of the Huron seeking Gray Fox in vain, he came to this town and abducted Ah-wen-ga."

His parents exchanged significant glances.

"I will return at once to the land of the Huron," Ja-gonh said harshly. "I will find Gray Fox and I will kill him—as much for my own sake and the sake of Ah-wen-ga as for the murder of Ghonka, my grandfather."

Renno shook his head and sent a messenger to summon Sun-ai-yee. "Wait, my son," he said.

When the portly old sachem appeared, Ja-gonh repeated his intention of going off again to the land of the Huron immediately. Sun-ai-yee shook his head. "Nothing would please me more than to see the punishment of him who had dared to abduct my daughter," he said. "But it is wrong of Ja-gonh to travel now to the land of the Huron. Gray Fox was not there when you went in search of him, and he is not there now."

"How do you know this?" Ja-gonh demanded.

His father sighed. "When we learned that Ah-wen-ga had been kidnapped," he said, "I sent my own brother with all possible speed to the land of the Huron. You had been there yourself only two days before El-i-chi arrived, and somehow you missed each other on the trail. The chief of the Huron swore to El-i-chi in the names of his ancestors that he and his people knew nothing of the abduction of the daughter of the sachem of the Seneca. They had no reason to abduct her, El-i-chi was told, and their reasons make good sense. They know we would go to war with them for such a deed and would show them no mercy. They know the Huron are no match for the Seneca in battle and that their braves would be slaughtered, their women made slaves, their children taken from them and brought up as

Seneca. It would be the end of the Huron nation. Therefore, I am satisfied that nothing is known by the Huron of
Gray Fox's vile act or the reasons he perpetrated it."

"Does my father think," Ja-gonh asked incredulously,
"that we can accept the word of the chief of the Huron in
this matter?"

Renno was weary and merely nodded.

"It makes great sense to accept his word," Sun-ai-yee
said. "It is true that the Huron would cease to exist as a
nation if they had participated in this plot. I am convinced,
as your father is convinced, that Gray Fox perpetrated this
deed for reasons of his own, just as he killed Ghonka for
reasons of his own. Quite possibly these originate with
those of his ancestors who are French, and not the Huron."

"He is the son of my ancient enemy, Alain de Gramont,"
Renno said, "and so he carries on an endless feud against
our family. It is very likely he kidnapped Ah-wen-ga
because he knew that you intended to marry her. That
would give him a further reason to act, in addition to his
well-known thirst for power and his desire to bring the
Iroquois nation to ruin."

"Then he must be found, and Ah-wen-ga must be
rescued before he kills her."

"He will not kill her," Sun-ai-yee replied. "Had he
wished to murder her, he had his chance in the forest. He
was taking her away from her people for another purpose.
We do not know that purpose."

"Sun-ai-yee speaks words of truth," Renno declared.
"Had the Huron half-breed wanted Ah-wen-ga dead, he
had many opportunities to kill her, but he fled with her
from the land of the Seneca. Perhaps he is holding her for
a ransom. If so, we will soon know it. But he probably has
some other purpose in mind, and in time he will reveal it."

"So it would be wrong," Sun-ai-yee said, "for Ja-gonh
to return to the land of the Huron. At best he could find
out little or nothing, and at worst he could place Ah-wen-
ga in greater danger. No one is more anxious than I for the
safe return of my daughter, but it is needful that we
exercise patience."

Ja-gonh wanted to retort that patience was a necessary virtue that a man acquired when he became old. When he was young and his blood was hot, he demanded action. His own thirst for vengeance against Gray Fox was so great that the desire overwhelmed him. At the same time, he knew that he had to listen to the opinions of the two highest authorities in the land, his father and his future father-in-law.

Renno recognized the strain under which his son was laboring and felt sorry for him. "That which Ja-gonh is asked to do is not easy," he said. "When a man has been wronged, his yearning for revenge is stronger than any other feeling on earth, but now is the time when Ja-gonh must demonstrate that he is worthy of the rank that he holds as a senior warrior of the Seneca. Be patient, my son, and the manitous will reward you."

"I seek no reward," Ja-gonh replied, "and I want no reward. First, I want the return of Ah-wen-ga to the house of her father unharmed, with her spirit as free as before she was made a captive. And no less do I seek the death of Gray Fox."

"I have lived for many winters," Sun-ai-yee said, "and I have learned that the ways of the gods are strange and the ways the manitous express their will is often even stranger. When we find out why my daughter was taken from us, we will be led to her or she will be returned to us. No harm will befall her. I am certain of this and feel in my bones that what I have said is so."

Regardless of how Ja-gonh might feel, he could not act on his own initiative. Though he found it exceptionally difficult to submit to a decision so alien to his own desires, he nevertheless bowed his head and then withdrew.

When he was gone, Renno and Sun-ai-yee exchanged a glance. Both of them understood precisely how Ja-gonh felt.

Renno leaned wearily against the rear wall of the house and closed his eyes for a few moments. When he reopened them, he saw Sun-ai-yee studying him with undisguised concern.

"You are not well." Sun-ai-yee made a flat statement rather than asking a question, and there was no doubt in his mind that his old friend and one-time protégé was ailing.

Renno did not deny the truth, but had no desire to have his illness blown out of proportion. He nodded and then said, "I am somewhat fatigued these days, but there is nothing seriously wrong with me. I could run for four days and four nights without pause, and I'm prepared as always to lead the combined armies of the Iroquois into the field if it should be necessary."

Sun-ai-yee, scrutinizing him carefully, saw the lackluster expression in his eyes and noted that his skin was beginning to look gray. "Does Betsy know of this fatigue?" he demanded.

"A woman doesn't understand these things," Renno said, "and I see no reason to alarm her needlessly. When I am recovered, I will tell her how I felt. Until then, I prefer to say nothing."

Sun-ai-yee knew his own hands were tied in the matter. He could not go to Renno's wife with news that Renno himself was reluctant to tell her. So he accepted his friend's decision as final. His worries over Ah-wen-ga put all other matters out of his mind.

Ja-gonh, meantime, was so restless, so filled with rage at Gray Fox that he needed time to cool off and regain his perspectives. He had just returned from a long journey, but instead of spending time with his mother and sister or asking El-i-chi in greater detail about his visit to the Huron, he sought the soothing solitude of the forest. He made his way past a thicket to a tiny clearing that he had known all his life, and there he perched on a rock and did his best to enter the mind of Gray Fox. Why *would* he want to abduct Ah-wen-ga a second time? The motive of revenge seemed obvious; was there perhaps a further reason— something connected with the French, as Sun-ai-yee had hinted?

He was so lost in thought that the drums of the sentries sounded for some minutes before they finally penetrated his consciousness. Then, listening more carefully, he realized they were informing the people of the Seneca town that two strangers were approaching, a white man and a white woman.

He assumed he knew them and was sure of it when the drums described the uniform worn by the man. He wore a tunic of scarlet and gold and trousers of black with a gold stripe on the sides, the most unsuitable of all attire for traveling through the wilderness.

In spite of himself, Ja-gonh chuckled. The visitor, he knew, could be no one but his good friend and former comrade-in-arms, Captain Roger Harkness, an officer in the British regiment of Grenadier Guards who was assigned as aide-de-camp to the governor of Virginia. The woman, he guessed, was Patience, Roger's bride, a member of the Wilson family of Fort Springfield. She was the daughter of his parents' good friends, the commander of the Massachusetts Bay militia and his wife. At one time, all four parents had held high hopes that Ja-gonh and Patience would marry, but the manitous had willed otherwise.

Listening to the drums, he ascertained the direction from which the couple were approaching the town of the Seneca, and then he went off at a run through the forest to intercept them.

He saw them long before they became aware of his presence. Instead of traveling single file as Indians would do in the forest, the couple walked side by side, much to Ja-gonh's amusement. He noted, too, that Roger was carrying his sword, which he used to hack away underbrush in his wife's path, though she made her way nimbly, evading fallen trees and branches with thorns on them.

Ja-gonh moved into the open, directly in the path of the oncoming couple.

Roger Harkness was startled and reached for the rifle slung over one shoulder. Then he recognized the white Indian, grinned, and extended his hand.

Ja-gonh returned the greeting. "Welcome, my friends," he said. "What brings you so far from Virginia?"

"We had a few weeks in which we could go where we pleased," Patience explained, "and we decided to visit

38

you. It is always good to see you, Ja-gonh. And your family," she added with a sudden smile.

That night the visitors dined at the lodge of Renno and Betsy, and because of Sun-ai-yee's position, he and Talking Quail were among the guests. Both Renno and Sun-ai-yee plied Roger with questions.

The English colonies, Roger told them, had rarely known a time of such universal peace. "The Huron and Ottawa and Algonquian, as well as the lesser tribes that are allies of the French, were beaten so badly in our joint campaign against them that they know better than to attack us again. The French themselves are quieter than they have been within the memory of our oldest officers. It's difficult to believe, but they seem to have abandoned their ambitions to take possession of our colonies."

Renno shook his head. "That is a very dangerous thought. I have known and fought the French since I was a junior warrior. I know them all too well. They may be licking their wounds and trying to regain their strength, but they will never abandon their ambitions; they will never give up their hope of someday combining the English colonies with their own and bringing all Indian nations in North America under their rule as well. How well do I remember the words of Ghonka, my father. How often he told me to beware of the French when they appear to be sleeping. I cannot ignore the prospect that they have a hand in this."

Roger listened carefully. He knew that his high regard for Renno was shared by the Great Sachem's brother-in-law, commander of the Virginia militia. Renno's views were to be respected and were to be reported at the highest level throughout the colonies.

"The Spaniards," Renno went on, "appear to be truly quiet. They are neither raising an expedition to conquer us; nor are they stirring up trouble among the Indian nations that lie to our south and to our west. I find it strange, but the attitude of Spain depends on the monarch who sits on the throne in Madrid. If he covets the colonies of the English, there is war. If he does not, there is peace.

I know nothing about the present Spanish ruler, but he has done nothing to cause alarm, and I believe that we can forget him, although it pays, always, to be vigilant.''

It was astonishing, Roger Harkness thought, that this white Indian who held the title of the head of the league of the six Iroquois nations was probably the best informed as well as the single most powerful leader in all of the New World. He lived in a primitive community in the remote wilderness far from civilization, yet he knew more about the state of affairs between the European powers that were colonizing America than did the governors of the English colonies, or for that matter, the administrators in charge of New World affairs in London.

Patience listened to the political talk less carefully than did her husband, and having expected to see Ah-wen-ga, she was surprised by her absence, particularly because her parents were present as guests. Unable to contain her curiosity any longer, she finally asked Betsy, ''Where is Ah-wen-ga?''

Her words seemed to have an astonishing effect. The men looked glum and disturbed, and the women quickly withdrew into their impenetrable Indian shells. Apparently, Patience thought, she had blundered by asking an improper question.

Ja-gonh broke the silence and explained what had happened. Roger was immediately alert and asked a number of questions, most of which Sun-ai-yee tried to answer. At last, it became apparent that the Seneca had explained all they knew about the mystery.

Patience was horrified. She had come to know and like Ah-wen-ga, and in a sense, gave her credit for her own happiness. Her own association with Ja-gonh had begun to taper off when he first showed signs of losing his heart to Ah-wen-ga. At the same time, pressures from both families that had been intended to bring them together began to decline. Coincidentally, she had become acquainted with Roger Harkness and had fallen in love with him, as he had with her.

Roger apparently had some specific notion in mind. ''I

am sure you recall the evil connection between Gray Fox and Major Henri de Bienville," he commented.

"Who is this major?" Sun-ai-yee demanded.

"He's been the director of intelligence for the government of New France," Roger explained, "and he's as shrewd and able an opponent as I have ever encountered."

Ja-gonh was bewildered. "Why would Major de Bienville have any interest in Ah-wen-ga?"

"I have no idea," Roger replied. "I'm just poking about, searching for clues, and I find myself coming back to the idea that Gray Fox is working for him in all of this. The evidence seems to sugest it."

"The father of Gray Fox," Renno said, "was a colonel in the army of France, and as much as I hated him, he was very competent. The son, however, resorts to murder and kidnappings and is not the man his father was."

Roger Harkness seemed lost in thought for a moment, and when he spoke, he addressed his wife but, in actuality, was speaking to all of the assembled group. "In the time remaining to us before I must go back on duty," he said, "we'll have time for a special journey. I think we'll go to Quebec."

She was surprised, and some of the Seneca were openly astonished.

"Is it safe for you to take your wife there?" Besty inquired gently.

Roger's reply was brisk. "Of course," he said. "England and France are at peace and intend to stay that way for the foreseeable future. I'm not only on the staff of the royal governor of Virginia, but I still hold my commission in the army. France, you can be sure, has no desire to start a war by doing any harm to my wife or to me."

Ja-gonh was puzzled. "What is the point," he asked, "of your making such a journey?"

Roger shrugged. "Call it a hunch, if you will, or attribute it to natural curiosity. I want to renew my acquaintance with Henri de Bienville and learn what I can about his activities these days. I'll be especially eager to find out how Gray Fox's activity ties in with his."

Ja-gonh saw an opportunity to become involved in action in spite of the ban imposed by his father and Sun-ai-yee. "You may know about such matters as espionage and counterespionage and sabotage," he said, "but if you're going to travel to Quebec, and take Patience with you, you need an escort. I volunteer my services."

Renno understood precisely what his son had in mind and shook his head. The possibilities that Ja-gonh might become involved in matters beyond his depth were endless. "We shall provide Major and Mistress Harkness with another, more suitable escort," he said. "Goo-ga-ro-no, you lived in Quebec for a time so you know the town well. Would you be willing to make a brief journey there?"

"I would be glad to," she replied instantly, "if I can help." Like a good Seneca, she dismissed from her mind the memory of her painful experiences in Quebec.

Renno looked pleased. "Good," he said, "and I shall send an escort of several warriors with you as well. I shall place No-da-vo in charge."

Ja-gonh couldn't help bristling. "Why No-da-vo?" he demanded.

"For a very simple reason," his father replied gently. "As I understand it, one of Major Harkness's reasons for going to Quebec is to see how Gray Fox and his evil work tie in with Major de Bienville. Of all our warriors, there are very few—other than you—who would recognize Gray Fox when they see him. No-da-vo is such a warrior and would know him."

Ja-gonh realized he should have known better than to try to outsmart his father.

Roger thanked Renno for his help but wanted to emphasize one point above all others. "I hope no one will expect miracles from this journey," he said. "I am merely intending to gain a general picture and won't necessarily find any answers to the question that perplexes you. I have no way of knowing whether we will find any clues to the whereabouts of Ah-wen-ga."

* * *

Gray Fox carried his captive northward through the wilderness, taking no chances and never allowing her to walk. When he reached a point several days' journey from Quebec, he sent one of his hired Huron braves to carry the word to de Bienville. Then, when he reached the south bank of the St. Lawrence, opposite the capital of New France, he remained concealed in the forest as he awaited word.

He did not have long to wait. Soon a message was received from the major, instructing him to carry out the intricate plans they had agreed upon before he left Quebec. At sundown that evening, he placed his captive in a canoe, concealed her by covering her with a blanket, and then slowly crossed the great river. In the port area on the north side, several ships rode at anchor, and after studying them in the half-light, he paddled directly to a large merchantman, *The Queen of Normandy*. He called out cautiously as he approached the vessel and several shadowy figures appeared on deck. A line was lowered and he wrapped it securely around Ah-wen-ga while she was still shrouded by the blanket. Then he signaled, and she was silently hauled upward. He followed her to the deck after turning the canoe over to a sailor who had joined him in the craft. Despite his misgivings about an ocean voyage, he asked no questions and sat down to wait for the arrival of the major.

Late in the evening, the captain's gig was lowered, and manned by four sailors and a boatswain, it was rowed ashore. There it was loaded with leather traveling boxes and other luggage, and it returned to the merchantman. It was sent ashore again, and this time the crew had to wait for about an hour before two muffled figures appeared and climbed into the stern seats. Henri de Bienville, discreetly attired in civilian clothes, and Arlene d'Amarante, her features hidden beneath a heavy veil, were carried to the ship. There, in the privacy of a passenger cabin, they were reunited with Gray Fox.

"You succeeded," the major said as they clasped wrists in the Indian style of greeting.

Gray Fox was proud of his accomplishment but merely nodded.

"You've paid off your Huron associates, I take it," the major asked.

"I have paid them and dismissed them," Gray Fox said. "They've gone back to their own town, which is located far in the interior near the fur trading post of Montreal that you French have established. It will take many months to locate them there, and even if they decide to talk out of turn, they know nothing that can harm us." He smiled complacently.

"Where is the girl?" Arlene asked.

Gray Fox pointed toward the adjoining cabin. Arlene squeezed past him and opened the door. Lying on a bunk, staring up at her, with wrists and ankles bound and a gag stuffed in her mouth, was Ah-wen-ga.

Arlene studied her critically from head to toe and was delighted. Ah-wen-ga's clean-cut, chiseled features and her slender, trim figure were far more attractive than she had even hoped, and she now felt certain that this savage Indian had the potential of appealing to King Louis.

Ah-wen-ga, her eyes unblinking, returned the other woman's gaze steadily. Arlene smiled to indicate a sense of kinship.

Ah-wen-ga continued to stare at her without blinking, her eyes indicating nothing.

"She's a human being, not a wild animal," Arlene said to de Bienville, behind her in the doorway. "When are you going to untie her?"

De Bienville referred the question to the Huron half-breed.

"I prefer to wait until we sail," Gray Fox replied. "You don't know this woman. She's the type who would jump overboard and try to swim to safety."

Even as he spoke, they heard commands shouted on the quarterdeck above, and the bare feet of seamen pounded on the hardwood deck over their heads. The clanking of metal told them that the anchor was being weighed.

"We're getting under way right now," the major said.

"So I daresay it's safe to release her. Besides, the sooner we have a talk with her and win her cooperation, the easier it's going to be for all of us."

Gray Fox hesitated, but removed the gag. Taking a knife from his belt, he slashed her bonds.

She made no move and uttered no sound until she was free of the rawhide thongs. Then, suddenly, she attacked her captor with a fury unlike anything that Arlene d'Amarante had ever seen.

A thrust of one knee caught Gray Fox in the groin, and as he doubled over, she grasped the hair of his scalp lock with one hand, and the nails of her free hand raked his face as she sought his eyes, obviously intending to gouge them out. She kicked him repeatedly with all her force, and when he managed to wrench his head from her grasp, she clawed at him with both hands, her strength far greater than seemed possible in one so feminine and slender.

Gray Fox did his best to protect himself from her attack. But that proved impossible. Kicking and flailing, beating and clawing, Ah-wen-ga was determined to exterminate this Huron who had dared to abduct her twice.

Under the fury of her unrelenting assault, Gray Fox toppled backward onto the bed. In one hand he still clutched the knife he had used to cut her bonds, and he was being subjected to such a severe trouncing that his instinct prompted him to try to use it to protect himself.

Henri de Bienville's amusement gave way to sudden alarm. This girl was far too valuable to be killed or injured. But when he joined in the attempt to subdue her, she turned on him and mauled him severely, scratching his face and neck.

The astonished Arlene was treated to the spectacle of two brawny men fighting for their lives as they attempted to subdue the Indian maiden. She had been wrong, Arlene thought, when she had said that the captive was no animal. Never had she seen a wild beast turn on its trainers with greater fury.

At last the men managed to hold down Ah-wen-ga's arms and legs long enough to immobilize her while staying a safe distance from her sharp teeth. Ah-wen-ga's instinct told her that the ship was in motion, taking her farther away from her beloved Ja-gonh and her people with each passing moment, and she was endowed with a supreme recklessness that she had never before possessed. She struggled to free herself, but could not, and to her dismay, new rawhide bonds now were tied to her ankles and wrists. Arlene watched in silence and finally addressed the major. "Henri," she said, "we cannot cross the ocean with a girl being held in such close captivity. We'll need the time to train her."

De Bienville wiped his blood from his face with a lace-edged handkerchief. "What do you suggest?" he said.

"Do you speak her tongue?"

The major indicated that he could.

"Very well," Arlene said, taking charge. "Let Gray Fox, whom she obviously despises, leave the cabin. I would prefer to speak to her alone, but you'll be needed as an interpreter, Henri, so I'll have to avail myself of your services." She glared at Gray Fox.

The half-breed wearily went out onto the open deck, glad to put distance between himself and the Seneca she-devil.

"I wish to speak with you," Arlene said to Ah-wen-ga as Henri de Bienville translated her words phrase by phrase. "All I ask in return is that you listen."

Ah-wen-ga realized that she hardly had anything to lose, and there was even a chance she had something to gain. Certainly she might learn the reasons she had been kidnapped.

"A great anger seethes within you," Arlene said sympathetically, "and I cannot blame you for feeling as you do. You have been cruelly mistreated and abused by men who do not understand what it means to be a woman. They should have come to you and explained to you the reasons for their urgent need for you."

Ah-wen-ga's nails dug into the palms of her hands, and she muttered solemnly, "No Indian tribe has the need for a woman of the Seneca as a captive. The Huron have no

46

such need, and those with the white skins who call themselves French have no such need either."

De Bienville hastily translated the girl's words.

Arlene looked at her earnestly. "You are wrong," she said. "You don't understand, and I certainly can't blame you after the way you've been treated. Let me explain. We had a need, not for any ordinary woman, but only for the daughter of the sachem of the Seneca. No one else would have been right or adequate. The King of the French people lives far from the New World. He is surrounded by men who are ignorant of the forests and the ways of the Indians and of the alliances on this continent. Therefore, it has proved necessary for someone to enlighten him and explain the true situation to him. We discussed this problem long and earnestly, and we finally decided that only you would be suitable."

In spite of herself, Ah-wen-ga was intrigued. "Why me?"

When de Bienville had translated her question, Arlene relaxed a trifle. She was well on the way to success now. Soon the captive would be sufficiently tamed to stop resisting, and then her essential training could begin.

"A great leader of the French—or for that matter of the English or of any other people in Europe—speaks as an equal only with those who are truly his equals. Had it been possible to persuade your father to make the journey to France, we would have welcomed him, but we knew he would not leave the land of the Seneca."

That much certainly was true, Ah-wen-ga had to admit to herself. No power could persuade Sun-ai-yee to make a journey by himself to a foreign place where people did not speak his language, had alien customs, and ate foods that would upset his digestion.

"You," Arlene continued, "are what the French would call a princess. You are the daughter of a sachem or a high-ranking official. Therefore, Louis of France will listen when you speak. When he learns from you that the nations of the Iroquois League wish to live in peace with their neighbors and that the English colonists have no

47

ambitions to acquire the land and property of the French colonists, he will welcome this news with all his heart. And when you present these truths to him, he will order his people in the New World to change their tactics. The French will no longer fight the English, and the Indian tribes, who are allies with the French, will gladly make their peace with the nations of the Iroquois League."

Unable to determine the truth of what she was being told, Ah-wen-ga nevertheless considered that the prospect being outlined to her seemed extremely attractive.

"You will be taught to wear the clothes of the French and to wear cosmetics on your face as I wear them," Arlene said. "You'll be taught the manners of the French, and above all, the language of the French. If you are an apt pupil, as I'm sure you'll prove to be, we will arrange for you to have an audience with King Louis as soon as you have mastered his tongue and the ways of his people."

Ah-wen-ga listened carefully. Then she shook her head slowly as if trying to clear it.

"Feel free to ask anything you like," Arlene told her. "If there's anything you don't understand, just speak up and it will be explained to you."

Ah-wen-ga thought hard. "Why is it necessary," she demanded, "for me to dress like a woman of the French and to paint my face the way a woman of the French paints her face? Why is it necessary for me to speak the language of the French and to know the manners of your people?"

Arlene laughed lightly, convincingly. "Louis may be a king," she said, "but he is also a man, just as your father may be a sachem, but he also is a man. A man is always impressed most favorably by a pretty woman who can speak to him in his own tongue and flatter him. You will resemble his people, and you will sound like one of his subjects. He will know that you have gone to great pains to learn the language and the ways of France in order to speak with him, and he will be deeply impressed. He will be far more inclined then to listen to the pleas for peace that you will make to him."

The story began to seem valid to Ah-wen-ga. At least

48

she knew now why she, rather than someone else, had been abducted, and she understood the alleged purpose of that kidnapping. She still had deep suspicions, to be sure, but she put them aside, at least temporarily.

Of one thing she was certain. If she continued to rebel, her abductors would be forced to keep her bound, hand and foot, as they carried her farther and farther from her homeland in this great ship that resembled a huge bird. In that respect, she had nothing to gain by continuing resistance. Perhaps, in spite of her bitter resentment of her abduction, and distrust of those who engineered it, she would be wise to accept the explanation—or at least seem to accept it. Yes, under those circumstances, she could learn the language and even wear the foolish clothes of the French women. In time, she would learn whether this red-haired woman was telling her the truth. And at that time, she would judge accordingly.

She could become a genuine heroine, Ah-wen-ga reflected, if she brought lasting peace to the land of the Seneca and to the English colonies. If she fought her captors, however, it seemed she would avail herself nothing.

She pondered all these elements for several minutes and then replied slowly. "I do not know whether you are to be believed, but I choose to believe you. I will do as you request until such time as I learn that your words are false."

Arlene was delighted and needed all of her willpower to refrain from looking in triumph at de Bienville.

"You have chosen wisely, my dear," she said to Ah-wen-ga. "We shall begin your lessons at once, and we shall hold them in private. Our inability to communicate with each other will prove to be no burden. You will learn my tongue quickly and I will share with you every woman's secret that I know."

Henri de Bienville almost choked as he translated Arlene's remarks. Not satisfied with the impression she had created on the naive young Seneca, Arlene went a step further. Raising a hand, she pointed a finger dramatically at him. "You may leave us," she said.

Her instruction was so blunt, so unexpected, that he hesitated.

"Go!" she ordered.

He had no real choice and left the cabin reflecting that if she lacked good sense, at least she was endowed with great courage. The young Indian woman might well attack and kill her the moment they were alone, but Arlene obviously was not in the least afraid of her.

When they were alone, Arlene allowed herself the luxury of a long, slow smile. "We will begin our first lesson," she said, "by teaching you the rudiments of grooming and a little of the French language. You don't understand a word I am saying, dear, but you soon will. I guarantee you that you'll make a very deep impression, indeed, on Louis. Far deeper than you can possibly imagine now."

Chapter III

General Jeffrey Wilson, as commander of the Massachusetts Bay militia, immediately threw the entire resources at his command behind the search for the young Seneca woman who would become the bride of Ja-gonh, son of Renno, his oldest friend.

With the help of his wife and the enthusiastic cooperation of Patience and her younger sister, Margot, a suitable wardrobe for an English colonist was provided for Goo-ga-ro-no. It was decided that since she spoke perfect English and her skin was as pale as that of Patience, she would masquerade as an English colonist and would call less attention to herself than if she appeared as a white Indian.

General Wilson supplied the party with an additional

escort of militiamen for the journey, and it was through his intervention that a trading sloop was provided for their further journey by water to Quebec. With the party aboard, the ship left Boston harbor and sailed quickly up the coast past the Maine District and Nova Scotia before entering the mouth of the St. Lawrence. To No-da-vo, never before in a seagoing ship, the entire experience was a novel one, and he took great pleasure in watching the captain and his men as they went about their duties on deck.

After sailing for a day or two up the St. Lawrence, the ship landed at a berth below Quebec City. There the captain, following his orders, would conduct his business slowly, so that he would still be on hand to return his passengers to Boston.

Roger found quarters for himself, his wife, and Goo-ga-ro-no at a lodging house that Goo-ga-ro-no, who was familiar with the town from her own sojourn there the previous year, had suggested to him.

No-da-vo parted company with the group and went off on his own to the nearby town of the Huron in search of information of the whereabouts of Gray Fox.

Prior to his departure from the land of the Seneca, Renno had advised him on how best to hunt for Gray Fox, and after he had arrived in Massachusetts Bay, General Wilson had given him further advice.

No-da-vo, being young and brash, had his own ideas on the subject. Confiding in no one, he inquired the way to the town of the Huron from a passing Indian on the streets of Quebec, who answered his questions reluctantly, and then he set out at the customary Seneca run for the town, some thirty miles distant. When he estimated that he was only a short distance from the town, he stopped and deliberately daubed his face and his torso with the yellow and green paint that marked him as a Seneca warrior.

As he approached the town and was seen by the Huron, the word that another Seneca was on hand spread quickly, and when No-da-vo arrived at the palisade, a reception committee of fifty to one hundred warriors, all of them heavily armed, awaited him. The fact that the third Seneca within a fairly short time had come to their town was as baffling and annoying as it was unusual.

They blocked his path, and before he could pass through the town gates, a war chief brusquely demanded to know his business. "I will tell that to your sachem," No-da-vo answered insolently, and rather than try to pry the information from him, they conducted him through the town to the house of the sachem.

The leader of the Huron hastily donned his war bonnet and his buffalo robe in order to greet this foe in full dignity. No-da-vo identified himself and then threw down the gantlet. "No-da-vo, of the Seneca," he declared in ringing tones, "has come to challenge a warrior of the Huron in personal combat. His name is Gray Fox, and I brand him as a coward."

His words created something of a sensation, and his hearers muttered to each other. One of the war chiefs and an elderly medicine man went up to the sachem and conferred with him in low voices.

Finally he nodded and turned to face the intruder. "We do not know," he said, "why you have chosen to challenge Gray Fox, as your brothers have. We do not know whether your charge that he is a coward is true or false. I do know that you will have to wait for the vengeance that you seek."

No-da-vo felt that his ruse was working, and he pressed still harder. "Why should that be?" he demanded with a sneer. "Is Gray Fox so afraid of the Seneca that he will not meet me in combat?"

The sachem's tone became chiding. "You jump too rapidly to a wrong conclusion," he said. "Gray Fox will not reply to your charges for many moons to come, because he is not present in this town. That is true now just as it was true when two of your tribe's warriors came with the same question."

"Aha!" No-da-vo struck a disdainful pose. "He is hiding from me!"

The sachem of the Huron shook his head and addressed him as one would speak to a wayward child. "Gray Fox," he said, "has now gone on a long journey. We know this, because he sent us a message not long ago, from the city the French call Quebec, saying not to expect his return for many moons—"

"I will follow him, wherever he has gone," No-da-vo interrupted.

All the Huron warriors laughed. "You will find that extremely difficult," the sachem said rather condescendingly. "He has by now sailed in a great white ship with white sails, and he has gone to visit the land of his father. This, too, was in his message."

No-da-vo was secretly elated. He had learned all that he had come to the land of the Huron to discover. Gray Fox's father, Alain de Gramont, had been French, and it appeared very definitely as though the half-breed had, for whatever his reasons, left the New World in order to sail to France.

No-da-vo struck a ferocious pose. "When Gray Fox returns," he said, "I will return also." Turning, he swaggered out of the house. Never deigning to look back over his shoulder, he left the town of the Huron.

Actually, No-da-vo was highly pleased. His bold, unusual strategy had succeeded, and he had learned exactly what he had wanted to find out about Gray Fox's whereabouts. He would report the information to Roger Harkness as soon as he reached Quebec again.

Parisians liked to believe that they were a breed apart, and that their city was unique in all the world. As it happened, the rest of the world agreed with them, and strangers who visited the capital of France marveled at the city, which was bustling and beautiful, bawdy but elegant.

Paris had a population of more than a half-million and even the poverty-stricken, who lived in hovels, carried themselves with an air. They were residents of the capital of the greatest city in Europe, and they never, for a moment, forgot it.

Most Parisians seemed to own methods of transportation. Nobles, the gentry, and the merchants who comprised the small middle class owned horses for riding, or were carried about the city in cumbersome carriages. Tradespeople and farmers owned carts pulled by donkeys and mules, and all of these creatures seemed to appear in the same streets at the same moment, creating monumental traffic jams that no one could untangle.

No one tried, of course. The King's Musketeers, members of the elite regiment that protected the monarch, would under no circumstances allow themselves to become embroiled in the disputes that inevitably arose when one tried to ease the traffic. The constables, too, were leery when they saw riders and vehicles piling up on the street.

The city was dominated by the great Cathedral of Notre Dame, located on a small island in the River Seine. Near it, on the right bank, stood the Louvre, the ancient palace that had been the home and the headquarters of kings of France since the Middle Ages. Now, however, it was occupied only by the employees who served in various government departments, and its magnificent gardens, the well-tended Tuileries, were all but deserted. This state of affairs had arisen because the late King Louis XIV had built himself a magnificent palace outside the city in the little village of Versailles, and the current monarch, Louis XV, continued to live and to keep his court there. As a consequence, not only was the Louvre not used for the functions for which it had been built, but the homes of most prominent nobles—many of them palaces in themselves—also were empty. Their owners preferred to live a cramped existence in the palace at Versailles, where they could be near the monarch.

Such a place was the home of Charles, Duc de Guise, the cousin of Lady Arlene d'Amarante. The duc owned a magnificent townhouse that would accommodate at least one hundred persons and twice that number of retainers and guards, but he, himself, was rarely there.

He loaned it to Arlene, however, after she and the members of her party had landed at Brest on the northwestern coast of France, and had moved on to Paris in two carriages.

Henri de Bienville was impatient, saying that a stop in Paris was a waste of time. But Arlene had strategic reasons of her own for the visit to the city. Her principal aim was that of dazzling Ah-wen-ga—and she succeeded brilliantly.

The largest communities that the young Seneca had ever seen were Boston, with a population of about ten to fifteen thousand, and Fort Springfield, which boasted no more than a thousand inhabitants. The mere fact that hundreds of thousands of people actually lived and worked in Paris was overwhelming to her.

Gray Fox was likewise impressed, but he made it clear that he preferred the forests and clear lakes of his homeland to the narrow, confining streets of the French capital.

Arlene took advantage of the party's sojourn in Paris to introduce Ah-wen-ga to several exceptionally talented dressmakers, who visited the Hôtel de Guise, and who created an entrancing, up-to-the-minute French wardrobe for her.

Shoemakers, milliners, haberdashers, and other tradespeople also were called to the de Guise home in large numbers, and as a result of their concerted efforts, a dazzling wardrobe was prepared for Ah-wen-ga.

"You are spending a fortune on the girl, you know," de Bienville told Arlene. "I hope she lives up to what you see as her promise."

"She'll do even more than that, Henri. I assure you that she'll be all we expect of her, and more. She's an exceptionally apt pupil, and she's learning our customs and our language rapidly. We couldn't have chosen a better subject."

"We have Gray Fox to thank for that," Henri reminded her.

She made a wry face. "No matter what we have to thank him for, let it be from a fairly considerable distance. Ah-wen-ga can't stand the sight of him, and perhaps she's influenced me, but I find it difficult to tolerate the fellow myself. The way he creeps around without making a sound annoys me, and I must say that sometimes I can't blame Ah-wen-ga for saying that she'd like to plunge a knife into his heart.

"Speaking of that—but really very seriously—she has

asked whether she could be given a small ivory-handled knife—one with a blade that disappears into the hasp—that she happened to see among my possessions. I expect to give it to her—it will make her feel more secure and therefore more amenable to all that I'm asking of her. I don't see how it can do any harm. She's really not going to attack even Gray Fox.''

De Bienville looked slightly dubious, but didn't object. He chuckled, and said, ''I must say that I find it ironic, my dear, that you're supposedly transforming Ah-wen-ga into a French lady, and in the process, you seem to be becoming something of a Seneca savage yourself.''

The party remained in Paris for several weeks, and as soon as Ah-wen-ga was equipped with the proper clothes, Arlene insisted that they take daily rides in an open de Guise carriage and that they eat at least one meal each day at one of the many public dining establishments which Paris boasted.

This exposure to the people of Paris was anything but accidental. Arlene had a double purpose in mind. For one thing, she wanted to make certain that Ah-wen-ga would become acclimated to the people of France. Even more important, she wanted to expose the Indian woman to the most critical of audiences. For Ah-wen-ga, in her new clothes, made for her by the most talented dressmakers in France, fulfilled the promise that her captors had seen in her when she had been abducted: she was ravishingly beautiful.

The French people responded to Ah-wen-ga with enthusiasm: everywhere she went, she unfailingly created a sensation. But she herself was somewhat bewildered by her transformation into a French lady. She realized that in her new attire, complete with a French coiffure and cosmetics, she looked European, but that didn't enhance her beauty in her own eyes. She was too much a Seneca for that.

Arlene, however, was more than satisfied. ''The girl really looks the part she's going to be required to play,'' she told de Bienville. ''I'm very much encouraged.''

"I think you're taking too great a risk by staying in Paris at this juncture," de Bienville responded. "There's already a buzz that arises every time she appears in public. Word of her unusual beauty is certain to reach Versailles, and our plans are doomed if King Louis learns about her prematurely."

Arlene considered the question and finally agreed. "I suppose you're right," she said. "She still has a great deal to learn, both about our moral standards—and why the aristocrats abandon them—and about our language. Yes, I think the time has come for us to move on to Gascony, in Charles's carriages. There we'll be isolated, and I can finish polishing her until she shines with the brilliance of the brightest star in the heavens."

In Quebec, Roger Harkness unwittingly used tactics remarkably similar to those employed at the Huron town by No-da-vo. While Patience changed into one of her most attractive frocks, he donned his full-dress scarlet and gold uniform of a captain in the Grenadier Guards. Then they walked together up the high cliff that was the core of Quebec life, and passed shops and offices where people stared at the unexpected sight of a uniformed British officer.

Ultimately, they came to the Citadel, the great fort that guarded Quebec and was supposedly invulnerable. The startled sentries on duty gaped and gripped their muskets all the harder when they saw the unfamiliar uniform.

Patience felt certain that one or the other of the two young French soldiers would try to challenge her husband with his bayonet.

But the officer in charge of the guard detail approached, and, behaving in a civilized manner, he saluted. Roger returned the salute. "We've come," he said, "to pay our respects to Major de Bienville. I'm Captain Harkness of His Britannic Majesty's Grenadiers, and I am accompanied by my wife. Major de Bienville will, no doubt, recall our previous meeting about a year ago."

The officer of the guard was apologetic. "I'm sorry to say, sir, that the major is unavailable, but I have no doubt that his deputy, Lieutenant de Malerbé, will be delighted to see you in his place." He summoned two other sentries from the guardhouse, and they escorted the British officer and his wife across the compound.

As they walked past barracks and fortifications—cannons that faced the river, high walls all made of thick stone—Patience could appreciate the feat accomplished by her father and Renno when they had actually captured the Citadel many years earlier. It was small wonder, she thought, that both had won lasting renown on that occasion. They came, at last, to a small, unprepossessing stone building, where a sergeant took charge of the visitors and led them to the private office of Lieutenant de Malerbé.

There, Roger introduced himself and Patience, telling the young officer what he had revealed to the head of the guard detail. Then he added, casually, "I regret to hear that the major appears to be out of town at the moment. I wanted to pay my respects to him and have him meet my wife, whom I've married since our last meeting. We intend to be in Quebec for several days while taking care of a business matter involving my wife's family, so perhaps he'll return before we leave."

"I regret to say he will not, Captain," the acting head of French Intelligence in the New World replied. "Major de Bienville is on an extended leave and has sailed for France."

Roger expressed astonishment at the news, exaggerating his reaction. "Was his journey rather unexpected?" he inquired.

"I believe he'd been planning it for some time," the French officer replied, "although he told no one of the details because of the delicacy of his journey."

"I beg your pardon, I had no intention of prying into French army business, Lieutenant," Roger said.

Lieutenant de Malerbé smiled as he shook his head. "Major de Bienville is on business that is strictly his own," he replied, taking the English officer into his confidence with rather indiscreet casualness. "He's taken leave. If madame will pardon the impropriety, he was being careful because of the involvement of ladies."

Patience felt her face redden, but her husband chuckled in seeming approval. "I didn't realize that Henri was that much of a ladies' man," he said, pretending to know de Bienville far better than was actually the case.

"Not many people know it, Captain, including his closest associates on the staff. But you may expect to hear the rumors if you're to be in town for several days, so I'll just tell you that he appears to have gone to France accompanied by two ladies, neither of whom was a relative."

"Two, eh?" Roger said and chuckled again. "Well, more power to him. I find that one is quite enough to keep me occupied, but, of course, I'm a married man, and I suppose that may make a difference."

The young French officer laughed dutifully.

Roger brought the conversation quickly to a close, and he and Patience took their leave. He was amazed, but pleased, that the inexperienced young officer had failed to ask any questions about details of their travel, in order to verify their authenticity.

He made no comment until they had left the Citadel behind them and were returning to their lodging. "I think we may have hit on something," he said. "I can't imagine an officer as experienced and as shrewd as Major de Bienville taking the risk of jeopardizing his entire future career by traveling with two women. The scandal would destroy his military career. So we must assume that at least one of those ladies is a person to whom he obviously would have no attachment."

"Are you suggesting," Patience wanted to know, "that perhaps Ah-wen-ga was one of those ladies?"

He held up a hand and smiled. "You're a mind reader, my dear, but let's not jump to conclusions. We'll figure out the next step with Goo-ga-ro-no."

When they reached their lodging, they found No-da-vo also arriving, obviously pleased with himself.

The young Seneca revealed to them the ruse he had

employed, and his resultant discovery that Gray Fox had sailed the previous week to France.

"The question that we must resolve now," Roger said, "is whether Ah-wen-ga was in the group that sailed to France with Major de Bienville. Goo-ga-ro-no, you spent a number of months here last year, I gather. Based on your knowledge of Quebec and its way of life, do you have any suggestions?"

She was lost in thought for a moment. "I remember an office on the lower part of this very hill that regulates shipping between France and this colony. In fact, I believe that it is said to be also responsible for shipping between Quebec and the French colonies in the West Indian Sea." She hesitated and fell silent.

Roger mistakenly thought that she was being shy. "Go on," he urged her.

"I'm thinking," Goo-ga-ro-no replied with great dignity. "I do not know this for certain, but I believe that in this office, there is listed the name of every passenger who is carried between Quebec and some other port, just as there is listed, in full detail, the cargo that is carried by every vessel."

"If the passengers are named," Roger said, "that could solve our problem."

"It does," Patience added, "provided that we can gain access to the list for the appropriate ship."

"We could break into the office at night after the people who work there go home," No-da-vo suggested, "and steal the list."

Roger shook his head. "I'm sorry," he said, "that may be a simple, direct way of doing things, and I can't blame you for thinking in such terms. But we're in New France, which considers itself civilized, and we can't afford a brush with the local constabulary. I've already been identified as a British officer, and if I or anyone associated with me were to be caught stealing, no matter what it is that's taken, a serious international incident could result. I'm afraid we'll have to think of something a little more appropriate."

Roger began to pace slowly, his spurs jangling.

"I believe," Goo-ga-ro-no finally said, a sly smile appearing in her eyes, "that I may have thought of the way. Let us suppose that Patience and I go there alone. You are, of course, wearing your wedding ring, Patience? Good. That will help to support my story if I explain that we are sisters from Massachusetts Bay and we are seeking the husband of my poor sister, who deserted her. We traced him as far as Quebec, and now we have learned that he may have gone to France on a ship that sailed recently from this port.

"We beg for the right to examine the manifest of that ship. Who will deny that privilege to a deserted woman? Who would be so hardhearted?"

Patience laughed aloud. "You're a genius, Goo-ga-ro-no," she said.

"There seems to be little doubt that you've inherited your father's mind," Roger said—and refrained from adding that any warrior who became Goo-ga-ro-no's husband might expect to have a difficult life as he tried to keep up with her.

"You approve then?" Goo-ga-ro-no asked easily.

"Of course," Roger replied. "We have everything to gain and nothing to lose by trying."

"We'll leave as soon you're ready, Patience," Goo-ga-ro-no said, and looking in the mirror, tugged at the white cuffs on the sleeves of her English settler's dress.

"I know of no time like the present," Patience said, and stood.

No-da-vo instantly jumped to his feet. "Where do you think you're going?" Roger demanded.

"I wish to accompany Goo-ga-ro-no to make certain no harm comes to her," the young warrior replied.

Roger shook his head. "It's going to be difficult enough for the girls to playact," he said. "If they've got to explain why a Seneca brave is hovering over them, it might prove to be too much. No, you'll stay here with me, No-da-vo, and we'll keep a vigil together."

No-da-vo grumbled, but subsided and sank into a chair.

The women were silent until they reached the street. "Do you still speak fluent French?" Goo-ga-ro-no asked.

"Yes, I do," Patience replied. "Because my mother is French, you know, we frequently use the language together, and so I have no chance to lose my familiarity with it."

"I myself learned enough from your mother to make myself usually understood," Goo-ga-ro-no said. "I think that for our purposes it will be best if I do the talking. You, meanwhile, should contrive to look sorrowful. I think we're likely to find out more if we appear to be bewildered and upset."

Her advice made sense to Patience, and she readily agreed. They made their way down the steep hill past shops and the working places of various craftsmen until finally Goo-ga-ro-no halted. "The place is still here," she said, and pointed to a sign that identified the second floor of a two-story building as the office of the Shipping Company of New France. After a bell announced their arrival, a middle-aged Frenchman approached them, removed his glasses, and made a move to smooth his almost nonexistent hair.

"What can I do for you, ladies?" he asked.

Goo-ga-ro-no launched into an explanation in her less than perfect French. As she explained that her newly married sister had been deserted by her husband, Patience drew a handkerchief from her sleeve and dabbed at her eyes with it.

The balding man looked properly sympathetic.

"We have been informed," Goo-ga-ro-no said, "that her husband only recently sailed from Quebec for France. We have no way of knowing whether this is true or not, and we have come to you to confirm it, if that is at all possible."

"Of course it is," the clerk said heartily. "The manifest will reveal whether your husband was on board. One moment." He pulled a large ledger from beneath the counter.

The girls exchanged a quick glance; the ruse appeared to be working.

"What was the name, if you please?" he asked.

Patience's mind suddenly became numb and refused to function.

Goo-ga-ro-no leaped into the breach. "Her memory is so painful," she explained, "that she can scarcely speak her husband's name. It is du Pont." She proceeded to spell it.

Patience lowered her head and pressed her handkerchief to her mouth. She made a strangled series of sounds that caused Goo-ga-ro-no to suspect that she was having an uncontrolled fit of giggling. Taking no risks, Goo-ga-ro-no kicked her sharply on the ankle. Patience winced and fell silent.

The clerk carefully turned the pages of the ledger, then came to a spot that he apparently was searching for and studied it at length. At last, he raised his head. "I'm sorry to report to you ladies that no passenger named du Pont was on board the brig that sailed most recently from Quebec for Brest."

Patience smothered her face again in her handkerchief, and her disappointment seemed genuine.

Goo-ga-ro-no was equal to the crisis. "If you please, sir," she wanted to know, "may we see the ledger for ourselves? I'm afraid that sorrow has left my sister almost deranged, and the only way she'll be convinced of the truth of the words that you speak is in seeing with her own eyes what is written in the ledger."

The request was rather unusual, but the clerk remained fully sympathetic. "To be sure," he said, and placed the ledger on the desk in front of them. "Here," he said pointing, "is the name of the ship, and here is the sailing date. And here you will find the full list of passengers who embarked for France."

Patience eagerly scanned the list.

Goo-ga-ro-no, as befitted her role of a sister, took her time, and then she too studied the list carefully.

"He is not listed here," Goo-ga-ro-no said sorrowfully. "I'm so sorry to have bothered you, monsieur."

"That's perfectly all right," the clerk replied. "I just
wish I could have given you better news."

"You are very kind, sir," Goo-ga-ro-no said as she
shepherded Patience back out of the office. They did not
speak as they descended to the street, and they remained
silent as they hurried back up the steep slope to their
lodgings.

There, Roger leaped to his feet and No-da-vo was
almost as tense. "Well?" Roger demanded.

Patience replied slowly. "I tried to memorize the names
of those who made the voyage," she said. "Major Henri
de Bienville was one. Gray Fox was another. A third was a
lady, Arlene d'Amarante, of whom I have never before
heard. Then a fourth was identified only as 'Indian girl.' "

"That's precisely right," Goo-ga-ro-no said. "I have no
idea, and I really don't care who this Arlene d'Amarante
may be, but I can assure you that I am quite positive the
'Indian girl' could be no one but Ah-wen-ga. Gray Fox
abducted her and disappeared with her. For whatever
reason, he has taken her on board a ship with Major de
Bienville and this lady and is taking her to France."

Roger frowned and ran a hand through his hair. "You
realize," he said, "that this seems to be as illogical as it is
unexpected."

"Indeed it is," Patience agreed. "But at least we now
know that Ah-wen-ga has been taken to France."

"But why?" Goo-ga-ro-no asked. "This is so distressing.
I know that France is a large country, and it would be
exceptionally difficult to find her there."

"It may not be as hard as you think," Roger replied,
trying to cheer them up. "Give me time to think about all
this, and I'll see what I can come up with to solve this
riddle."

Later that day, Roger sent word to the ship that was
waiting for them that he and his party were ready to
depart, and that evening they set sail for Boston on the late
tide. Roger knew that he had to take the lead in finding
some key to this puzzle.

*   *   *

Gascony, a province of rolling hills and fertile valleys, of mountains and cliffs and ever-changing landscape in southwestern France, was noted for its potent brandywine, the courage of its fighting men, and the beauty of its women. It was also renowned throughout France because of the predominance of red hair among the inhabitants, and it was said that all Gascons had evil tempers. This, however, was not entirely the case.

Ah-wen-ga soon discovered that the Gascons whom she encountered were amiable and courtly and that they went out of their way to be helpful to her. For the first time since she had been abducted, she even felt relatively at ease.

Her immediate surroundings had more to do with these pleasantries than she realized. She and her escorts had taken up residence in an ancient castle that dated back to the early Middle Ages, constructed on the edge of a precipice overlooking a lush valley below. The castle, with stout ramparts and high walls, which was located about two miles from the little town of Tournay, dominated the countryside around it. It was not only inaccessible but seemed virtually impregnable. This suited the purposes of Arlene d'Amarante and Henri de Bienville.

They were taking no chances, however, and had been escorted by fifty so-called household retainers of the Duc de Guise. "Household retainers" was a diplomatic way of saying that these men belonged to the duc's private army. Only the greatest nobles were allowed to raise their own military forces, and all of those who wore the green uniform of de Guise were veterans of French infantry. They had seen action at home, in Alsace, and abroad. They were commanded by Captain de Sanson, a ruggedly handsome bachelor who, having no domestic attachments, enjoyed the military life and particularly relished the high salary that the duc paid him.

Ample room was available for all members of the party. The military contingent occupied the ground floor, where the soldiers were on sentry duty, and they had little or no cause to encounter Lady Arlene's group.

As befitted a relative of the Duc de Guise, they were also attended by a number of servants, including chefs, butlers, housemaids, and ladies' maids for Arlene and Ah-wen-ga.

The party was housed on the upper floor of the castle, and beyond the French windows of the bedchambers stood an open verandalike area that extended all the way to the three-foot-high parapet, from behind which they could look down on the surrounding countryside. Arlene and Ah-wen-ga occupied the two largest bedchambers, handsome rooms with small sitting rooms, and fitted with numerous conveniences that ladies of high rank expected.

Henri de Bienville also occupied a large chamber, but spent most of his time in the drawing room.

Only Gray Fox had inferior quarters—a small chamber that normally was a valet's room. He was insulted by Arlene's decision to quarter him there, but he had learned to expect nothing good from her. Not only was the very sight of him still anathema to Ah-wen-ga, but she had communicated her dislike of him so thoroughly to Arlene that the young noblewoman also openly detested him. Nevertheless, he refused to part company with the group. Had it not been for his efforts, Ah-wen-ga never would have arrived in France, he often thought to himself—and he intended to protect his interests. Only in this way, he conjectured, could he share in the glory resulting from her presentation to King Louis, and he looked forward to his reward.

What he hoped for was nothing less than a commission as a full colonel in the French army, and the command of a regiment. When the senior officers of the army learned that he was the son of the noted Alain de Gramont, he reasoned, they would welcome him into their midst gladly, and like his father before him, he would make them proud to call him a colleague.

Arlene drilled Ah-wen-ga for hours each day in private, and the results were obvious. She was learning to speak and understand French with facility, and her progress in other ways was equally remarkable. Aside from her dark skin, black eyes, and blue-black hair, she looked and acted like a lady of the French court. Since Arlene was training her with a specific purpose in mind, the resemblance she bore to a somewhat dissolute lady, careless of her personal morals, was quite marked.

Arlene realized how well she was succeeding with her pupil when de Bienville made a point of paying more and more attention to Ah-wen-ga. He often watched her surreptitiously. And Captain de Sanson appeared to be openly smitten with her. As for Gray Fox, although under strict orders to keep his distance from her, he, too, eyed her frequently. And it was Gray Fox who created the first trouble.

At the end of each day, shortly before sundown, Ah-wen-ga had fallen into the habit of wandering out onto the terracelike roof and over to the parapet, where she would stand for a long time, admiring the view. The sight itself was rather spectacular, to be sure, because it offered unlimited access to a scene that stretched for miles in three directions.

Actually, she was indulging in some private daydreams. The French countryside spread out below, as such, meant nothing to her, but after a hard day of study with Arlene, she liked to pretend that she was back in the land of the Seneca, secure in the home of Sun-ai-yee and Talking Quail, her parents, and betrothed to Ja-gonh. These harmless excursions into fantasy made her lonely existence far more bearable. At such times, her tediously irksome captivity and bitter thoughts of her captors faded into the gathering twilight.

Her routines became known to the entire staff, of course, and it was hardly accidental one day—when she was even lovelier and more seductive than usual, in a dress of black silk with a fitted bodice, plunging neckline, and low back—that Captain de Sanson happened to wander in her direction from the drawing room.

Ah-wen-ga was so lost in her thoughts that she was unaware that he had come near.

The captain cleared his throat and bowed rather awkwardly. "Forgive the intrusion, mademoiselle," he said, "but I'm just checking on security and want to make sure that you're all right."

"I'm just fine, thank you," Ah-wen-ga replied in French, and favored him with a smile and a long, burning look, techniques that had been drilled into her by Arlene. She was not, in her innocence, deliberately flirting with the officer, but merely responding—appropriately, as she saw it—to her training. Nevertheless, the result was immediate. Captain de Sanson reacted at once, preening, squaring his shoulders, and making his interest in her very evident.

Ah-wen-ga instinctively felt that such a flirtation, which she had never previously known during her years of Seneca life, was pleasurable and gratifying to her ego. Not only did it enhance her opinion of her own attractiveness, but it demonstrated to her—beyond any doubt—the considerable power that she, as a woman, could exert over any man whom she chose to favor.

As she continued to smile steadily at the captain, de Sanson became so flustered that he stammered a few words, bowed, and hastily took his leave.

Basking in a warm, feminine glow, Ah-wen-ga gradually slipped back into her daydream. But a new, jarring element intruded on her harmless pastime.

Her lifetime training now came to her assistance. Her ears picked up a soft but unmistakable sound of someone behind her, creeping closer and still closer to her.

She had no need to turn and look in order to realize that it was Gray Fox who was drawing nearer. Only an Indian who had received rigorous training could have moved so quietly, and certainly no Frenchman was capable of such a feat.

Because she was wearing such a snug-fitting skirt, Ah-wen-ga had not deposited Arlene's knife in her garter, where she had been in the habit of placing it since acquiring it in Paris, but instead carried it beneath one voluminous sleeve of her gown. She quietly lowered her hand, and as the blade descended from its handle, her fingers closed around the hilt. She was ready now, and tensed.

Now came the most difficult part of her wait. She had to time her attack carefully, and she stood motionless, pretending to be unaware of Gray Fox's presence as he gradually drew closer.

When she gauged that he was almost within arm's reach, she wheeled on him suddenly and brought the sharp, double-edged blade up to chest level. In astonishment, Gray Fox found the point of her knife penetrating his leather shirt.

Ah-wen-ga addressed him in her own tongue. "If you come any closer," she said, "you will die. If you do not believe me, just raise a hand against me."

His ardor cooled abruptly, and he sought in vain for some mollifying remark that would soothe her and perhaps put her off her guard.

To his astonishment and to Ah-wen-ga's surprise, he had no opportunity to reply. Suddenly, the muzzle of a pistol jabbed him in the back, and Henri de Bienville spoke crisply, coldly. "Raise your hands high above your head, Huron," he said, "and try no tricks or I shall be obliged to blow you into the land of your ancestors."

Gray Fox slowly raised his hands above his head.

Relieved beyond measure by the unexpected help she had received, Ah-wen-ga lowered her knifeblade and it vanished again up her sleeve.

"You were very brave," de Bienville told her, "but fortunately I became aware of Gray Fox's presence soon after he appeared out here. Something in his manner convinced me he was up to no good, and when I realized he planned to make advances to you, I decided that I should do something quickly to help you."

Ah-wen-ga's smile was full and limpid. "I am more grateful to you than I can tell you," she said.

Her seeming interest in him and her obvious gratitude stirred the major. It wasn't often that a woman as lovely and desirable as the young Seneca signaled—as she seemed to do—that she was available.

He dealt brusquely with Gray Fox. "You know that you are to keep away from this lady at all times," he said. "You may consider yourself fortunate that I'm not doing away with you at once, and instead I'm allowing you to live. Approach her again, however—come near her just once—and I promise you that you will regret it."

Desire had turned to hatred in Gray Fox's eyes, and he glared at Ah-wen-ga before turning abruptly on his heel and stalking off. His surprise at the stern and hostile response by his friend de Bienville stunned and irritated him.

She continued to flirt with the major. He deserved her attention, she thought, and because he had helped her, she was eager to please him.

When Roger Harkness and his party returned to Boston from New France, they received another escort of militiamen and went promptly on to the land of the Seneca and to the lodge of Sun-ai-yee. Ja-gonh, who had been fretfully passing the weeks with only his ordinary routines to while away the time, hurried to join them there.

Roger explained in full what they had learned in Quebec, and the others—Patience, Goo-ga-ro-no, and No-da-vo— related the parts they had played and passed along what they had learned.

Soon after the recitals began, Renno and Betsy slipped into the house and unobtrusively joined the gathering. The tensions were so great that no one really noticed that Renno was walking with some difficulty and that his normally rugged complexion had taken on an unhealthy pallor.

When the young people had finished their recital, Sun-ai-yee broke the silence. "I do not understand," he said. "Gray Fox apparently acted on behalf of the French when

71

he abducted my daughter. But what possible use could she be to them—and why have they taken her across the great sea to France?''

Ja-gonh spoke succinctly and curtly. "It is useless for us to speculate, just as it is useless for us to send a rescue party for Ah-wen-ga without knowing where she might be. There are hundreds, and even thousands, of places in a land as vast as France where she could be hidden from us and where we could search for many years without finding her.''

Renno cleared his throat, and the others gave him their full attention. "It strikes me," he said, "that we need help with this problem. We need the assistance of people who know France and the French. We need help from someone who can trace the movements of the French major and his party from the time their ship lands until they arrive at whatever their destination may be.''

Sun-ai-yee regarded him hopelessly. "How do we get such help?''

Roger immediately interrupted the conversation. "The governor of Virginia, my superior," he said, "is not only a powerful figure in the New World, but he has great influence in the Old.''

Betsy now intervened. "I think my brother could be of considerable help to us, too," she said.

Ja-gonh nodded eagerly. "Of course!" His uncle, Ned Ridley, was not only prominent in the shipping business, but as head of the Virginia militia he had countless contacts. And inasmuch as England and France were officially at peace with each other, it was possible he even had influence in French military circles.

They decided to write him at once, and Ja-gonh promptly volunteered to accompany Roger and Patience to Virginia, not only to deliver the letter but also to see the governor and his uncle, Ned. They would leave as soon as it was feasible.

No one could think of a better plan, and so they agreed on that as the next course of action. As Sun-ai-yee commented privately later to Renno, the scheme offered only a slim hope—but any hope was better than none.

Perhaps it was the appearance of a full moon that had made Ah-wen-ga pensive; perhaps it was the events of the afternoon. For whatever reason, she could not shake off her feeling of depression, even though she changed into even more glamorous clothes. And a splendid evening meal failed, too, to raise her spirits.

So, later in the evening, she found herself wandering back to the parapet on the terrace. She had no idea what was bringing her here, but she did not fight the urge.

Arlene, standing inside the door of her suite, watched the young woman. She was in no way surprised when the major appeared from within the drawing room and followed Ah-wen-ga into the open. It was all too evident to Arlene that he was even more taken by her than was Captain de Sanson; if not smitten, at least he wanted her badly.

As de Bienville strolled toward Ah-wen-ga, the way he held his shoulders and arms, the way he moved, indicated his great tension.

Ah-wen-ga saw him bleakly, realized that he was approaching her, and understood that he intended to make advances to her. For a long moment, she stood indecisively, uncertain how to react.

Certainly, she didn't feel drawn to him, nor did she crave his lovemaking. On the other hand, she owed him a debt of gratitude for his help earlier in the day, when he had sent Gray Fox packing so efficiently.

She weighed her chances and decided that it would be best to seem to go along with him, rather than to try to avoid him. She had few enough friends in France, and she needed the major's support. And to oppose him would avail her nothing.

Furthermore, she would have no chance to reach for the little knife she carried in her garter. She knew, too, that her physical strength was no match for the powerfully built

French officer, and, as before, some inner voice warned her not to transform him into an enemy at this time. It should be a simple matter to win his sympathy, and the cost would be slight.

Therefore, she willingly raised her head, and her lips parted for his kiss. De Bienville kissed her hungrily, a surge of passion rising within him.

Feeling nothing, An-wen-ga was unmoved by the physical contact with him. She was not surprised by this because, she told herself, only Ja-gonh had the power to cause her to react. But she was so feminine that she needed no instructions to guide her, and simulating intense pleasure, she curled her arms around the major's neck and pressed still closer to him as their lips continued to meet.

From the living quarters of the suite, Lady Arlene d'Amarante watched the scene closely. She conceded wryly that Ah-wen-ga not only was an apt pupil who responded well to instruction, but was a woman who had a natural instinct for intimacy with a man. Having this quality herself in abundance, Arlene understood its relative rarity, and she congratulated herself: when her pupil ultimately was presented to Louis XV, the monarch would be almost certain to find her irresistible.

For the present, she considered that Ah-wen-ga had gone far enough—and so had Arlene's own lover. Before they were both carried away, and indulged in an affair before they could stop themselves, it was time for her to call a halt.

Just inside the open doors that faced the terrace, Arlene stirred noisily the contents of a glass with a silver spoon. Then, pausing to clear her throat, she stepped into the open.

De Bienville immediately stepped back, leaving a distance of some three feet between himself and Ah-wen-ga, who—obviously unaffected by the experience—looked tranquil and smiled pleasantly at her instructor. She had been obeying orders, after all, and saw no reason to be upset.

Henri de Bienville, however, was far more flustered. He was conscious that quantities of Ah-wen-ga's scarlet lip

74

rouge undoubtedly were smeared around his mouth. His passions, though curbed, had not yet subsided. Although he was a man accustomed to rapid thought and rapid action, he now did not know what to say or do.

Arlene saved him the trouble. "Here you are!" she exclaimed cheerfully. "I've been searching the castle for both of you, and it didn't occur to me that you might be out here enjoying the view. Isn't it a gloriously clear night?"

De Bienville agreed rather lamely that he found the weather perfect.

"You know," Arlene said brightly, "we should arrange to have some chairs brought out here so we can watch the scenery at our leisure. We really don't want to miss any of the pleasant weather before the snow and rains come."

It seemed inconceivable to de Bienville that she had somehow missed seeing him embracing Ah-wen-ga, but her cordial manner was that of a tranquil young lady, not that of a mistress who has been given ample cause for a jealous outburst. He breathed more easily. He had been fortunate, he told himself, in having escaped unscathed, so all was well.

The next time he tried to make love to Ah-wen-ga, he would see to it that nothing would interrupt him.

Chapter IV

Alexander Spotswood, the retired royal governor of Virginia and now deputy postmaster general of the American colonies, was one of the most able and distinguished English administrators in the New World. He was also, by far, most enthusiastic about the potentials of America, and he had elected to spend the rest of his days in Virginia, where he had acquired vast tracts of land.

A summons from Spotswood was almost tantamount to a royal command, and when Ned Ridley—Betsy's brother and uncle of Ja-gonh—received a request one day during the summer that he call on the former governor, he lost no time in riding over to the comfortable Spotswood home in Norfolk, one of several that the former governor owned.

Spotswood suffered from the gout, but otherwise enjoyed robust health, and he looked far younger than his years. "I'm sorry to have to bring you here on such a hot day, General Ridley," he said, "but I have news for you, and I know you're eager to receive it."

Ned Ridley nodded eagerly as he sat opposite the older man in his study. "You've received word from France already, Your Excellency? It has not been that many weeks, I believe, since you sent off your letter of inquiry."

Spotswood nodded. "I am as surprised as you are, but it appears that the information I sought was easy to obtain. Also—fortunately for us—the commercial agent to whom I wrote is one of the most competent in France." He picked up a letter and glanced at it briefly. "He informs me that the people you seek, Major Henri de Bienville, Lady Arlene d'Amarante, and a half-breed Indian, son of Alain de Gramont, were visitors in Paris until recently and dwelled in the mansion of the Duc de Guise. They were accompanied by an Indian girl, who was quite comely, according to our agent, who emphasizes that nothing further is known about her. He assumed that she was in the service of Lady Arlene."

Ned barely concealed his excitement. "That's precisely the kind of information that I required, Your Excellency," he exclaimed. "Does your informant have any idea where the party may have gone when they left Paris?"

"Indeed," Spotswood replied, and searched the letter for the appropriate reference. "Ah, here we are. Southeast of the market town of Tarbes in Gascony lies a much smaller community, Tournay. Located a short distance from the town—a few miles, apparently—is an ancient, well-defended castle that belongs to the Duc de Guise. As Lady Arlene is related to the de Guise family, it is believed that she and her companions may have gone there. The reason so much is known about her whereabouts, I gather, is because of the interest she generates as a former mistress of King Louis."

Ned asked for the privilege of making notes on the present location of the party and, thanking Spotswood with great sincerity for his enormous help, rode home to inform his wife.

Consuelo was excited and amazed when her husband told her the news. "Why would Ah-wen-ga be abducted and forced into the French woman's service?" she wanted to know. "Surely the French nobility has no lack of servants."

"I know no more than what Governor Spotswood has passed along to me," Ned said. "Your guess is as good as mine."

At supper that evening, they broke the news to Ja-gonh, who felt a sense of excitement surge within him. "At last!" he almost shouted.

"What will you do now?" Consuelo asked.

The young Seneca gazed at his aunt stolidly. "Obviously," he said, "I must go to France and rescue Ah-wen-ga!"

Consuelo was dismayed and Ned was startled. "Not so fast," he said. "You don't know France, and you're not really familiar with the language."

Ja-gonh's look was eloquent. It was evident that he intended to allow nothing to stand in his way.

Having known and admired Renno for more than three decades, Ned Ridley recognized certain qualities that Renno's son had inherited. Ja-gonh had the same stubborn courage, the same disregard for obstacles that stood in his path, the same determination to complete a mission successfully.

Ned sighed. "I had a notion you would feel this way," he said. "That's why I've taken the liberty of asking Roger Harkness to call."

When Roger arrived at the house within the next half hour, they brought him up-to-date on developments. "I intend to go to France," Ja-gonh told him. "Not only will I have the opportunity to find Ah-wen-ga and bring her home, but my enemy, Gray Fox, is there. My confrontation with him has been postponed for far too long, and the spirit of my grandfather cries out for justice."

"I've pointed out to Ja-gonh," Ned interjected, "that what he proposes will not be a simple matter. He is unfamiliar with France, and his knowledge of the French language is very limited."

"Those handicaps can be overcome easily enough," Roger replied. "I plan to go with you, Ja-gonh. I believe I can easily get approval for such a mission."

The young Seneca was highly pleased, but Consuelo was not satisfied. "You know the Gascon region of France, Captain Harkness?"

"I know it well, Mrs. Ridley," he replied. "We've been at peace with France, at least on the surface, for quite a few years, and I've spent long holidays there—ostensible holidays, you might say, duly encouraged by the Department of War. I spent an entire summer on a walking tour of Gascony, and I know the little town of Tournay. I may even be familiar with the de Guise castle. As to the language, I speak French almost as well as I speak English. So Ja-gonh will have no problems on that score, either."

"How will your bride react to the fact that you're going away on this mission so soon after marrying her?" Consuelo persisted.

Roger looked regretful, but nevertheless spoke firmly. "It is unfortunate that we must be separated," he said, "but I can see no alternative. Ja-gonh faces a great crisis, and I would be unworthy of our friendship if I failed to do everything in my power to help him. I believe the governor will approve, and I'm sure that Patience will understand and will agree that this separation can't be avoided."

"I was very fond of Ghonka," Ned said. "In fact, I was about the age of you two young men when I met him, and I shall never forget him. I was in awe of him, and I respected him to the end of his days. The very least I can do is to offer you what help I can in this expedition. I have a seagoing brig at anchor in the port of Norfolk at present, and it will be easy enough to fill it with goods to send to the French. The master will be ordered to put into the port of Marseilles. That's within striking distance of Gascony. He'll be given plausible reasons to delay his homeward voyage until you return escorting Ah-wen-ga. How does that suit you?"

"I shall be more than ever in your debt for all time, Uncle Ned," Ja-gonh said solemnly.

Ned shook his head. "You will not," he replied. "Consuelo and I are permanently in Renno's debt, and we'll consider the dispatch of my brig only as payment of part interest on it.''

''If your wife is too upset,'' Consuelo told Roger, ''perhaps we can help to persuade her that you are doing the right thing. We've known her all of her life, so it may well be that we'll be able to influence her reaction to your leaving.''

''I thank you,'' Roger said, ''but I anticipate no troubles.'' He rode home soon thereafter, arranging to meet with Ja-gonh the following day to make final plans for their long voyage.

Patience listened without comment as he explained. ''This information only serves to confirm what we learned in Quebec. Now there can be no doubt. Ah-wen-ga is in France, and the informant assumed that she was working as a serving maid to the woman who was traveling with Major de Bienville. Of course, there must be a great deal more involved in this situation than we know, but we will find out soon enough.'' Roger went on to tell her of Ja-gonh's insistence on going to France, and then he disclosed that he had volunteered to accompany the young Seneca, because he was thoroughly familiar with the Gascon territory and language.

Patience accepted her husband's news quietly. In fact, her reaction was almost docile.

''How soon do you plan to set sail for France?'' she asked, her voice and expression innocent.

''We're leaving as quickly as the ship can be made ready,'' he said. ''They'll need only a day or two to load her cargo and then we'll go.''

''And about how long do you expect to be away?''

He paused to consider. ''We'll spend about six weeks on the high seas going, another six returning—that's about three months. And how long we'll actually spend in Gascony, I can't tell, of course. It all depends on our success in getting Ah-wen-ga away.''

''That makes it as much as four months, I suppose,'' she murmured.

''I hope you don't mind this separation too much,'' he

said apologetically, "but it really can't be helped. Ja-gonh needs my aid desperately, and I'd disgrace the name of friendship if I let him down."

"By all means, do what you must," Patience told him earnestly.

Roger was vastly relieved. Had he known her as well as her parents did, he might have guessed—as they would have done—what was in her mind. As it was, he happily accepted her attitude for what it appeared to be.

The preparations for the journey were necessarily hectic. Ja-gonh had one suit of English clothes at the Ridleys' house, but at their insistence he had several others made and bought shirts, shoes, boots, and stockings.

"You'll be wise to let your hair grow in on both sides of your scalp lock," Ned told him. "Any American Indian is, after all, a rarity in France, and a white Indian is bound to arouse enormous curiosity. You'll be seeking anonymity and won't want to draw attention to yourself in any way. So the more nearly you resemble an ordinary Frenchman, the less noticeable you'll be." Ja-gonh accepted the advice gratefully.

The tailor rushed his new clothes, and Captain Fred Grey, the master of the brig, saw to it that the hold was filled at the earliest possible hour with merchandise to be sold in France. He took on fresh provisions for his officers and crew of eighteen, but urged the two passengers, who would be fortunate in having separate cabins, to carry their own supplies of fruit, fresh meat, and bread.

As the hour for sailing neared, Ja-gonh wrote a long letter of explanation to his father, and Ned added his own postscript of endorsement before sending it off by courier to the land of the Seneca.

Ned and Consuelo accompanied Ja-gonh to the ship, and they were surprised, when Roger appeared, to find him deeply perturbed.

"I expected Patience to be on hand so I could bid her an appropriate farewell," he said, "but she's nowhere to be found, and one of the servants told me that she had left the house an hour ago."

Consuelo tried to soothe him. "Her disappearance is only natural," she said. "After all, Patience is still a bride, and it undoubtedly hasn't been easy for her to contemplate this separation. So, by absenting herself, she's saved both of you the pain of parting."

Roger was only partly mollified. He and Ja-gonh, who looked like a young Virginia gentleman complete to his long sword and the pistols he carried in his belt, boarded the ship and were greeted by Captain Grey.

"Now that you're here, gentlemen, we'll weigh anchor at once," he said.

They went to the rail, and Roger searched the shore in vain for any sign of Patience.

"Good luck, lads, and good hunting!" Ned called as the brig cast off. The anchor was weighed, the sails filled gradually, and the merchantman made her way out of Norfolk harbor for the voyage to the Mediterranean port of Marseilles.

Ja-gonh and Roger remained on deck for more than two hours, reluctant to go to their cabins to unpack while land was still in sight. Then, as the Virginia shore gradually faded on the horizon, they finally went below.

Roger opened the door of his cabin, then halted abruptly, blinked in astonishment, and his jaw dropped.

Patience stood facing him, her manner half-defiant, half-tentative. "I'm sorry, darling," she said, "but I saw no reason why I should not help in this mission, for I feel sure I can be of great help to you. I do speak French like a native, you know, and I refrained from telling you that I, too, even know something of the Gascon countryside."

He continued to stare at her, shaking his head.

She came to him and placed a hand on his arm. "The Ridleys made the arrangements for me," she said. "Both of them thought it was a good idea for me to accompany you on this adventure, but they agreed that you wouldn't permit it if you knew in advance."

Roger finally was able to speak in a calm voice. "Are you a stowaway, or does Captain Grey know you're on board?"

She smiled somewhat apprehensively. "Oh, he knows," she said. "General Ridley confided in him, and he personally sneaked me on board."

Roger seemed to be on the verge of losing his temper; the color rose to his face, his eyes flashed, and he clenched his fists. Then, suddenly, he began to laugh. Patience was encouraged and beguiled.

He laughed even more loudly. "If it would do any good," he said, "I'd lose my temper, but I'm afraid you're incorrigible." He reached for her, drew her to him, and kissed her.

Patience clung to him. "I really will be a big help to you in France. You'll see."

He regarded her fondly. "We'll find out soon enough whether you're a help or a hindrance," he said, and sighed. "It's just as well, in any event. I would have missed you too much had you been left behind."

Patience hoped that Ja-gonh would accept her presence with the same equanimity. She soon had an opportunity to learn his reaction. The young Seneca, hearing voices in the cabin adjoining his, came to investigate. Taking in the situation at a glance, he raised his eyebrows eloquently.

Feeling compelled to explain, Patience began to offer him her rationalization for sneaking on board the brig.

Ja-gonh held up a hand to silence her. "Just keep in mind," he told her solemnly, "that we are making no pleasure trip. I have taken a sacred vow to kill a man, and his blood will stain my tomahawk before I return to the land of my people."

Of all the warriors in the entire Seneca nation, perhaps none was more typical of his people than No-da-vo. He not only looked like a prototype of a senior warrior, but his actions seemed to shout his nationality. Unlike the Great Sachem and his family, who had strong ties in the English colonies, No-da-vo had spent his entire life in the wilderness, and knew almost nothing of the civilization of the white man, or of the attitudes of the settlers.

"It is because No-da-vo is a Seneca of Seneca," Betsy told Ena one afternoon when they were drying corn together in the early autumn sunlight, "that Goo-ga-ro-no is drawn to him."

Ena stopped cutting kernels of corn from their cob, and put down her knife. "You think she is reacting, then, because she went so far in the opposite direction last year and caused so much trouble?"

"Exactly so," Betsy replied. "She threw herself at a Frenchman, one completely unworthy of her, and went scampering off to Quebec with him because she was rebelling against her Seneca background. She learned her lesson, and it is the very qualities that No-da-vo has that make him most attractive to her."

"Whatever her reason, I do admire her taste," Ena said.

"Renno and I quite agree, as you know," Betsy declared. "It wouldn't surprise me in the least if a wedding ceremony were to take place in the near future."

But Ena frowned. "I am thinking of the pledge that No-da-vo made concerning the kidnapping of Ah-wenga."

"That was unnecessary," Betsy conceded. "Whatever he may do to help, the matter of avenging her abduction is really Ja-gonh's responsibility. But since No-da-vo made a public pledge, I suppose that the manitous are certain to hold a man to his word."

"I think not in this case," Ena replied unexpectedly. "I have worshiped the manitous all my life, and only now, as I grow old, do I begin to understand them. They realize, to be sure, that No-da-vo is young and hot-blooded. They undoubtedly recognize his rash gesture as one made in the heat of anger against one who is a Huron. I think it very unlikely that the manitous would insist that No-da-vo honor his pledge."

Betsy did not pretend to understand the religious faith of the Seneca but was willing enough to accept her mother-in-law's view. "May I tell this to Goo-ga-ro-no? She has not discussed the matter with me, but I know that she and No-da-vo are worried about it."

Ena's mouth formed a thin, uncompromising line. "I think it best that you say nothing," she replied. "It is often preferable that the young worry themselves into some gray hairs. Only in this way do they mature. The manitous will find ways to create in Goo-ga-ro-no and No-da-vo the enlightenment that eventually will make them far happier. They will suffer first, but later they will be relieved."

Accepting her mother-in-law's word as final, Betsy bowed her head.

Both women resumed the task of cutting corn from the cob and spreading the kernels on planks of wood to dry in the sun. "Renno is late," Ena remarked. "He has kept the council in session for the entire day."

Betsy nodded. "Yes, it appears that way."

"Did the council have many decisions of importance to make?"

The younger woman shrugged. "I didn't discuss the meeting with Renno. He hasn't been in an especially talkative mood lately."

"He looks very tired to me," his mother said.

"I think he is more worried about Ah-wen-ga than he indicates, and he grieves also for Ja-gonh's sake," Betsy replied.

"There is more than that behind his behavior," Ena said.

Betsy became thoughtful. "You may well be right. He's had very little appetite lately, and when Renno loses interest in food, I begin to worry about him."

Both women looked up as a brave, wearing the feathered bonnet of a war chief, appeared hurriedly around the edge of the house. It was El-i-chi, Renno's younger brother, who now looked very solemn. "Betsy," he said gravely, "prepare yourself for a blow. My mother, call on the manitous to give you strength."

"What is amiss?" Betsy demanded.

"Renno," his brother said, "is ill. He fell into the Big Sleep during the council meeting, and we could not awaken him. The principal medicine men of the nation have tried, and they have not been able to rouse him."

Neither woman became visibly flustered or upset. "Where is he now?" Betsy asked.

"He is being brought to this house," El-i-chi replied, and gestured toward the center of town.

They did not have long to wait. Renno, unconscious and pale, was carried on a pallet by four young warriors. His buffalo robe, the mark of his high office, had been thrown over him for warmth. Betsy and Ena started forward at once. Neither gave in to her feelings. Betsy directed her husband's limp body be placed on his bed, while Ena immediately hurried to the cooking fire to instruct Goo-ga-ro-no, who was already preparing the evening's meal, to be sure to make a quantity of broth, which they could try to feed to Renno.

The bearers withdrew, and Betsy stood with her brother-in-law, looking down at Renno, who appeared to be resting comfortably despite the bright spots burning in both his cheeks indicating that he was running a high fever.

A chill passed through her when she saw her beloved Renno brought to her in such a pitiful state. Yet her years of exposure to the Seneca ways came to the fore, and she forced herself to speak in an even voice.

"I have heard it said," Betsy declared, "that the Big Sleep has found many victims in other places. It attacked the main town of the Mohawk, and there a number of men and women died. It also appeared in Fort Springfield, and many failed to awaken."

Like Betsy and Ena, El-i-chi, who now folded his arms across his bare chest, showed no sign of the inner panic that was assailing him. "The Mohawk," he said, "know of no cure for the Big Sleep. I discussed it only a few days ago with one of their war chiefs."

"Have the physicians at Fort Springfield found a cure or at least an antidote, to your knowledge, El-i-chi?"

"The physicians of the English," he replied, "do not confide in me."

Betsy unhesitatingly hurried to her private quarters in the adjoining building. She took a jar of carefully hoarded ink, a quill pen, and a sheet of parchment. Scribbling rapidly, she wrote a message to Renno's oldest and dearest friend, Jeffrey Wilson, at Springfield.

I implore your help, if it is possible for you to give it. Let me know at once if any antidote has been found for the Big Sleep. I regret to say that Renno has been stricken.

"I don't know whether they've found anything useful, but it can do no harm to find out, and surely we must try," she said to El-i-chi. "I would like this to be carried by our swiftest messenger."

A faint smile touched the corners of El-i-chi's mouth, as he looked in the direction of the young warrior who had just joined Goo-ga-ro-no, and was speaking to her in a low tone. "I know of no man more capable than No-da-vo," he said.

Betsy instantly hailed the young man and asked if he would carry her letter to General Wilson. Within a few minutes, No-da-vo was on his way, running through the forest at a rapid, steady gait.

When the broth was cooked, Betsy held Renno in her arms, while Ena raised a steaming gourd to his lips. Both women were encouraged when he responded sufficiently to their ministrations. Then, without having opened his eyes, he slumped once again in his wife's grasp and drifted into the sleep from which it was impossible to fully rouse him.

El-i-chi, assured that everything possible would be done to help his brother, went to the house of the sachem of the Seneca. Sun-ai-yee had eaten an early supper and in spite of the cool weather, was sitting on the ground, leaning against the outer wall of his house, as he smoked a pipe.

El-i-chi sat down beside him, produced a pipe of his own, and stuffed it with tobacco. Sun-ai-yee plucked a piece of coal from the fire with a forked stick and passed it to the younger man.

El-i-chi lit his pipe. "Could you see any improvement in the condition of Renno?" Sun-ai-yee asked.

El-i-chi merely puffed on his pipe.

"Because his wife," the grizzled sachem said, "comes from the English colony, Virginia, in a time of crisis her ways are not our ways, and her beliefs are not our beliefs."

El-i-chi weighed the statement. "Sun-ai-yee is right as far as he goes," he said, "but there are other factors to be considered. When Ena, as the mother of Renno, decides that the time has come to call upon the medicine men of the Seneca to summon the attention of the gods, she will call on them. And they will respond to her bidding."

"That is so," Sun-ai-yee said, sounding relieved.

El-i-chi told him in detail about the letter that Betsy had sent to Jeffrey Wilson.

"I have no faith in the physicians of the white man," Sun-ai-yee responded abruptly.

El-i-chi drew on his pipe. "It is always bad when a leader is stricken," he said, "but I consider that the illness of Renno has come at a very bad time for the Seneca and for the other people of the Iroquois nations."

"It is a very bad time," Sun-ai-yee agreed.

"The Iroquois League," El-i-chi said, "has endured many shocks and many attempts to pull it to pieces. Now, however, it may be threatened from the inside."

"If it were not for Renno, who is so strong and determined in the high post of Great Sachem," Sun-ai-yee said flatly, "the Iroquois League would founder. Only the Seneca would remain steadfast in their purpose. The Mohawk would go in one direction, the Oneida and Onondaga would go in another, the Tuscarora would heed their own leaders, and the Cayuga, as always, would strive to stand apart."

"The Iroquois League," El-i-chi replied, "is the single greatest political work that has ever been constructed in all the lands of North America. We are at peace with each other, and our strength is so great that other nations keep the peace with us. In every land there is prosperity; in no land is there mourning for warriors who have been killed. This is a tribute to the efforts of Renno, who has held the league together when it might have fallen apart."

"If I could," Sun-ai-yee said, "I would make a speech to the leaders and the warriors of all Iroquois. I would beg them to stand together now, shoulder to shoulder, as they have done for so many years in the past, and I would remind them that together, we can overcome all of our enemies. But I will keep silent, because I know they would not heed my words."

"They will not listen to me, either," El-i-chi said. "They heed the voice of no man except Renno."

"I fear that the league—like a bear trap that has seen better days and has grown old—soon will break apart."

"If it does, only Renno has the wisdom and the skill to put it together again."

They puffed their pipes in silence for a time and suddenly Sun-ai-yee demanded, "What would become of the Iroquois League if Renno did not recover from the Big Sleep?"

El-i-chi took his pipe from his mouth and stared at the burning coals. "In that case," he said, "the Iroquois, like Renno, would die and be no more."

Sun-ai-yee clenched a narrow fist. "That must not be allowed to happen!" he declared passionately.

"We will do our best to salvage the alliance," El-i-chi said, "but I have no hope that you and I—or anyone else, other than Renno—can influence the sachems and war chiefs of the other Iroquois nations. The fate of Renno will determine the destiny of the great nations that inhabit this continent."

Chapter V

No-da-vo neither slept nor rested on his journey through the wilderness from the land of the Mohawk, until he reached the Wilsons' fine old farmhouse outside Fort Springfield. There, he was served an elaborate meal —of which he partook sparingly—and offered the full hospitality of the place, while Jeffrey and Adrienne, his still-attractive French wife, read the letter from Betsy. Both were deeply disturbed.

"This is terrible news!" Jeffrey exclaimed.

"I know," Adrienne replied. "Renno has done so much and has come through so much that one doesn't ordinarily think of him as mortal. But he *is* made of flesh and blood, just like everyone else."

"We've got to move quickly," Jeffrey said. "I don't know if we'll be able to accomplish much for him, but at least we can try. Please invite Dr. Bowen to dine with us today, if you will.''

She grasped his intention at once, and immediately wrote a note to the physician, which she dispatched by messenger. A scant hour later, Dr. Bowen sat with them at their mahogany dining table, eating a simple meal of pot roast with carrots, onions, and potatoes from the Wilson farm.

Jeffrey showed him the letter from Betsy, then added, "I'll greatly appreciate any information you can give us about his peculiar ailment, Doctor.''

The physician settled his spectacles on the bridge of his nose and sighed. "The Indians have invented the most accurately descriptive phrase for the sickness, when they call it the Big Sleep,'' he said. "We've had a number of names and none of them do as well. I'm sorry to say that we know very little about the ailment. It has never reached epidemic proportions, fortunately, but we still don't know whether it can be passed from one person to another. It strikes people in every walk of life. From figures we have accumulated here in the colonies and in England,'' he continued, "we've gathered that most of the victims are men. Furthermore, there seems to be no doubt whatsoever that those who are exposed to the illness can develop a strong immunity to it. For example, as you know all too well, the Reverend Obadiah Jenkins—may the Lord have mercy on his soul—was taken from us. His wife, Deborah, who attended him during his illness, developed an immunity to it that, more or less, is permanent. It's a virtual guarantee that she'll never become a victim of the disease.''

"What I'd like to know most of all,'' Jeffrey said, "is what kind of help we can offer to Renno—whether there is any medication you might be able to prescribe for him, or whether there's some kind of a regimen that his family could follow.''

"I wish there were something, but I'm afraid that, though they're working on the problem at Edinburgh University, no cure has been discovered. Your friend, you say, is an Indian—''

"He's the famous white Indian, actually born here in Springfield," Adrienne interjected. "He was the head of the Seneca, and now he's the chief of the whole Iroquois League."

"Ah, yes," the doctor replied, "now I know the man you mean. I'll say this for him, even though I live some hundreds of miles from him and haven't examined him: his chances of recovery are fairly good—provided he receives the proper care and attention. I assume he has a fairly rugged physique—"

"I doubt if there's a man anywhere who is stronger," Jeffrey said, "or is in better basic physical condition. Renno is my age, but his stamina is phenomenal."

"In that case," the doctor replied, "I'd say the prognosis for him is fairly good. What kind of care is available to him in the land of the Seneca?"

"His people are extraordinarily devoted to him," Jeffrey explained, "and his wife, who was a colonist from Virginia, will do everything she can for him."

"Unfortunately, however," the physician said with a frown, "she's unfamiliar with the illness, I gather."

"When her husband was stricken, it seems to have been her first experience with it."

The doctor ate in silence for some minutes. "You're truly concerned about this man Renno?" he asked at last.

"As concerned," Jeffrey replied passionately, "as I'd be about my own brother."

"Well," the doctor said, "to be totally frank with you, I'd feel far more confident, and would regard his recovery as far more certain, if someone who is familiar with the disease were with him and could take charge of his day-to-day care. Well-meaning people often do the wrong thing, you know, and in cases like this, an experienced hand can be a very valuable help."

They turned to other subjects, and after the doctor took his leave, Jeffrey asked Adrienne to join him in his library, then carefully closed the door behind them. "I'm going to tell you something," he said, "that must go no farther than this room. Many years ago, when all of us were quite young, and you were still in Europe, Deborah Jenkins—she was Deborah Alwin then—was kidnapped by rogue Indians. Renno rescued her and took her back to the town of the Seneca. There, I gather, they had an affair.''

Adrienne exclaimed her surprise. ''I had no idea—''

''No,'' her husband cut in, ''and neither does anyone else. I'm inclined to doubt that Renno has ever mentioned it to Betsy because it all happened so long ago. I know that Deborah told Obadiah about it before she married him, but it made no difference to him.''

''Why do you bring all this up now?''

He replied with great care. ''Deborah's cousin, Walter Alwin, joined the Seneca many years ago, as you know, and has lived successfully among them ever since, and has even become a distinguished war chief. He happens to be married to Renno's sister, Ba-lin-ta. So, that makes Deborah almost a relative of Renno and his family.''

''I can see the connection, although it is stretching a point somewhat,'' Adrienne said.

He smiled at her briefly, and then sobered again. ''I'm seriously thinking of asking Deborah to go out to the land of the Seneca and nurse Renno through his illness. She has, after all, helped with nursing care of several other victims. What do you think?''

Adrienne thought at length. ''I'd say it depends on Deborah's own attitude,'' she said finally. ''She's borne up well since Obadiah passed away. Her children are grown now and don't need her anymore, so she might want to accept because she would feel that she would make herself useful. But I surely can't speak for her.''

''You don't see anything wrong with my making the request?''

''If you're referring to any romance between Deborah and Renno long ago, certainly not.''

Jeffrey was very much relieved. ''I'll ride into town right now, and get Deborah's reaction,'' he said. ''With Renno seriously ill, I'd rather not delay in getting the question settled.''

A horse was saddled for him, and he rode straight to the

Jenkins house. He was greeted by Deborah, still slender and attractive; the only signs of her recent ordeal were dark smudges beneath her eyes.

She was pleased to see Jeffrey, who lost no time coming to the point. First he showed her the letter from Betsy, and then told her of the physician's conversation.

Deborah listened carefully. "You're asking me," she said, "if I would be willing to go to the town of the Seneca and take charge of nursing Renno in an attempt to help see him through this ailment."

"Exactly," Jeffrey replied.

"When Obadiah and I visited the town of the Seneca," she said, "Walter and Ba-lin-ta made us feel very much at home there. For that matter, so did Betsy and Renno." She stared for a long time out of the window at the leaves that had fallen from the trees to the ground, and then she smiled. "I have a soft spot in my heart for Renno. He saved me when I was in despair, and he treated me with great kindness and consideration. I'll always be grateful to him for it, and now I have the opportunity, unexpectedly, to repay a favor from long ago."

"You may want a little time to think this over," Jeffrey Wilson suggested.

She shook her head. "I'll be honest with you, Jeff," she said, "I've dreaded the thought of spending the autumn and winter by myself here. Obadiah's replacement at the church has taken charge there now, and with everybody feeling sorry for me, I know I'd have a tendency to feel sorry for myself, too, and that simply wouldn't do at all. I very much prefer to go out to the land of the Seneca and look after Renno."

"If you're quite sure that this is what you want to do—" he said.

She grasped his forearm. "I'm very sure," she said. "I'll have the chance to do some good for an old friend—and it will be a godsend for me!"

The decision having been made, Jeffrey Wilson moved swiftly. He persuaded No-da-vo to wait until Deborah was ready to leave, and to act as her guide. While she selected

95

and packed belongings for her journey, he assigned a full platoon of infantry scouts to accompany her through the wilderness and insure her safety on the trail to the land of the Seneca.

Adrienne joined her husband in seeing Deborah off on her journey. The widow was visibly excited about her coming mission.

After exchanging farewells with her, the Wilsons watched as, with No-da-vo in the lead, Deborah made her way down the trail surrounded by the members of her militia escort. Adrienne sighed, but her husband saw a fixed smile on her lips. "Share the joke with me," he suggested.

"It's no joke," she said. "I've just been marveling quietly at the way this mission has given Deborah new energy and new purpose. It's rather remarkable."

"I'm glad she feels that way," Jeffrey replied.

Adrienne lifted an eyebrow. "Quite right," she said, "provided Betsy doesn't misunderstand."

Female subtlety was beyond Jeffrey Wilson, and he became somewhat annoyed. "When I broached the idea, she admitted to me that she's always had a soft spot in her heart for Renno because he saved her life when she was badly threatened. I am sure there's no more and no less to her feelings than that. In the years that have passed, Renno has found happiness in marriage and has sired two children. Deborah brought a daughter and a son into the world, and in all the years of her marriage to Obadiah, you can be certain that she never as much as looked at another man."

He was so indignant that Adrienne thought it prudent not to remind him that because Obadiah Jenkins was no longer among the living, his widow might be far more vulnerable than even she realized.

But there was no point in looking for trouble. The paramount consideration was that someone familiar with the ravages of Renno's debilitating ailment would be on hand to look after him and ease the great burden he faced as he fought for his life.

* * *

Ah-wen-ga realized only dimly that she had been transformed into a ravishing beauty. The kohl she wore around her eyes made them enormous, compelling; everyone who came into her presence was mesmerized by them. Her full lips were emphasized by scarlet rouge and the scent that she wore, a perfume made exclusively for women of the de Guise family, was a flauntingly exotic fragrance. Her gown of pale tan silk, setting off her bare shoulders and low neckline so magnificently, clung to her almost magically, revealing every alluring line of her body. She had mastered the art of wearing high-heeled shoes, thanks to her natural grace, and her hips swayed seductively as she walked, even though she wasn't conscious of it.

Overcoming his abashed reaction to her response in their first meeting, Captain de Sanson approached her when she had appeared in the garden inside the high walls of the castle an hour earlier, and he had not left her side since that time. Now, as she returned to her suite, he insisted on accompanying her and climbed the narrow, winding stone stairs, directly behind her. The scent of her perfume, combined with his view of her light, slender body as she mounted the stairs, seemed to intoxicate him so that he scarcely knew what he was doing. By the time they arrived at her sitting room, he felt that he had to kiss her regardless of the consequences.

Ah-wen-ga, though very much aware of the French officer's nearness, saw no reason to treat him other than politely. So she smiled at him blandly as she drifted into the room.

That smile was all the captain could stand; saying nothing, he stepped forward boldly, took her into his arms, and pressed his head forward to kiss her.

Ah-wen-ga averted her face just in time, and his fervent kiss landed on her cheek.

At once she comprehended the meaning of the expression she had been reading in his eyes, and putting her

97

hands on his shoulders, she exerted considerable strength and pushed him away. Captain de Sanson fell back several paces and stared at her, obviously crushed by her response. He stammered an apology. Ah-wen-ga saw no need to explain her actions. Her yearning only for Ja-gonh, though she thought him to be thousands of miles away in the forests of North America, was strictly her own business.

She recovered her poise swiftly, and having gained total control of the situation, knew she could afford to be generous. "You are forgiven, sir," she told him in lilting French. "You have no need to apologize. We are all human, and therefore, we all make mistakes from time to time." Her comment sailed over the captain's head. All he cared was that she was not angry with him, and he began to breathe more freely.

Removing his plumed hat, he touched the floor with it as he bowed low to her. Thanking her for her generosity, he began to take his leave, but as he reached the door, he stared at her hungrily again before he departed.

Lady Arlene, who had witnessed the entire scene through the open door, was eminently well pleased. Ah-wen-ga, she thought, had a natural instinct for handling herself in the presence of men.

Ah-wen-ga seated herself on a divan that looked out beyond the parapets to the rolling French countryside, and though she seemed composed, her expression was very distant.

At times such as this, Arlene had no idea what her charge might be thinking or feeling. Perhaps she was brooding; perhaps she was yearning for her own people; perhaps her mind was blank.

Arlene was about to join her when she heard heavy footsteps approaching, and she waited just inside the door of her own sitting room.

Major de Bienville paused at the door of Ah-wen-ga's room, across from the divan and, delighted to find her alone, studied her at length. She had become by far the most desirable woman he had ever seen, and he found her charms irresistible. Calling a greeting to her, he slowly walked toward her.

Ah-wen-ga, now aware of his presence, smiled politely.

"Would you care for a drink?" the major asked. She thought it far too early in the day for brandywine so she declined.

Paying no attention to her response, he poured liberal quantities of brandywine into two glasses, which he placed on a table in front of the divan.

To Arlene, silently listening close by, it was plain that her lover had a seduction very much in mind, and his mistress had no intention of interrupting him—yet.

He handed Ah-wen-ga a glass, raised his own, and drank a considerable quantity. She took a token sip, which burned as it slid down her throat. Among the many customs of the French that she found strange, none mystified her more than their drinking of alcoholic beverages. She regarded the taste as unpleasant as that of the mashed roots that her mother had forced her to drink when she was ill, and, even worse, the brandywine made her feel ill.

De Bienville took another swallow, put his glass down, and suddenly reached for her. One hand began to fondle her breasts through their thin covering of chiffon; with the other hand, he held her close and kissed her passionately.

Caught completely off guard, Ah-wen-ga's instinct again told her not to struggle, so she went limp, seemingly yielding to him.

But, recalling the earlier attempts at wooing her, she was seething inside. For two men to have made advances to her in quick succession was infuriating to her. She had no real idea why she'd become the object of their urgent attentions, but she didn't care: enough was enough. Allowing the major momentarily to do as he pleased, her right hand crept slowly up her leg, reached under her dress, and plucked Arlene's knife from its resting place beneath a garter.

De Bienville was so aroused that he failed to recognize his danger until the knife's cold, hard metal point pricked his throat. He released her at once, and moved back to what seemed a safe distance from her.

Ah-wen-ga regarded him with scorn and continued to hold the knife blade at his throat.

Arlene intended to intervene, but she was in no rush. Henri had earned the "reward" that he was now receiving, and she wanted to see his punishment prolonged.

Without intending, Ah-wen-ga reverted to the language of the Seneca. "You think me a woman of the Huron or Erie who has been captured, and is available for the sport of warriors," she spat out contemptuously. "But that is not so. Ah-wen-ga is a free woman of the Seneca. She will marry Ja-gonh—and she will have no other man."

Henri tried to edge away from the knife that was exerting pressure against his Adam's apple.

But, as he moved backward, Ah-wen-ga, her hand and arm remarkably steady, moved forward. "You shall die!" she announced calmly. "I will carve out your heart, and I will have it roasted for my evening meal. None will mourn you."

It was plain that she was in earnest, and de Bienville now recognized the full seriousness of his plight: if he raised his voice to call for help from the de Guise sentinels, it would be a simple matter for her to slit his throat before anyone could come to his assistance. He could only try to dissuade her from murdering him.

"Think of all that is planned for you, Ah-wen-ga," he whispered huskily in French. When she did not immediately press him further, he felt momentarily encouraged and went on, his voice hoarse with fear. "If you kill me, you will be imprisoned, and then you, too, will be put to death. These are the laws of France, and they must be obeyed by everyone who sets foot in this country."

She replied in her own language. "The laws of the French mean nothing to me. I am tired of being handled and mauled by men. I've been touched for the last time!" She exerted a slight pressure, and the knife blade turned crimson with de Bienville's blood.

Arlene realized that the time had come when she must intervene. It was obvious from Ah-wen-ga's actions, as well as her tone of voice, that she had no intention of compromising. Arlene saw that if she hesitated, de Bienville could be killed before her eyes. She walked quickly into the room.

The tortured expression of fear and pain on the major's face gave way to a look of great relief.

"He may deserve to die," Arlene said, "but you must allow him to live, Ah-wen-ga. He holds a high place in the government of France, and it would not go well with you if you kill him."

Ah-wen-ga considered the appeal and reluctantly removed the knife from the man's throat. Almost casually, she wiped it on his breeches in order to remove traces of blood from it.

Arlene was elated. This was a lesson that de Bienville would remember for the rest of his days.

He took out a handkerchief from his pocket and pressed it against the cut in his throat to stop the bleeding. There was nothing he could say in defense of his behavior, and having completely lost face, he took his leave quickly, scarcely bothering to bow to Arlene before he fled from the suite. Later, he would argue fruitlessly with Arlene that the knife should be taken from Ah-wen-ga.

After the door closed behind him, Arlene laughed aloud. "You have no idea how much I enjoyed that," she said. "I'm so pleased that I let you borrow that knife."

Ah-wen-ga calmly placed the knife for safekeeping beneath her garter and tried to understand the series of events. She had no idea why Arlene was so amused, and—far more important—she was curious to learn her version of why both Captain de Sanson and Major de Bienville had made impassioned advances to her.

Speaking in French slowly, haltingly, she asked for an explanation. Arlene decided the time had come to disclose the real reason she had been brought to France and trained in feminine wiles. "You've received advances," she explained, "because you are enormously seductive. No man can look at you and think clearly. All he knows, when he sees you, is that he wants you."

"But why should that be?" Ah-wen-ga was still mystified.

Arlene spoke carefully. "That is the whole point of what you and I have been doing together," she said. "You are being trained to be as seductively appealing as it is possible to make you."

Ah-wen-ga looked at her in surprise as she tried to absorb this information.

"In due course of time, when you are ready for it," Arlene said, "you will be presented to King Louis XV. He will react to you as these other men react. When you become his mistress, you will enjoy great wealth and great power. All of France will bow low before you, and you may have anything in this world that you wish."

Ah-wen-ga felt as though she'd been suddenly immersed in the icy waters of the lake of the Seneca in midwinter. Now, at last, her abduction, her journey to France, and the odd training she had been undergoing all fitted together and made sense. She understood that her kidnappers hoped to prepare her for an existence as a mistress of the King of France. She was too startled to protest.

Even the reasons behind these surprising developments were coming clear to her. She was aware that she was basically attractive, but had seen many girls in Paris who were equally appealing. Why, then, had she been singled out for preparation to become the King's mistress?

As much as she was repelled by the idea, she realized that it was because she was different. She was an American Indian, hence her skin was copper-colored, rather than white. Her blue-black hair, her dark eyes, also were unusual. No matter what the plans of Arlene, de Bienville, and Gray Fox, Ah-wen-ga was certain she could not go through with it. Under no circumstances could she allow King Louis, a total stranger, to make love to her.

Never had she yearned so desperately for Ja-gonh. Never had she missed him so much, nor sought the comfort of his presence as greatly as she yearned for it now.

In spite of her feelings, a sense of caution warned her not to reveal them to Arlene. Her immediate situation, viewed realistically, appeared to be virtually hopeless.

She was thousands of miles from the land of the Seneca, separated from it by a vast ocean that she had no means of crossing alone. She was in a strange country where she was just learning the language and customs, and where she stood out as an alien. Even if she succeeded in escaping, it would be easy for her abductors to trace her movements and recapture her. She had no funds of her own, and was just beginning to comprehend the importance of money in European civilization. She was completely alone and had no one to help her, no ally with whom she could plan or conspire. In brief, she was helpless.

If she revealed to Arlene and de Bienville that the very notion of becoming the mistress of King Louis was repugnant to her, they would certainly go to great lengths to break her spirit and to force her compliance with their wishes. Therefore, common sense told her to keep her opinions to herself. In time, perhaps, she would find some way to avoid the fate that Arlene and her companions had in store for her. Meanwhile, she could devote every waking moment from now on to devising ways of gaining her freedom and of avoiding being handled like an inanimate object. She knew she would die rather than become the mistress of Louis XV.

But she was conscious, too, that she was no ordinary person—she was Ah-wen-ga, daughter of Sun-ai-yee, betrothed of Ja-gonh. Even among the proud Seneca, she stood alone. She refused to abandon hope and knew that within her she had the capacity to outsmart those who would shame her.

Lady Arlene had no idea of the thoughts that were going through Ah-wen-ga's mind, but she was surprised that she seemed to accept the news of her future with a degree of equanimity. Her expression had remained unchanged, and her face had not registered revulsion, fear, or even a sense of upset.

So Arlene felt encouraged by the response to the revelation that she had made. Now that Ah-wen-ga understood what was in store for her, her progress should be even more rapid as she was carried toward the goal of becoming the complete temptress.

The brig dropped anchor in Marseilles, a Mediterranean port of growing importance, and the three passengers disembarked immediately and hired horses for their journey into Gascony, which lay to the northwest. If Ah-wen-ga was recovered, the trio would return with her to the port, and sail for home on board the brig. If anything untoward should happen in the meantime, however, Roger promised that he would send the captain a communication freeing the brig to sail in its own good time.

At the end of the second day of travel, they arrived in the area dominated by the de Guise castle. Ja-gonh's heart pounded when he saw the stone ramparts high on a cliff directly ahead of him, and realized that Ah-wen-ga, in all probability, was in the castle at that very moment.

Luck was with the travelers, and they found a small but exceptionally comfortable country inn located no more than two miles from the castle. It was on a narrow, little-used road, and the only other buildings of consequence in the area were a nearby farmers' market and a small group of shops.

While Roger and Patience talked with the proprietor of the inn and his wife, they engaged a room for themselves, and another adjoining chamber for their "cousin." The innkeeper and his wife paid scant attention to Ja-gonh, whose hair had grown out so he no longer had a scalp lock. When dressed in fashionable European clothes of the period, he looked like an English or colonial gentleman. Nothing in his looks or manner suggested that here was a celebrated Seneca.

At supper that evening, Patience, engaging in small talk with the innkeeper's wife who served them their meal, learned that the castle, though vacant for several years, was currently occupied. A relative of the Duc de Guise was in residence, the woman reported, accompanied by several other persons. In addition, the permanent sentry detail had been more than doubled.

This news was sufficient to convince the trio that Ahwen-ga and her abductors were indeed present in the castle. But it was evident to them that, in order to learn more, they would need to do their own investigating.

After dinner, Ja-gonh excused himself and went up to his room on some mission he did not bother to explain. Roger and Patience watched the sunset from the terrace of the inn, and then retired to their own room. Soon thereafter, they heard a rap at the door, and when Roger opened it, Ja-gonh came in. He was no longer wearing his civilized attire; instead, he was clad in a buckskin shirt, trousers, and moccasins. Over his shoulder he carried a quiver of arrows and in one hand he held his bow. In his belt were his two favorite weapons, a knife and his tomahawk. Except for the lack of the feathered headgear of a senior warrior, and the war paint that he habitually used in the wilderness of North America, he appeared now as he did at home.

Roger was surprised. "What's the meaning of the clothes?" he wanted to know.

A flicker of a smile crossed Ja-gonh's face. "When I have work to do," he said, "I prefer my own kind of comforts. I know that I can be quieter in the clothing of a Seneca, and also inconspicuous enough, considering the darkness in which I shall be proceeding."

They immediately guessed what he had in mind. "You're going to investigate the castle?" Patience asked.

"I will not climb the face of the cliff tonight. I prefer to wait until I become more familiar with it by daylight. But I shall approach the castle from the rear."

"Be very careful," Roger warned him. "We've heard

twice now about the de Guise sentinels who are guarding the place. We have no idea how many of them there might be or what arms they may carry.''

''When a Seneca does not wish his enemies to know his presence,'' Ja-gonh said, ''he makes himself invisible. Then he is neither seen nor heard.''

''Be very careful, all the same,'' Roger told him. ''I assume that the sentinels use firearms, and as they're undoubtedly veterans of Louis XIV's wars, they're bound to be expert shots.''

''Ja-gonh will not be their target,'' the Seneca said, and slipped out into the night.

He left the road that headed in the direction of the castle, and instead swung around through the open countryside toward the back of the precipice on which the castle was located. The rocky terrain bore some resemblance to the forest wilderness of the New World. A few olive trees stood in a small grove, and he passed some large bushes that bore berries, but the only cover was grass which a herd of sheep kept short. In brief, there was almost no place where a man could conceal himself. A half-moon rose in a clear, star-filled sky, and Ja-gonh soon realized with fear that he was casting a distinct shadow. In the event that the troops in the castle were keeping a close watch on the approaches to the property, they were almost certain to see him drawing nearer.

He studied the walls and ramparts at length; this was an enterprise that could not be rushed.

As well as he could judge, no one was keeping a watch from the ramparts on the ground below. That was merely a guess, however, and he could not be sure that he was right. Preferring to take no chances, he looped far around to the rear of the castle, and avoiding the lights that he saw glowing in several cottages, he approached the heights far more gradually.

At last he came to the stone wall that surrounded the property. Several feet thick, it soared to a height of at least twenty feet above the ground and cast a shadow. Ja-gonh was quick to take advantage of that situation. By staying close to the wall, he avoided exposure. He climbed onto much higher ground as he followed the wall around the castle, and he paused when he came to a heavy inlaid door of stone and metal. To his amazement, it swung slightly ajar at his touch. Had a careless guard left the door open? He paused only the briefest of moments to ponder the question: after all, the castle's remoteness and its very impregnability could well have caused the guards to grow complacent.

Drawing his tomahawk and holding it in his right hand, Ja-gonh cautiously opened the door a few more inches. The hinges squeaked loudly, making so much noise that he felt certain the entire sentry detail would be alerted.

He waited for at least a quarter of an hour, and to his surprise and relief, no one appeared. He had no idea where the sentries might be stationed, but it was apparent that none were in his immediate vicinity.

Drawing a deep breath, Ja-gonh stepped swiftly and boldly onto the castle grounds, then shoved the door almost shut behind him, leaving it no more than slightly ajar. If necessary, he would use it as an exit.

Looking at the complex of buildings ahead, he slowly familiarized himself with the layout. Directly ahead was a stone building, perhaps two stories high, that appeared to be built into the fortifications. Here was the castle itself! Flickering candles glowed in several windows; and as the night was mild, a couple of the windows were open, and the young Seneca could hear voices and the occasional clinking of glasses inside. The voices were all male, so he guessed that these were quarters for the sentries.

Far above ground level, toward the very top of the castle, were a number of windows with oil-burning lamps. He assumed that these were the chambers that were occupied by Ah-wen-ga and her abductors.

Now he had to proceed with great caution. In spite of his overpowering desire to reach Ah-wen-ga, he realized that if he alerted Gray Fox and her other kidnappers, he would face an impossibly difficult time extricating her from the castle.

It was far better, he decided, to develop a thorough and complete plan of action, rather than to blunder into a situation he could not foresee or be prepared to handle. It would be wise to work out details with the help of Roger Harkness, who better understood the mind of the European military planner.

His greatest, most potent weapon, was surprise. Surely, Gray Fox, Major de Bienville, and any other foes who might be in the castle, had no idea that he had followed them to this remote corner of Gascony from the New World.

Common sense finally prevailed and Ja-gonh persuaded himself to withdraw. He retraced his steps, left the castle grounds and, still following the back route, began to descend to lower ground.

Suddenly he halted, and his heart seemed to leap into his throat. The face of the moon was momentarily obliterated by a familiar shadow. Only one bird in all the world—the hawk—had such a body and such wings.

Ja-gonh marveled. He was far from the land of the Seneca, farther than he could even estimate, yet the manitous were watching over him and Ah-wen-ga. His ultimate victory was assured.

He gazed in reverent fascination at the majestic hawk that swooped in wide circles high overhead. He would not have believed it possible that the manitous could have kept watch on him so far from his own land, and on this soil that was as alien to them as it was to him. Yet, the hawk's appearance was a sure sign that he was favored by the gods; he accepted that presence gratefully and joyfully. He stood transfixed to the spot as he watched the hawk glide still higher.

Ja-gonh clenched his fists until his nails dug into his flesh as the hawk seemed to hover above a window in which an oil lamp was glowing. He needed no explanation of the significance of that move. He doubted that Roger and Patience would accept his interpretation—much less believe it themselves—but he did not care.

He knew, in his own mind—beyond all doubt—that

Ah-wen-ga was inside that room. The manitous who guided him had pointed out her precise location through their messenger, the hawk.

Having grasped the message, Ja-gonh was in no way surprised when the hawk soared still higher, far above the castle, and disappeared as it flew off to the west.

Continuing to walk toward the inn at an ever-increasing pace, Ja-gonh felt that the weight of the world had been lifted from his shoulders. His companions might be too civilized, too sophisticated to accept the sign he had just been given as conclusive proof, but he knew better. Ah-wen-ga was alive and well in the castle—and it was his destiny to rescue her.

It was his destiny, too, to have his climactic meeting with Gray Fox and to live up to his vow to his grandfather to avenge his death. The days of Gray Fox's stay on earth were limited.

Chapter VI

Renno had occupied the same lodge in the main town of the Seneca as a young senior warrior more than thirty years earlier, but several new rooms had been added, and it now was far more spacious, although it was still basically simple.

Deborah Jenkins stood in the chamber and looked around in nostalgic wonder. The shelf on which a bed of corn husks had been made for her was identical to that on which she had slept when Renno had first brought her here years before. The cooking utensils hanging from pegs on a wall near the outdoor, brick-lined hole in the ground that was used for cooking, could have been the very utensils that she herself had used. She was transported in time to the days of her own youth.

Betsy came into the house and broke the spell. "I was told you would arrive," she said, "and I must apologize for not being on hand to greet you."

"Not at all," Deborah replied, equally pleasantly. "You have better things to do, I'm sure, than to look after unwanted guests who foist themselves on you."

"Not unwanted, I promise you," Betsy said. "Jeffrey Wilson has written to me in detail regarding the opinions of the Fort Springfield doctor and why you seem to be just perfect for the volunteer mission. I am more thankful to you than you will ever know, and I am sure Renno will be, too, when he is able to express himself."

"How is he?" Deborah wanted to know.

"See him for yourself," Betsy told her and led the way into the sickroom where Renno lay unconscious with a blanket beneath him and another covering him. His normally robust frame looked wasted and frail, and his color was pale. In fact, he was so pale that Deborah was uncertain whether she would have recognized him elsewhere. She went to him, placed a hand on his forehead, and said, "He's suffering a high fever."

"I know," Betsy replied, "but I've had no way of ridding him of it."

"May I make a suggestion?"

"He's your patient now," Betsy said wearily. "Do what you will."

Goo-ga-ro-no and No-da-vo were waiting in the background, anxious to hear Deborah's opinion of the sick man's condition. So she summoned them at once.

"Fill three gourds with cold water," she said, "the coldest water you have available." She recalled her own youth. "If the water that you draw from a spring is chillier than the lake water, let the gourds be filled with spring water. If the lake water is colder, use it. And bring me also a towel."

No-da-vo was perplexed by her order, and Goo-ga-ro-no

shook her head. "We have no towels in the land of the Seneca, I am afraid," she said.

"Of course," Deborah hastily corrected herself. "I should have recalled that fact. Please bring me a clean loincloth instead."

They raced off to do her bidding, and when they returned, she provided the fever-stricken Renno with some primitive, but effective aid. She placed his hands in two water-filled gourds, and after dipping the cloth in the third, put it on his forehead. He moaned softly in his sleep, but made no move.

"The water will remain cool for about a half hour," Deborah said. "Have other gourds on hand, ready to replace these when the time comes."

Again, the young couple hurried off to do as she directed.

Betsy had been a silent witness. "On reading Jeffrey's letter again," she said, "I realize now why you know so much about this ailment. I'm very sorry, Deborah, and you have my great sympathies."

"It was the will of the Lord that Obadiah be taken from me," she said. "We had many wonderful years together, and my memories of that time are rich and full. I have much for which to be thankful, and I make no complaint."

Betsy quietly hoped that she could be as courageous in the face of stark adversity, and she prayed that Renno would be spared.

"I urge you to stay here beside me," Deborah said. "This method of reducing fever is crude, but it's fairly effective, and in my experience, the patient often awakens and is rational for a short period."

"Really?" Betsy asked hopefully. "Renno has been suffering from the Big Sleep for more than two weeks now, and I don't think he's been rational for more than two hours in all that time."

"I think we can improve on that record in short order," Deborah said cheerfully, "and let me suggest that we have some nourishing broth waiting for him when he awakens, because it will be much easier to feed him when he is in his right mind."

"Of course," Betsy said, and hastened to the nearby house of her mother-in-law.

Ena, carrying a steaming metal caldron of soup, returned with her daughter-in-law and heartily embraced Deborah. "It is good to see you again, my daughter," she said, speaking in the tongue of the Seneca. "I am so grateful to you for coming to help my son."

Deborah astonished Betsy by replying in the same language. "It is good to see you also, my mother. It is my honor to try to help."

After the gourds were changed and a fresh, cold poultice was applied to Renno's forehead, he stirred and opened his eyes. "Well," he murmured. "We have quite a gathering here."

Betsy, at a gesture from Deborah, began to feed him the broth. "You're going to get well, and that is all that matters," his wife said.

"Indeed it is," Deborah added. "You always claim that a Seneca has the constitution of a bear, and now you have the chance to prove it."

Renno blinked in surprise. "You are here, Deborah?"

She smiled. "I've come to help you get well."

"Did Obadiah come with you?" he asked weakly.

Deborah had no intention of telling him that her husband had died of the ailment with which he was now stricken. "He couldn't come," she said, "but he is with me in spirit." The reply was to Renno's liking, and he smiled as he continued methodically to take spoonful after spoonful of the soup.

"How soon will I recover?"

"That depends entirely on you and on your will," Deborah told him. "Those who want to shake off this ailment can do so."

"Then I'll do it," he said and promptly dropped off to sleep. Betsy eased him back onto his bed.

"If he follows the usual routines of the illness," Deborah

114

said, "he should sleep now until morning without waking. But we'll need more gourds of cold water shortly after dawn."

"I'll bring them," Goo-ga-ro-no said.

"So will I," No-da-vo indicated.

"I'm afraid," Betsy told her, "that we can offer you very little in the way of diversion."

"I haven't come to be entertained," Deborah told her, "and I know this town and the customs of the people, so please don't worry about me. I'm glad that you've given me a room adjoining this one, and I'll look in regularly at Renno and make sure that he doesn't want for anything."

"I so hate to impose on you," Betsy began.

"Nonsense," Deborah replied firmly. "You need a respite, if nothing else. You've been attending him constantly for two weeks, and you need relief."

"Yes, I must admit that I will welcome it."

"I didn't leave Obadiah's side for several weeks, and when I was finally forced to look after myself, I scarcely remembered how it felt. I'll have you summoned fast enough if he wakes or if he should take a severe turn for the worse, I promise you. In the meantime, visit friends, go elsewhere for meals—and try not to think too much about the patient. His recovery won't depend on your concern. That's the most difficult lesson, I think, that a wife is obliged to learn in a situation like this."

Betsy was grateful to her and, following her advice, went to Ena's house for her supper.

Deborah, remaining near Renno, was pleased to see El-i-chi, who brought her meal to her. He greeted her shyly. "You have not changed," he said, "in all the moons that have passed since you lived in the town of the Seneca."

Deborah's laugh was unfeigned. "I never knew that you were a flatterer, El-i-chi," she said. "My hair is gray, my daughter has the figure now that I had when I was here, and I've become an old widow."

He bowed his head. "It grieves me," he said, "to hear

115

that the Reverend Jenkins has gone to the land of his ancestors. He was a fine man, and he was good with a musket. We often hunted for deer together.''

"So you did." Deborah recalled her husband's friendship with El-i-chi.

"If Deborah intends to take care of Renno, she will need much rich food to give her strength," El-i-chi said. "She will require steaks of venison and of bear and will eat the liver of the buffalo. I will hunt for her, and I will bring her these foods." He could have made no greater offer, and Deborah was touched.

"Thank you, El-i-chi," she said, "I appreciate your kindness."

"It is nothing," he said abruptly, and took his leave.

As she returned to Renno's sickroom to keep watch over her patient, it occurred to her that El-i-chi had changed drastically since she had first known him. He had been a young boy then, almost her own age, and now he was a distinguished war chief of his people, with a long and honorable record in combat to prove his worth. His character was reflected in his face, and she realized that although he and Renno were not blood relatives, they were truly brothers. Both had their fine characters stamped in their features.

The Seneca, Deborah concluded, were by no means as savage and primitive as most colonists thought. She had been convinced of it when she had lived in this very building, and she was even more certain of it now, more than three decades later.

As the days followed each other and became weeks, Deborah devoted herself to Renno and his welfare. As she well knew, he was fighting a long, uphill battle which had become hers, too. She bathed his wrists and forehead in cold water whenever his temperature rose. She saw to it that he was given only basic, simple foods. Usually she fed him, but Betsy sometimes replaced her.

Her most difficult task was in preventing the Seneca medicine men from practicing their rites before the Great Sachem. Every two days, a delegation appeared at the door, determined to conduct a ceremony, complete with drums, chanting, and dancing around Renno's bed. Each time Deborah held firm, and they departed unhappily.

She was aided in holding the well-meaning medicine men at arm's length by El-i-chi, who understood enough of civilization and its ways to agree with her that the incantations and noise might do his brother more harm than good. It was a personal gesture on his part, indicating respect and regard for Deborah. In truth, El-i-chi was well persuaded of the powers of the manitous and the gods.

Actually, El-i-chi was more than faithful in his regard for his brother, and called daily at Renno's house. Always pleasant, he invariably paused to chat for a time with Deborah, and he made it a practice to bring her gifts. Sometimes he appeared with a brace of wild ducks or rabbits. On other occasions, he carved a venison steak for her or brought her fish fresh from the lake. She was always grateful for his thoughtfulness and was appreciative of his efforts. The thought flickered through her mind that perhaps El-i-chi was forming a sentimental attachment to her, but she dismissed the notion as rapidly as it occurred to her. She was a mature woman now, not a romantic young girl, and she knew the time had come to put such thoughts behind her.

Renno's condition varied, as she had known it would. One day he was lucid for hours at a time and the next he was out of his mind. One day he was able to sit up and take nourishment himself, and the next he was so weak that he had to be fed. Experience with her own husband had taught Deborah that the condition of her patient would swing wildly, offering hope one day and despair the next. She saw to it that in Betsy's presence, at least, she always maintained a calm and cheerful facade.

In spite of his illness, Renno had lost none of his shrewdness, and one day, somehow suspecting that Deborah had lost her husband to the ailment from which he himself was suffering, in a moment of lucidity he tricked her into admitting it. Then he seemed to lose interest, and made no mention of Obadiah for another ten days.

One morning while Betsy was straining soup through a square of linen for her husband's next meal, she heard voices from the next room and knew at once that Renno was in his right mind that day.

"I have no right to ask you something, Deborah, but I'm curious."

"I'll answer you if I possibly can," Deborah replied.

"Did Obadiah know about—you and me?"

"Of course!" Deborah replied firmly. "I told him while he was courting me, before he ever had a chance to propose."

"It didn't matter to him, then," Renno said and sounded relieved. "I'm very glad. I'd hate to think that I was responsible for causing you and Obadiah the slightest unhappiness."

In the next room, Betsy's hand faltered as she poured more soup through the strainer. She wanted to flee into the open, but it was too late for that, and she knew she had no choice but to remain where she was and hear the rest of the conversation.

"Does Betsy know?" Deborah asked.

"No," Renno replied slowly. "That's one thing I've never told her. Perhaps I was wrong to conceal it from her, but I saw no reason to hurt her unnecessarily. We were both very young, scarcely old enough to know what we were doing."

"That's true," Deborah agreed with a smile. "And yet I've often thought about those days and have wondered whether we were right or wrong to part. I felt strongly then that it was wrong to mix the cultures of the colonies into the Seneca, yet that's precisely what you did when you married Betsy. And you've both been happy together for many years."

"I know," Renno replied. "All I can say now is that perspectives change. But, looking back, I'm quite certain of one thing. If you and I had married we could have found happiness together. We would have insisted on creating happiness in our own way. That's the kind of people we are."

Deborah laughed gently. "I honestly think you're right, Renno," she said. "I've never thought of it in that light, but I'm sure you're quite right."

Betsy was crushed and bewildered and numbed by the conversation she had inadvertently overheard. Though many years ago she had guessed that Renno might have been intimate with Deborah, that possibility had long since faded from her thoughts.

Certainly, she understood that she had nothing to fear, since Deborah was forthright and honorable in all things. Nevertheless, she was still an exceptionally attractive woman, and it was all too painfully clear that she had been Renno's first love. Now she was devoting herself to him, night and day, helping him to fight a terrifying illness. Naturally, he was far more vulnerable to her than he otherwise would have been.

Betsy faced a terrible but delicate dilemma. If she continued to accept Deborah's help, she conceivably would risk losing Renno to the widow. But if she curtailed that assistance—which was certainly within her rights—she would be risking her husband's life.

In the final analysis, Betsy recognized that she had no real choice. She must do everything in her power to preserve Renno's life, even if it were to mean the loss of his affections. So, she steeled herself, and pretending she had not overheard the conversation between her husband and Deborah, she acted as though she knew nothing of their romance of years past.

But as day followed day, it was increasingly difficult for her to keep her resolve. When Renno was in his right mind, which was about half the time, he showed his deep gratitude to Deborah for the unselfish care and attention that she devoted to him. Betsy was forced to carry on as though she were unaware that anything untoward was happening, but she became more and more apprehensive and worried about the day when her husband would be pronounced cured. Then, only, would she know for sure whether she had lost him.

* * *

Saying nothing to Roger and Patience Harkness until he was in a position to give them a full report, Ja-gonh returned to the de Guise castle. Knowing what to expect, he took certain added precautions: he wore a knitted cap to cover his blond hair, and although he did not go so far as to apply Seneca war paint, he rubbed dirt onto his face and hands in order to make them less plainly visible.

Once again, he found the gate set in the high wall unlocked and slightly ajar. Although he again heard voices from the guards' rooms on the ground level, he saw no sentry on duty. So he was free to wander where he pleased and studied the layout of the place with infinite care.

His experience with castles was extremely limited; he had known of only two in his life: the French headquarters in Quebec, and the great fortress of Louisburg on Cape Breton Island, and all he knew of the latter was what his father had told him. But he had one natural asset to aid him in his search: his keen eyesight, developed since earliest childhood in accordance with the most rigorous Seneca standards, was almost perfect. Like certain wild animals and birds of prey, he was endowed with virtually unerring night vision.

Taking his time, he committed to memory every detail of the fortifications and of what he could see of the various rooms of the castle from the outside. He actually spent more than two hours conducting his search. Suddenly, on the top floor of the castle where oil lamps burned in several rooms, he saw a French woman in a trailing silk gown emerge through a pair of opened French doors and stand on the terrace near a wall that surrounded it. Shrinking against the wall so she would be certain not to see him, he stood very still.

He felt as though a bolt of lightning had struck him! The woman standing on the heights above him was no French lady, but was Ah-wen-ga! Her hair, arranged in the latest French style, was piled precariously high on her head. Her elegant, revealing gown was undeniably of French styling. But there was no doubting Ah-wen-ga's identity.

Peering at her eagerly, Ja-gonh was startled by her

obvious heavy use of cosmetics in the French manner. It was small wonder that he had mistaken her for a lady of France! Now he faced a critical problem that required an immediate solution: he wanted to call himself to Ah-wen-ga's attention and notify her that he was near, while concealing that fact from her captors. Only one solution occurred to him and he put it into action immediately.

Drawing one of his Seneca arrows from the quiver he carried on one shoulder, he notched it into his bow, and then took careful aim and let fly. Instantly, he returned to the deep shadows of the wall.

Ah-wen-ga heard a familiar singing sound that she had not heard since she had left the land of the Seneca, and she could have sworn that it was that of an arrow in flight. Then, she glanced up at the pine paneling of the wall directly behind her and froze. There, quivering as its head was buried deep in the wood, was an arrow!

She examined it, and her sense of excitement mounted. Early in her childhood she had learned to distinguish arrows by their makers, and she could tell from a glance at the arrow's carving and the tufted feathers in its tail that this particular weapon had been made by Ja-gonh. She was as certain that it was his as she was sure of her own identity.

She knew, too, that only Ja-gonh could have achieved such superb marksmanship, shooting from a distance and missing her head by only inches.

Ah-wen-ga stood very still, curbing the sense of exultation that bubbled up within her, and forced herself to think rapidly. It was plain that Ja-gonh had somehow learned her whereabouts and—miracle of miracles—had managed to follow her to France. He had chosen a foolproof method of notifying her of his presence, but she knew, as he obviously did, that at all costs this fact had to be kept from the others in the castle.

Now she knew what had to be done, and Ah-wen-ga sprang into action. She pulled at the arrow, tugging with all her might, trying to remove it from the wall panel, but it would not budge. She was tempted to break off the arrow, but was afraid that even the presence of a stub could be dangerous. Finally it came out, and as she held it in her hands she wanted to fondle it. The arrow was more than a symbol of Ja-gonh—it was his property, crafted by him, and he had sent it to her to inform her that she was no longer alone. She looked at it for a long moment, then deliberately broke it over her knee into two pieces and took them to the hearth, where a small fire burned. The fire flared as the hard wood caught hold, and then it gradually died down again.

Common sense told Ah-wen-ga not to be obvious in her search for Ja-gonh's whereabouts, but she could not resist peering out into the night. Though her own eyesight was far superior to that of most people, she could see nothing. Ultimately, hiding her disappointment, she retreated to her room through the French doors and closed them behind her.

Only then did Ja-gonh emerge from the shadow of the wall. He was strongly tempted to wave or otherwise further reveal his presence to Ah-wen-ga, but he knew that nothing would be served by such a gesture and that he would be increasing the risk of discovery.

Now, exercising great caution, he left the grounds of the castle. Only when he was some distance from the stone wall did he break into a run.

Patience and Roger had not yet retired when Ja-gonh rapped at the door that connected their chamber with his. They listened as he told them in full detail about his exploits of the past two evenings.

Patience could scarcely control her excitement. "You actually saw Ah-wen-ga?" she asked breathlessly. "And you thought at first she was French?"

Ja-gonh repeated that portion of his story for her. Far more important matters were on Roger's mind. "You're quite certain that she removed the arrow from the wall so that it could be burned?"

"I am very sure," Ja-gonh replied. "I had to control an urge to shout a reminder that she must be sure to get the arrow out of the wall. But she did it on her own."

"Then she knows you are in the vicinity and intend to help her," Roger said.

Ja-gonh grinned broadly; Roger leaned back in his chair, then sat forward again abruptly and crossed and uncrossed his legs. "You realize, I trust, what a tremendous task awaits us," he said.

"I know it will not be easy," Ja-gonh replied somberly. "I will draw a diagram as best I can of the interior of the castle, and you can be sure that it is going to be extremely difficult to gain access to Ah-wen-ga's chamber."

"We must also consider human factors," Roger pointed out. "I've been talking to the innkeeper about the de Guise retainers who are on duty at the castle. They're all army veterans, and they're known throughout Gascony for their ruthlessness. The Duc de Guise seldom uses the castle, but no robbers would ever think of raiding the place, even though the Gascon hills are full of bands of thieves. The retainers shoot to kill, and they're all first-rate shots. What's more, I gather several dozen of them are on the castle grounds right now."

"I will admit there are quite a few," Ja-gonh said.

"In addition, Gray Fox and Major de Bienville must be living at the castle, along with Lady Arlene d'Amarante, who is related to the de Guises. How many others may be involved, we don't yet know."

"I assume we'll find out readily enough when we attack," Ja-gonh said.

Roger frowned. "The whole point I'm trying to make," he replied, "is that it would be the height of foolishness to openly attack the castle. We'll be vastly outnumbered and no matter how hard and how bravely we might fight, I can't see how we could overcome such enormous odds."

"We'll have to find some other way to get into the property and to rescue Ah-wen-ga. We do have one great advantage which we must keep," Patience said, entering the conversation for the first time. "Not only do her captors have no idea that Ja-gonh is near, but they know nothing of you and me either. I say we can use this advantage very handily."

123

Her husband challenged her. "How?"

She thought for a moment and then smiled. "Suppose I go alone to the castle," she said, "and ask for Henri de Bienville. I believe he'd be certain to see me. I'll address him in French, of course, and he'll naturally assume that it's my native language. Remember that I learned to speak a perfect, accentless French from my mother. I don't know yet what I'll say, or just how I'll say it. We'll have to work all that out, but I hope that I can learn how many people are guarding Ah-wen-ga and what the purpose of de Bienville and his associates was in bringing her here. When we have such information, we'll be far better able to cope with the problems that we face."

"I'll grant you," Roger replied, "that any information that we might add would be all to the good, and it could be very helpful. Unfortunately, my dear, you are forgetting that by going alone to see de Bienville you would be walking into the lion's den, and I can't allow you to take such a risk."

She drew herself up proudly. "You have no right to refuse me the privilege that I claim as mine," she replied. "I know that you and Ja-gonh are prepared to risk your own lives in battle to save Ah-wen-ga if it becomes necessary. I should not be refused the right to take a far lesser risk."

Ja-gonh knew he should not interfere with Patience's participation in the rescue effort.

"You admit," she went on vigorously, "that we stand to gain a great deal from such a visit to the castle."

"There's no question of that," Roger replied impatiently. "Anything and everything you find out could be worth its weight in diamonds to us, but what if de Bienville learns your identity and decides to hold you prisoner, too? Then you've only compounded our problem—and seriously."

She smiled calmly. "You're letting your fears cloud your judgment, my dear," she replied. "Henri de Bienville has never met me, and unless I am mistaken, he's had a meeting with you."

"That's correct," Roger said.

"I see no reason, then, why he should connect me with you in any way. I'll think up a foolproof story, and we must proceed on the assumption that he and everyone else at the castle will accept it. I haven't come all this distance to stand aside at a crucial time!"

In spite of the care that Deborah lavished on Renno, he failed to respond consistently to her ministrations and gradually became more feeble. He failed little by little, and no longer was in his right mind at any time. He lost his appetite, too, and neither Deborah nor Betsy could persuade or force him to take any nourishment other than a little water and an occasional sip of soup.

Little by little, Renno slipped deeper into a trancelike coma. "I have seen others stricken with the deep sleep," El-i-chi said one day, "and when they looked as my brother now looks, all hope for them had to be abandoned."

"We *can't* give up hope!" Deborah declared. "All we can do is to continue to carry out the instructions of the physician and hope that Renno will take a turn for the better."

Ena, however, had ideas of her own, and that evening she called a family council around the fire behind her house. "We have waited patiently for many days," she said, "while Deborah has applied whatever magic the white doctors have, but my son grows worse. Surely we have not forgotten the ways of our Seneca ancestors. Surely we have not turned our backs to the manitous at a time when we most need their help."

Betsy, who realized what was coming, looked around the circle and could see no one who would support her reluctance to rely on the manitous. El-i-chi stood squarely behind his mother. Goo-ga-ro-no, too, having wholeheartedly adopted the Seneca approach, rejected all others. Ba-lin-ta, Renno's sister, and her husband, Walter, Deborah's cousin, who had recently returned to the village, looked on in apparent agreement, and they, at least, had valid reasons

125

for their attitude. Walter, born deaf, had regained his hearing years earlier due, it was said, to the intervention of the manitous. Naturally, they agreed with Ena.

For many years, Ena and Betsy had seen eye to eye on most questions. Now, however, they stood on opposite sides, and the widow of Ghonka was not afraid to confront her daughter-in-law openly.

"Betsy," she asked rhetorically, "prefers that Renno live with her in the land of the Seneca, rather than to bid him farewell and watch him as he goes alone to the land of his ancestors?" Betsy bowed her head.

"For a full moon the magic of the white doctors has been tried and it has failed to cure my son. Now his sickness is much worse, and if he does not soon recover, the manitous will carry him across the great river to the land of his ancestors. The time has come for the Seneca to reveal their faith in their gods and in the manitous who stand between the gods and humans. Does Betsy agree that the Seneca must have the chance to prove the strength of their faith?"

Betsy knew that it was impossible for her to refuse Ena's request. If she rejected it and her husband died, she would be regarded as his murderer, and be put to death. "The mother of Renno," she said, speaking softly but distinctly and trying with all her might to conceal the despair that she felt, "may of course do as she pleases and may call on the manitous to restore Renno to health. The wife of Renno would not think of interfering." She folded her arms across her breasts and lowered her head.

Only Walter and Goo-ga-ro-no realized fully what the response had cost her.

As the family council came to an end, Ena went off to make the necessary arrangements for the Seneca ceremonies, and Betsy hurried back to her own house. Renno was asleep, as he had been day and night, and did not stir. Deborah, who sat cross-legged on the floor beside him, looked up, and seeing Betsy's face, was alarmed. "What's wrong?" she asked.

"Renno's mother has demanded the right to try to cure

him with Seneca magic, because she claims the 'magic of the white doctors' has failed. Perhaps I was cowardly, but I could not refuse her demand.''

Deborah sighed deeply. "You had no real choice, I'm afraid, and I don't suppose it will do Renno much harm to be subjected to the ordeal."

"Have you ever seen such a ceremony?" Betsy asked bitterly.

"Once, many years ago," Deborah replied. "Renno is in such a deep sleep that I don't think even the ceremony will awaken him."

"And," Betsy added, "it can't possibly do him any good." Even as she spoke, they could hear drums throbbing in the distance and the sound grew louder. Soon a half dozen of the tribe's medicine men, all of them smeared with green and yellow war paint, and carrying crude spears and primitive shields, surrounded the house. Some of them were standing outside the open windows of Renno's sickroom, while others came into the room itself. The sound of the drums throbbing in unison became louder and more rapid, and the medicine men started to dance, throwing themselves about with abandon and occasionally emitting earsplitting shrieks.

Betsy and Deborah exchanged a glance, and Betsy knew that the other woman felt precisely as she did—that this barbaric rite at best was a waste of time, and at worst could badly disturb Renno.

Renno's relatives now crowded into the room in single file, their faces smeared with white paint, and they, too, swayed to the beat of the drums and occasionally uttered loud cries. They were followed by Sun-ai-yee, and the old chief led all the senior warriors of the nation through the sickroom, with the junior warriors bringing up the rear. Everyone in the town entered the chamber and spent some moments there before being replaced.

Betsy, developing a headache from the beat of the drums and the shrieks of the dancers, hoped that the ceremony finally was coming to an end, but instead, a number of elders appeared wearing the grotesque half-animal, half-human masks known as the great faces. They stayed in the sickroom for some time and danced interminably. Betsy was grateful that at least they kept silent, and ultimately, after they withdrew, the drums were silent and peace was restored. Betsy pressed her hands to her throbbing temples and peered anxiously at Renno.

"He appears none the worse from the experience," she conceded.

Deborah leaned down and studied him with great care. "I am not so sure," she said. "It seems to me that his breathing is shallower and more labored than before all that nonsense began."

Betsy pulled herself wearily to her feet. "If I thought it had done any good," she said, "I'd tolerate the racket and the nonsense for a whole day and night. Under the circumstances, I just wish that they'd leave Renno alone, and if he's going to die, let him go in peace."

Tears welled to her eyes, but she managed to curb them, and retaining her dignity, she went off to rest.

She was soon interrupted when Goo-ga-ro-no unexpectedly returned, accompanied by No-da-vo. They stood in the entrance and raised their left arms stiffly in formal greeting to her. Betsy realized they wanted to talk with her, and she wearily dragged herself to a sitting position on her bed.

"The mother of Goo-ga-ro-no saw and heard the people of the Seneca seek to appease the manitous?" her daughter asked.

"Yes," Betsy replied, "I saw and I heard."

"But the father of Goo-ga-ro-no is no better," Goo-ga-ro-no went on. "The evil spirits that lurked in his body still reside there."

"He appears to be no better," Betsy agreed.

Goo-ga-ro-no exchanged a long, significant glance with No-da-vo. "The reason the evil spirits still occupy the body of my father," she said, "is because my mother does not believe in appeasement of the manitous."

Obviously she had come a very long way for someone who had only months earlier rejected the tribal beliefs of the Seneca.

"I don't see how my views can affect the result," Betsy said, so exhausted that she finally gave in to her annoyance. "I allowed the ceremony to be held, and almost every man, woman, and child in town came into your father's room. Can you ask more than that?"

Goo-ga-ro-no wanted to reply but fear gripped her, so No-da-vo felt compelled to answer. "It is not what Goo-ga-ro-no thinks that matters to the gods and to those who interpret them to us. It is the manitous themselves who decide these things, and it is well known that when even one person does not believe in the manitous and accept their powers, they will not act."

"That is so," Goo-ga-ro-no said emphatically. Then she caught her breath and added, "The manitous wait for my mother to appease them."

This was too much for Betsy. Her ragged nerves, her fear of his impending death, and the long, inane ceremony overwhelmed her. She glared at her daughter and at the young warrior beside her. "I have done everything in my power to help my husband, whom I love more than I could love any other person in this world. Go now and leave me in peace. If he hears the sound of our voices, you will only be disturbing him."

She lay down, pulled up her blanket, and closed her eyes. Goo-ga-ro-no and No-da-vo slowly and reluctantly withdrew from the room.

What really mattered, Betsy thought helplessly, was that the days of Renno, the Great Sachem, appeared to be numbered, and there seemed to be no way that anyone could save him.

On the day after the ceremony, it was evident that Renno had not improved in any way. Sun-ai-yee reluctantly and sadly dispatched messages to the other Iroquois nations, informing them that the Great Sachem was dying.

Soon, the leaders of the other nations began to arrive in the land of the Seneca to pay their last respects to the great Renno. Their war chiefs and their medicine men insisted on visiting him, and it was impossible for Betsy and Deborah to keep them out.

When all the leaders of the other nations of the league had arrived and had viewed Renno, they retired to the Council Lodge to confer. The Seneca town realized that in the privacy of the lodge, consideration would be given to choosing the next Great Sachem. The post was always kept filled, and in this way the Iroquois assured the continuity of their leadership.

Mi-shal, the sachem of the Mohawk, largest of the Iroquois tribes, made a long, graceful speech, reciting Renno's many virtues.

Sun-ai-yee was gratified; the tribute paid by the Mohawk was no greater than it should be. The next speaker was the relatively young sachem of the Oneida. Da-kay, known as an ambitious man, had recently made his mark as a warrior, defeating the Erie in a brief but ferocious war. His voice was deceptively mild.

"At last," Da-kay said, "the mighty nations of the Iroquois are about to be relieved of the burden they have carried for so long. They soon will elect a new Great Sachem whose skin will be the color of their own, whose hair will be black, and whose eyes will be dark. No longer will they bow to a white man as the Great Sachem."

Sun-ai-yee openly displayed his shock and indignation. The attack on Renno was totally unwarranted, and he looked aghast at Da-kay. The other sachems responded somewhat less violently. They knew that the Oneida had long resented the election of Ghonka's white son as the Great Sachem, and they were willing to concede that Da-kay had a point.

Da-kay continued to speak. "The league made a great error in the days when Ghonka was the Great Sachem," he said. "The fault was not his, however, but his son's. His son influenced him and persuaded him that the nations of the Iroquois should become the allies of the English. That is because Renno was himself descended from English settlers. Why should the English be favored, rather than the French? France offers many gifts to the nations that become their allies. The Huron and the Ottawa, yes, and even the stupid Algonquian have all become wealthy since they allied themselves with France. But the Iroquois proudly keep their distance from the French and remain loyal to Renno's friends, thc English—who do nothing for the Iroquois but persuade the Iroquois to fight their battles for them.''

Cold anger welled up within Sun-ai-yee, but he held his tongue. No matter how many lies the Oneida told, the Seneca would not be accused of being inhospitable to a visiting sachem.

"When Renno dies as he deserves to die," Da-kay said, "a new Great Sachem will be chosen by those who are present now in this council hall. I tell you that if you choose me as the new Great Sachem, I will make an alliance with the King of the French and all the people of the Iroquois will enjoy great and bountiful gifts.''

A long silence followed his words. His open suggestion that he would cancel the alliance with the English colonics and would instead become a brother of the French was near heresy, and the other sachems were too stunned to react to it.

As it happened, the entire speech was overheard by several young senior warriors of the Seneca, who made it their business to loiter beyond the entrance to the Council Lodge, just out of sight. No-da-vo was among them, and he was so outraged that he hurried off to find El-i-chi, to whom he related what he had heard. El-i-chi listened in grim-faced silence, then stalked off to the Council Lodge.

The sachem of the Onondaga was just concluding a brief speech in which he sought to calm the troubled session. El-i-chi entered the lodge and looked around at the gathered sachems. "You know me, and I know you," he said. "I have heard of the words of Da-kay, sachem of the Oneida. I have heard that he believes Renno deserves to die and that he and my father, Ghonka, before him, are traitors to the Iroquois cause." Slowly, deliberately, he drew the tomahawk from his belt. "Let Da-kay meet me in fair combat, here and now," he challenged, "and we will see whether truth prevails.''

Da-kay was on his feet instantly and started forward.

But Sun-ai-yee, in spite of his advanced years, was too quick for him and stood between the two antagonists. He knew, as did every other leader in the council chamber, that a personal grudge fight between Renno's brother and Da-kay of the Oneida would rip apart the entire fabric of the Iroquois League. The union that had withstood so many trials would be rendered impotent if the fight took place.

"Will you insult the manitous by fighting in this lodge where brotherhood prevails?" Sun-ai-yee demanded in a deep, rumbling voice, his considerable bulk separating the two men who seemed on the verge of leaping at each other. "Will you call the wrath of the gods onto the heads of all the Iroquois?" He glared at Da-kay, then turned to El-i-chi and glowered at him. As he did, however, a strange phenomenon took place.

With his face averted so that the Oneida could no longer see it, he dropped one eyelid in what was very emphatically a wink.

El-i-chi was so startled that he managed to recover his emotional balance. He had no idea what the wily Sun-ai-yee had in mind, but they had been associated with each other for so many years in times of peace and in war, that he was willing to trust the older man as he trusted no living person other than Renno. He promptly subsided and slipped his tomahawk back into his belt.

The admonition of the old Seneca chief hit home with Da-kay, too, and the Oneida took a step backward, muttered an apology, and quickly left, making his way to the quarters that had been provided for him.

Quiet settled over the Council Lodge after he left. Then, Sun-ai-yee shook his head sorrowfully and a sad caricature of a smile appeared on his lips. "How many ways do you know to skin a deer, El-i-chi?" he demanded.

The war chief was surprised by the question and thought for a moment before he answered. "There are more ways than I can count," he replied.

"Exactly," Sun-ai-yee declared in triumph, and looked at each of the other heads of the Iroquois nations in turn.

"What was proposed here today by Da-kay was treason," he said. "Treason to his own people, treason to all Iroquois. But if El-i-chi had acted or if any of us raised our arms today and killed him on the spot, we would have destroyed the league. The Oneida would have lost faith in us, and nothing we did or said would have convinced them that we were anything other than perfidious."

His listeners exchanged sheepish glances. As always, Sun-ai-yee made great sense to them.

"How much better it is," he continued, "to have been forewarned. Now we know that the heart of Da-kay lies with the French, rather than with the English, because the French have bought his loyalty with gifts. Now we know what we must do to protect the Oneida from themselves, and to safeguard the future of the Iroquois League."

Several ideas occurred to his listeners, but they knew better than to interrupt.

"We will take turns," he explained. "Each of the other Iroquois nations will send an experienced senior warrior to the principal town of the Oneida. Each of us will have his own reason for the warrior's visit, and it will differ from the reason of the others. When the visit of the Mohawk ends, the visit of the Seneca will begin. When the visit of the Seneca ends, the visit of the Onondaga will begin, and so it will go."

The others were quick to grasp his meaning. "Ah, I see," the sachem of the Mohawk declared. "Each of us will have a spy who will keep watch on Da-kay and will let us know immediately if he takes any direct action that would place the nations of the Iroquois in jeopardy."

"That is correct," Sun-ai-yee said. "In this way we will not be called upon to remove Da-kay from office until his deeds are those of a traitor, just as his words now are those of a traitor."

As the meeting ended, the chiefs of the tribe were well satisfied with the arrangements, feeling reasonably certain that their interests would be adequately protected under the scheme that Sun-ai-yee had outlined.

Once the old man and El-i-chi were alone, Sun-ai-yee

sighed ponderously. "We have avoided terrible trouble today," he said. "The manitous have shown us their mercy and have spared us a breakup of the Iroquois League."

El-i-chi started to apologize for his hotheaded role in creating the crisis.

Sun-ai-yee silenced him with a wave of the hand. "Now," he said, "we must pray hard that the manitous will extend their mercy to Renno and will restore him to health. I fear that many problems, like that which arose today, will plague us in the future if Renno remains ill with the Big Sleep."

El-i-chi knew he was right. Renno, like Ghonka before him, was the firm foundation-stone on which the alliance of the six powerful Iroquois nations was based. He alone possessed the strength and the wisdom to maintain the league and prevent it from disintegrating. If he failed to recover, the troubles that lay ahead, not only for the Iroquois but for all the Indian tribes of North America, threatened to become cataclysmic.

"Our concerns are many," Sun-ai-yee said. "My heart is heavy as I worry about the fate of my daughter."

"If anyone can help Ah-wen-ga, Ja-gonh can do it," El-i-chi assured him.

Sun-ai-yee sighed. "I have faith in Ja-gonh because I must," he said. "He and my daughter are in an alien land far from home, and I pray that the manitous will guide them and bring them back to us in safety."

Patience Harkness studied her reflection in a full-length pier glass and was satisfied. Her hat, with its enormous plumed feather curling back across the crown of her head, showed off her honey-colored hair to excellent advantage. Her gown of dusty rose-colored silk was snug-fitting enough to show off her figure, but in no sense could it be considered flamboyant. Her high-heeled shoes were attractive, but were not so high that they hampered her ability to walk, and her makeup, applied with great care, was just right to bring out the best of her features.

Smiling and winking jauntily at her reflection, she raised a hand in salute and then went into the adjoining sitting room of the suite where her husband and Ja-gonh awaited her.

Ja-gonh looked at her in approval.

But Roger seemed far from pleased. "I really don't want you to take this great risk," he said. "We already know that Ah-wen-ga is in the castle."

"What we don't know is how to approach her quarters from the inside," Patience replied. "And it seems to me that such information is going to be vital in any attempt to rescue her." She put a hand on his arm. "Please don't worry about me, dear, I assure you that I will make out just fine."

"Because your parents engaged in a number of wild escapades in their youth and escaped with their lives, that is no reason to assume that you're going to be as fortunate," he said.

"My parents' adventures," Patience replied brightly, "give me the confidence that will make it possible for me to carry out this little mission. You may take my word for it, Roger, not one person in the castle will know that I'm anything but French. I'll carry off the deception perfectly."

"But what convincing reason can you give them for appearing out of the blue?" he demanded. "That worries me."

"I'm formulating a plan in my mind, and I don't want to express it prematurely," she said. "I beg you, have confidence in me, that's all."

Roger turned to his friend and spoke gloomily. "We may have to rescue two of them rather than just one, Ja-gonh," he said. "So we'd best be prepared for anything."

Ja-gonh smiled encouragingly at Patience. He had long recognized her cleverness and had faith in her ability to carry off this deception and obtain the vitally needed information.

Doing his best not to further distress her, Roger fervently kissed his wife, and then he and Ja-gonh accompanied her to the courtyard of the inn where a sidesaddled mare awaited her. She was carrying no weapons, which both men regarded as somewhat foolhardy, and she was in high spirits as she started out, turning once to wave a cheerful good-bye to them. She covered the distance between the inn and the castle quickly and approached the forbidding main gate. Not until she saw the de Guise retainers on sentinel duty, resplendent in their green uniforms, did she begin to lose her nerve. Their muskets looked business-like, and the bayonets that protruded from the ends of the weapons made her shudder slightly. But the sergeant in charge of the detail smiled gallantly as he opened the gate for her, and she decided that an attractive young woman could expect to get away with almost anything. Her nervousness quickly dissipated.

"I believe," she said in faultless aristocratic French, "that Major Henri de Bienville is currently residing here."

"He is, madame," the sergeant replied respectfully.

"Splendid. Would you be good enough to take me to him?" She spoke firmly, confident that the man would do as he had been requested.

The sergeant hesitated only briefly and considered the request. Had some ordinary person come to the castle seeking Major de Bienville, he would have been subjected to an interrogation. But this lady obviously was a member of the upper class, and the sergeant well knew that if one wanted to get ahead in the world, he did not jeopardize his prospects by arousing the ire of aristocrats. "Whom shall I tell him is calling, madame?" he inquired respectfully.

"Madame Adrienne de Longe," Patience replied glibly, combining her mother's Christian name with the married name of an aunt who had followed her mother to the New World.

The sergeant appeared satisfied, and after leading her horse to a stable located in an outbuilding near the main castle, he helped Patience dismount and then offered to show her the way. "The castle is large," he said, "and one could easily get lost."

"I appreciate your concern," she told him, and a dimple appeared in one cheek as she smiled at him.

He led the way through a great hall where the furniture was covered with sheets of linen, and a layer of dust coated everything. It was obvious that this chamber was not used. Directly behind it was a wide, winding staircase, and Patience, following close on the heels of the sergeant, mounted it slowly, pausing every dozen steps to catch her breath. Apparently these stairs led directly to the tower, and this information was very much worth remembering. Other approaches might lead to the top floor of the castle, but this staircase seemed to offer direct access.

When they reached the top, Patience was surprised to see that the staircase opened directly to a large, pleasantly furnished living room much like the parlor of her parents' farmhouse. The furniture was comfortable rather than elegant. The tapestries hanging on the walls and the thick rugs were intended for warmth rather than decoration, and though the day was pleasant, a small fire was burning in a huge fireplace at the opposite end of the room. A young woman was seated near the windows, which offered a breathtaking view of the surrounding countryside, and she rose to her feet when she saw the visitor approach.

Patience disliked her on sight. Her gown was expensive and its cut was almost too perfect; her overabundant use of cosmetics and her brilliant red hair contributed to her flamboyant appearance.

"Lady Arlene d'Amarante, may I present Madame Adrienne de Longe." The sergeant was obviously proud of his ability to remember names, and rolled them off his tongue like a majordomo announcing arrivals at a grand ball.

Arlene took in Patience's appearance at a glance. Her clothes, though costly, were slightly old-fashioned. Clearly, they had not been made by a Paris dressmaker. "What may I do for you, madame?" she asked.

Patience tried to conceal her dislike and replied civilly. "I'm here to see Major de Bienville."

"Oh," Arlene was curious. "May I know the nature of your business with him?"

Patience stood her ground. "I make no secret of it, milady, and I'm sure that Major de Bienville wouldn't in

137

the least mind telling you whatever it is that you want to know.''

There, she thought, the direct rebuff should stop further questions.

Arlene was insulted. Glaring at the visitor, she drew in her breath sharply and stood very erect.

Before she could reply, however, Henri de Bienville came into the room. He had overheard the conversation and was mildly puzzled to find an attractive young woman, a total stranger, awaiting him.

Patience moved forward and extended her hand to him. "Ah, Major de Bienville," she said. "I would know you anywhere." She deliberately allowed her hand to remain in his for some moments longer than necessary.

"Do I know you, madame?" the major asked with a half-smile.

"Not directly," Patience replied glibly. "I am the sister of the Marquis de Fontaine, the lieutenant colonel who commands the wilderness battalion at Quebec."

De Bienville searched his mind frantically, but could not recall a Colonel de Fontaine. This was not surprising, as he was a mythical character invented on the spot by Patience.

But she had reasoned that de Bienville would be reluctant to admit that he couldn't place an officer who held the high rank of a marquis, and she was banking on the prospect that he would pretend to recall such a man.

The gamble succeeded. De Bienville forced a smile and said only a trifle tardily, "Of course."

Patience's heart hammered less loudly in her ears, and she breathed more easily.

"Won't you sit down?" he invited.

She needed no second request, and promptly sank into a chair before her shaking legs gave her away.

Arlene had no intention of being left out of whatever had brought this stranger to the castle. She seated herself, too, and the long fingernails on one hand beat a quiet tattoo on the arm of her tapestried chair.

The wedding ring on Patience's hand was her own, and it, at least, was genuine.

Henri thought rapidly. This lady, obviously married, was the sister of a marquis and, therefore, was not to be subjected to any cavalier treatment. He immediately rang for a servant and ordered refreshments.

In a remarkably short time, tea was brought.

Patience had done well——exceptionally well—in stalling for time, but she knew she would need to make the reason for her visit clear, and she was prepared for that, too.

"My husband and I have a small country estate not far from here," Patience explained. "It's about an hour and a half from the castle. When I received a letter recently from my brother, he told me that Major de Bienville, holder of a most elevated and respected position in our government in the New World, would be sojourning at the de Guise castle. So I felt it suitable to call on you and offer our greetings in welcome. My husband joins me in hoping that you can dine with us in the near future."

"That's very kind of you, madame," the major murmured.

Arlene was puzzled; at least one point in the story was peculiar. "How did the marquis know that Major de Bienville would be coming to this particular place?" she asked. "After all, we were none too sure of it ourselves until we reached Paris."

A sticky situation now confronted Patience, but she had an answer ready. She spread her hands in a gesture that indicated she was absolving herself of all responsibility. "I have no idea how he knew the major's plans, milady," she said sweetly. "I assumed they must have discussed the matter in the Citadel at Quebec or somewhere thereabout."

The explanation seemed very logical to de Bienville, even though he could not place Colonel de Fontaine. He assumed that in discussing his plans briefly with one or two colleagues before leaving Quebec, he might have mentioned the possibility, at least, of coming to the de Guise property in Gascony. Come to think of it, he had been not at all surprised when Arlene had told him that her relative had made the place available to them, so he must have known it ahead of time.

He smiled. "Of course," he said. "The colonel isn't a clairvoyant, I'm sure, so I must have indicated to him before leaving Quebec that I thought it likely we'd be spending a little time down here."

His response did not really satisfy Arlene, but she hardly could press the issue further.

Suddenly, Patience almost started from her chair.

Ah-wen-ga had come into the room in a daringly low-cut gown and carrying a wicker basket over one arm. "I've just picked what seems to be the last of the autumn berries," she said, "and we shall have them for supper. They do look lovely."

As she became aware of the presence of a visitor, she apologized for her interruption. Neither de Bienville nor Arlene bothered to introduce the exotic Indian to "Mme. de Longe."

But Patience held her breath, and with good cause. She was already well acquainted with Ah-wen-ga—far too well acquainted. In fact, Ah-wen-ga had stayed at the Wilson farmhouse shortly before Patience's wedding and had slept in a "civilized bed" for the first time when she had shared a chamber with Patience and her sister.

Any sign of recognition now would instantly plunge both of them into great peril.

But Ah-wen-ga promptly demonstrated that she could handle herself superbly in an emergency. She looked at Patience, recognized her instantly, and then her lifelong Indian training saved her. Her face became totally expressionless, her eyes and mouth registering nothing. She was apparently looking at Patience for the first time and felt only indifference toward an utter stranger.

"I'll leave these berries with you, Arlene," she said, "and trust you'll give them to the chef. I'm going off to my chamber."

Patience counted her blessings and, behaving as superbly as Ah-wen-ga had done, pretended to pay no further attention to the Indian. She noted, though, that Ah-wen-ga went to a door at the far end of the drawing room, near the fireplace, and she was quite sure she could accurately point out its precise location on a chart of the castle.

Henri de Bienville had no desire to become involved socially with the local gentry, but felt it would be rude to reject the visitor's request too abruptly. It was unfortunate that Ah-wen-ga had come in while "Mme. de Longe" was present, but she appeared to make only a slight impression, if any, on the visitor, and he was grateful for that much.

"I'm rather occupied these days on a project that I'm not allowed to discuss," he said, taking refuge in alleged military secrecy. "But any time that I'm free I'd be delighted to accept your hospitality, madame."

The session had gone well—almost too well.

"Shall we set a date now?" Patience asked as she rose.

De Bienville shook his head. "I prefer to wait until I can see ahead a little more clearly," he said vaguely.

"In that case," she said, "I shall return in the near future and perhaps we'll make a definite engagement then."

She shook hands with Arlene, then with the major, and said, "Don't bother to show me out, I can find my own way."

Disregarding her protest, he nevertheless rang for a sentinel, and a uniformed sentry appeared to conduct Patience to the front gate. Apparently, no chance was being taken that strangers might wander where they pleased through the palace itself or the grounds.

Arlene said nothing as she watched the other woman leave. Patience felt her eyes burning into her back and realized that she probably had made an enemy. Well, that couldn't be helped; in all, she had good reason to feel pleased with herself. She not only had discovered the location of Ah-wen-ga's room, but their chance encounter had served to notify Ah-wen-ga that Ja-gonh had not come to France alone. Surely, she would be alert from now on.

Patience was in high spirits as she returned to the inn. Good fortune had attended her, and the captors of Ah-wen-

141

ga suspected nothing. The only unfortunate aspect was Arlene's antipathy, but that struck her as a relatively minor matter.

Roger had been awaiting his wife, and he shouted the good news to Ja-gonh the moment he spotted her approaching at a distance through his field glass. They met her in the inn's courtyard, and Roger was so relieved that he hugged and kissed her as he lifted her out of the saddle to the ground.

Saying nothing in the presence of the groom or other hired help, Patience waited until they reached the privacy of their suite before she gave a verbatim account of what had happened at the castle.

They listened carefully, and although Ja-gonh wanted to interrupt, he remained silent until she had completed her report.

Then he said, "You make it sound as though Ah-wen-ga has the run of the castle. I was afraid she was being held prisoner in one room."

"No," Patience replied. "Her situation doesn't appear to be desperate. She had been gathering berries, as I told you, and the only thing I found incongruous was her dress. She looked like a . . . like a courtesan of some substance, if you'll pardon the observation."

"I find that odd," Roger said with a frown.

Ja-gonh impatiently dismissed the remark without delving into its significance. "Ah-wen-ga is well and has not been mistreated. That's the most important thing. As to why she wears French clothes—that is confusing to me. It is beyond my comprehension, but that does not really concern me at this moment. We now have the benefit of knowing where her room in the castle is, and I intend to rescue her at once."

Patience was startled. "Surely, you're going to make a careful plan," she began.

Ja-gonh interrupted. "We've come a great distance and have made enough plans to last a lifetime," he said. "It should be easy enough to get into Ah-wen-ga's room and get her out. We'll have a horse waiting for her here, and we'll ride like fury to Marseilles. If we are followed, those who dare would do so at their own peril."

"You make it sound so simple," Patience said with a faint smile.

"The trouble with European civilization is that it makes everyone too cautious. In the land of the Seneca, when we face a problem, we go straight to the heart of it and seek a solution. The solution to this problem strikes me as very simple."

"It may be simple," Roger replied, "but it surely isn't going to be easy. I'll come with you, Ja-gonh, when you go to rescue Ah-wen-ga. That's the least I can do for you."

"You'll be subjecting yourself to too great a risk," Patience protested.

Her husband laughed at her. "You took what I regarded as great risks, and fortunately you escaped unscathed. You can't deny me the same opportunity."

She realized it would be unfair to try to restrict him after he had come so far to help Ja-gonh free the captive.

"Very well," she said. "Go with Ja-gonh tonight—and may God go with both of you!"

Chapter VII

E ven when Ghonka was alive, Ena had made all the final decisions in family matters. That had been the custom of the family, and she had never shirked her responsibility, always doing what she considered right and proper. Now as she watched her elder son wasting away under the dreaded influence of a seemingly incurable ailment, she formed certain convictions.

Renno's illness had to be halted. It was essential for the good of the Seneca, for the future of the entire Iroquois League, that he be cured and restored to good health. A lesser woman might have resigned herself to his death, and would have comforted herself with the knowledge that he would find the happiness he deserved in the land of his ancestors. But the living needed Renno—and Ena was determined that Renno would live. The meeting of the sachems that very day had emphasized that need.

That evening, when she summoned her younger children to supper, they knew this was no ordinary invitation. El-i-chi appeared early, and his brother-in-law, Walter, arrived a few moments later. Ba-lin-ta had already spent the entire afternoon helping her mother prepare the meal.

They ate in silence; although El-i-chi and Walter were both war chiefs, neither dared to speak.

The food was excellent, as always, and the bachelor, El-i-chi, overate slightly as he always did at his mother's house. Walter, who was inclined to put on weight, could not follow his example because Ba-lin-ta was watching him too closely and would be certain to express herself freely if he overindulged.

At last the meal was done, and the men lighted pipes. Now, as had been the custom even in Ghonka's day, was the time for Ena to speak.

"Unless something is done," she said, "Renno soon will die." She crossed her arms over her breasts and looked across the fire at her son, daughter, and son-in-law.

All three nodded. Renno's condition was increasingly precarious, and he was in a bad way. He had not been in his right mind for several days, and they knew that he was taking no nourishment now except water.

"Betsy, the wife of Renno," Ena said, "is a fine woman, but she is still a colonist and does not truly understand the ways of the Seneca. Neither does Deborah, who attends Renno. Both are devoted to him, but he sinks lower each day, and I fear that soon he will slip from the land of the living and will cross the invisible river into the land of his ancestors."

El-i-chi knew he was expected to respond. "That is possible," was the best he could manage. He couldn't quite agree with his mother's assessment of Betsy and Deborah, but he knew it was useless to argue with Ena when her mind was made up. She had certain ideas in mind, and nothing would change them.

"The men and the women and the children of the town

146

asked the gods to preserve the life of Renno, but their pleas were not heard. Now," Ena said forcefully, "I must do what only a mother is able to do. I must perform the ceremony of the ashes and beg the manitous to spare his life."

Walter and Ba-lin-ta exchanged a quick glance, and then both looked at El-i-chi. It was his place, as the second son of the family, to tell his mother that Renno's wife and Deborah would protest strongly against such a ceremony, which they regarded as not only useless but certain to upset the patient. El-i-chi, however, was a true Seneca to the core. Like Ghonka, his father, and Renno, his brother, he had never shirked his duty, and he could not start now in middle age. It was his mother's privilege to conduct a ceremony of the ashes, no matter how wearing it might be.

He bowed his head and said flatly, "So be it."

"So be it," Ba-lin-ta and Walter echoed.

A long, uncomfortable silence followed. "Who will tell Betsy and Deborah of my decision?" Ena finally asked.

El-i-chi opened his mouth to reply and then closed it again. The truth of the matter was that he had grown very fond of Deborah and had no desire to upset her and see her in tears. Nor did he wish to be responsible for causing Betsy to cry. White women were less stoic in their attitudes than the women of the Seneca and gave in to their emotions far more easily.

Ba-lin-ta knew it was not her place to pass on the message. She—like her sister-in-law and Deborah, her husband's cousin—was only a woman and lacked the ultimate authority necessary in this highly charged, dramatic situation.

Walter squared his shoulders and tugged at the collar of his buckskin shirt. Inasmuch as Deborah was his blood relative, he knew he could not evade the inevitable, and he accepted it with as much calm as he could muster. He stood, adjusted the tomahawk in his belt, and walked swiftly around the house and crossed the road. Ba-lin-ta watched him until he disappeared into the dwelling of Renno. Walter was a fine man, whose courage was underrated. Under such circumstances, at least, he was more courageous than El-i-chi, but Ba-lin-ta had no desire to point this out to her brother.

Walter found Deborah and Betsy in the sickroom, keeping watch at a distance on the unconscious Renno as they picked at a light meal of fish and squash.

Betsy knew at once that this must be a visit of particular importance. Customarily, Ba-lin-ta would have accompanied her husband.

Deborah was genuinely pleased to see her cousin. She had actually grown accustomed to seeing him wearing a scalp lock with Seneca war paint smeared on his face and torso, and she no longer regarded it as strange that he should have become transformed so completely into an Indian.

"Ena grieves," Walter said, speaking in English, "because the manitous have not heeded the pleas of the people of the Seneca town, and her son is still ill."

"Indeed he is," Betsy replied in a leaden voice, and she gestured toward the emaciated body of her unconscious husband. "We think his illness is coming to a climax."

"I'm quite sure it is," Deborah said. "I've seen half a dozen victims of the ailment suffering, and I'd say we'll know in the next forty-eight hours whether Renno will live."

Walter steeled himself. "I must tell you," he said, "that Ena has decided to conduct a ceremony of the ashes in an attempt to persuade the manitous to intervene with the gods on Renno's behalf."

Betsy gasped, and Deborah looked questioningly at Walter.

"The ceremony of the ashes," Betsy explained to her in a stifled, horrified voice, "is one of the more primitive of Seneca practices. Drums beat far louder than they did during the other ceremony they held here. They burn feathers and leather and heaven only knows what else, and they scatter the ashes on the sick person. The noise will be bad enough. But Renno is likely to suffocate from the ashes that are poured over him, and—the whole thing is just too dreadful even to contemplate. If his illness is truly coming to a climax, I can think of nothing worse for him than to be forced to endure that ceremony.''

"I remember now," Deborah said thoughtfully, "that when, many years ago, Renno's aunt—Ghonka's sister—became very ill, they subjected her to such a ceremony. She survived it, and I always have considered that rather miraculous.''

Both women turned to Walter in silent appeal. He shrugged. "Ena is the widow of the Great Sachem and the mother of the Great Sachem," he said. "Who in all the land of the Seneca has the strength and the power to deny her wishes? Surely, I don't.''

"El-i-chi—" Deborah began.

Walter shook his head. "El-i-chi would not dare to oppose his mother for fear of offending the manitous. No man in this land would deny Ena the right to conduct the ceremony that she wants.''

Deborah was becoming desperate. "Sun-ai-yee appears to be a sensible man," she said. "Surely he—"

Betsy interrupted her with a harsh laugh. "Sun-ai-yee is a Seneca of Seneca," she said. "Sensible or otherwise, I can assure you that we can expect no help whatsoever from that quarter.''

"Then we're to stand aside?" Deborah demanded heatedly, "and do nothing while Renno is killed by sights and smells and excitement beyond his capacity to endure?''

"What choice do we have?" Betsy replied bitterly. "I've been a Seneca wife for thirty years, and I've made their ways my ways, to the best of my ability. I can't accept this pagan ritual, but I'm helpless to prevent it.''

Walter cleared his throat. "When I was young," he said, "I could not speak. As you know, I was born dumb. I moved to the land of the Seneca because I was accepted here, and the gods of the Seneca became my gods. My hearing was at the root of my trouble, and one day a great miracle occurred. A musket exploded near me, and suddenly I could hear. By dint of great effort and the loving teaching of my wife Ba-lin-ta, I had found my voice, and in time I became as other men also. So, I can only say to you who do not understand the gods of the Seneca and the powers of the manitous, do not despair, they are greater than you realize.''

He had done his duty, and having defended his beliefs and those of Ena and his people to the best of his ability, he withdrew hastily. He saw no point in arguing further with these women who held the views of English colonists.

Betsy had lived with the Seneca for so long that she had learned to control her emotions rigidly. She did not weep now, but she found herself staring bleakly at Deborah.

''I was so sure when I married Renno and came here to live,'' she said, ''that my ways would never conflict with the ways of the Seneca. Now, too late, I discover a conflict too great to be resolved. I would do anything possible to prevent Ena from conducting this barbaric ritual. But her mind is made up and I can do nothing.''

''My aunt, Ida, who was a wonderful, wise woman, was fond of quoting that saying about what to do when in Rome. That's all well and good, but the thought of a brave, good man dying because of pagan superstition is too much to bear. But we'll have to stay near Renno during the ceremony. That's all there is to it.''

''Yes, I'm afraid you're right,'' Betsy said. ''And if we see that he's sinking, I'll have to think of some way to bring the ceremony to an end and to clear the house. Tomorrow, I'm afraid, is going to be the most difficult day of my life!''

Ja-gonh and Roger Harkness, having decided that this time they would ride to the castle, set out after dark. They halted their horses in a grove of trees about twenty yards from the high wall that blended into the castle. There, they waited impatiently for the oil lamps in the private apartments to be extinguished for the night.

Both were clad in buckskins, and both had darkened their faces and hands in order to make themselves less visible. Ja-gonh wanted to smear war paint on his face, but had been dissuaded by Roger's argument that if they unexpectedly encountered passersby, it would be a grave error for him to be too noticeable.

At last, the lights on the upper story went out, one by one, but it became evident that those on the floor below would burn all night as one sentry detail succeeded another.

Rather than risk discovery by making their way to the high parapet from inside the castle, Ja-gonh decided it would be best to scale the wall on the outside, and Roger, after some hesitation, agreed with him. In addition to his bow and arrow, tomahawk, and Seneca knives, Ja-gonh carried over one shoulder a length of thin, strong rope. He preferred his own weapons, he explained, because they would make no noise. Roger, however, carried a rifle and a brace of pistols; if a battle should develop, he wanted to fight with maximum efficiency.

The wall of the castle that soared above was not as solid a mass as it had appeared from a distance. The castle was very old, and over the centuries stones had eroded and chipped, so, as Ja-gonh was quick to note, it was possible to climb the wall. His sense of balance was so good, his night vision so keen, that he ascended rapidly. When he had gone about fifty feet he paused atop a flying buttress, and there he tied one end of the rope around his waist and lowered the other end to the ground.

Roger's climb was far more gingerly, but the rope around his middle gave him a feeling of security, and he, too, reached the top of the buttress safely.

Then they resumed their climb. Anyone approaching the castle would have been startled to see two human figures blithely scaling the heights. The sentinels inside the building remained unaware that security was being breached.

At last, Ja-gonh reached the parapet at the top and, still breathing easily, held the rope tightly while Roger made his final ascent. Then they dropped a few feet down to the terracelike roof.

They stood for some moments while Roger caught his breath and gradually brought his trembling arms and legs under control. As he looked down at the ground far below, he marveled that he had been able to scale the wall with the ease of a monkey.

They were outside the castle's bedrooms, and only the open French doors separated them from Ah-wen-ga and her captors. There was a need for silence, and Roger marveled at the speed and agility of Ja-gonh. The moon disappeared behind a bank of clouds, but the darkness into which the scene was plunged offered no problems to the young Seneca. Roger, following closely, could only hope that he didn't stumble upon some unseen object.

Ja-gonh paused to get his bearings. The open French doors directly ahead would lead to Ah-wen-ga's chamber, according to his sightings from below. He gestured, and Roger knew what was expected of him.

Ja-gonh would enter the chamber, awaken Ah-wen-ga, and then return with her. Meantime, Roger would stand guard outside the doors. He stood close to them in order to be less visible, while Ja-gonh glided like a shadow into the bedchamber.

One hand on the handle of his tomahawk, Ja-gonh stood still, allowing his eyes to become accustomed to the darkness of the room. Gradually he made out the form of Ah-wen-ga on the bed, and as he gazed at her, he became strangely disturbed.

She was wearing a flimsy nightgown of French silk that almost revealed her nudity, and this made an even greater impact on him than if she had been totally unclad. Her hair, hanging loose, fell forward across her face, and this, too, was completely new to him. His nostrils were assailed by a musklike scent that she wore; he could not remember a time in the past when either she or any other Seneca woman had worn perfume. His mother and sister used a scent, to be sure, but only when they visited relatives in Virginia. When they were in the land of the Seneca, they followed the custom of the nation and used no scent.

The musklike odor clung to Ah-wen-ga, and in spite of himself, Ja-gonh was aroused. He had not anticipated reacting in this way and was stunned.

As he looked at her, Ah-wen-ga stirred and finally began to open her eyes.

Not wanting her to cry out, he spoke to her softly in the language of the Seneca. "Fear not," he said. "You are protected by a fellow member of the Bear Clan."

Recognizing his voice instantly, Ah-wen-ga smiled as she searched the room for him and finally found him standing some feet from her bed. "I knew you would come here, Ja-gonh," she whispered. "I couldn't believe my good fortune when you shot the arrow into the wall to tell me of your presence, and ever since that moment, I have been awaiting you." She sat up in bed.

More conscious of her semiclad state than ever, he stirred uneasily. "Roger Harkness has come with me," he said. "We will spirit you away from this place immediately."

She rose effortlessly from the four-poster bed and donned a peignoir of silk that matched her nightgown. Then she sat on the foot of the bed and patted a place beside her. "Sit, Ja-gonh," she said. "We need to talk."

He was impatient, anxious for them to be on their way. "Perhaps," he suggested politely, "we would do best if we leave now and save the exchange of words until later."

She shook her head. "We must speak now," she said. "But don't worry—it's safe enough here, as long as we're quiet. No one will come in, and we will remain undisturbed."

Grudgingly he took a place beside her, more conscious than ever of her now that they were so close.

"No doubt you know," she said, "how I come to be here at the hands of Gray Fox, Major Henri de Bienville, and the woman known as Lady Arlene d'Amarante. We crossed the Atlantic Ocean; they took me first to Paris, then here."

"I know that Gray Fox is motivated by his hatred for me and for the Seneca," Ja-gonh responded somberly, "and I know a good deal about his thirst for power and his ambitions for himself and his people. But I am still at a loss to know exactly why he and Major de Bienville, and this Lady Arlene d'Amarante, have gone to the trouble and

153

expense of abducting you all the way to France. Tell me what you know of their plan."

"Their plan is a subtle but effective one. They have been preparing me to become more attractive to Frenchmen, particularly to King Louis XV. They hope he will take me as his mistress when they present me to him, and that they will consequently win his favor. They seek ultimately to gain his support in their effort to win the New World for France and for their allies, the Huron."

Ja-gonh ground his teeth with rage. So angry was he that he could only sputter in reply. Though he—and Roger, too—had suspected the outlines of their opponents' scheme, its very breadth and its far-reaching implications took Ja-gonh's breath away.

Ah-wen-ga put a hand on his arm to calm him. "I was outraged, too, when I first learned of the scheme," she said, "but now I can view it more peacefully."

Ja-gonh was on his feet. "We will make your escape immediately," he said. "Change into other clothing—you can't climb in all those silks."

Ah-wen-ga pulled him back beside her. "I really don't believe that I wish to escape," she said, "and when you hear what I have in mind, I think you will not wish it either."

Scarcely believing he was hearing her correctly, he could only stare at her.

"The King," she said, "will be interested in my body. But he shall not have it. I have promised myself to you, Ja-gonh, and only to you."

He was only somewhat mollified.

"All the same," she said, "I can see a way, perhaps the only way, to gain the King's full attention. Think of it! I shall be alone with him, and he will be forced to listen to me. I will plead with him to make peace in the New World, and I shall make it clear to him that he—alone in all the world—has it within his power to decide whether there will be peace or war. I will let him know he has a simple choice. Maybe New France will cooperate with the English colonists and their allies of the Iroquois League in maintaining the peace. But I will tell him that if he strengthens the Indian nations that are the allies of France and sends more troops and arms to New France, we and the English will fight because we value our freedom above all. I'm sure he will listen to me, because not even the King of the French wants the weight of the burden of a new war on his soul."

Ja-gonh was startled. The very idea that Ah-wen-ga was refusing to flee with him was alien to all of his thoughts about her. Her proposal to use her opportunity to speak personally to King Louis was so unexpected that he had no idea whether it was good or bad.

"For six moons," she continued, "I have been a prisoner. I have undergone training with only one end in the minds of my captors. I have suffered too much for too long, and I seek a complete victory, which I intend to achieve in my own way. All that will remain unfinished will be the killing of Gray Fox. And I will leave that to you."

"I can think of many reasons why your plan may be a bad one," Ja-gonh responded finally. "The most obvious is that the King may not listen to you and may demand that you submit to him as a woman. Then what would you do?"

She smiled slightly as she reached under her peignoir and produced Arlene's little knife.

He shook his head vigorously. "If the King of France is protected, as I believe he must be," he said, "you would be executed for assassinating him. In any event, this is neither the time nor the place to discuss such ideas. Come with me, and we'll hear what Roger and Patience have to say."

"If I leave now," she replied, "I can never return. If I go, I become a fugitive from the French, and we will be required to make our way back to our people as best we can."

"If you come with me now, tonight," he replied, "a ship awaits to take us back to the New World."

Ah-wen-ga was torn but held firm. Her plan helped see

155

her through many days of misery and discontent, and she had no intention of abandoning her scheme lightly. "I am grateful to you, Ja-gonh," she said, "and to Roger and to Patience, too, for risking your lives for me. I owe each of you a personal debt that will be very difficult to repay. So the least I can do is to think about your offer and weigh it along with my own plan. Can you return here tomorrow night as you have come here tonight, silently and secretly?"

He had to admit that he felt sure that what he and Roger had accomplished once they could achieve again.

"Very well," she said, "come at this same hour tomorrow, after all of us have had time to think. When you return, we will be able to decide what is best for me to do. If I am to stay here and see the King, we will have to sacrifice our personal happiness for a time. If I am to come with you, I will be prepared to leave immediately." She stood.

He rose, too. She looked at him long and intently in the dark, and then suddenly leaned toward him, her face raised for his kiss.

He swept her into his arms, and they kissed fervently as they embraced. Then, not trusting himself to speak again, he silently departed.

Roger Harkness, waiting outside, had become concerned because Ja-gonh was taking so long inside Ah-wen-ga's bedchamber. When the warrior reappeared, Roger was surprised that she was not accompanying him. Now was not the time for questions, however, and when Ja-gonh beckoned, Roger silently followed him over the parapet.

The two men laboriously lowered themselves to the ground on the outside of the castle, and it was only then that Roger learned the astonishing news that Ah-wen-ga was reluctant to accept immediate freedom because she saw a new opportunity to serve the cause of the Seneca.

The day began badly, ominously for Betsy. As the sun rose over the great forest that lay to the east of the principal town of the Seneca, Renno awoke—color burned unnaturally in his cheeks, his eyes were glazed, and he appeared not to recognize her as he asked for water. She dipped into a gourd, supporting his head, and he muttered his thanks, still not knowing her identity.

Then Deborah came in from the next room, intending to bathe his wrists and forehead in cool water. In spite of his condition, he knew her at once.

Betsy was sorely troubled. It was difficult for her not to attribute significance to the fact that her husband treated her like a total stranger, but had instantly known the woman who had been his mistress so many years earlier.

Then, through the open window, she heard the loud cries of the Seneca medicine men, their voices rising and falling in a curious, rhythmic cadence. The ceremonies in which Ena would seek the intervention of the manitous on behalf of her stricken son had begun.

Betsy and Deborah silently exchanged looks of helplessness compounded with anger. Both knew only too well that anything they might say would be superfluous.

The voices of the medicine men grew louder, and through the open window Betsy caught a glimpse of several of them wearing the masks reserved for the most solemn rites. Some of the medicine men stationed themselves outside the window, and the others trooped unbidden into the house and came into the sickroom. Their chants became louder and the air turned gray with a thick, nauseating smoke.

The two women saw that the medicine men held in their left hands brands made of dampened bird feathers that smoldered rather than burned openly.

In their free hands the medicine men carried carved, painted containers filled with the ashes of feathers that had been previously burned. They scattered handfuls of them at regular intervals as they chanted, and soon particles of ash were everywhere in the room. Looking anxiously at Renno, who paid no attention to the commotion, Betsy saw that his breathing appeared more labored. It was small wonder, she thought; the ashes were undoubtedly clogging his nose and throat.

Ena came into the room, her face and hands smeared with ashes, and she was followed by Goo-ga-ro-no and No-da-vo, both of whom had also smeared themselves liberally with ashes. They began to march around Renno's sickbed, each occasionally shaking a fist defiantly at the evil spirits who continued to possess the Great Sachem.

Goo-ga-ro-no and No-da-vo, entering wholeheartedly into the spirit of the occasion, followed close behind Ena, joining in her chants. From time to time they dipped into a container of ashes, flinging handfuls of the sticky substance into the air.

In the meantime, the medicine men in their hideous masks continued to cavort and to make their loud, rising and falling cries. The rites seemed interminable. Watching the dancers' incessant movements made Betsy unbelievably weary. The smoke from the torches of burning feathers made the air hazy and thick. What the ordeal might be doing to Renno, she couldn't bear to imagine, but she tried to prepare herself for his sudden strangulation.

For a time, Deborah bore the ordeal with a fair degree of equanimity, but eventually, the sounds and the odors left her gasping for breath. She was angry, but she was incapable of stopping the primitive rite.

The stamina of the dancers played an integral part in the significance of the ceremony. Noon came and went, and the hours of the afternoon crawled past, but still the dance went on and on.

Renno lay motionless, with his eyes still closed. His blanket was covered with ashes and soot, and his breathing had become even more labored. Betsy, sitting beside him, leaned over and called him by name, but he did not open his eyes nor stir.

She was afraid the end was drawing near, and she gazed apprehensively at Deborah, who also was trying to steel herself for what she regarded as the inevitable.

By late afternoon the chanting seemed to be reaching a climax.

Suddenly, Betsy saw Deborah's lips move, and although she couldn't hear the words, she recognized what the minister's widow undoubtedly was saying. She instantly joined in.

Our Father who art in Heaven, hallowed be Thy name.

The dancers lighted fresh plumes of feathers.

Thy kingdom come, Thy will be done on earth as it is in Heaven.

Although Ena was an old lady, she appeared fresh and confident, as though she were just beginning her exertions.

Give us this day our daily bread, and forgive us our trespasses as we forgive those who trespass against us. And lead us not into temptation, but deliver us from evil.

The medicine men seemed to inspire Goo-ga-ro-no, and her leaps became wilder and more unrestrained.

For Thine is the kingdom, and the power, and the glory, for ever and ever. Amen.

Betsy could not recall a time when she had spoken the Lord's Prayer with as much fervor.

She looked at her daughter in utter astonishment. The true Seneca, who had crowded into the building and were cavorting outside it, had believed naturally in their own god and in the manitous. But Goo-ga-ro-no had been reared as much in the faith of the Anglican Church of Betsy's family in Virginia as in the faith of the Seneca; nevertheless, today she betrayed no training other than that of a complete Seneca. Her eyes glowed as fiercely as her grandmother's. She moved with unrestrained energy around the room, and like Ena, she was absorbed in her entreaties to the manitous.

Betsy stared at her daughter in undisguised horror. Through the years she had freely allowed both Ja-gonh and Goo-ga-ro-no to be brought up as Seneca, to know and appreciate the heritage of their people, but this exhibition was so alien that she felt she no longer knew her own daughter.

Renno lay very still, his breathing painfully labored, his skin waxen, his eyes closed. It appeared that he was in a crisis and could not last more than a few moments.

Suddenly, he galvanized into action. Sitting bolt upright, he joined in the chant to the manitous, his voice loud and his words enunciated with great clarity.

Betsy and Deborah were utterly astonished, but the Seneca did not regard his unexpected burst of activity as unusual. They appeared to accept it as a sure sign of his recovery, and they immediately rejoiced. Ena and Goo-ga-ro-no stopped their chanting and stood at the foot of Renno's bed, their arms around each other as they listened to his chant. Both were smiling broadly, and it was evident that they felt the manitous had heard their pleas for help and were responding to them.

Betsy, with bewilderment, saw that her husband's behavior seemed that of a man who had recovered from the Big Sleep. He was alert and wide-awake. Above all, he showed no sign of the physical weakness that had made the slightest movement torture for him.

Apparently truly recovered, he spoke to Betsy above the continuing chant of the medicine men. "Do not worry, my love," he told her. "I will be well now. I drifted close to the shores of the river that separates us from the land of our ancestors, but now I have returned safely and surely to the near bank."

He turned to Deborah and smiled at her. "I'm in your debt, too," he said. "I appreciate, from the bottom of my heart, all that you've done for me during these terrible weeks."

The word spread rapidly throughout the town that the Great Sachem was indeed recovered from his ailment—that the plea to the manitous, led by his mother, had been successful. The members of the tribe were eager to greet Renno personally, and long lines formed outside the house. Among those present were the leaders of the other Iroquois nations who had not yet returned to their own homes following their council meeting.

At last the chanting of the medicine men stopped, and the burning brands were removed from the sickroom. The air became clearer, and the women found breathing relatively easy again.

Knowing how long it would take for Renno to greet the people of the Seneca individually, Betsy and Deborah quietly moved out-of-doors. Both were exhausted by their ordeal, and they walked slowly to an isolated spot just inside the town palisade. There they sat down in the late afternoon sunlight and without a word enjoyed both the quiet and the fresh air.

Betsy finally broke the silence. "I can't explain the miracle we've just witnessed," she said.

"Nor can I," Deborah replied. "But Renno has returned to the living from the near dead, and his cure seems complete."

Betsy was lost in thought for some moments. "Never again," she said, "can I deny the power of the manitous."

"You are fortunate that you can be so malleable," Deborah replied. "As one who was married for many years to a devoted clergyman, I am forced to reject what's happened, even though I've seen it and heard it with my own eyes and ears."

"Do you suppose it is possible," Betsy asked, "that the Lord heard *our* prayer and answered it?"

"I'd like to think so," Deborah said. "I'd like to believe that our prayer, rather than the pagan appeals of the Seneca to the manitous, could be responsible for Renno's recovery, but we'll never know."

Betsy, sighing tremulously, realized that her grueling

nightmare apparently had finally come to an end. She probably would never find the answer, never know just what was responsible for Renno's miraculous recovery. All she knew for certain was that his health had been restored. And recalling the love in his eyes when he had looked at her, she was assured that he was hers and hers alone.

Chapter VIII

The crisis that had placed the future of the Iroquois in jeopardy was resolved and the leaders of the league were content. The restoration of Renno to health was accepted by his brother sachems as normal and natural, and after extending their congratulations to him—and seeing for themselves how well he was faring—they were content to begin their delayed departure for their own homes.

Da-kay of the Oneida was an exception, however. His hatred and resentment of Renno continued to smolder, and the invisible chip he carried on his shoulder became larger and more burdensome. His escort of twenty-five Oneida warriors awaited him for their return to their own land, which lay directly east of the land held by the Seneca. Da-kay went to bid his official farewell to Sun-ai-yee. The sachem of the Seneca, as luck would have it, had just visited Renno himself and stood in the main street of the Seneca town exchanging a few words with El-i-chi before he proceeded to his own home.

Da-kay approached, extended his left forearm in formal greeting, and then exchanged wrist-grasps with the older man. "It was my hope," he said, "that the illness of Renno would end the problem that the league faces, but we must struggle with it anew."

Sun-ai-yee was determined to keep the peace and responded mildly. "Problem? I know of no problem."

"It is a problem I discussed in the Council Lodge," Da-kay replied, his eyes glittering. "Renno betrayed our interests to the English colonists, and his brothers in the Iroquois League must overcome the shoddy peace that he arranged."

El-i-chi, standing by, knew he was being baited, but he could not help rising to it. He considered it bad enough for the Oneida to insult his brother gratuitously; it was quite another, far more serious matter for Da-kay to insinuate that Renno was accepting bribes from the English settlers.

El-i-chi now forcibly injected himself into the conversation. "I trust," he said, "that you can prove this so-called shoddiness of Renno's arrangement with the English colonists?"

Da-kay laughed unpleasantly. "I have no need for such proof," he replied, "when every Iroquois warrior knows that what I have said is true."

El-i-chi could tolerate no more. Drawing his tomahawk slowly, he dropped it so that it landed between the Oneida's feet, with the blade imbedded in the ground. "Every Iroquois warrior well knows," he said, "that Da-kay of the Oneida is a notorious liar."

Sun-ai-yee sighed imperceptibly. The personal combat that he had sought to avoid would now be fought. Da-kay's impudence could not be allowed to go unpunished, and he deserved to be taught a lesson that all Iroquois would remember.

As El-i-chi had anticipated, Da-kay quickly picked up his challenge and accepted it. Word spread swiftly through the town that the sachem of the Oneida had insulted Renno, the Great Sachem, and that El-i-chi, war chief of the Seneca, had taken up the cudgels on his brother's behalf.

Soon, scores of warriors began to gather in the open area beyond the grain and vegetable fields outside the town palisade. The sachems of the Mohawk and Onondaga, Tuscarora and Cayuga, postponed their leave-taking so they could witness the fight. Dozens of Seneca also trooped to the site of the coming combat, and most of them were in an ugly mood. Their joy over Renno's recovery was stifled by the insults from the leader of the Oneida.

Betsy and Deborah received word of the impending bout from No-da-vo as they were considering a return to Renno's bedside.

Deborah was exasperated. "Men are all the same, regardless of whether they are supposedly civilized or they're savages," she said. "They insist on pumping up their chests and protecting their so-called honor. They make me so angry."

"I won't tell Renno about the fight until later," Betsy said. "He'll worry about El-i-chi, so it will be time enough to tell him after El-i-chi takes care of himself."

"You sound confident that El-i-chi is going to be the survivor," Deborah said.

"The sons and grandsons of Ghonka," Betsy replied with a smile, "never lose battles, including personal combat. That simply isn't their way. Are you coming with me to see Renno?"

Deborah shook her head. "No," she said. "You and Renno deserve a little time to yourselves, even though he is so weary that he can't converse and falls asleep. I'll join you presently."

She deliberately lingered behind as Betsy went on to the

house. Then, as though drawn by an invisible magnet, Deborah found herself following the crowds to the field beyond the town palisade. Men of every age and rank were present, but only a handful of women had seen fit to attend the bout. Feeling she would be even more conspicuous if she withdrew now, Deborah stayed, but her uneasiness increased when a number of Seneca warriors made way for her and she unexpectedly found herself in the front rank.

Da-kay was the first of the principals to appear. He had stripped to his loincloth and was heavily greased from head to toe for the fight, with his vermilion and white war paint prominent on his face and chest. Then El-i-chi appeared, similarly dressed and greased, wearing the familiar green and yellow paint of the Seneca. His arms swung freely at his sides, but in his belt he carried his tomahawk and a knife. He greeted no one as he approached the open area in the center of the arena where Da-kay awaited him, intending to greet only Sun-ai-yee, which would have been proper. Then he caught sight of Deborah, and he stopped short.

To her acute embarrassment, he raised his left arm stiffly in a full-fledged formal salute to her.

She felt impelled to reply in kind, and saluted him as best she could, although the gesture was unfamiliar to her.

El-i-chi grinned at her. Deborah found it much easier to return his smile.

Then he raised his hand a second time, in salute to Sun-ai-yee, and turned to face his enemy.

Da-kay repeated his accusation, charging that Renno accepted the bribes of English settlers, who had paid him for the treaty that the Iroquois had made with them.

A dangerous rumble erupted in the ranks of the Seneca warriors.

El-i-chi drew his tomahawk and silenced his compatriots. "Every warrior in the Iroquois League," he said loudly and clearly, "knows that Da-kay of the Oneida is a liar and that he cannot utter words of truth."

That was the signal for the combat to begin. Both men sprang at each other and began to circle warily, each grasping a tomahawk in one hand, and a knife in the other. Each sought an opening, some sign of a mental lapse or carelessness that would give the initiative to the warrior who was wise enough to seize it.

Deborah had not witnessed personal combat between Indians since she had seen Renno fight in a similar engagement more than three decades earlier. Sorry that she had come, yet not quite understanding her reluctance to leave, she stood miserably, one hand slowly creeping up to cover her mouth. She reflected that perhaps she was avoiding a temptation to scream.

The combatants appeared to be fairly well matched. Both were in their early fifties and in superb physical condition. El-i-chi was taller and had the advantage of a somewhat longer reach, but Da-kay was heavier by about ten or fifteen pounds and was more broad shouldered.

The crowd was strangely silent. Deborah reflected that nowhere but in this Indian world would partisans refrain from cheering for their representative.

Da-kay struck first. Feinting with his tomahawk, he leaped forward, his knife held high above his head, and brought it down in a swinging arc as he lunged. Had he struck his target, nothing could have saved his Seneca opponent. But El-i-chi was too wise in the ways of combat not to recognize the ruse. He knew that his foe would not deliberately deprive himself of his tomahawk at this early stage of a fight. So he concentrated, instead, on his opponent's foot movements. Consequently, when Da-kay lunged, El-i-chi easily sidestepped, and the Oneida's knife cut through thin air, but made no solid contact.

Da-kay appeared slow to learn. He repeated his tactics identically, and El-i-chi avoided him precisely as he had done the first time.

Some of the younger Seneca warriors chuckled aloud derisively.

Their laughter stung Da-kay, and he became still more aggressive toward his foe. His tomahawk was held at head-height; his other arm, above his head, was poised to plunge his knife into the Seneca.

El-i-chi remained remarkably cool, precisely as Ghonka had taught him and his brother to do from the time they had been small boys. He made no move until the last possible moment, remaining motionless until Da-kay was virtually on top of him. Then he ducked skillfully and stepped forward, slipping under the surprised Oneida's guard.

El-i-chi creased one side of the Oneida leader's face with his tomahawk as he engaged in close combat and then hastily drew back out of arm's reach again.

The crowd rocked with laughter, breaking a prolonged silence. The gesture was magnificent, and they appreciated its meaning.

The significance of what El-i-chi had done dawned more slowly on Deborah. Ultimately, she realized that he had inflicted a minor injury on his opponent deliberately, as if to say, "I have marked your face with my tomahawk, and if you live you'll bear the scar forever. Regard it as a scar of shame, because I could have killed you as easily as I inflicted the wound on you."

Nor was the meaning of El-i-chi's move lost on Da-kay. His eyes gleamed, and brushing away the blood that oozed from the thin wound on his face, he took a fresh grip on both his weapons. He intended to make short work of his foe and bring the combat to an end. But he made the mistake of revealing his plan too plainly to his opponent. El-i-chi saw that the Oneida intended to move in for a kill, and he was equally determined to prevent just that.

A flurry of thrusts followed—a quick exchange of blows in which both the Seneca and the Oneida jabbed with their knives and swung their tomahawks at each other. They moved with such graceful speed that only one trained in Indian combat could know precisely what had happened.

Deborah realized only that both men were still on their feet, and El-i-chi seemed to have fared somewhat better in the exchange, although he, too, had suffered.

Da-kay had sustained another cut, this one on the shaved portion of his head, and El-i-chi had suffered a nasty gash in one shoulder. He seemed to be losing considerable quantities of blood. He gave no sign that it bothered him, but Deborah feared he must be in excruciating pain.

Suddenly, the pace of the battle increased as the combatants seemed to explode in a frenzy of activity. Both had been wounded; both realized they would be weakened in any protracted struggle, and consequently they hastened their efforts in an attempt to finish each other off.

Deborah's heart pounded wildly as she watched knives and tomahawks clash. Da-kay was intent on first crippling his opponent and then dispatching him. El-i-chi was equally sure in his own mind that he must render his opponent totally harmless.

The two men dodged and squirmed, each catlike in his agility and seemingly possessed of as many lives as the legendary cat. The Oneida struck again and again with his knife, then brought his sharp tomahawk down with a vengeance. How El-i-chi managed to survive was beyond Deborah's imagination.

But El-i-chi was equally active, equally aggressive. His movements were less sweeping than those of his opponent but his chops with the tomahawk were more measured.

The fight ended suddenly when Da-kay staggered, dropped to the ground, and lay still, his face in the dust.

Deborah knew from the awkwardness of his position that he was dead. But she was not interested in him—what concerned her was El-i-chi.

Breathing hard, the Seneca war chief moved under his own power, walking slowly away from the opponent who had paid for his insults with his life. Not bothering to glance in Da-kay's direction again, he dropped slowly to the ground and folded his arms.

Sun-ai-yee declared him the winner, and the warriors of the Oneida sorrowfully removed the body of their fallen sachem from the field of combat.

El-i-chi continued to sit, and he seemed at peace, but Deborah realized that his labored breathing indicated that he was encountering some difficulty.

But the Seneca did not believe in pampering a warrior who had been wounded in battle. The spectators returned singly and in groups to the town, leaving El-i-chi to manage as best he could.

Their barbarism stunned Deborah, who remained behind in order to render whatever assistance she could. She hurried to the lake, and tearing off two generous pieces of cloth from her petticoat, she soaked them in the cold water and then carried them to El-i-chi. She wasted no time on words of sympathy. Wiping the congealed blood from El-i-chi's wound with one of her sopping cloths, she applied the other to his cut and held it there.

He gasped involuntarily but silently, and shuddered slightly, but made no complaint.

"I will apply the powdered red root of a healing plant to my cut," he reassured her, "and by tomorrow it will be much better."

"You're sure?"

"Very sure," he replied. "I have sustained many wounds in a lifetime of battles."

Deborah lowered herself to the ground beside him. She looked at him searchingly, her expression grave. "Perhaps you'll tell me something I very much want to know," she said. "Why is honor so all important to you? Why did you deliberately choose to risk your life in combat simply because Renno had been insulted by a vicious-tempered man?"

El-i-chi smiled and replied deliberately in English. "I like to think of myself as a civilized man," he explained. "I am one who lives in the eighteenth century, as you colonists count time. But there is much you fail to understand about the temperament of the Indian."

She was surprised; apparently his reasons were more complex than she had realized.

"The Indian warrior, regardless of his nationality," El-i-chi said, "is obsessed with honor. Maintenance of his honor means more to him than food or drink, or even the welfare and future of his wife and children. It is wrong, perhaps, for him to feel as he does, but the fact is that his belief is as much a part of him as is the breath that he draws in and out of his body."

170

So far, she understood the point he seemed to be trying to make, and she nodded.

"Had Renno been well, he would have been obliged to respond to Da-kay's challenge. In fact, I am doubtful that Da-kay would have said what he did, had Renno been able to defend himself. The Oneida attacked him only because he thought he was safe."

"But you felt that your family honor demanded that you respond and fight him?"

El-i-chi shook his head. "That is not quite as it seems," he said. "I rose to his challenge because the warriors of the Seneca expected and demanded it of me."

He was trying to make a point that eluded her, and she was puzzled. He hastened to explain in detail. "If I had accepted the insults of Da-kay," he said, "the warriors of the Seneca would have wondered about the Oneida's words. Soon they might begin to suspect some truth in them. They would say to each other that perhaps it was true that Renno had accepted money or land or other favors from the English settlers in return for the alliance with the Iroquois League. The good name of Ghonka would have been destroyed, and the good name that Renno inherited from him would have been no more. Renno's children would have been disgraced, and his grandchildren would have been driven from their homes—all because the people of the Seneca would have become convinced by then that Renno was, indeed, a criminal."

At last, Deborah understood what he meant and was deeply impressed by his reasoning.

"I knew in my heart as well as in my mind that Renno was innocent of wrongdoing," El-i-chi continued. "All of us who are related to him knew it, but if I had not forced a confrontation with the sachem of the Oneida, we would have been alone in our beliefs. Never again would Renno or any of his family have been able to hold up their heads."

Instead of being concerned with honor, Deborah now saw, El-i-chi had acted as he had done because he had the welfare of the entire Seneca nation in mind. She saw the fight now in an entirely different light and realized he had no choice but to fight in order that his brother's reputation be maintained in the land of the Seneca. "By the standards of my people," Deborah told him forcefully, "you've done a very wonderful and courageous thing."

El-i-chi shrugged. "I did what was needed," he said. "My brother would have done the same for me. So would my sister's husband, and so would Renno's son. In order for the men of a nation to stand together, it is first necessary for the men of a family to stand together."

Deborah took the cloths, returned to the lake, and after rinsing them, brought them back to El-i-chi. "Here," she said, placing one on the wound. "It looks much better already. The bleeding has stopped, and the swelling is vastly reduced."

He smiled at her somewhat lopsidedly. "A Seneca warrior is not accustomed to being treated with so much kindness," he said. "You spoil me."

"That's all right," she replied lightly. "You deserve spoiling."

"You will never know," he declared, "how surprised I was to find you in the crowd that had gathered for my fight with Da-kay. What caused you to come?"

"I was concerned for you," she said simply.

El-i-chi stared at her, his gaze piercing.

As Deborah felt herself reddening beneath his scrutiny, she felt it absurd that she, a woman who had been married for many years and had two grown children leading independent lives of their own, should be reacting like a flustered schoolgirl.

"We are the same age," El-i-chi said, "but girls mature more rapidly than boys, so when you first came to the land of the Seneca, you were already a woman, though I was barely a junior warrior. Not only were you a woman, but it was plain to me, as to all who saw you, that you were Renno's woman."

She was embarrassed by his candor and wondered what he was trying to tell her.

"You never knew," El-i-chi said, "that I lost my heart

to you. The only person who knew I loved you was my mother, and I swore her to secrecy. She would never betray that promise."

His confession was so surprising that Deborah was at a loss for words.

"Through the years," he went on, "I made it my business, always, to be included in any party of Seneca that visited Fort Springfield. Always, I sought you out, although you did not know it, and I merely viewed you from afar. I rejoiced for the happiness you found in your marriage. I was pleased at the health of your son and of your daughter, and I was happy for you when they grew to manhood and womanhood and went off to lead their own lives in their own way."

Deborah was deeply touched. "What are you trying to say to me?" she asked. To her surprise, her voice was tremulous.

"Over the years," he said, "I satisfied the needs of a warrior by visiting the huts of the women who were captured from the Erie and the Huron. But I did not marry. Many Seneca sought me as a husband for their daughters because I was the son of Ghonka, the brother of Renno, and because my own advancement progressed steadily. Even in recent times, since I have been a war chief, there are many who have indicated to me that they would be pleased if I would become the husband of their daughter. Always, I have declined."

She discovered that her fists were clenched, her nails digging into the palms of her hands, and that she was holding her breath.

"I have never taken a wife," El-i-chi said solemnly, "because my heart has belonged all these years to Deborah."

Her mind whirled and she found it difficult to think clearly. She was astonished by El-i-chi's declaration of love for her. Yet, at the same time, she had more or less expected it; she had guessed from his attitude toward her during the weeks she had spent in the town of the Seneca, taking care of Renno, that El-i-chi was enamored of her. She had even gathered that, finally having cast off all

173

restraints, he was building up to a declaration of his feelings for her. Now, the only question in her mind was whether she cared enough for him to become his wife. Was she willing to give up her home in Fort Springfield and live for the rest of her days in a Seneca dwelling? In facing the issue squarely, she recognized—just as Betsy had so many years earlier—that the sacrifices she might be called on to make would be well worth the effort. Certainly her children no longer needed her, and if she returned to Springfield, she would live out her days as a much-honored, partly pitied widow.

When Deborah, through this process, made up her mind, she raised her head and returned El-i-chi's steady gaze. What he saw in her eyes encouraged him, and he looked at her even more intensely. They had no need for a further exchange of words. What he saw dumbfounded and then elated him. Ignoring his half-forgotten wound, he reached out a hand to her.

Deborah unhesitatingly placed her small white hand in his large brown one. They thus sealed their betrothal, and their joint future was now assured. In the back of Deborah's mind was the realization that she would need to become acclimated once again to the ways of Seneca. Had she agreed to marry a fellow English settler, he would have sealed the bargain with a kiss. El-i-chi, however, under no circumstances would kiss her in a public place and would wait until assured of total privacy before he engaged in so intimate a gesture.

They rose together, and the spring in El-i-chi's movements indicated that he would suffer no ill effects from the wound that had been inflicted on him.

"I would like to tell our news to Renno and Betsy," Deborah said, "and then I want to write a letter to my children."

"I will arrange that No-da-vo, who travels like the wind, will deliver your words to your son and daughter," he assured her.

She touched his arm in a gesture of thanks, and for a

long moment they stood side by side, smiling at each other.

Deborah knew that many parishioners of her late husband's in Fort Springfield would never be able to understand her decision to marry again, much less to a Seneca war chief. But her decision was sound and good. Instead of living out her days in respectable obscurity, she would play a vital role in the annals of her people and of the Seneca, whom she had so long admired.

As she and El-i-chi walked slowly past the palisade and across the town to the house of Renno and Betsy, their shoulders touched occasionally, and she knew again that she had made the right decision. In a sense, her whole life had been a preparation for this day, and she felt certain she would face the future with confidence, never looking back over her shoulder at what could have been.

"I think Ah-wen-ga's attitude is dangerously naive," Patience said. "If King Louis finds her sufficiently attractive to want her as his mistress, he'll insist on having her. He'll perhaps let her make her political speech about wanting freedom for all the people of the New World—but then he'll bed her. Or, he may just tell her that he isn't interested in her political views."

Roger agreed with his wife. "I agree as wholeheartedly with Patience as much as I tend to disagree with Ah-wenga. She underestimates the danger that she faces. She has no important friends at court, no alternatives in case Louis decides to cut off her line of retreat. What will she do if he wants her? She can hardly ask you and me to appear out of nowhere and fight the entire regiment of King's Musketeers. No, I'm afraid she must view the situation that's come up realistically and sensibly—which means that she must leave the castle with us, and return without delay to the ship that awaits us in Marseilles."

Ja-gonh, listening with infinite care to the words of his friends, absorbed them slowly. They were dealing in a realm that was almost totally unfamiliar to him. His only experience with powerful colonists had been with Uncle Ned Ridley in Virginia and with General Wilson in Massachusetts Bay. Neither could compare, even remotely, in stature with the monarch of the French.

If Patience and Roger were correct—and he had every reason for assuming that they were—once Ah-wen-ga was presented to Louis XV, her attitude would be of little consequence. For all practical purposes, she might then become his property. He could do with her as he pleased, making her his concubine, and rejecting her—or, if it pleased him, holding her indefinitely as his prisoner. He stood above the law in France, and in fact, whatever he chose to do, was the law.

Ja-gonh had to admit that his companions seemed to make complete sense. Furthermore, he trusted their judgment.

"Ah-wen-ga was very firm in her opinion," he said, "but I can see that her mind must be changed."

"And I can see no doubt of that," Patience said. "She'll be playing into her kidnappers' hands if she tries to persuade the King to adopt a new attitude toward the English colonies and the Iroquois. What reason does he have to change?"

"Exactly!" Roger asserted with great emphasis. "He could expect to add considerably to his realm if the present tactics of his government are successful. Any gratitude shown by the English colonies and the Iroquois for being left in peace is of little consequence to a man like Louis, who is accustomed to ruling large numbers of people."

"I will tell her all that both of you have told me and will try to compel her to be sensible," Ja-gonh said.

"The trouble, I think, is that she has been in captivity for so long that her captors have swayed her mind and her heart. She is not sure now what she really wants," Roger said. "You will have to try to convince her that we haven't come all the way to France and endured great risks just to lose at the last moment."

"Furthermore," his wife added, "for safety's sake, you had better go to the castle alone tonight, Ja-gonh. When

Roger goes with you, the chances of exposure are doubled. If you go alone and something untoward happens, Roger is here, close by, to back you up and intervene on your behalf. If I were left by myself, I could do little or nothing for you or for Ah-wen-ga.''

Roger was reluctant to see his friend in danger alone, but he realized, too, that his wife's advice was sound, and he gave his approval. "I think Patience is right," he said. Go alone and, if it is at all possible, bring Ah-wen-ga back with you. Then we'll go from here together.''

Ja-gonh was in a fever of mounting impatience, but waited until well after dinner. Then, but only then, did he ride off to the castle, leaving his horse tethered in the forest where it could not be seen by those inside the great stone structure.

After he had gone, Roger turned to Patience with an observation that she found so unexpected that she almost gasped in astonishment.

"I've been thinking—and rethinking," he declared as he paced the floor in a large circle, "about Ah-wen-ga's idea and about our reaction to it. I've begun to conclude that we have responded quite naturally—but also hastily. Now I'm by no means so certain that we would be acting properly to force her to leave against her will and, more important, against her own judgment. After all, she is the one who has been on the scene. It is she who knows—and very possibly understands—these people and their scheming. She has heard more—undoubtedly much more—about the King than we have, and she may have attained insights that would surprise us. And she has had this one subject to ponder for all these months. It's hardly something that she hasn't had ample opportunity to give consideration to.''

Patience, who had heard him out in increasing appreciation of the turbulent thoughts that had been growing within his mind for the several past hours, indicated her understanding of his new observations.

"And perhaps most important of all," Roger concluded, "don't forget that Ah-wen-ga is a Seneca. Who can doubt that she is capable of following through on any action that she chooses to undertake? I feel that we must really rethink what course we are going to take from now on—and how we should advise her!"

Although Ja-gonh could see lights burning in the sentinels' quarters on the ground floor, darkness prevailed on the top floor of the castle. He gained access precisely as he had done the preceding night, scaling the wall. His agility had improved with practice. No longer concerned because of Roger's presence, he climbed with surefooted rapidity, and in a surprisingly short time he reached the top, swung over the parapet, and dropped soundlessly to the terrace.

Still taking no chances, he listened carefully for any sounds that might indicate that someone was still awake. The silence was absolute, and he made his way noiselessly to Ah-wen-ga's room.

This time she was awake and fully dressed, greeting him warmly as soon as he entered.

"I was beginning to think that something unpleasant had happened to you," she murmured. "It's been a very long wait."

"I prefer to come late enough to make sure that we're not disturbed," Ja-gonh explained, then plunged into his argument. "I have talked today at great length with Patience and Roger. I respect them both, and they are convinced it would be a tragic mistake for you to be presented to the King in order to change his mind on his policy toward the New World colonies. If he wished, and he is a ruthless man, he could keep you with him by force and compel you to do his bidding."

Ah-wen-ga protested. "You forget that I carry a knife and would be perfectly ready to use it."

"And what you forget," he replied, "is that the King of France knows no authority except his own. He rules as he pleases, and if he wants you he will take you. No power on earth is strong enough to stop him from exerting his will."

"Yes, I do see your point," Ah-wen-ga replied, a note

of doubt creeping into her voice for the first time. "Perhaps you could come with me to my meeting with him."

Ja-gonh didn't know how to respond. The idea appealed to him, but he knew he must again ask Patience and Roger for their opinion.

"That," he said, "is something that we can decide in due course. Meanwhile, we are wasting time. Come with me now and I will see to it that you are safe."

Before she could reply, he heard a sound behind him and turned, grasping his tomahawk as he whirled.

A bulky figure stood in the doorway that opened onto the roof terrace. To Ja-gonh's horror, he spoke in the familiar tongue of the Seneca. "I thought I heard voices in here," Gray Fox said, "and I could have sworn that they were speaking in the language of the wilderness. I was not dreaming."

Even in the darkness, Ja-gonh knew he had at last come face-to-face with his mortal enemy, the murderer of Ghonka and the abductor of Ah-wen-ga.

Gray Fox heard his sharp intake of breath and instantly was aware that this was no ordinary confrontation. Though he had only once seen Ja-gonh, he quickly guessed his identity. The male voice he had heard had been speaking the Seneca language faultlessly.

Ja-gonh was armed with his tomahawk and a knife. Feeling himself to be well equipped to fight, he contemplated the possibility of hurling himself at the half-breed without warning. But that was not the true way of the Seneca: in order to truly avenge his grandfather, he knew that justice demanded that he declare to the Huron his identity and his mission.

Gray Fox began to back slowly toward the terrace. He was armed with both a cavalry saber and a French pistol, and these weapons gave him sufficient confidence so that he felt certain he would be the equal of any Seneca. As the son of Colonel Alain de Gramont, he had his own fierce pride, and under no circumstances would he deign to call for help. If he shouted, he might rouse the garrison of de Guise retainers, but his father, watching from the land of his ancestors, then would have only scorn for him. Consequently, Gray Fox was determined to fight the Seneca man to man.

Ja-gonh followed the Huron, and they stepped onto the terrace.

"I am Ja-gonh," the Seneca declared softly, "and I am here to take revenge for the death of my grandfather, Ghonka!"

"I know that," Gray Fox replied, his tone mocking. "I've been looking forward to an encounter with you for a long time. But I never thought I'd have the pleasure of meeting you in France."

Ja-gonh disdained a reply, but slowly advanced toward him. With equal care, Gray Fox retreated.

Ah-wen-ga knew that only one would survive this confrontation. She was too well grounded in the ancient, inviolable traditions of her people to interfere, to attempt to join the combat on Ja-gonh's side. She knew that the spirit of Ghonka would be watching this fight, and that to raise a hand in interference would be a terrible mistake. So she hung back. A time came in the life of every man when he had to meet his destiny. Such a time had arrived for Ja-gonh, and she was willing to leave his fate in his own, extraordinarily competent hands. The climactic struggle that he had been seeking for more than a year was undeniably at hand.

When Gray Fox felt the stone wall behind him, he knew he could retreat no farther and leaped onto the three-foot-wide parapet, simultaneously flipping his saber from its scabbard. Perhaps, he hoped, he could take advantage of the greater height to prevent his foe from following him onto the parapet. But Ja-gonh was too quick for him. Showing scarcely any effort, he jumped onto the parapet, too.

Ah-wen-ga caught her breath, for she knew that a sheer drop of at least two hundred feet to the ground below awaited the man who made a misstep.

Ignoring his opponent's sword, Ja-gonh took one step closer, then stepped again. He held his tomahawk in his

180

right hand, his knife in his left. To his surprise, now that the actual moment had arrived when he could taste and see potential victory ahead, he felt no emotion.

Regardless of what might become of him, he was resolved that Gray Fox had to die. Even if he himself should perish along with Gray Fox and thus be unable to rescue Ah-wen-ga, he could not rest while Gray Fox still lived. The hour had come when he was finally in a position to fulfill his vow.

Gray Fox saw the steely expression in the white Seneca's pale eyes and was shaken. He recognized what he should have taken into account—that he faced a foe who was determined to take his life, no matter at what cost.

Very well, Gray Fox reflected. He would make that cost astronomically high. Halting his retreat along the parapet, he lunged suddenly and unexpectedly with the saber.

Ja-gonh, blessed with reflexes as remarkable as his eyesight, knew instinctively that the blow had been struck from too great a distance to do him any serious damage. Placing one foot behind him, he then leaned backward, and the tip of the saber barely grazed the black sweater that Roger had given him for his evening's adventure.

Gray Fox, deeply chagrined, recognized his error and did his best to compensate for it. He took a long step forward, but suddenly hesitated, seeing Ja-gonh's knife poised.

At such a short distance, as both men well knew, it would be difficult to miss a blow if the knife was well thrown. Gray Fox had heard enough of Ja-gonh's prowess to realize that his foe undoubtedly could throw the knife with deadly accuracy.

Halting abruptly, the Huron began to retreat again, half-crouching to present a smaller target.

Ja-gonh grunted in satisfaction, although his expression did not change. That backward step, he knew, had been a fatal error on the part of Gray Fox, because it had indicated for the first time that he was fearful. As Ja-gonh understood intuitively, fear was the emotion that most often robbed a man of victory, whether in a major battle or in individual combat. He was now confident, even though his opponent carried superior weapons. The Huron's fear was robbing him of whatever advantage he had enjoyed.

Suddenly a shadow appeared over the moon, momentarily obliterating it from view. Ja-gonh inadvertently flicked a brief glance upward.

His heart leaped to his throat; only through untold self-discipline did he refrain from shouting a joyful war cry that would have echoed and reechoed across the hills of Gascony. A hawk, appearing out of nowhere, was watching the battle from on high, swooping and dipping as it flew.

Ja-gonh could not watch the hawk because he did not dare take his eyes from his foe again. But it was enough to know that the manitous had sent the hawk to tell him that they were supporting him.

Ah-wen-ga became aware of the hawk's presence almost as soon as Ja-gonh, and she smiled softly to herself. She knew the tradition in the family of Ghonka that he and Renno, El-i-chi and Ja-gonh, all had enjoyed the protective, benevolent influence of hawks at critical moments. This was such a moment of moments, and the appearance of the hawk in the middle of the night could mean only that Ja-gonh would triumph.

But Ah-wen-ga's joy was short-lived. A door creaked open, and Henri de Bienville came onto the terrace, a cocked pistol in one hand.

Ah-wen-ga saw him before he caught sight of her or of the two figures moving in seeming slow motion on the parapet. She reacted instantly, instinctively. Reaching under her skirt, she drew her knife and crept up behind him. He became aware of her presence only when the knife cut through this clothes and its sharp point pricked him in the back.

"If you fire your weapon or cry out for help," Ah-wen-ga said softly, "you will die. I guarantee it. I mean these words from the bottom of my heart."

De Bienville realized that she had him trapped. As he froze, he saw the two duelists on the parapet and stared hard at the stranger. The man had a full head of blond hair and, dressed all in black, was wearing a high-necked sweater, breeches, and boots. Nothing in his appearance suggested that he might be an Indian from a North American tribe.

The riddle was too great for de Bienville; he had to focus on the unwelcome surprise that Ah-wen-ga seemed to have acquired a totally unexpected ally.

"Drop your weapon," Ah-wen-ga commanded in a cold voice, emphasizing her words by prodding the major in the back with her knife.

He contemplated trying to trick her in some way, but hastily changed his mind. She had acquired the patina of an erotically attractive French woman, but he realized anew that at heart she was still a savage Seneca and that she would not hesitate to keep her word if he disobeyed her.

Reviling himself, but helpless to do anything, he dropped the pistol.

Ah-wen-ga swiftly bent down and scooped it up. Had she known anything about firearms, she would have uncocked it immediately in order to make certain that it would not discharge and bring the entire de Guise garrison to the castle roof. In her ignorance, she flung it away from her, and it sailed over the parapet and landed on the ground far below. Her luck held, however, and for reasons that no one who later learned of the incident ever could understand, the pistol failed to discharge. It struck the ground as only a useless mass of metal.

Now the duelists had two witnesses. Ja-gonh became concerned when he realized that Ah-wen-ga had been joined by a man. But because of her stance, half behind him, he knew that she had found some way of immobilizing the newcomer. So much the better, but he realized, too, that he must not tarry in disposing of the Huron. Reinforcements for Gray Fox might be arriving at any time, and the mere thought of losing another opportunity to kill his hated foe filled him with near panic, and his energies surged.

Suddenly, Ja-gonh's lips moved as he addressed his grandfather. "Great Ghonka," he said, "hear my words from your eternal sanctuary in the land of our ancestors. I have waited long for this opportunity to keep my vow to you by avenging your murder. At last I have come face-to-face with the Huron who surprised and killed you when you least expected it. Watch me now as I even the score with the Huron nation on behalf of your son, Renno, and most of all on your own behalf, beloved Ghonka!"

And then, he knew the moment had come for him to act.

Ja-gonh moved in for the kill, but was conscious of the weapons that his opponent still wielded. Somewhat illogically, he was none too concerned about the pistol, believing that such weapons could be unreliable, often failed to discharge, and that even when they did, the bullets often went wide of the mark. The saber, to be sure, was far different, and he had to neutralize it.

This he did in a simple, direct manner. Raising the hand that held the tomahawk, he threatened the Huron with repeated gestures.

Gray Fox, fearing that the Seneca intended to throw the tomahawk at him, slashed at Ja-gonh's wrist with his saber.

Ja-gonh had created precisely the situation that he wanted. While the Huron's eyes were riveted on the hand that held the tomahawk, Ja-gonh carefully measured the few feet that separated him from his adversary and then, with a sharp movement of his wrist, he released his knife. The blade flew the short distance through the air, traveling with great speed and force.

The blow was remarkably accurate: the knife buried itself in Gray Fox's heart.

As Gray Fox felt the blade striking him, he knew that he had lost the combat, and with it his life. Before he could speak, however, he crumpled onto the parapet, an ironic half-smile still twisting his lips, and then plunged off it to the ground far below.

A sense of peace and fulfillment flooded Ja-gonh's soul.

184

He had kept his word to his grandfather and had brought the slayer of Ghonka to justice. And he had meted out deserved punishment to the abductor of Ah-wen-ga.

A sudden movement in the sky above him caught his eye, and he raised his head in time to see the hawk swoop low, coming within no more than some fifteen yards of the place where he stood. Then the bird soared again and disappeared into the night. The messenger of the manitous had fulfilled its own obligation and was leaving until the intermediaries for the gods might have need of it again.

"The blood of Gray Fox," Ja-gonh said aloud, "has washed clean the stain of the crime he committed when he slew you, Ghonka. Rest now in peace, beloved Grandfather, now and for all time."

Ah-wen-ga, deeply moved by what she had witnessed and still maintaining pressure with her knife on de Bienville, felt the urgent need of adding a word of her own to the proceedings. "Your future granddaughter, Ghonka," she said, "and the mother of your great-grandchildren wishes you peace for all eternity and knows in her heart that you will have it."

The sound of her voice jarred Ja-gonh and forcibly reminded him of her presence. Still gripping his weapons, he leaped to the terrace and hurried to her side. The danger was far from over even though Gray Fox had been eliminated for all time. "What have we here?" he demanded.

"Major de Bienville," Ah-wen-ga said, "was going to intervene in your fight—until I stopped him."

"Perhaps he also should die," Ja-gonh declared harshly.

De Bienville was saved the need for replying when a clamor went up from the guardhouse below. A bell clanged repeatedly, a bugle was blown, and guard dogs began to bark furiously.

Ah-wen-ga and Ja-gonh exchanged a quick, startled look. Their personal foe, the foe of all the Seneca, was dead, but perhaps they themselves had deferred too long their escape.

Ja-gonh intended to determine the outlook as rapidly as he could. So he leaped again onto the parapet and what he saw below caused him to frown. At least twenty or thirty sentries, all of them armed with muskets, were milling around inside the castle walls and even were roaming outside it. Some had guard dogs on leashes, and if they had not already found Ja-gonh's mount, it could only be a short time until they discovered it.

If he had been trying to escape alone, Ja-gonh would have risked climbing down the steep wall and taking his chances. But the need to take Ah-wen-ga with him limited the possibilities, and he knew that she could not make such a climb, especially if the sentinels began to fire at them. He could not subject her to such extreme danger. Instead, he must quickly take command of the situation.

A sergeant of the guard climbed the stairs that led to the tower and reported to de Bienville on the terrace, addressing him briefly in French. Ja-gonh instantly made it clear to the sergeant that the major's life was the price if the military acted against the invaders.

Ah-wen-ga understood the man, but Ja-gonh did not.

"He says that some people have come here and are demanding to see him and Lady Arlene," she translated for Ja-gonh, who was confused, and it appeared that de Bienville was also nonplussed.

"Major," Ja-gonh said, addressing the officer in English, "you and your sergeant are to precede us, but take heed of my warning. If I must, I will kill you with as little mercy as I showed Gray Fox! If you try to trick us or to take us captive, your associates may succeed but you will not be alive to witness their success. Stay in front of me at all times." He drew his tomahawk and motioned with it for the major to lead them down the stairs.

De Bienville began the descent. Ah-wen-ga, leaving the problem of controlling him to Ja-gonh, fell back and brought up the rear.

A surprising sight awaited them when they reached the great hall. Seated, facing a perplexed Arlene, were Roger and Patience Harkness, both smiling and apparently very much at ease. Roger held a pistol and clearly was very much in charge. Standing near them was Captain de

186

Sanson, whose hand hovered near the hilt of his sword. Apparently he was having difficulty in deciding whether to try to challenge the Englishman.

"Ah, there you are, Ja-gonh!" Roger called, speaking in the language of the Seneca. "We followed you here from the inn, and when the body of Gray Fox crashed to the ground from on high and the alarm was sounded, we reasoned the time had come for us to intervene. Greetings to you, Ah-wen-ga. We rejoice that you are safe."

It immediately became apparent to both Ah-wen-ga and Ja-gonh that de Bienville spoke the Seneca tongue because he obviously had understood every word that Roger had said. They merely bowed their heads in silent greeting.

Arlene was still trying to piece together the events that had taken place with such rapidity. She knew that Gray Fox was dead, and, never having liked or trusted him, she did not mourn his passing. But the man who had done him in caught her full attention and fascinated her. She had heard of Ja-gonh from Ah-wen ga, to be sure, but she was astonished that this blond, blue-eyed man who looked like a typical English aristocrat should be a Seneca warrior. He was superbly built and ruggedly handsome, and she could see at a glance why Ah-wen-ga would favor him in preference to a king.

"You remember me, I am sure, Major de Bienville," Roger said as he bowed. "Captain Harkness of His Britannic Majesty's Grenadier Guards. My dear," he said to Patience with a smile, "I have the honor to present you Major Henri de Bienville, the chief of military intelligence operations in New France. This is my wife, Major."

Neither Patience nor the major bothered to acknowledge their earlier meeting.

De Bienville's mind was still spinning. "And who are you?" he demanded, jabbing a finger in the direction of Ja-gonh, who still held his tomahawk ready for immediate use.

Ja-gonh minced no words. "I am the son of Renno and the grandson of Ghonka," he said. "I am a warrior of the Seneca." His pride in his identity was complete.

"What I have to say, Major," Roger declared, "is intended exclusively for your ears and those of Lady Arlene d'Amarante."

De Bienville took the broad hint and dismissed the captain of the guard.

"That's better," Roger said, and stretched out his legs in front of him. "We have gone to a great deal of trouble in tracking you down to this place," he said. "It is only in the last twenty-four hours that we've learned for certain your motive for abducting Ah-wen-ga from her people."

"Your knowledge will do you no good," Arlene countered, smiling complacently, "for there is absolutely nothing you can do about the situation. Bringing some kind of criminal charge against us would be totally out of the question: you're in France now, and my relative, the Duc de Guise, is enormously powerful at the court of King Louis. You would find it very hard to find any judge in France willing to convict us on a charge of supposedly bringing a native Indian girl from the forests of North America."

Roger shook his head and grinned cheerfully. "I am sufficiently aware of the way the world operates, Lady Arlene. The thought of bringing you and Major de Bienville to the bar of justice for your deed never crossed my mind."

"By the same token," Patience said, "I trust you realize you can't deal with us as you have dealt in the past with Ah-wen-ga. I am the daughter of the general commanding the Massachusetts Bay militia, and my husband, as you know, has connections with the Foreign Office and the military authorities in England. If we should meet with foul play, a great many people would be thoroughly aroused. You'd have the devil's own time explaining why you knowingly instigated a war."

"Now you know," Roger said pleasantly, "that we mean business. However, we are prepared to be amicable in the current situation, and as a sign of that let me state that I am confident Ja-gonh will refrain—at least for now—from paying you, as he paid Gray Fox, for the roles that both of you played in the abduction of his future wife.

188

But let me warn you that he and I are your determined captors, and any covert effort to change that status will result in instant reprisal. You will inform your captain of that fact and see that this warning is heeded scrupulously."

Ja-gonh realized that he was witnessing a game that he did not completely understand, and he was at a loss as to how to reply. So he confined himself to a quick nod of reluctant acquiescence to what Roger was saying.

"We have thought through your scheme," Roger continued, "and we have no objection to its basis. In other words, we now can see a great deal to be gained by a presentation of Ah-wen-ga to King Louis. We shall accompany you to his palace to make certain that it is carried out promptly."

Arlene, stunned, made no attempt to hide her surprise.

De Bienville was a more accomplished dissembler and his mind worked rapidly. "You have something to gain," he asked pointedly, "if she becomes the favorite of Louis XV?"

Roger's smile was unfaltering. "No, I wouldn't go quite that far," he said. "In fact, Ja-gonh, as her future husband, wouldn't like that idea at all."

Ja-gonh still had no idea what game his friend was playing, but he wanted one point made very clear. "Ah-wen-ga," he said in faultless English, "will not become the mistress of King Louis. This I promise all of you. No matter who it is necessary for me to kill, she will be wife in name and fact only with Ja-gonh of the Seneca." He glowered first at the major, then at Arlene.

It was the first time he had appeared to take note of Arlene's existence, and she lost no opportunity to impress herself on him. Letting her eyelids droop and allowing her mouth to fall into a pout, she looked at him seductively.

Ja-gonh, so inexperienced in the ways of the world that he failed to realize that she was flirting with him, was nevertheless struck by the full impact of her gesture.

Ah-wen-ga was conscious of it, too, and her eyes narrowed. Just as Ja-gonh rightly demanded that she be faithful to him, she demanded his fidelity in return. She owed nothing to Arlene, who had been kind only because of what she hoped to gain from a friendship. Well, friendship was impossible if she made advances to Ja-gonh. A woman of the Seneca was able to look after her own interests; in fact, she could be fully as competent as any of the nation's warriors.

"It may be," Roger said, "that Ah-wen-ga will wish Ja-gonh to accompany her when she is interviewed by the King."

Ah-wen-ga immediately indicated enthusiastic assent. "I will definitely want that," she said. "With Ja-gonh beside me, I will know that no harm can come to me."

The very idea of having a husky, handsome young man present at the meeting with Louis was patently absurd. But de Bienville treated the statement with seeming seriousness and in no way showed his true feelings. The nosy young English officer and his colonial wife seemed to be capable of upsetting the most carefully made plans. As for the young Seneca, his violence was unrestrained and unpre-dictable. But he viewed it as better by far to pretend to agree to whatever was offered—and then find a suitable way out of the dilemma later.

To Arlene's astonishment, he even appeared to agree with the proposal. "You make good sense, Captain Harkness," he said with a straight face, "and I can see no reason why we should object to your amendment to our scheme."

Arlene bit her tongue and bided her time. Surely, Henri hadn't lost his senses?

"We were just getting to the point of discussing when we would journey to the palace at Versailles," de Bienville said. "Perhaps if we can all meet again tomorrow, we would arrive at a mutually agreeable meeting of minds."

Roger Harkness was vastly relieved. He and Patience had gambled on their making a sudden, unexpected ap-pearance at the castle as soon as they learned of the death of Gray Fox, and their strategy appeared to be paying dividends. At least, de Bienville and the shrewd Lady Arlene were amenable to the idea that Ja-gonh be present

190

when Ah-wen-ga met King Louis. The reasons for their attitude were quite apparent: if they objected, they were afraid that Ah-wen-ga would withdraw completely from the entire scheme. Having spent months, with considerable expense, in preparing to present her to Louis, they were being cooperative because they could see no alternative.

Roger rose and offered his arm to Patience, who promptly stood, too. "Do you wish to come with us or do you prefer to stay here, Ah-wen-ga?" he asked with seeming innocence.

She thought quickly. She had only a surface acquaintance with Roger Harkness, but knew that he was giving her the ostensible choice of leaving the castle and spending the night elsewhere—but only because he wanted to lull the suspicions of Henri and Arlene. He could have no other reason for making the request of her.

So she smiled and said, "It's far more convenient for me to stay here." Now her captors could know that she was not intending to run away, and so Roger's strategy was working.

Ja-gonh had his own firm ideas on the subject. "Then I, too, will stay here," he said. "Ja-gonh will sleep on the terrace outside Ah-wen-ga's window." His tone made it emphatically clear that his intentions were firm, and that nothing could persuade him to change his mind.

Henri de Bienville had to simulate pleasure at the idea. "That is settled, then," he said, "and I suggest that, it being quite late now, we meet again here tomorrow at noon."

The atmosphere had become so amicable that Ja-gonh went off to fetch his horse from the forest so it could be lodged in the castle's stables. Roger and Patience withdrew, both of them reasonably satisfied with the outcome, and Ah-wen-ga quietly retired to her chamber.

She undressed slowly, and as she finally climbed into bed, she caught a glimpse of Ja-gonh through the open French doors, making himself at home on the terrace. She needed no explanation for his failure to bid her good night after the tumultuous events of the evening.

He knew, as did she, that if he drew near to her again, they would be unable to resist staying together for the rest of the night. The situation was already so complex that it was wisest for him to keep his distance, and on reflection Ah-wen-ga agreed with him. All the same, she couldn't help wishing that he were less circumspect.

In the great hall, Lady Arlene and Major de Bienville sat in silence for quite some time after the others had departed. "Damnation!" Arlene exclaimed.

De Bienville did not reply but instead strode to a cupboard and splashed generous quantities of potent brandywine into two goblets. Returning to the divan on which she was seated, he handed her one, then dropped into a medieval chair opposite her.

"The English," Arlene said, "are naive beyond words. I first thought that Captain Harkness was joking when he suggested that the blond Indian accompany Ah-wen-ga to her meeting with Louis. My God! Do they think the King is either totally insensitive or a complete fool? Do they think that he actually arranges his liaisons while the fiancés of his future lovers act as their chaperons? The presence of this Ja-gonh would be insane. It would totally inhibit Louis—and enrage him!"

The major smiled, then sipped his drink. "I urge you to relax, my dear. This is some of the best brandywine from the de Guise cellar, and it has a superb bouquet."

"Don't play cat and mouse with me, Henri," she said irritably. "You know I can't stand it."

"Very well," he replied briskly. "Certain facts have seemed self-evident to me, and if they haven't to you, I'm sorry, but I'll spell them out for you. To begin with, I have no intention of allowing the white Indian to be present when Ah-wen-ga meets His Majesty. Good Lord! If the King as much as reached out and touched her hand, I think the swine-fellow, Ja-gonh, would try to scalp him. Can you imagine the uproar?" He shuddered delicately.

In spite of herself, Arlene had to laugh. "It is a terribly

funny concept, you know," she said, and then her smile faded as she sobered. "But how will we get rid of him, and also those busybodies, the Harknesses?"

He pondered the question thoughtfully. "The Harknesses will present no problem. I promise you that I will take care of those most unimaginative people very effectively— when the proper time comes."

Gaining her self-control, Arlene sniffed the brandywine appreciatively and then sipped it. "So far, so good," she said.

De Bienville suddenly looked directly at her. "You found the white Indian attractive, did you not?"

"Was I that obvious about it?" she murmured.

"No—but then, I know you quite well and can read your face like a book. In any case, I think *there's* the answer that we seek."

Her response was a questioning look.

"Let us say that you meet in private with Louis and arrange a rendezvous for the following evening for him to meet Ah-wen-ga. At the time the meeting is to take place, I think you could be relied upon to keep Ja-gonh occupied elsewhere—to keep him so busy that he totally forgets Ah-wen-ga and any problems she might encounter with Louis."

Her face cleared, and she agreed emphatically. "Of course!" she said. "It's so obvious that I wonder I didn't think of it myself immediately."

"I'm rather surprised, too," Henri observed mildly. "Be that as it may, you'll not only keep Ja-gonh occupied, but you'll thoroughly enjoy the experience."

She smiled smugly, complacently.

"That leaves just one major problem to be solved," he said, and frowned.

Arlene was surprised. "What is that?"

"We haven't yet learned why Ah-wen-ga is so amenable to the idea of meeting Louis. Surely she isn't interested in becoming his mistress, even though you've told her that the purpose of the rendezvous is to ensure just such a relationship. She plainly has something else in mind."

"I'll see if I can learn what it is from her." Arlene said. He regarded her attitude as a trifle too casual.

"Please be sure you do," he told her. "Everything depends on her willingness to enter a liaison with Louis."

"If it isn't just like a man," Arlene said, "to be forgetting the key element in all this."

He looked at her questioningly.

"You forget the role that Louis himself is going to play," she elaborated. "He's going to be a principal, not a casual bystander. Furthermore, you give no credit to the impact that he will have on Ah-wen-ga—the impact that he has on any woman. He's a man of overpowering charm, and I daresay that no matter what motive she may have in mind for her meeting with him, Louis himself will see to it that she forgets it once she is alone with him. I can assure you he's persuasive and insistent, and that what he wants, he gets. Not just because he is King Louis—but because he's a man whom any woman finds irresistible!

"But, in any case," she continued, "it will be very much in our own best interests to expedite our departure for Versailles, on the basis of the news that came today through the de Guise retainers to Captain de Sanson."

De Bienville raised his eyebrows. "You probably haven't heard this yet, but it turns out that Cardinal Fleury has been recently a belated victim of the childhood disease, mumps. It seems that it has affected him most severely, with very painful complications. The aftereffects apparently will keep him infirm and confined for several weeks yet. Inasmuch as he happened to be on a visit to Rome when he became ill, he is immobilized there—and consequently is away from Versailles and out of direct touch with Louis for an unexpectedly extended period."

"That is indeed a stroke of good fortune," Henri de Bienville replied, startled at the news.

"Yes," Arlene went on, "and we'd best take advantage of it by getting up to the royal court immediately. Without needing to ask for Fleury's advice, Louis may be expected to be both more accessible—and more vulnerable."

Chapter IX

Betsy was thunderstruck by the betrothal of Deborah Jenkins and El-i-chi. "What I find so hard to believe," she told her rapidly recuperating husband, "is that their romance developed right here under my nose. I was so concerned about you that nothing else entered my mind."

Renno chuckled. "I'm glad for both of them," he said. "I know El-i-chi often has been very lonely in his life, and Deborah was destined for a life apart from the mainstream of the community in Springfield after Obadiah's death. It's good for both of them."

"Ba-lin-ta and Walter are delighted, of course," Betsy said.

Renno reached absently for a length of jerked beef and chewed on it thoughtfully.

Betsy said approvingly, "Ba-lin-ta and Walter have always been very close to Deborah. They have had what you might call a special relationship with her. She and El-i-chi will have a good life together. My only regret is that they are a little too old to have children.''

"Not necessarily,'' Renno replied.

"Necessarily!'' Betsy said firmly.

Renno knew little about such matters and was willing to defer to his wife's judgment. "I suppose you're right,'' he said mildly.

"Only the young should have babies,'' she said. "Young like Goo-ga-ro-no and No-da-vo.''

He raised his head and peered at her sharply. "Are you trying in a subtle manner to give me information?'' he demanded.

"Good heavens! Nothing was further from my intentions,'' Betsy replied with a laugh. "That isn't what I meant. I don't think we need to worry about Goo-ga-ro-no. She's become too committed a Seneca to have an affair with any man, including the man she loves. In fact, I think I can safely predict that you will be having a visit from No-da-vo in the near future asking for the right to marry Goo-ga-ro-no.''

Renno became thoughtful. "I missed a great deal during the weeks that I was ill,'' he said, "and apparently I saw very little and knew even less of the romance developing between Goo-ga-ro-no and No-da-vo. Do you approve of him?''

Betsy sighed gently and averted her face. "You want a true opinion, of course?''

"Naturally,'' he said. "That's what I always expect from you. And what I always get.''

"He is a complete Seneca in every way, at all times and at all things,'' she said. "Nothing that he does or says could cause me to disapprove of him.''

"But you're still holding back somewhat,'' Renno commented.

"I find it hard,'' Betsy explained, "to put my feelings into words. I didn't grow from childhood to womanhood as a Seneca. All that being a Seneca entails was imposed on me from the outside when I came here as your wife after I had become an adult. So I can see certain things more clearly, perhaps, than can you who have known Seneca ways almost since birth. I find No-da-vo to be the epitome of all that being a Seneca entails. What makes me even slightly uncertain is that he's almost too good to be true!''

To her relief, Renno didn't laugh or scoff, but seemed to be weighing her statement carefully. "You might be right," he said. "At any rate, I realize that you do feel uneasy about him, which is your privilege as a mother. I shall take that into account when he comes to me to ask for Goo-ga-ro-no's hand.''

Betsy was a good enough Seneca wife to drop the subject; it was enough that he agreed to pursue the subject later.

With each passing day, Renno showed fewer signs of his debilitating illness; gradually he acquired greater stamina. He went fishing regularly, and on three afternoons each week he went hunting in the deep forest with El-i-chi. Although he didn't tell Betsy, he had begun to practice the renowned "Seneca trot" whenever he could in the wilderness, and he was gratified when he could run again for hours at a time without losing his breath or feeling unduly tired. He believed that he truly was totally recovered from his ailment.

One night when he and Betsy—together with Ba-lin-ta and Walter, and Deborah and El-i-chi—were invited to the house of Ena for supper, Goo-ga-ro-no appeared with No-da-vo in tow. The meal had been planned to discuss the wedding of Deborah and El-i-chi, and Betsy thought that the timing of the two young people was unfortunate. Goo-ga-ro-no, she reflected, should have known enough to wait until Renno's mind was clear.

The young couple sat meekly and in silence throughout the meal, neither of them daring to irritate their elders. El-i-chi and Deborah presumably were seeking Renno's approval, but in actuality, they were obtaining the authentication of Ena.

Because of their age, El-i-chi and Deborah said, they

wanted neither an elaborate ceremony nor a general cele-
bration afterward. They preferred to be married quietly by
the principal medicine man of the Seneca, then would
travel to Springfield where they would repeat their vows in
the church that had been Obadiah Jenkins's.

Renno carefully but surreptitiously kept watch on his
mother's reaction, and when he saw Ena smile, he spoke
briskly. "It shall be as Deborah and El-i-chi wish," he
said, adjusting his heavy ornamental buffalo robe of office
over his shoulders. "I will provide you with an escort to
see you safely through the forest to Springfield." He
looked purposefully at the quiet No-da-vo and said, "You
will command the escort, No-da-vo, and will select twenty
warriors of your own choice for the journey."

Deborah felt moved to protest. "I don't want a big fuss
made over us," she said. "Can't we just go by ourselves?"

Renno shook his head firmly. "Deborah does not understand," he said. "As the wife of a war chief and as
sister-in-law of the Great Sachem, she would be a great
prize if she were captured by our foes. They would enjoy
mocking and humbling her, and would place an exorbitant
price on her return to us. The Seneca have gone to war
with nations like the Erie and the Huron and the Ottawa
for incidents similar to that which I have just outlined to
you."

"I'm so naive," she said in dismay, "that sometimes I
can scarcely believe it myself."

Goo-ga-ro-no and No-da-vo lingered after the meal, and
at last Renno looked at them curtly, giving them no chance
to speak as he said, "I know what is on your minds and
what you wish to say. It must wait until a more appropriate
time. No-da-vo, when you escort El-i-chi and Deborah to
Springfield, you will wait for them and return with them.
Then we will discuss that which you have in your minds."

They had no choice but to swallow their disappointment
and do as he had bidden them.

That night, as he and Betsy were preparing for bed,
Renno gave her a clue to his treatment of the young
couple. "I was deliberately rude to No-da-vo and Goo-ga-

ro-no," he said, "even though I felt unhappy on her behalf. But I have decided to put No-da-vo to the test. I wish to push him to the limits of his patience and endurance, and then we shall see for ourselves what his true nature may be—whether he *is* the perfect Seneca."

Two days later, in a quiet ceremony attended only by family, Deborah and El-i-chi were married. The bride's long dress of doeskin, made for her by Betsy, was decorated with porcupine quills. The principal medicine man exhorted the gods of the Seneca to watch over the couple.

"I hope that I can adapt as successfully to the ways of the Seneca as you have done," Deborah told Betsy immediately after the brief ceremony.

"You'll do splendidly," Betsy assured her. "Just trust your instinct."

"My instinct—and my husband," Deborah replied.

El-i-chi and Deborah spent their first night as husband and wife in the simple hut of the bridegroom in the town of the Seneca. Ordinarily, a newly married couple would have gone off into the wilderness for their bridal night because their contemporaries would have found irresistible the urge to play tricks on them. But El-i-chi's rank was too exalted, and men who had served under his command in various campaigns and knew him as a strict disciplinarian were reluctant to play practical jokes.

The following day, the couple departed for Springfield, accompanied by twenty young warriors under the command of No-da-vo. Goo-ga-ro-no had wanted to go, too, and ordinarily her parents would have permitted her to make such a journey, knowing that Jeffrey and Adrienne Wilson would welcome her on her arrival and that Deborah and El-i-chi would chaperon her on the journey. But when her father did not suggest such a journey on his daughter's part, Goo-ga-ro-no responded like a model Seneca daughter and did not ask for such a privilege.

"Seneca warriors are accustomed to traveling very rapidly through the great forests," El-i-chi told his bride, "but this journey will be very different for them. You will set the pace, and they will adapt their speed to yours. I do not want you to overdo or to burden yourself. When you are tired, we will rest, and we will travel only when you feel fit." Deborah smiled her thanks.

The warriors in their escort were secretly amused that the pace of the journey was slow, but they kept their views to themselves. No-da-vo, acting as a scout, went ahead alone through the wilderness. He maintained at first a distance of about a hundred yards from the main party, but by the third day he had increased this to more than two hundred yards.

El-i-chi was anticipating no troubles and therefore was astonished on the third afternoon when No-da-vo crept silently back through the underbrush and materialized, seemingly out of nowhere, directly in front of him.

The young warrior wasted no words. "A party of Oneida is ahead," he reported, "and they are preparing an ambush. It must be us that they are planning to attack because no other travelers are using this route. We have seen no sign of anyone else anywhere on the trail."

El-i-chi immediately halted the group. He should have known, he told himself, that he would be a natural target for relatives of Da-kay seeking revenge for the death of their chief. And now, thanks to his lack of foresight, Deborah would be threatened. But it did no good to blame himself, and he needed to concentrate on the very immediate problem that he faced.

"How many of them are there?" he demanded.

"I'm not certain," No-da-vo replied carefully. "I counted enough to guess that there must be about forty in the entire party."

El-i-chi now realized the danger was even greater than he had thought. He was outnumbered by two to one, and the prospects were not good for emerging safely from an encounter.

Deborah had paid no attention to the exchange between her husband and the young warrior, but the expression on El-i-chi's face told her that he had learned bad news. Rather than wait until he elected to communicate with her—as the women of the Seneca would have done—she went to him at once. "What's wrong?" she asked bluntly.

When El-i-chi told her the truth of their situation, she did not appear surprised, and for the sake of No-da-vo and the other braves who clustered around them, she replied in the language of the Seneca. "You say we are outnumbered by two to one." Here, she forced a broad smile. "Those odds appear to be almost exactly right for guaranteeing a Seneca victory."

That she had struck precisely the right note became evident at once. The young warriors preened, grinned, and exchanged proud glances.

"Did the Oneida see you?" El-i-chi asked No-da-vo.

The young warrior shook his head.

"Were they carrying rifles or the bows and arrows of their ancestors?"

"The Oneida," No-da-vo said in obvious disapproval, "carried rifles."

El-i-chi was somewhat relieved. The Massachusetts Bay militia had been providing firearms for the members of the Iroquois League for some time, but few, if any, of the younger warriors of the other tribes had learned to use them with the skill of the Seneca. Prior to his illness, Renno had intended to establish special classes of instruction and practice in the use of the weapons, but the Big Sleep had interrupted this plan. So El-i-chi considered it safe to assume that though the rifles were impressive for purposes of display, the young Oneida, in all probability, were not altogether adept in their use.

"We will use only our bows and arrows," he ordered. "They are silent weapons, and they do not reveal our location in the wilderness. Hear me, O warriors, and I will explain my plan of battle. We will move very quickly from one place to the next. We will discharge an arrow, then move to another place in the forest before we fire again. Do not use your arrows indiscriminately. Always have a target clearly in sight before you release the string on your bow. Then move swiftly to another spot and fire again.

You'll be given no orders during the battle, and I want total silence maintained. Do you understand?''

No-da-vo nodded in assent, as did his colleagues.

El-i-chi stood quietly, and his manner remained calm, as though he were accustomed to meeting such crises regularly. But Deborah was deeply worried, and her heart pounded so hard that she felt her temples throbbing.

Her husband sensed her apprehension and, smiling at her, patted her shoulder. "No harm," he said, "will come to the wife of El-i-chi. She will stay close beside him. He cannot tell her where he will go next, and he will make many turns and twists as he makes his way through the wilderness. She must remain alert and do her best to keep up with him."

Deborah realized that his demand for silence was not intended for the warriors alone, but that she was included. She could only do her best to follow his orders.

"Who among you," El-i-chi demanded of the warriors, "wishes to create a diversion?"

Much to the disappointment of his colleagues, No-da-vo instantly raised his hand. The war chief selected him for what all regarded as a position of honor because it entailed a great risk. Then he clasped the younger man's forearm and waved him away.

One moment No-da-vo stood in plain sight facing his superior, and in the next instant, he had vanished. He made no sound as he went off through the forest in the direction of the Oneida. Had Deborah not seen him disappear so completely, she would not have believed it possible.

Not until she heard No-da-vo crashing through the underbrush at a considerable distance from the main party did she realize the strategy that her husband was employing. The young warrior was acting as a decoy, deliberately luring the Oneida to come after him. In the meantime, El-i-chi and the rest of the band would set on their foes from the side and from the rear.

El-i-chi now merely raised a hand and pointed ahead in the direction of the Oneida. It was the only order he gave.

Deborah was deeply impressed by the disciplined reaction of the young braves, who formed in two groups, each in single file. Then they, like No-da-vo, vanished into the forest.

El-i-chi stayed close by Deborah, casually fitted an arrow into his bow, and then finally beckoned to her. She followed him as quietly as she could, praying that her moccasins would not land on a twig or on dry leaves. Then she realized that El-i-chi was choosing a path for her with great care. The ground was clear underfoot wherever she stepped.

He raised a hand to warn her to halt. Drawing his bow, he released his arrow. Deborah heard a faint, whistling noise, and then she was certain she heard the arrow make contact with something solid.

But she had no opportunity to investigate. El-i-chi beckoned, and she followed close on his heels as he circled to his left. Suddenly, she caught a glimpse of green and yellow war paint only inches ahead of her, and she realized that the entire party of Seneca was circling to the left, apparently having surrounded their foes.

No specific commands were given. El-i-chi released a second arrow and then a third. In the meantime, his warriors were shooting arrow after arrow, too, and Deborah, concentrating on studying her husband's face, thought that he seemed satisfied with the results his subordinates were achieving.

El-i-chi shifted and moved sharply to the right instead of to the left. Deborah did the same, almost tripping and falling in her anxiety to follow.

Again came the crashing sounds of someone noisily moving through the wilderness, and she realized No-da-vo now was off to their right. How he had correctly divined the movements of El-i-chi and the others, she could not even guess. The timing of every individual's moves blended perfectly into the whole.

What struck Deborah most forcibly was the deep silence that pervaded the wilderness. Neither the Seneca, nor those who had lain in wait for them, made a sound. She had no idea whether Seneca arrows were finding their targets, but if they were, the Oneida were making no sound as they fell. It was an extreme example of Indian stoicism unlike anything she had encountered after a lifetime in a community on the edge of the wilderness.

The battle ended as abruptly as it had begun. No-da-vo uttered a war cry so loud and so piercing that Deborah jumped nervously.

No-da-vo's shout was one of victory. The badly outnumbered Seneca once again had demonstrated that they were unique in battle and that no warriors, even perfidious turncoats, were their equal.

For the first time since the battle had begun, El-i-chi stood erect and smiled. The other Seneca did the same, and Deborah, amazed, saw that they were spread out over a considerable area of the forest.

El-i-chi spoke to her now. "Stay where you are and wait for me," he told her sternly. "Under no circumstances follow after me now."

Without explanation, he moved forward.

The other Seneca also were spreading out and were making no attempt to be quiet now.

Deborah had no idea why El-i-chi had issued such specific orders to her, but she obeyed them with care. And then she caught a glimpse of something that No-da-vo held aloft in one hand: a length of human skin, with hair attached to it, and dripping with blood.

Her stomach turning, Deborah realized that the victors were exercising their custom of gathering the spoils of combat and were collecting the scalps of those whom they had killed.

Forcing herself to breathe deeply, she wondered if she had made a mistake by marrying a Seneca. Perhaps she had been guilty of romanticizing the whole tribe because of her youthful experience with Renno. She had seen scalps hanging from the belts of Seneca, including Renno and El-i-chi, but they had been dried, and so she had not needed to think of them as those of warriors who had lost their lives.

When El-i-chi turned and came toward her, Deborah

knew at a glance that he was carrying three fresh scalps in his belt.

But his smile was warm, his expression loving and considerate, and she decided that she was probably making an issue where none existed. Certainly she did not—and never would—approve taking scalps from enemies who had fallen. All the same, was it right to condemn men as savages because they engaged in the practice? Her views were changing.

Militiamen at Fort Springfield did not emulate the Indians and gather scalps, but she could recall the early period of her marriage to Obadiah Jenkins, who had accompanied the militia regiment on several campaigns. He had been deeply upset by barbaric practices in which they had engaged in battle and had refused to discuss particulars with her, but she had gathered that they were as primitive and as uncouth as the Indians.

All men became barbarians when they engaged in battle, Deborah reflected, and she told herself not to judge her new husband—or anyone else—by his behavior after winning a victory. El-i-chi had loved her before going into combat, and he loved her still. He had demonstrated repeatedly his concern for her and had shown her every consideration. There was little more that she could ask.

The party was on the move again, and late in the day two of the warriors shot elks, which the Seneca regarded as a great delicacy. Not until they called a halt for the night and the meat was roasting on an open fire, did Deborah learn that No-da-vo had been wounded in the battle. An ugly gash inflamed one side of his face, which was laid open by a blow, presumably from an enemy tomahawk.

She insisted on bathing his injury in cold water from a lake and was not satisfied until El-i-chi had provided her with ground red leaves from a medicinal plant that the white settlers would later know as sassafras. These she applied as a poultice to the young warrior's wound.

No-da-vo squirmed and seemed on the verge of sudden flight the entire time that Deborah was treating him. At best, he was thoroughly uncomfortable.

His thanks were perfunctory when she completed her ministrations, and it was plain to her that he hardly appreciated the care and attention she had given him.

El-i-chi was privately amused by her bewilderment, and not until they sat near the fire while several of the younger men stood sentinel duty did he explain.

"No-da-vo is a warrior of the Seneca," El-i-chi told her. "When a brave of our nation suffers an injury in battle, he bears his wound in silence, telling no one of it and never faltering. The less attention he seems to pay to his wound, the higher becomes the regard of his brother warriors."

"Oh, dear," Deborah said. "I certainly didn't mean to embarrass him. But I was worried about him, and I was thinking really of Goo-ga-ro-no."

El-i-chi grinned and waved a hand deprecatingly. "Do not worry," he said. "You are known as the aunt of Goo-ga-ro-no, and every Seneca realizes that No-da-vo wishes to marry her. So your attention to his injury did him no harm. Besides, the other young braves would not dare to speak out on the subject and tease him, because No-da-vo has a fierce temper and would challenge them to a wrestling match. I know of no one who would enjoy the experience. I would not look forward to it myself."

Reassured by him, Deborah became drowsy because of the warmth of the fire and soon dropped off to sleep. Her last recollection was that of seeing El-i-chi sitting beside her, his blanket on the ground, as he smoked a pipe and stared into the night.

Deborah had no idea how long she slept, but when she awakened, the fire had been reduced to a low glow. All the young warriors, except the sentinels, also were asleep, but El-i-chi continued to sit statuelike. He did not appear to have moved for several hours.

Realizing that something was troubling him, Deborah reached out and touched him. As he turned toward her, he smiled.

"You're worried about something," she said.

"It is of no concern to a woman," he replied shortly.

206

"You may as well understand one thing about our marriage right now," she told him firmly. "Anything that worries you is also a matter of worry to me."

"I am afraid," he explained with a sigh, "that I shall have to notify Renno of our encounter today. I dread telling him, but as the sachem of both the Seneca and the Oneida—as the overlord of all Iroquois—he has the right to know. It would not be fair to him to try to conceal the truth from him. Many of our young warriors distinguished themselves in battle and deserve the sachem's praise. Besides, when they return home, their relatives and their friends will see the fresh scalps they carry in their belts and will want to know how they were acquired. So the truth is bound to get out."

"I don't understand," Deborah said. "Why would you want to hide the incident from him?"

El-i-chi was silent for some moments. When he spoke again, his voice was sorrowful. "The Iroquois League was formed in the time of the grandfather of Renno and El-i-chi," he said, "but it was Ghonka, our father, who made it into the great alliance it became. Ghonka dealt harshly with the warriors of any tribe in the league who dared to raise their hands against their brothers in other tribes. Renno has kept that tradition. Not long ago, he himself had trouble with the Mohawk, the largest of the nations in the league. He showed great patience and wisdom, and the trouble passed. But what happened today cannot be excused. The warriors who lay in wait for us, and would have taken our lives, were the relatives of Da-kay, the sachem of the Oneida, whom I defeated in fair combat."

"You're afraid that Renno will react angrily when you break this news to him," Deborah said.

"It upsets me," El-i-chi replied, "because I know that Renno is required by the tradition established by his father to take strong action against the Oneida. He cannot allow this act to go unpunished."

"It seems to me," Deborah said, "that you and the members of our escort have already inflicted a severe

207

punishment on them. About forty men in the forest awaited us, and by the time you were finished with them, I gather that none survived. So, although they were traitors to the alliance of Iroquois nations, they paid for their treason with their lives.''

"That is true,'' El-i-chi replied. "But that must be only the beginning of the punishment inflicted on the Oneida. The cousins and brothers and nephews of Da-kay could not have plotted such a major expedition in secret. Many other members of their tribe—warriors and medicine men, women, and even children who will someday become warriors—must have known their plans. Yet not one messenger arrived in the town of the Seneca to warn us of their treachery. You and I might have lost our lives today and our scalps would be hanging from the belts of Oneida.''

Though his arguments were primitive, they had a crude justice to them, Deborah conceded to herself.

"If Renno does not punish the Oneida,'' he said, "you may be sure they will plot again—and the next time the Great Sachem himself will be their target. Not only will the Oneida lose respect for him, but so will the Mohawk and all the others. If the Oneida are not punished, every nation in the league sooner or later will rise up against brother nations. The league will become nothing but a memory.''

Deborah hadn't been able to foresee such events that would create a most serious situation. She did know that the league was the backbone of Indian support for the English settlers and that if the Iroquois should be disrupted, the blow to the security of every English colony would be severe.

"I begin to see the implications," she said. "They're frightening.''

"I know war, and I hate the shedding of blood,'' El-i-chi told her. "My brother Renno knows war even better than I do and hates it with all his heart. But it is my fear that we will be forced to go to war in order to teach the Oneida a great lesson. I can see no other way, and my heart is heavy within me.''

Deborah's first instinct was to reach out for him, cradle him in her arms, and comfort him. But El-i-chi was a Seneca, not an English settler, and he would react like a Seneca. It was beneath the dignity of a war chief to require comfort. She recognized the shame he would feel if she made such a gesture in the presence of subordinates.

It was absurd, she knew, to feel that she was responsible for the incident that had taken place that afternoon. Da-kay, jealous of Renno, had deliberately quarreled with the Seneca, and El-i-chi had defeated the Oneida leader in a fair and open fight. She was not responsible, certainly, for the craving for revenge that had motivated his relatives to establish today's ambush.

The problem, she could now see, was far more complex than she had imagined. She still had a great deal to learn about life as the wife of a leader of the Seneca nation.

Having decided to leave Gascony and set out for Versailles while Cardinal Fleury was still detained in Rome, Henri de Bienville and Lady Arlene—together with the Harknesses, Ah-wen-ga, and Ja-gonh—left the de Guise castle and began the journey northward.

Before the group departed, Roger sent a message to Captain Grey at Marseilles, releasing him from any further need to wait for their return.

Both de Bienville and Lady Arlene were convinced that Ah-wen-ga's training had been successfully completed. All that remained was her presentation to the King. Conferring privately before the departure, they also concluded that it would be wise to dispense with the services of the de Guise military contingent. An escort of fifty men on the high road would be almost certain to call unwanted attention to their entourage, and word of the striking beauty of Ah-wen-ga might well leak out prematurely. With scores—perhaps hundreds—of men in France seeking an opportunity to be of service to their King, some well-meaning opportunist could easily ride ahead to Versailles with word that a rare beauty was heading in the direction of the palace. Not only would the element of surprise be lost, but Henri and Arlene might not gain credit for Ah-wen-ga's presentation.

They had agreed to travel by horseback instead of the slower carriages, in order to arrive at Versailles as quickly as possible and carry out their mission. Trunks with their individual effects, including Ah-wen-ga's extensive new wardrobe, were to arrive by carriage somewhat later.

Ja-gonh experienced a strange feeling as he rode peacefully side by side with his enemy. It was stranger, still, to realize that Arlene was indeed an enemy who had played a major role in the abduction and captivity of Ah-wen-ga. He was not accustomed to thinking of a lovely and charming young woman as a foe.

Because horses were virtually unknown in the land of the Seneca, Ah-wen-ga had to grow accustomed to the mount she was given to ride. She acclimated herself with relative ease, although her elaborate French gowns, complete with sweeping skirts and a half-dozen petticoats, made it necessary for her to ride sidesaddle. She found this unnatural and difficult, but she learned to emulate Arlene and soon became skilled.

Their routines were very similar day after day. They stayed at small inns, leaving after an early breakfast and traveling most of the day, pausing only briefly at noon time to eat a meal that had been packed for them by the hosts of the previous night. As a rule, they rode until sundown and then pulled into the courtyard of yet another inn to obtain food and a night's lodging.

Ja-gonh frequently found himself puzzled and somewhat confused, in part because Ah-wen-ga bore only a remote resemblance to the girl she had been. With her liberal applications of cosmetics and her daring, strikingly attractive French wardrobe, she looked like a great lady of France rather than the daughter of the sachem of the Seneca.

His confusion was compounded by the attitude that Arlene deliberately adopted toward him. She consistently flirted with him at every opportunity, deferred to him, and used every trick in her arsenal to gain and hold his attention. He could not help responding to her, although he had no idea of the reasons for his attitude. Accordingly, he found it odd to be drawn to this French beauty when he loved only Ah-wen-ga. He said nothing about his perplexity for several days, but finally, as the party approached the southern foothills of the Auvergne Mountains, he confided in Roger.

Unable to give him the answers he sought, Roger referred his questions to Patience. She dropped behind her husband, giving up her usual place in the procession in order to ride beside Ja-gonh.

"The problem," she told him, "is far simpler than you think."

His expression indicated that he was totally mystified.

"You and Ah-wen-ga love each other," she said, "and if you were in your own wilderness, everything would fall into place. But remember you're seeing each other and the world around you through strange eyes. You're both in Europe, following European customs, so your sense of values is jarred. To make matters still worse, you've been exposed to the machinations of Lady Arlene, who has a very great sexual appeal."

"She knows that I care only for Ah-wen-ga," Ja-gonh said. "Why should she throw herself at me?"

"Roger and I have discussed it," Patience answered flatly, "and frankly we don't know the answer, although we agree that the problem certainly exists. You haven't been fully aware of the effort that Arlene has been making because you've had so little experience with women of her sort."

Ja-gonh glanced ahead inadvertently at Arlene, who was riding with de Bienville at the head of the little caravan, and studied her.

Becoming aware of his scrutiny, she promptly rewarded him with a dazzling smile.

"There!" Patience said softly. "You see what I mean?"

"She seems very nice," Ja-gonh muttered.

Patience sighed, aware that it was difficult to explain the

true situation to someone so inexperienced in the ways of European women. At the same time, she sought to warn Ja-gonh. "She is a woman whose every move is calculated— always! Believe me, this is so. What her reason is for flirting with you in this instance is beyond us, but we intend to keep our eyes and ears open, and we hope eventually to discover her motives."

The tempo of the travelers' pace slowed considerably as they made their way along the narrow paths that wound up and down through the Auvergne Mountains. The views from the heights were spectacular, and both Ja-gonh and Ah-wen-ga had to conquer an inner feeling of uneasiness as they passed by deep crevasses. Accustomed to the gentler hills and valleys of Iroquois country, both of them felt ill at ease as they sat on their mounts and looked out over miles of countryside beyond sheer drops. The end of the mountains now was beginning to come in sight, however, and de Bienville announced that, at the end of another day's ride, they would arrive at the market town of Clermont, the northern anchor of the Auvergne chain. Then they would descend into the valleys of central France and would be able to increase their pace once again.

As they negotiated a particularly hazardous hairpin turn, Ja-gonh smiled confidently at Ah-wen-ga. He had mastered the art of riding a horse, and he even felt at home in the mountains. What he failed to take into consideration, however, was that, in these strange surroundings, his normal instincts were dulled.

Consequently, he failed to become aware of a band of highwaymen until too late. Six masked men, all armed with swords and very large pistols, appeared from behind boulders and ordered the travelers to raise their hands.

"Do as you are told," the leader said, "and no harm will come to you. Gentlemen will throw their purses and wallets to the ground, one by one, and the ladies will remove their jewelry and drop it. After you've done this, you'll be released and permitted to go on your way."

TOMAHAWK

De Bienville and Roger Harkness weighed their chances and decided that loathsome though the idea was, they had no real choice but to obey. The presence of the young women in their midst made them vulnerable, and they were afraid someone might be badly hurt if they balked.

The robbery would have been routine, perhaps, if one of the bandits had not overreached himself. Fascinated by the charms of Arlene and Ah-wen-ga, he rode closer to their horses and, reaching out, snatched their reins.

"Where do you think you're taking us?" Arlene demanded haughtily.

The brigand laughed coarsely, but offered no reply. Ah-wen-ga, hearing the laugh, instinctively knew that serious trouble loomed. Without hesitation, she reached beneath her skirt, drew her knife and, leaning in her saddle toward the brigand, plunged the blade deep into his back. A crimson patch spread rapidly on his shirt, and the man died, an expression of incredulity on his coarse features.

The other members of the party knew instantly that they no longer could avoid an all-out fight.

Ja-gonh was the first to react. Snatching his tomahawk from his belt, he hurled it with all his might. As always, his aim was accurate. The blade cut into the head of the leader of the brigands and struck with such force that he was knocked from his saddle to the ground. There he sprawled, almost certainly dead.

Roger had engaged in wilderness combat enough times to realize that he must react instantly and follow up the advantage that Ja-gonh had created. Instead of taking his purse from his pocket as he had already started to do, he drew his brace of pistols, cocking them as he removed them from their holsters. Taking quick, careful aim, he fired both of them at the nearest bandit.

De Bienville was not far behind. He, too, drew a pistol which he fired, and discovering he had missed, he quickly snatched his sword from its scabbard and slashed at the brigand closest at hand. He inflicted a severe wound in the man's shoulder, and the ruffian drew back, howling in pain.

Ja-gonh was enjoying himself, as he always did when in a fight. He reached over his shoulder for an arrow from his quiver and, notching it in his bow, fired at yet another of the brigands whom he wounded in the upper arm.

The two remaining thieves had seen enough and took to their heels, with their pair of wounded companions bringing up the rear. Two bodies were left behind. De Bienville dismounted, made certain the men were dead and, after helping himself to their weapons, contemptuously nudged their bodies out of the path with a booted toe.

Ja-gonh sprang from his saddle to the ground, too, recovering both his tomahawk and Ah-wen-ga's knife, from which he wiped blood, using the brigands' clothing as a blotter. Then, before presenting Ah-wen-ga with her blade, he horrified Patience, Arlene, and de Bienville by scalping the two thieves. Conscious that he would spatter blood on his clothes, he looped both scalps over his saddle and then grinned as he gave Ah-wen-ga her knife. "When the scalp of the man you killed is dried," he said, "I will present it to you. You have earned it with your own efforts."

She inclined her head in thanks, Seneca-fashion.

Patience felt queasy, but knowing the ways of Indians, she—like Deborah—was able to overcome her feelings.

Arlene's recovery was rapid. "What a magnificent young brute he is," she murmured.

De Bienville heard her comment, raised an eyebrow, and peering at her, realized she was sincere in her admiration for Ja-gonh.

The ride was resumed, and they soon reached their destination for the night, an inn in the bustling market town of Clermont. As they gathered for supper in the taproom, Henri offered a toast: "I drink," he said, "to our Seneca companions. They saved our purses today and possibly our lives."

By this time, Arlene, having had time to absorb the lessons of the experience, recognized anew that Ah-wen-ga was not as malleable and easygoing as she appeared. She had acted without a second's hesitation, calmly killing a man who had dared to take hold of her reins. What might she do if she resented the advances that Louis undoubtedly would make at their initial rendezvous? The possibilities of what might take place in that encounter—in spite of all the careful training in French ways that Ah-wen-ga had been given—made Arlene shudder.

Perhaps, Arlene thought, she should alter her plans, at least to the extent of allowing Ah-wen-ga and the King to become acquainted before permitting them to be alone together.

Chapter X

Deborah's return to Fort Springfield as the wife of El-i-chi created a sensation in the community. Some residents of the town, including a number of Obadiah's parishioners, were openly critical. But they were far outnumbered by Deborah's adherents, who declared flatly that a woman of her age and good sense was entitled to lead any life that she pleased. In addition, they recalled that her cousin, Walter, had joined the Seneca years earlier and had not only recovered his health there, but had found happiness with the warrior nation.

No one was more delighted with the marriage than was Jeffrey Wilson, who had served in several campaigns with El-i-chi and recognized the fine qualities of his old comrade-in-arms. Jeffrey and his wife, Adrienne, gave a party for the newlyweds after their vows were repeated in the Springfield church. Scores of guests came to the Wilson yard to eat roast beef and wild turkey, sweet potatoes in their skins, salad greens, corn, and squash. For dessert, they ate steaming apple pies.

Deborah took up temporary residence with El-i-chi in her old house and packed the clothes that she thought suitable for her future life in the land of the Seneca, as well as a variety of household goods that she would be able to use. Only one thought concerned her, and when the Wilsons came to dine, she confided in them: "I have no long-term use for a house here in Springfield," she said. "I hate to see it stand idle when so many new immigrants from England are arriving on the frontier."

"That matter is easily solved," Jeffrey said with a chuckle. "Name me as your agent and I'll sell it for you."

Deborah shook her head. "I don't believe it would be right to accept money for this house and land," she said. "I wouldn't feel right in taking it. Obadiah and I knew too much happiness here, and I don't want a materialistic taint to color my memories."

"What is more," El-i-chi added, "what would we do with money? We have all the cloth and the clothes and the weapons and the cooking utensils and other tools that we need. The Seneca have no use for money. We exchange wampum in our formal dealings with other nations, but even its use is very limited. The pounds and shillings Deborah would receive would become coated with dust."

Jeffrey was puzzled. "Do I gather," he asked, "that you have something in mind?"

"I do, indeed," Deborah replied. "I think I'll present the property to Obadiah's church, and I'll stipulate that the title be presented to married immigrants with children who need a place to live but lack the funds to build or buy a house. I believe this would be a truly fitting use for what was my home for so many years."

The Wilsons approved heartily, and that afternoon after dinner she and El-i-chi called on Obadiah Jenkins's successor and astonished him by presenting him with the deed to the house.

"You've chosen the most effective means anyone could

imagine," the clergyman said, "for silencing the few who criticize you for becoming a heathen, as they put it. You are demonstrating a degree of Christianity that few people, anywhere, possess."

A few days later, the newlyweds returned to the land of the Seneca. The warriors of their escort, with No-da-vo at their head, carried the few boxes of Deborah's clothes, personal effects, and household utensils. As they drew nearer to the town, El-i-chi's good humor gradually vanished, and he became increasingly silent and withdrawn.

Deborah had no need to ask what was troubling him: he was still concerned by the dilemma that the attack by the Oneida had created. As soon as they reached their own house, El-i-chi hurried to see Renno.

The Great Sachem, his health plainly much improved, greeted his brother cheerfully and asked many questions about friends in Springfield, as did Betsy. But El-i-chi believed that such gossip must wait, and told in slow, measured tones of the ambush made by the Oneida relatives of Da-kay.

Renno sat silently, listening attentively, his face impassive. To both Betsy and El-i-chi, his attitude was reminiscent of Ghonka; he was truly the son of Ghonka as he listened, his mind already at work on the problem that the attack had created.

El-i-chi concluded by relating the way he had outwitted the Oneida braves in achieving a victory over a force so much larger than his own.

Renno wasted no time in offering congratulations to El-i-chi for doing his duty; that was to be expected, and he dismissed the heroics briefly. Only if the young warriors had failed to act as they had would he have commented.

The first sign that a major decision was in the making came when Renno donned his elaborate feathered headdress and the buffalo cape that were the symbols of his high rank and went off to the Council Lodge.

Soon thereafter, El-i-chi and Walter joined him, both in full war paint and wearing the regalia of war chiefs. It was clear to all who saw them enter the council house that the senior male members of the ruling family were holding an almost unprecedented formal, private conference, prior to the more traditional gathering of all the members of the Seneca warrior class, which would doubtless follow.

Finally, a junior warrior was sent to summon Sun-ai-yee, who, having anticipated just such a call, responded promptly. A few minutes later, the rolling of drums beckoned all the elders, the medicine men, the war chiefs, and the senior warriors to the lodge. Heavily armed junior warriors were posted around the building to prevent eavesdropping.

Sun-ai-yee opened the expanded meeting with a brief statement, and then deferred to Renno, who addressed his fellows in ringing tones. "My brothers," he said, "we face a grave crisis. What we decide here and now, on this night, will determine whether the Iroquois League survives or founders."

El-i-chi rose and related again the account of the Oneida ambush in the wilderness. Some of the warriors had already heard of the incident; an angry murmur, like the buzzing of bees, filled the council chamber.

Renno stood again, raising his hand for silence. "If we make war upon the Oneida," he said, "we will be as guilty as they of breaking a sacred vow never to attack fellow members of the league."

A young senior warrior rose and asked, in a tortured voice, "What can we do then to protect our honor and to prevent future attacks? If we do nothing, every other nation of the Iroquois will assault us, and all our enemies will believe that the Seneca have lost their courage, and they too will attack."

"I do not for one moment propose that we do nothing to retaliate," Renno answered quickly. "I think I can propose a way that will maintain the honor of the Seneca, convince our allies and our foes alike that we do not lack courage, and teach the Oneida a lesson they will never forget. I propose that we send one warrior to the land of the Oneida and let him challenge their greatest fighter to individual combat. The Oneida may choose the type of combat they wish. The fight shall be conducted as they please, whether with tomahawks, bows and arrows, or the weapons of our white allies."

The Seneca absorbed his words in silence. At last an elder seated cross-legged in the front row rose laboriously to his feet. "I do not see how it is possible for one courageous warrior issuing a challenge to accomplish all that the Great Sachem has said will be accomplished," he declared.

Sun-ai-yee rose ponderously and adjusted his own feathered headgear that marked his station as the sachem of the nation. "It is true," he said, "that this task can be performed by any Seneca among us. I am sure that we have no lack of volunteers for the task—"

He was interrupted by the wild eager war cry of the younger senior warriors. At least two hundred were on their feet gesticulating, waving tomahawks and knives, and clamoring for the right to represent the nation.

Sun-ai-yee and Renno made no attempt to hide their pleasure. They exchanged a swift glance, and although neither changed his expression, the light in their eyes indicated their appreciation of the spirit that they hoped would prevail.

Then Renno spoke. "He who goes to the land of the Oneida," he declared in ponderous tones, "will not merely be a Seneca warrior who represents all this nation. He will be recognized as a personal representative of the family of the Great Sachem and of El-i-chi, the war chief who, together with his wife, was subjected to a vicious ambush."

A hush fell over the assemblage. Now everyone present understood the full significance of the private meeting of male members of Renno's family, which had preceded the larger council.

Renno looked around slowly until he saw No-da-vo sitting with the other young senior warriors, and he beckoned majestically. No-da-vo rose, conscious that all eyes were on him. He stood very erect, then walked to the center of the lodge beneath the opening that emitted smoke. He stood before Renno, his arms folded across his chest.

TOMAHAWK

"You have asked for the right to marry the daughter of the Great Sachem," Renno said. "I have forced you to wait until I could devise a plan whereby you would be given a fitting test to determine whether you are suitable to be admitted to my family. Now I have made a decision. My brothers, El-i-chi and Walter, have conferred with me, and they agree that the test I have devised is a fair one. Goo-ga-ro-no will give to No-da-vo a token of her favor that all will recognize and it will identify him as one who has won her favor and who hopes to marry her in the immediate future. Then No-da-vo will travel alone to the land of the Oneida and issue his challenge. He will fight the champion of the Oneida and will prove his skill by the victory that certainly will be his. In this way, he will secure the honor of our family and of the nation. His act of daring will convince the allies and foes of the Seneca alike that it is not wise to raise a hand against the men and women of this nation." That was in accord with the highest Seneca tradition: he who wished to marry a daughter of the Great Sachem was required to prove that he was endowed with qualities superior to those of ordinary men.

No-da-vo was delighted and instantly accepted the challenge. "I will do as the Great Sachem has directed," he declared, "and I shall defeat in battle the champion of the Oneida."

Goo-ga-ro-no said farewell to No-da-vo in the best Seneca tradition. Her face wooden, reflecting none of her feelings, she wished him well on his mission.

He, too, was a complete traditionalist. He accepted her good wishes, assured her that he intended to succeed and, turning away without a backward glance, trotted off around the edge of vegetable fields until he disappeared in the forest.

They had not made physical contact with each other, and no words of endearment were exchanged. Goo-ga-ro-no departed from the nation's custom only to the extent that she watched until the young warrior disappeared from sight in the forest. Then she went about her ordinary business with seeming calmness.

Betsy and Renno, very much aware of her attitude, quietly marveled at the change that had taken place in their daughter, transformed from a rebel who rejected Seneca life to a complete traditionalist.

No-da-vo was a Seneca warrior in every sense. He moved through the great forest at a steady trot, his pace rarely varying, and he did not stop for rest at any time. He ate a few handfuls of parched corn and several strips of jerked beef that he carried with him, and he halted very briefly on occasion to drink from a swift-flowing brook. But he did not tarry.

At last he put the Seneca domain behind him and moved into the somewhat smaller land of the Oneida. He deliberately wore full war paint, and he could hear the Oneida sentries' drums, announcing his arrival. Their code was different from that employed by the Seneca, but he had no doubt of the contents of the message that was being conveyed. So it was not surprising when he arrived at the main town of the Oneida to find a large number of warriors gathered outside the palisade.

Their greeting was cordial, as befitted a welcome accorded to an Iroquois ally, but nevertheless they showed a degree of reserve. They had not forgotten that Da-kay, their sachem, had been killed by a Seneca war chief, nor that his relatives had been slain.

No-da-vo was conducted with due ceremony to the Council Lodge, where the new sachem of the Oneida, Bre-jo-be, awaited. Tall and rugged, he was surprisingly young, only a few years older than No-da-vo, and he bore a strong resemblance to Da-kay. The realization dawned on the Seneca that the new sachem probably was a younger brother of the slain leader of the Oneida nation.

Greeting the sachem courteously, No-da-vo raised his voice so that all the warriors who had gathered in the council chamber could hear. He described in detail the perfidious ambush on El-i-chi and his white bride while they had been en route to Springfield, and he related with some relish the destruction of the attacking force by the escort of which he had been a proud member.

When he finished, a dead silence followed. Neither Bre-jo-be nor any of his subordinates reacted, and it was difficult for No-da-vo to believe they had actually heard what he had said.

Were they ashamed of the role that their fellow countrymen had played and thus too embarrassed to respond? Such would be the worst of all possible reactions that No-da-vo could have anticipated. Unless he aroused them to a fighting pitch, no one would accept his challenge.

He had an idea, and reaching for his belt, he removed from it a dried, dangling scalp. "This was the leader of the Oneida expedition," he declared, and after exhibiting the scalp, replaced it in his belt. He then drew each of three other scalps in turn, taking care to stress that they were from the heads of Oneida.

His strategy, he could see, was working. The warriors were becoming restless, exchanging glances. Several were fingering their knives and tomahawks, and it was apparent that they were eager for personal combat.

"A great wrong has been done to my people," No-da-vo said loudly. "The brother of the Great Sachem of all the Iroquois, himself a war chief of the Seneca, was subjected to an attack by those who call themselves his brothers, members of the Oneida tribe. The sacred blood of the Seneca has been sullied. The honor of the Seneca, which is more important than is life itself, has been questioned. I have come to seek satisfaction. I challenge the Oneida to name a representative who will meet me in fair combat and will try to salvage what remains of the honor of a nation that has sunk low in the esteem of the Seneca and of all honorable Iroquois."

Precisely as he had anticipated, his remarks created an uproar, and the Oneida warriors roared their defiance. Scores of them clamored for the right to represent their nation in combat.

Bre-jo-be rose, settled his war bonnet more firmly on his head, and drew his buffalo robe cape more tightly around him. He waited for the noise to subside, and finally the chamber became quiet enough for him to speak.

"The Oneida," he said, "show great valor in combat. But their fame is as nothing compared to the renown of the Seneca. The Seneca have won the favor of the gods, and they are called the most ferocious and best fighting men in the world. We Oneida know that is not the truth. We stand second to none as warriors. But the Seneca have misled the manitous. That is why my brother, Da-kay, died at the hands of El-i-chi. That is why my cousins were trapped and slaughtered by a party of Seneca in the wilderness. This will not happen again. The eyes of the manitous must be opened, and through them the gods must learn the truth of the situation."

He was speaking such gibberish that No-da-vo could not help but laugh aloud.

This reaction infuriated Bre-jo-be. "My brother died at the hand of a Seneca," he repeated. "My cousins were killed by Seneca, and one of their warriors dares to flaunt their scalps before my eyes. My brothers, I can understand your eagerness to meet this impudent Seneca in personal combat and to teach him and his nation a lesson that they will never forget. But you have made me your sachem, and I would not be living up to my obligations if I shirked my duty. I will meet this Seneca in combat myself."

The warriors shouted and stamped their feet in approval so boisterously that No-da-vo immediately realized that Bre-jo-be had achieved a measure of renown in the Oneida nation as a fighting man. He was pleased that he would not face an ordinary warrior.

"I would test his skill and his courage now, without delay," Bre-jo-be declared, "but if I did, the warriors of the Seneca would claim that he was tired after his march through the wilderness. So I shall curb my impatience and meet him tomorrow morning. Until then, let every honor be given our guest during his final hours in the land of the living."

No-da-vo could find no fault with his treatment. Escorted to a private hut where fresh pine boughs were provided for his bed, he was given a thick blanket of English wool to ward off the night chill. Several senior warriors were in attendance and brought a large meal of hot venison stew and a corn, onion, and fish soup that was an Oneida specialty. He ate heartily, making up for some of the meals he had missed while on his journey. At dusk, he went to bed, suspecting that he would be awakened early.

Not yet asleep when he heard someone creeping into his tent, he immediately grasped the long knife that rested beside him. To his astonishment, his visitor proved to be a young Indian woman. She was surprisingly handsome, with her hair hanging loose rather than in the usual pigtails. Her dress was unusual, too; her gown of silk resembled the clothes that the English and French colonists wore.

"Who are you and what do you want here?" No-da-vo demanded brusquely.

The girl answered in a soft voice. "I am a member of the Ottawa nation who was captured by the Oneida, and the warriors of this tribe make sport with me. I was told to make myself available to the great warrior of the Seneca, and I am here. Do with me as you will."

No-da-vo realized that his hosts were taking Bre-jo-be at his word and were providing him with a female captive to whom he could make love.

"I thank you for your offer," he said, "but I need my strength for the combat to the death tomorrow with the sachem of the Oneida."

The girl was terrified. "Please!" she said, "I beg the great Seneca warrior to take me. Otherwise the Oneida will think that he did not find me attractive, and they will beat me with whips."

No-da-vo felt sorry for the captive, but he saw no reason to tell her that under no circumstances would he be interested in her; that he loved Goo-ga-ro-no, the daughter of the Great Sachem, and did not care to make love to any other woman.

"Of course you may stay," he said, "and as far as I'm

concerned you can let the Oneida know that we were together and that I very much enjoyed the experience.''

The girl, much relieved, bowed deeply in a gesture of gratitude and respect.

No-da-vo didn't trust her sufficiently to fall asleep when she was still on hand. It was no trouble to stay awake for a while, though he made no attempt to converse with her. After what he regarded as a reasonable length of time, he felt himself growing drowsy and signaled to her. ''The time has come, I believe, for you to go now,'' he said.

She stood, walked to the door and hesitated there. ''You are fighting Bre-jo-be in the morning,'' she said, clearly reluctant to say more, but then she continued. ''Tell no one that I have mentioned this to you, but I urge you to beware of his feet. His kick is as powerful as that of a wounded buffalo calf.''

Promptly putting the girl out of his mind, No-da-vo dropped off to sleep.

Dawn was breaking over the lake that lay to the east of Oneida town when a group of senior warriors arrived to awaken No-da-vo. He became alert the instant they entered the hut.

They presented him with a large breakfast, from which he chose to eat sparingly of broiled fish and two small corn cakes. It was far wiser, he knew, not to eat too heavily before going into combat.

They gave him a loincloth, then applied bear grease to his entire body, from head to toe; the odor was overpowering.

To his consternation, he saw that one of the Oneida was picking up his weapons. He curbed a surge of anger. ''The tomahawk and the two knives that you have picked up,'' he said, ''are my property.''

''You will fight our sachem,'' one of the warriors replied, ''using weapons of the Oneida.''

''When I fight,'' No-da-vo said, his voice soft but becoming firm, ''I use the weapons of the Seneca.''

One of the warriors shook his head. ''The manitous have given their blessings to the weapons of the Seneca

227

and made them more deadly," he said. "That is why our medicine men have decreed that you will use weapons of the Oneida."

No-da-vo was indignant but, on second thought, realized that if he could beat the sachem of the Oneida while using Oneida weapons, his victory would be even more pronounced. Then the losers could not claim, once again, that the gods had favored the Seneca.

"I will agree to use Oneida weapons," he said, "but they must be of my own choosing. Let me test a tomahawk and some knives, and I will select those that please me. If none are offered that please me, it will be necessary for you to bring still others."

His conditions were eminently fair, and the Oneida, after obtaining the silent approval of his comrades, agreed. The junior member of the group hastened away and soon returned with a collection of weapons. Taking his time, No-da-vo tested the balance and weight of four or five tomahawks, almost selected one, but then discarded it because the blade was insufficiently sharp. Another seemed right for his needs. It was solid, well made, and he could hardly distinguish it from his own. Let the Oneida think that he had gained possession of a weapon that the manitous had not blessed.

His selection of two knives was equally painstaking. At last all was in readiness, and he left the hut with his escort.

In spite of the early hour, the entire community was on hand for the coming fight. Even the women had gathered and the small children sat quietly with their mothers, not daring to mar the solemnity of the occasion by their usual running and shouting.

As No-da-vo was conducted to an open area beside the lake, the spectators, including warriors and the elders of the nation, moved aside to clear a path for him. His face was expressionless as he followed his escort.

Bre-jo-be awaited him, and similarly greased and also wearing a loincloth, he inclined his head a fraction of an inch.

No-da-vo astonished the entire assemblage by raising his

hand in salute. He felt no fear, not even a sense of excitement. He was only gratified that at last he had a supreme opportunity to serve the Seneca, as he had always hoped he might—this was fully sufficient.

Grasping the tomahawk in one hand and a knife in the other, he planted his feet apart and stared up at the brightening sky overhead. "Hear me, O manitous," he called.

The people of the Oneida, who had been conversing in low tones, suddenly fell silent. The Seneca, it appeared, was on the verge of communicating with the manitous, and they wanted to miss no part of this rare experience.

No-da-vo's gesture had been sincere, but the sudden hush told him of the reaction, and he smiled to himself. Let them continue to believe that he, as a Seneca, enjoyed a special rapport with the manitous and through them with the gods who ruled the heavens and the earth.

"O manitous," he called, speaking loudly for the benefit of his audience and especially of his opponent, "hear the words of your brother and subject of your favorite people, the Seneca. As you know, I have come to the land of the Oneida to teach a lesson to these people who have dared to break their vow of eternal friendship and have attacked a war chief of the Seneca. Intercede for me with the gods as you have so often interceded for the warriors of my nation, and ask them to protect me from harm as they have protected me so often in the past. Render the tomahawk and the knives of my opponent harmless during our struggle and allow no evil to befall me, as is your custom in dealing with the Seneca, who acknowledge you as supreme because you have done so much to favor us above all other nations on this earth."

As nearly as No-da-vo could judge, even Bre-jo-be was impressed by his words. Now Bre-jo-be began to chant. His words were in the ancient tongue of the Oneida. The chant meant nothing to No-da-vo—and possibly had no meaning to Bre-jo-be himself, for that matter—but the young Seneca knew that this was part of the ritual in which Oneida always indulged before going into battle, and he

229

became a trifle nervous. His own words had been spoken strictly for their effect on his enemy, but it was possible that the manitous and even the gods heard the call of Bre-jo-be for help and were planning to intercede for him.

Wanting to eliminate needless risks, No-da-vo let loose with the war cry of the Seneca, shouting at the top of his lungs. It had the desired effect. His audience seemed stunned, and warriors stared at one another uneasily. Bre-jo-be continued to chant but lowered his voice to little more than a mere mutter.

No-da-vo, eager for the fight to begin, swung the tomahawk in a wide circle.

Bre-jo-be was quick to respond. The combat could start at any time now, according to the time-honored customs of the Iroquois. The sachem of the Oneida would be unable to fault his opponent if the Seneca grew tired of waiting and suddenly attacked. So the chant ceased abruptly, and the two foes faced each other, both with tomahawks raised and knives poised to strike.

As a junior warrior, No-da-vo had been trained by El-i-chi and had fought in a campaign under Renno's personal supervision. So he tried now to remember all that the renowned brothers had told him about combat. Sizing up his opponent with great care, he saw that Bre-jo-be outweighed him by as much as fifteen pounds, perhaps more. The Oneida also had the advantage of longer legs and arms, and the Seneca did not forget the Ottawa girl's warning. He would take special care to stay out of range of his foe's kicks.

He intended to exploit to the full, two advantages of his own. One was his greater speed, which made him more agile. The other was purely mental, the fact that he wore the dreaded green and yellow paint of the Seneca.

He darted toward his foe, feinting with his tomahawk, and then slashed with his knife before retreating out of range. Neither blow struck home, but that didn't matter to him. He was trying, initially, to intimidate the Oneida sachem and convince him that he could not win in a fight against a foe who was invincible.

Bre-jo-be advanced slowly, trying to hem in No-da-vo between the lake and a large elm tree that grew in an open field. No-da-vo saw no reason why he couldn't enjoy himself. He waited until the last possible moment, then retreated swiftly behind the trunk of the tree. The gesture was intended to make the Oneida look clumsy and ridiculous. Unfortunately, No-da-vo had his eyes fixed on the man rather than the ground and he tripped over a half-exposed tree root. Losing his balance, he sprawled on the ground, and only by gripping his tomahawk and knife hard was he able to avoid losing them.

He was mortified by the mishap. Even a junior warrior was familiar with the ground underfoot and didn't allow himself to be thrown to the ground because he stumbled. The myth of Seneca invincibility was damaged.

No-da-vo remembered the words that Renno had drummed into the minds of his young warriors:

The unexpected frequently happens in battle. He who allows himself to be surprised by such developments inevitably is defeated and frequently loses his life. Always be prepared to take advantage of the unexpected. Instead of being surprised, use tactics that will surprise your foe. Never hesitate. Act swiftly and with certainty and the victory will belong to you!

No-da-vo quickly realized what he had to do. Still lying on the ground, he threw his knife at Bre-jo-be, putting his full force into the blow. The move followed so rapidly on the heels of his fall, that it appeared as though he had planned the entire gesture.

The blade whipped past Bre-jo-be, and missing his head by inches, it sailed into the lake where it dropped harmlessly into the waters.

No-da-vo sprang to his feet, taking advantage of his opponent's preoccupation with the thrown knife, while regaining his balance and snatching his remaining knife from his belt. He had learned something in the experience. In a fight to the death it did not pay to mock one's

231

opponent. Every move, every gesture was intended to count.

Bre-jo-be seemed more confident as he moved forward again. His opponent had missed him; perhaps the manitous were not as favorably disposed to his cause as the Oneida had assumed. In any event, Bre-jo-be, conscious of his greater size, was ready to move in for the kill.

No-da-vo hastily applied another of Renno's maxims:

Whenever you appear to be caught in a tight corner or an impossible situation, act boldly. The greater courage you show, the more easily you will extricate yourself and will escape unharmed.

Very well. No-da-vo uttered the dreaded Seneca war cry again and leaped through the air directly at his foe.

Bre-jo-be was caught off guard and had to sidestep in order to avoid being knocked to the ground by the thrust of his exuberant young opponent.

In moving, he lowered his arms for a moment—and that was all the time No-da-vo needed. Seneca, as El-i-chi had so often reminded junior warriors, didn't wait for opportunities in battle, but created their own. No-da-vo knew the time had come to throw his tomahawk, and he realized, too, that he was so close to the Oneida sachem that it was almost impossible to miss his target. He balanced the weapon in his hand, then flicked it toward his foe. His gesture was expert, the result of long and difficult practice. The Seneca, unlike lesser tribes, rarely threw tomahawks with force but merely lofted them through the air, relying on accuracy rather than power in order to create the required damage.

He was gratified when he saw the blade bury itself deep in one side of Bre-jo-be's neck, and he knew that he had inflicted a serious wound.

What he failed to recognize was that the desperate Bre-jo-be had just enough strength left to release his own tomahawk. Its blade caught the young Seneca in the shoulder, causing a deep, painful wound that bled profusely.

Bre-jo-be, staggering, dropped to the ground. His eyes were glazed and he was no longer capable of carrying on the combat.

But No-da-vo, although blurry-eyed and suffering excruciating pain, nevertheless was determined to finish off the engagement. Standing directly above his foe, he drove his knife into the Oneida's heart.

Scores of women and the younger children gasped.

Too dizzy to stand, No-da-vo slowly lowered himself to a sitting position on the ground. After a time, he realized that someone was attending to his wound. By focusing hard he recognized the Ottawa girl who had visited him the previous night. She was stufffing red leaves into his open wound, ignoring the blood that continued to pour out. No-da-vo shuddered involuntarily because the pain was so intense, but he made no sound.

Ultimately the bleeding stopped; the red leaf was a common cure for the wounds used by all the Iroquois in battle. His injury robbed him of the ability to use his left arm, but he had escaped with no other injury, and he was grateful. He murmured his thanks, and the girl, afraid of antagonizing her captors, hastily retreated into the crowd.

"No-da-vo of the Seneca has defeated Bre-jo-be of the Oneida in fair combat," he called and was surprised by the thickness of his own voice. "But the Seneca and Oneida are united in the Iroquois League, so I will not dishonor your sachem by taking his scalp. He may keep it and take it with him to the land of his ancestors."

There, No-da-vo thought, he had made a conciliatory gesture that, he hoped, would help to heal the rift between the Seneca and the Oneida. Common sense told him that he would be wise to rest for several days, sleeping and attending to his wound, and that he should not attempt to travel until his health improved. But, conscious of maintaining the myth of Seneca strength and invincibility, he walked boldly to the lake. He rinsed the bear grease from his body and then called for his clothes and weapons. They were returned to him, and he took the pouches containing his jerked beef and parched corn. Weighing them in his hands, he decided he had just enough food to see him home. The warriors and the elders of the Oneida crowded around him as he dressed. He was relieved that the poultice of red leaves not only had stopped the bleeding but had acted as an anesthetic. His shoulder now felt numb.

"The Seneca who defeated the sachem of the Oneida will stay here as the guest of this nation until he is strong enough to return to his own people through the wilderness," an elder called out.

No-da-vo shook his head. "I go to my own land," he said, "to carry the word of my victory to the Seneca."

His listeners were astonished. "We will send a messenger to carry the word of your victory to the Seneca," a war chief told him.

"No," No-da-vo replied. "They will expect to hear the news from me and to see me."

"But surely it is too dangerous for you to travel unattended through the wilderness after you have sustained such a severe cut in your shoulder," a medicine man said to him. "You should spend a few days here and assure yourself of your safety."

No-da-vo drew himself up proudly. "I am a Seneca," he said, "so I have all the protection that I need. As for strength, I have ample to see me to the conclusion of my journey."

The Oneida exchanged glances; they could not argue with a man who was as determined and firm. A sudden thought struck No-da-vo. "It is my right," he said, "to claim a boon from the Oneida, and I do claim it."

His listeners braced themselves. He could demand wampum or weapons, and they would be obliged to fulfill his demand.

"A girl captive of the Ottawa visited me last night," he said, "and attended to my wound after the combat ended today. She has earned her freedom and should be returned to her own people."

The Oneida were relieved by the modesty of his request. "Do you wish to take her with you to the land of the Seneca?" a war chief asked.

The last thing, of course, that No-da-vo wanted was to arrive home with an attractive prisoner in tow; it would be difficult, at best, to convince Goo-ga-ro-no that he had not engaged in relations with the girl. It would be best not even to mention the Ottawa captive when he told the story of his activities.

The Oneida escorted him back to the hut he had occupied and insisted on giving him additional food supplies for his journey. Having won a victory of consequence, No-da-vo graciously accepted the offer.

While he waited, the girl of the Ottawa came in and stood timidly inside the entrance. "I owe you my freedom," she said. "You have demanded nothing of me in return, but ask what you will and I will grant you all that is within my power."

"I want nothing from you," No-da-vo replied. "I seek for myself only that which I have been fortunate enough to obtain for you—freedom and dignity."

Tears came to her eyes but, ashamed of her momentary weakness, she blinked them away. "I will always remember the warrior of the Seneca," she said. "I will regale my people with tales of his exploits, and it is my hope that our paths will cross again one day so that I may, in some way, repay my debt to you."

A short time later, after the captive girl had been dispatched homeward with a small escort, No-da-vo began his homeward journey through the wilderness, and he soon regretted his impetuous decision to leave the Oneida town without delay. The cut in his shoulder began to throb painfully again.

Having started his homeward journey, he could not stop now. He was still in the land of the Oneida, and the nation's sentries would see his movements. If he stopped to rest for twenty-four hours, they would know it and would undoubtedly look down on him. The Oneida had been taught a great lesson, and in order to keep it fresh in their minds for all time, they should think of a Seneca warrior as a member of a breed apart.

So he continued to trot evenly at a steady pace, ignoring

the pain in his shoulder, though it became excruciating and spread throughout his entire body.

In true Seneca fashion, he refused to allow himself to dwell on it. He emptied his mind and did not halt until he stumbled. Only then did he pause beside a stream to drink water, pour handfuls over his head, and finally to bathe his wound. The shock of the cold water in his wound sent sharp pains through him, but he did not move a muscle until the agony subsided somewhat. Then he forced himself to eat a portion of the food that the Oneida had given him. He ate some cornbread and some cold venison. He would have preferred his parched corn and jerked beef, but he knew that the other foods were more nourishing and that he would need all his strength to reach home safely.

No-da-vo resumed his journey immediately after finishing his meal. Again he trotted endlessly until long after midnight. Then, when his feet felt like heavy metal that would tear him from his ankles, he decided to halt briefly beside a small stream and sleep.

When he awakened in the morning, the wound in his shoulder had become infected and had caused a high fever that robbed him of his reason. But a Seneca was so drilled in the requirements of wilderness travel that No-da-vo reacted instinctively to the challenge that he so unwittingly faced. He ate more venison and cornbread and washed them down with large quantities of water. He washed his shoulder again, and again he suffered great pains until the throbbing subsided. Then he resumed his journey and trotted onward toward the land of the Seneca. He had no idea that he was moving on raw courage alone.

Only the rigorous Seneca training—harsh by the standards of even the most warlike of Indian nations—saved his life. The fever that gripped him robbed him of his ability to think, but he reacted automatically to his situation. He trotted because he knew he had no choice. Occasionally, when pangs of hunger reminded him that it was time to take nourishment, he reached for the parched corn and the jerked meat in his pouch, forgetting the

236

Oneida's food. Because of his fever, his thirst often was overpowering, and he stopped often at swift-running streams to drink and bathe his face.

It was these stops that undoubtedly saved his life. Again, and again, he paused to drink more of the cold, life-sustaining waters. The cool liquid felt so good on his face that he bathed in it repeatedly, plunging his arms into the streams up to his elbows. This, as Betsy and Deborah realized, when he finally reached home, held his fever in abeyance and enabled him to survive.

How No-da-vo found his way home was a miracle to anyone but a devoted Seneca. The warriors of the nation took his feat for granted when he staggered across the fields toward the town palisade, seeming more dead than alive.

When Goo-ga-ro-no heard that he had arrived, she hurried to him, and a single, swift glance told her he was seriously ill. He failed to recognize her, which was thoroughly alarming. At her mother's suggestion, she put him to bed, and then Ena examined him.

No one knew more about the plants that cured many ailments, and Ena's reputation was recently enhanced by Renno's complete recovery. So Goo-ga-ro-no stood, respectfully silent, while she waited for her grandmother to complete her examination of the patient.

Ena prescribed that the wound should be poulticed with the familiar medicinal red leaves and that he be fed a brew of the root of a bitter herb that grew tiny yellow flowers to rid him of the infection.

No roots were on hand in the town, and Goo-ga-ro-no hastened into the forest to search for some; this was her duty as the future wife of No-da-vo. She welcomed the opportunity to make herself useful, and searched long and diligently, but with no luck. Beginning to feel a sense of panic, she prayed to the manitous for guidance. Scarcely had she spoken when she saw a cluster of the tiny yellow flowers nearby.

As she reached eagerly for the plant, intending to pull it

out by the roots, she heard an ominous rattle and quickly drew back. There, coiled in knee-high grass, was a deadly rattlesnake about to strike.

Goo-ga-ro-no once would have been immobilized by the sight of the vicious snake, but the knowledge that No-da-vo's welfare depended on her safe return with the necessary medication gave her courage and strength. The mere fact that the manitous had answered her plea so rapidly gave her heart.

She quickly drew her one weapon, a knife, from the girdle that encircled her waist, and unhesitatingly plunged it into the rattlesnake, the blade penetrating directly below the head. The rattler died instantly but continued to thrash convulsively for some moments.

Wise in the ways of the forest, Goo-ga-ro-no conducted a swift but thorough search of the immediate vicinity to make certain that a second snake was not nearby. Having assured herself, she pulled up the root, then picked up the dead snake, and returned to the town with her trophies.

Ena was delighted, and removing the sac of poison from the throat of the dead rattlesnake, she said sagely, "Your worries are at an end, Goo-ga-ro-no. That snake was a carrier of evil, and by killing it you have rendered harmless the forces bent on the destruction of No-da-vo. Now we need have no doubt that he will recover."

Goo-ga-ro-no chopped the root of the herb and dropped it into a pot to simmer with a small quantity of water. Ultimately the root disintegrated and Ena then instructed her granddaughter to feed the medicinal tea to No-da-vo. He was resting fairly comfortably, thanks at least in part to the poultice of red leaves. He opened his eyes when Goo-ga-ro-no came into the room but still failed to recognize her.

Placing a hand behind his head, she hoisted him to a sitting position and then presented him with a gourd filled with the steaming brew. "Drink this!" she commanded.

No-da-vo took a small sip and shuddered. As any of the warriors seriously wounded in battle could have told him, the taste of the herb tea was horrid; some braves declared it worth any risk to avoid tasting the tea.

But Goo-ga-ro-no would tolerate no nonsense. "Drink it, I say!" she said sternly.

No-da-vo, as a warrior trained in obedience, did what he was told, making a face and shuddering, but draining the gourd.

Soon he dropped off to sleep, and Goo-ga-ro-no busied herself preparing the rattlesnake skin for preservation. She would make a headband of it and would wear it always as a memento of her betrothed's recovery.

Without doubt, No-da-vo's recovery was in truth underway. When he next awakened, his fever had subsided, and Goo-ga-ro-no knew when she saw his eyes that his sanity had returned. She summoned her father.

No-da-vo submitted his formal report to the Great Sachem, telling in detail how he had fought and defeated the new leader of the Oneida in fair combat. "The warriors of the Oneida," he said, "appeared to have learned a lesson and were ashamed of the treachery of their comrades."

Renno was well pleased. Not only had No-da-vo preserved the peace and prevented the Iroquois alliance from disintegrating, but equally important, he had acted with valor and dispatch. He had truly earned the right to marry Goo-ga-ro-no.

"No-da-vo has done well," Renno said. "He deserves the daughter of Renno and the granddaughter of Ghonka as his bride."

This was the reward the young warrior had sought, but it would have been unseemly for him to display emotion in the presence of Renno. He contented himself with bowing his head in acceptance of the Great Sachem's verdict.

But Goo-ga-ro-no betrayed her white antecedents and the days she had spent as a child and an adolescent in Virginia; for once forgetting the Seneca ways which she had so enthusiastically espoused, she broke into a smile and, with cries of delight, thoroughly embarrassed Renno by throwing her arms around him and kissing him.

Renno would have been outraged had any other Seneca so blatantly ignored the nation's traditions. But Goo-ga-ro-no held a special place in his affections and, as her mother had often commented, could get away with almost anything in her relations with her father. As usual, Betsy was right. Renno returned his daughter's hug and then hastily left the room, averting his face so neither of the young people could see his amusement.

Only when they were finally alone did No-da-vo smile at his future bride. He extended a hand to her, and she came to him at once, bending over him and kissing him tenderly.

Only now did she show him the rattlesnake skin and tell him of her near brush with death.

No-da-vo was deeply impressed. "It is true that we have won the favor of the manitous," he said, "and we are among the blessed on earth. Soon we will marry, and our children will bring great glory to the Seneca and to the family of Renno!"

So it happened that, less than a week later, after No-da-vo had recovered his strength, they were married in the presence of all the Seneca who were in the town at the time. The ceremony was conducted by the principal medicine man, as befitted the daughter of the Great Sachem, and two elks which Renno had killed for the occasion were quartered and roasted on an open fire so that all could eat and enjoy the occasion.

Betsy's pensive mood was the privilege of the mother of the bride. But her thoughts actually were far from Goo-ga-ro-no, and after the ceremony, in an exchange of glances with Talking Quail and Sun-ai-yee, she knew that their thoughts, like hers, were far from home.

They were hoping and praying, as she was, that Ah-wen-ga was safe, that Ja-gonh had found her, and that he was bringing her home. She could not discuss her son and Ah-wen-ga with anyone—not even with Renno. But she mentioned the young couple fervently every morning and every night in her prayers.

240

* * *

The palace of Versailles, commissioned in the middle of the previous century by Louis XIV and built by three famous architects, made the name of a tiny village outside Paris synonymous with the greatest glamor ever achieved by the royal house of Bourbon.

The palace, worthy of the Sun King and of his great-grandson and successor, Louis XV, contained so many hundreds of rooms that no accurate count had been made. A smaller palace, the Grand Trianon, was on the grounds, as well as almost innumerable temples, grottos, gazebos, and other ornamental structures. The gardens, extending for thousands of acres, included fountains, reservoirs, and sculptures by the finest artists in France. A special machine was built to supply the great amounts of water required by the fountains.

As had been the custom during the reign of King Louis's predecessor, when the monarch was in residence most of the nobles of the realm were also in attendance. So many crowded into the palace that rooms originally intended for servants were occupied by counts and countesses who made no complaint, but regarded themselves as fortunate that they could sleep under the same roof that King Louis did.

The monarchy was a highly centralized institution, and this was both the strength and the weakness of France. The King's ministers were in constant attendance at Versailles, as were the chiefs of the armed forces and even of the judiciary. No decision of importance was made without the approval of the monarch. It was highly unusual for influential leaders to be absent, as now unavoidably was the case with Cardinal Fleury, detained at Rome because of his untimely illness.

The ladies had nothing better to do with their time than to compete with each other in gaudy, expensive dresses that would catch the eye, perhaps of the King, or at the very least, that of an influential nobleman. Gentlemen who found time heavy on their hands played cards and other games of chance—and inevitably engaged in liaisons.

The court was vastly corrupt. As Voltaire, one of the dominant literary figures of the age, observed, the ladies were lacking almost completely in virtue, and honor was unknown to the men. Card games began soon after breakfast, and only the most fortunate had an opportunity to engage in any constructive work approved by the Crown.

Intrigues were endless, and those closest to the throne were subjected to almost as intense flattery as that lavished on the King. Anyone who aroused the royal ire became a pariah, and to be dismissed from Versailles meant the end of one's career.

Every newcomer was carefully scrutinized, even by the highest-ranking nobles, and everyone indulged in the pastime of deciding whether to cultivate or ignore a new arrival. A mistake in judgment could turn out to be ruinous.

Lady Arlene received more than the usual share of attention, not only because she was a member of the wealthy and powerful family of the Duc de Guise, but because almost everyone at Versailles recognized her as a previous favorite mistress of Louis XV. She appeared to be even lovelier, and her self-assurance was as great as ever. Wherever she had been, she obviously had not been pining away.

Major Henri de Bienville, unknown to many at the court, was recognized by certain high-ranking army officers and members of the Department for the Colonies. Once he had been categorized as merely the chief of military intelligence for the New World, he could be shunted aside rather safely.

Roger and Patience Harkness, unknown quantities, attracted interest principally because of Patience's attractiveness. When it was established, however, that they were English rather than French, most of the court promptly lost interest.

But precisely as Arlene had predicted, Ah-wen-ga created a sensation. The combination of her dark, sultry beauty and her almost exaggeratedly chic French clothes were irresistible lures. Speculation regarding her identity was intense. Some thought she was an Arab, and it was rumored that she was related to the Emir of Algiers or the Bey of Tunis. A vocal minority insisted that she must be a native of Constantinople, a Turkish princess ranking high in the family of the Sultan of the Ottoman Empire.

No one guessed that she was an American Indian, and thanks to the intense tutoring by Arlene, it was impossible to determine her background from her accent. She spoke a passable French and, following Arlene's shrewd instructions, turned aside all questions with a bland, noncommittal smile.

Ja-gonh created a furor almost as intense. On the morning that the party was due to arrive at the palace, he had startled his companions by appearing in full Seneca regalia and with his head shaved on either side of his scalp lock. He wore a buckskin shirt, trousers, and moccasins. On his face and, where visible, also his torso were the yellow and green streaks that marked the war paint of the Seneca. He proudly carried the weapons of his people. Over one shoulder were slung his quiver of arrows and his bow; in his belt he carried his tomahawk and the delicately balanced knives that could be thrown or be used in a warrior's hand. Hanging from his scalp lock were the three hawk feathers that marked him as a senior warrior of his people. As he remarked to Roger, "Let the French call themselves prince or duke or count—none of them is greater than a senior warrior of the Seneca."

Many of those at court considered Ja-gonh an untutored savage and dismissed him from their thoughts. But others, who took the trouble to learn more about him, were astonished to discover that this white Indian spoke impeccable, accentless English and could be as civilized as any settler from England's New World colonies.

Arlene's reaction to Ja-gonh's appearance in his native attire was identical to that of many of the women at Versailles. Extraordinarily handsome, he exuded an almost animallike magnetism that made him seem irresistible to them. Arlene believed that it would not be difficult for her to try to seduce him when she arranged a rendezvous for Ah-wen-ga with King Louis. In fact, she found that she was looking forward eagerly to the prospect.

As luck would have it, King Louis had retired to a private hunting lodge with a current mistress only a day before the party's arrival at Versailles. He did not reappear for a fortnight, and the court became thoroughly bored. Only the cabinet officers and other ministers of state who had duties to perform were busy. The rest, deprived of the spectacles they enjoyed at the monarch's levees, found time hanging heavy on their hands.

It was almost inevitable that some of the men, particularly the young and adventurous, should try to create a measure of instant renown for themselves by using Ja-gonh as a foil. Some bumped into him deliberately when they passed in the busy corridors of the palace or encountered him in one or another of the public rooms. Others made insulting remarks in his hearing. They were deliberately trying to prod him into challenging them to duels.

Roger Harkness was familiar with the idiosyncrasies of royal courts. "The young Frenchmen," he said, "are trying to create names for themselves at your expense because they regard you as something of a colorful freak. Don't allow yourself to be goaded into challenging them."

"That's easier said than done," Ja-gonh replied. "I don't mind their making jibes at me, but if I hear anything untoward regarding Ah-wen-ga, I won't guarantee not to lose my temper."

"But that's just what you must not do," Roger cautioned. "We've come a long way to Versailles, and we stand on the threshold of a meeting with the King. Depending on your skill and Ah-wen-ga's, I believe you could help guarantee peace in the New World. But suppose you were to fight and kill some prominent nobleman who happens to be one of the King's favorites. Our cause would be doomed, and the King probably wouldn't even be willing to grant an audience."

"You're asking forbearance such as I've never before

been obliged to show," Ja-gonh objected. "A Seneca must be patient in all things at all times, but he cannot permit his honor to be stained or insults directed at his woman. You may be asking more of me than I am able to give, Roger."

Ah-wen-ga, who had been listening to the conversation, interrupted. "In wandering around this enormous place today," she said, "I saw two spots of great interest. One appeared to be a range where the French warriors practice shooting. The other was a large hall where many were at practice with their long knives." She corrected her Seneca expression by adding in French, "Their swords, I mean."

"You're quite right," Roger said. "I understand that the military has instituted these practice grounds so that their officers don't get rusty while at the court hoping to catch the King's attention."

"Then I know how to silence those who make jests and insults at Ja-gonh's expense," Ah-wen-ga said. "Let Ja-gonh go to the practice range and take with him a long rifle and two pistols of the English. I have no idea how expert the French officers may be, but I think they would have a great distance to go before they are the equal of Ja-gonh."

"You are absolutely right," Roger said, chuckling. "He's a superb marksman, even if he does prefer the weapons of the Seneca."

"There's a good reason why I can shoot fairly well with firearms," Ja-gonh said modestly. "My father and uncle, Ned, began to instruct me in their use when I could barely walk."

"Very well," Roger said. "Ah-wen-ga has sharpened her shrewd mind while forced to associate with the French. You and I will go to the practice range tomorrow, and you will show off your skills with both rifle and pistol. I daresay that will silence some of those who seek to build their reputations at your expense."

"Do not forget the hall where they practice also with swords," Ah-wen-ga added softly.

Roger stroked his chin. "Ah, I have it," he said. "We'll

245

arrange to borrow two sets of foils and masks, and we'll brush up on our swordplay. I'm sure both of us can stand the practice."

"I'm none too certain," Ja-gonh replied dubiously, "that I am sufficiently accomplished with the sword to achieve the purpose that you and Ah-wen-ga have in mind."

Roger laughed aloud, and a hint of amusement appeared in Ah-wen-ga's eyes. "I think we'll find," Roger assured him, "that your skill is greater than you are ready to admit—and that the French gentry of Versailles will give you a very wide berth once you've demonstrated your proficiencies."

Ja-gonh had no choice but to accept his word. Versailles, a strange and confusing place, was to him one where values were badly distorted.

The following morning he met his companions in a great, mirrored hall lined by long tables. There gentlemen in suits of velvet and silk, with their ladies in gowns suitable only for the most formal occasions, sat down to a breakfast of beef served on trenchers of bread, broiled fish served with exotic sauces, and a specialty of Versailles—chickens stuffed with pigeons which in turn were stuffed with olives. Those who dined here were the court syco-phants who lived at the palace but did not rate private apartments where their meals could be served to them.

Arlene had come to breakfast with Ah-wen-ga, and she looked curiously at Ja-gonh when the young Seneca appeared with a brace of pistols in his belt and a frontier rifle in his hand. The rifle was vastly different from the short, squat French muskets, which featured bayonets attached to the muzzles.

She inquired as to the meaning of the firearms, and Ah-wen-ga explained their purpose. "If women were only permitted on the practice range," Arlene said, "I'd come and watch you perform, Ja-gonh. I think the whole idea is wonderful!"

After breakfast, Ja-gonh and Roger left the women and walked rapidly to the practice range behind the main building of the palace. Located in a secluded grove, the range was cut off from the palace by a thick screen of poplars. Roger was quick to note that aside from two young infantry officers, he and Ja-gonh would have the area completely to themselves.

"We'll wait," he decided, "until a somewhat larger crowd appears." Ja-gonh was agreeable, but for the next hour, no one else arrived on the scene. Ja-gonh was beginning to grow restless when at last a group of full colonels, led by two generals in gold-trimmed uniforms, strolled onto the range from the direction of the palace. Roger looked at Ja-gonh and winked solemnly.

The young Seneca needed no other signal. He loaded his rifle quickly and efficiently and with a seeming lack of effort. Then he searched in vain for a target.

One of the colonels realized that the gaudily painted Indian and his companion were new to the ways of the range, and called for an attendant to set up a target.

Ja-gonh was disconcerted, as was Roger, when a liveried attendant appeared carrying a cardboard dummy in a uniform consisting of a bearskin hat, scarlet tunic, and black, red-striped trousers—the uniform of the Grenadier Guards. It was typical of French humor to take practice with targets wearing British uniforms. Noting that Ja-gonh seemed confused at first, several of the French officers chuckled.

Ja-gonh, who did not share their humor, felt nonetheless at ease, in spite of his alien surroundings. His weapon was familiar; he knew precisely what he could do with it and was aware of its limitations. Looking down the length of the barrel, he carefully measured his target and aimed for the forehead of the dummy. The torso would have given him a much larger target, but he was in no mood to trifle. Holding his rifle firmly and preparing for the weapon's kickback, he squeezed the trigger. The shot echoed across the vast gardens.

The French officers stared at the target and murmured in awed approval. The bullet had penetrated the center of the forehead. But the expressions of several others suggested that perhaps the white Indian's marksmanship was largely luck.

Moving swiftly, efficiently, Ja-gonh reloaded and this time aimed for the dummy's heart. Again he squeezed the trigger, and again his results were eminently satisfactory. One of the French generals whistled under his breath.

Again, Ja-gonh reloaded, and to emphasize that his marksmanship was anything but accidental, his third bullet penetrated the dummy less than a half-inch from his previous shot. Then Roger called out to the attendant, "Be good enough to provide me with a new target."

The entire group gaped as the servant removed the dummy and replaced it with another.

Ja-gonh drew his pistols, checked to make sure they were properly loaded, then fired twice, first with his right hand and then with his left.

The senior French general applauded vigorously when he and his companions saw that one of the bullets had penetrated the forehead and the other the heart of the dummy. The French officers had never seen such shooting.

The general approached, his spurs clanging, and bowed stiffly. "I am Etienne Leclerc, a lieutenant general in the service of His Christian Majesty," he said. "I must congratulate you, sir, on your shooting. I have never known anything to equal it." He spoke in French and Roger quickly translated for Ja-gonh's benefit.

The general peered at him. "Since you probably do not know French, I will address you in English," he said. "Your marksmanship is little short of superb."

In spite of his attire, Ja-gonh responded as an English gentleman, even clicking his heels—or rather trying to in his soft mocassins—and bowing from the waist. "You're very kind to say so, General, but among the people of my nation I am considered an ordinary marksman. I am Ja-gonh of the Seneca, the son of Renno, the Great Sachem of all the Iroquois."

General Leclerc was immediately impressed, as were several other officers who understood English. According

248

to their standards, the son of the Great Sachem of the Iroquois was necessarily a prince.

"I would be very pleased," General Leclerc said, "if you should see fit to honor me by joining my staff and teaching marksmanship to the troops of the divisions under my command."

Ja-gonh was flattered but kept the offer in perspective. His expression unchanging, he replied gravely. "My people, the Seneca, belong to the Iroquois League. All the nations of the Iroquois are bound in a solemn treaty with their blood brothers, the settlers who owe their allegiance to England. England has been the enemy of France, and I cannot take part in the instruction of French soldiers who will shoot to kill my allies and my brothers."

General Leclerc was unaccustomed to such blunt talk, but had to admire the young man's courage. "Nothing is as changeable as political alliances," he said. "Those who are our enemies one day become allies the next. If a change takes place and England and France become allied, remember that my offer is always open to you." He took his leave, followed by the other officers.

Roger grinned broadly. "I'd say you accomplished your objective magnificently," he said. "They were greatly impressed, and the word is going to be passed along that you're a marksman of special stature."

Ja-gonh reflected that here was another of the ways in which civilized nations were very strange: a man's reputation rather than his actual accomplishments were responsible for much of his success or failure.

In any event, he was achieving the goal that Roger had set for him and had reason to be satisfied with the results so far. Taking their time, they left the range and strolled to the so-called Hall of Arms, a barnlike structure adjacent to the palace. It was used exclusively for practice with swords, and other countries were beginning to copy its concept. The windows were oversized, admitting far more light than customary. The hardwood floors gave a smooth surface for those who clashed with swords.

An attendant handed Ja-gonh and Roger foils, masks, and padded armless jackets. They donned their gear, and as Roger had anticipated, they became the object of considerable attention from the nearby forty men who had been practicing swordplay. All other activities in the large hall stopped as he and Ja-gonh faced each other.

They raised their foils to each other in the usual salute and then launched into a spirited exchange. Although Roger was concentrating on his opponent's tactics, he was nevertheless aware of the astonishment of the onlookers. The mere fact that the white Indian could handle a sword properly and was familiar with the etiquette of dueling was as impressive to them as it was surprising.

Ja-gonh felt far less confident than he looked, and far more ill at ease than on the shooting range. He had used swords so little that the blade felt like an alien weapon in his hand.

His actual technique left nothing to be desired; his thrusts and parries were smooth and well coordinated, and he appeared to be an accomplished swordsman, thanks to his rigorous training by Uncle Ned Ridley. But he knew, as did Roger, that he was far inferior to the Englishman and in a real encounter would have been no match for him.

Roger was aware, too, of the need to present Ja-gonh in the most favorable possible light. So he deliberately increased the pace of their mock duel, thrusting repeatedly while making certain that none of his blows struck home.

Ja-gonh realized what his friend was doing and couldn't help grimacing. He appreciated Roger's concern but hated to win under false colors.

Persisting in his deception, Roger was sufficiently clever and nimble that he made it appear that Ja-gonh was by far the better swordsman. Gradually, Roger allowed his opponent to assume the offensive, and he began to fall back under the fury of Ja-gonh's assault. The competitive spirit had been aroused in Ja-gonh, and more angry with himself than with Roger, he exerted all his limited skill and all his effort into achieving a legitimate victory.

Roger was surprised by the intensity of his friend's

drive, but understood that Ja-gonh's spirit would not permit him to falsify or dissemble.

Little by little, Ja-gonh actually gained the ascendancy, and Roger smiled wryly as he had to exert all his skill in order to avoid a humiliating defeat.

Suddenly Ja-gonh saw a slight opening and exploited it, delivering a lightning thrust that penetrated Roger's guard. The tip of his foil left a chalk mark on the young Englishman's padded jacket directly over his heart. Had the duel been real, Roger would have died instantly.

The duel was over and both contestants fell back and removed their masks. The astonished spectators burst into spontaneous applause. Not only had the white Indian demonstrated style, but his victory was genuine, and the onlookers were sufficiently experienced to recognize that his developing skill had won him an encounter with a far more experienced opponent.

Ja-gonh stood still, his expression unchanging, and he seemed unaware of the applause.

"They're congratulating you," Roger said to him in an undertone. "Acknowledge their applause with a bow or a salute."

Remembering the purpose of the exhibition, Ja-gonh raised his sword over his head, then bowed slightly but graciously.

He was relieved that the exhibitions were concluded, and he hastened to hand his dueling equipment to the attendant. It was good to breathe the crisp air when they moved outdoors.

Chapter XI

F ew men in France had a higher rank, more money, or greater power than Charles, Duc de Guise. In the hierarchy, he stood immediately behind his close friend and ally, the Duc de Vendôme, who was a great-grandson of Henri IV. The de Guise family was not of royal blood, but it was their private contention that they were far worthier to rule the country than the Bourbons, who sat on the throne of France.

The duc was a shrewd, ambitious man of forty whose red hair and beard were reminiscent of his hot-tempered ancestors. Unlike them, he kept his emotions under strict self-control and was said to have ice water rather than blood flowing through his veins.

Henri de Bienville, who knew the duc only slightly, was somewhat ill at ease when he responded to the summons of

253

Charles de Guise to join him in his Versailles apartment for dinner. He was not in the least surprised to find Lady Arlene already on hand.

The exalted rank of the duc entitled him to one of the finer apartments in the great palace, and he had a series of sitting rooms, a comfortable dining room, and his own spacious kitchen, in addition to sleeping quarters for himself, his wife, and for the various mistresses whom he entertained.

The meal was the rich, sumptuous fare typical of Versailles. The first course consisted of delicately flavored seafood rolled in thin pancakes and served with a white wine sauce from a recipe that the de Guise chef kept secret. Next came a chicken-based soup, followed by a small omelet and then a very large roast flamed in cognac. Salad greens were an inevitable course; for dessert the duc and his two guests were served bowls containing a half-dozen sherbets. A different wine accompanied each course.

Unaccustomed to such a rich meal, de Bienville ate and drank sparingly.

At the end of the meal, the duc offered de Bienville a *segaro* from the French colonies in the Caribbean and, lighting one himself, sat back in his chair. Now that his hunger and thirst had been satiated, he was ready to discuss business.

"Well, Arlene," he said jovially, "I've asked you and the major to dine with me today because I am most curious. What mischief are you up to?"

"None, I assure you, Cousin Charles," Arlene replied demurely.

Charles de Guise chuckled coarsely. "I find that very hard to believe. You went off to the New World to get away from the court after your affair with His Majesty inevitably ended, and you've returned with a ravishing Indian girl who not only speaks French but has many mannerisms of a great lady. I smell something out of the ordinary."

De Bienville was alarmed when he saw that Arlene was

on the point of confessing their scheme to her relative. She hastened to reassure him.

"You may relax, Henri," she said. "In the de Guise family, blood is thicker than water, and family blood is thicker than royal blood. I can assure you that Cousin Charles is very discreet and fully understands how to keep a secret."

Exhibiting considerable pride in her achievement, Arlene related how the daughter of the sachem of the Seneca was abducted, and how she had trained her with only one goal in mind—that of making her the mistress of Louis XV.

"What of the others who came with you?" the Duc de Guise inquired.

Arlene identified Ja-gonh, Roger, and Patience, and then added, "They will not be in the way when Ah-wen-ga has her meeting with Louis. I intend to ensure personally that the white Indian is fully occupied."

Charles de Guise looked very pleased as he puffed on his cigar and blew a thin stream of smoke toward the ceiling. Raising his cognac glass, he sniffed its bouquet appreciatively and then sipped it before he deigned to speak again.

"As it happens," he said, "your plans dovetail with mine. You have no idea how grateful I am to you, Arlene, for helping to solve a number of problems for me."

Arlene's smile was unwavering but a wary expression crept into her eyes.

"What I'm about to reveal to you," the duc said, "is private information of the highest order and is to be released to absolutely no one outside this room."

Arlene indicated agreement, and de Bienville, thoroughly confused, did the same.

"The days of Louis XV on the throne of France are numbered," de Guise declared. "Like my father and grandfather before me, I have grown tired of seeing incompetents from the House of Bourbon ruling this nation. France has the resources and the wealth to be the most powerful nation in Europe, but she has frittered away her potential by becoming soft and corrupt. The gathering of all nobles under one roof has drained France of spirit and has turned bluebloods into mere sycophants. France needs to be reborn and revitalized.''

A chill crept up Henri de Bienville's spine. The duc appeared to be planning the overthrow of Louis XV, yet he spoke as casually as though discussing his menu for the evening meal.

Arlene appeared to be neither surprised nor disturbed. ''You're intending to take the throne yourself, Cousin Charles?'' she asked almost casually.

''It's not that I crave the power and personal satisfactions of sitting on the throne,'' he said, ''but I know of no one else in the realm other than the Duc de Vendôme who could bring the nation to the stature that she deserves. As it happens, Vendôme already has agreed to be my first minister, so we shall have not only my own talents, but his as well in the service of our country.''

It appeared evident to the horrified de Bienville that the plot was well advanced. Although ruthlessly unscrupulous in performing his duties and endowed with a soaring ambition, he realized that what he was hearing was nothing short of high treason. Laws protecting the monarch were very severe, and the penalties for those who might try to kill the ruler were uncompromising. Ever since several attempts on the life of Henry IV, an attempted assassin or anyone connected with any plot to do away with the monarch was whipped until he lost consciousness; then, after he regained his senses, he was drawn and quartered. The mere contemplation of such punishment caused de Bienville to shudder.

Charles de Guise read his mind and smiled pleasantly. ''You're wondering, Major, and you, Arlene, whether it is worth your time and effort to participate. I appeal to you, as patriotic French, to join us. I assure you that you won't regret it. You, Major, have a splendid record in the New World, and I know of no reason that you couldn't be promoted to the rank of general and be given command of all the troops in Quebec.''

The prospect was dizzying and caused de Bienville to hesitate. He wanted to weigh the possible consequences before he gave a final answer. Arlene, meanwhile, gave every appearance of being comfortable with participating in such a hazardous and treasonous undertaking.

The duc gave them no opportunity to think. "My associates and I," he went on, "have planned our moves with great care over a long period of time. We know whom we can trust and whom we cannot. To preclude our being betrayed and executed before we put our scheme into operation or during any of its stages of development, we have taken certain highly necessary precautions. Among our associates are some who will not openly declare in our favor until our plan is complete. But if anything should happen to me or to those close to me in the meantime, those comrades will even the score with anyone who talks out of turn. I trust that I make my meaning quite clear."

"It is very clear indeed, Your Grace," de Bienville muttered. If he went to the authorities and revealed the plot, he could expect that his days would be strictly numbered.

Arlene, whose mind was working with great rapidity, underscored that prospect in summing up the situation. She was cheerful as she always was in times of stress. "It strikes me, my dear," she said to the major, "that we have no real alternative. Now that Cousin Charles has honored us by making us privy to his plan, we should be deeply flattered. I will join him cheerfully, and as for you—you'll not regret your association with him, I am sure, because Cousin Charles is noted for his great generosity to those who serve him loyally.

"On the other hand," she went on, "if you are foolish enough to go to the colonel commanding the King's Musketeers with news of Cousin Charles's plan, I regret to say you would live a very short time."

De Bienville sighed gently. "In other words," he said, "whether I like it or not, I have a simple choice. Either I become a party to treason, or my own existence will be terminated rather swiftly."

"And none too pleasantly at that," the duc added with a tight smile.

The major made up his mind and acted accordingly. "I am flattered to be taken into Your Grace's confidence," he said, "and you may consider me enrolled as your faithful supporter."

"That's very wise of you, de Bienville," the Duc de Guise said. "I commend your sagacity." He turned back to his cousin. "The Indian girl will play a key role," he said, "in the isolation of King Louis. We must time our attack in such a way that no one will know for some time that he has been assaulted, much less who is responsible. Once he is disposed of, I shall need approximately three hours to rally certain elements to my own banner, particularly the top-ranking officers of the army and navy. So no one, including servants, must know that poor Louis has lost his life."

Arlene laughed. "The best way of ensuring his isolation," she said, "is to arrange a rendezvous with a new candidate for his personal interest. On such occasions everyone is dismissed and even his servants are absent. I find your thinking brilliant, Cousin Charles."

"What will become of Ah-wen-ga?" de Bienville asked.

"As she will be the only witness to His Majesty's demise," the duc said, "I am inclined to think it will also be necessary that she lose her life as well. It's unfortunate, perhaps, that an innocent bystander should suffer, but on the other hand, I can take no risks that a witness would betray me or any of my subordinates."

"Perhaps the double death could be made to look like a lovers' rendezvous with death," Arlene suggested. "It would require very little to spark talk in the court that Louis had been in love with her, but because of her nationality they had decided that they had no future together and determined to end their lives jointly. That would be quite fitting, I think, and I'm sure that the majority of courtiers would gladly accept it. People do, after all, love juicy tidbits of gossip."

"That's a perfectly brilliant idea," the duc said coolly, "and it solves any number of problems."

"I will see that Ja-gonh is taken care of," Arlene said, her enthusiasm growing. "And I presume you will want Henri to keep Roger Harkness and his wife busy."

"I'm inclined to think," he said, "that Major de Bienville can perform a far more important function by leading the Indian girl to the place of rendezvous with Louis. We shall work out the details in due course; now all we need to do is to await the King's return to the court and his inevitable sparking of interest in her." He raised his glass of cognac in silent salute and drank slowly.

Watching him, de Bienville stirred uneasily. He was no stranger to assassinations and bizarre plots, but this cold-blooded approach was eye-opening to him. Never had he known anyone as cruelly determined to have his way. The stakes were incredibly high, of course, and should the duc be successful, he would become Europe's most powerful monarch.

The return of Louis XV to the court at Versailles caused subtle but distinct changes in the routines of the nobles and their ladies who waited on him.

The gaming tables became deserted at the hours when the monarch held audiences. The younger and more attractive women wore heavier cosmetics and fewer, more daring clothes. The high-ranking officers spent less time on the practice ranges and considerably more time standing interminably in the audience chamber and dutifully laughing at the mild jokes made by the King.

The man who was the center of attention was habitually dressed in cloth-of-gold, and even his shoes and stockings were fashioned of gold. Robbed of his exalted rank, he would have seemed among the most ordinary of mortals. He was thin, with narrow drooping shoulders and the prominent nose and chin that marked all members of the Bourbon family. He lacked the intellect of Henri IV, the charm of Louis XIII, and much of the wit and grandeur of Louis XIV. Some at his court, in fact, privately considered him to be slightly stupid and more than unduly influenced by the women to whom he was so fatally drawn—and who, in turn, were invariably attracted to him.

Louis was married, but his wife played no part in the business of the nation, and her existence in no way deterred her husband from his endless rounds of affairs. Maria Leszczynska was the daughter of the deposed King of Poland. Louis had given him refuge in Lorraine, where he now made his home. As Maria was shy, retiring, and not particularly good-looking in any sense, most of the court could not understand why the monarch had chosen to marry her. The reason most frequently expressed was that she could take on a regal mien, and minded her own business, which gave him a free hand. These were aspects that no one tried to deny.

Queen Maria had the good sense to avoid her husband's public levees in the audience chamber. So, too, she avoided being humiliated in the presence of her subjects. Whatever her opinions of the philandering, she was able to keep them to herself.

Some twenty-four hours after King Louis's return to the palace, the court chamberlain let it be known that His Majesty would be pleased to meet any newcomers to the court scene. The word spread quickly.

Arlene hastened to prepare Ah-wen-ga for this long-awaited event, and she supervised her makeup and selected the gown she was to wear. It featured an exceptionally low-cut, tight-fitting bodice of pale, peach-colored silk, and a full skirt which achieved a floating effect by virtue of having several overskirts of pink silk net.

Roger and Patience dressed carefully for the event, but Ja-gonh contented himself with applying a fresh coat of war paint to his face and torso.

The news that the exceptionally lovely Indian woman would be presented to Louis soon became common knowledge, so the audience chamber was crowded with curious nobles, officials, and other courtiers crowding in to watch what promised to be an edifying spectacle.

Arlene, who elected to present these newcomers herself, was wearing a new gown made for this occasion. Its pale green silk set off her red hair to good advantage, and she was conscious that she had never been more attractive.

King Louis, wearing a shoulder-length powdered wig and holding a walking stick fashioned of solid gold, sat on a thronelike chair on an elevated dais at one end of the hall.

At the chamberlain's glance, Arlene approached and curtsied low. "Your Majesty," she said, "I have the honor to present several newcomers to the court, including an English couple, Captain and Mistress Roger Harkness of London, and more recently of the British Crown Colony of Virginia."

Louis's attitude indicated that the formalities of such an occasion bored him to distraction. He nodded vaguely and opened his eyes wider just long enough to inspect Patience. She failed to interest him, and it appeared that he was about to turn his attention elsewhere.

"I have the honor also to present Ja-gonh," she said, "of the Seneca nation."

Louis sat bolt upright in his chair, gripping his walking stick hard as he stared at the paint-smeared white Indian.

Though instructed to bow low from the waist to the King, Ja-gonh had no intention of obeying the rules of France. His father and grandfather had held the highest rank in the Iroquois League, and he regarded himself as the equal of French royalty. So he raised his left arm in Seneca fashion and addressed him in English. "Ja-gonh, son of Renno, Great Sachem of the Iroquois League, greets his brother, Louis of the French."

Almost without exception the audience gasped. Never had anyone shown such familiarity with the monarch, and they fully expected the King to lose his temper and order the strangely clad Indian banished from his presence forever.

Louis, however, demonstrated his lively sense of humor.

He smiled broadly and, shifting his walking stick to his right hand, raised his left in imitation of Ja-gonh's gesture. "We are very pleased to make the acquaintance of our brother," he said, with only a hint of amusement in his voice.

Members of the court laughed dutifully, and Louis looked pleased with himself. Ja-gonh, lacking a translation, knew that they were amusing themselves at his expense, but the reasons for the laughter were beyond his comprehension. The ways of the French were far too difficult for him to bother to understand.

Then, as Ah-wen-ga came forward, the courtiers fell silent. A strange tension was in the air; it was so strong that it could be felt and almost seen.

Arlene knew that her long campaign was a success. Watching the King carefully as Ah-wen-ga approached the dais, she saw Louis's eyes open wide and the knuckles of the hand that gripped the head of the walking stick turn white. He was fully as interested as she had hoped.

"Your Majesty," she said proudly, "I have the honor to present the Princess Ah-wen-ga, daughter of the sachem, or leader, of the Seneca nation."

Ah-wen-ga wanted to respond in true Indian fashion as Ja-gonh had done, but her training had been too thorough. She spread her skirts and sank to the floor in a deep, graceful, and seemingly effortless curtsy.

By this time everyone in the audience was aware that the attention of Louis XV was riveted on her. He studied her intently and appeared to be memorizing every detail of her face and figure.

Arlene curtsied again and withdrew with Ah-wen-ga to the rear of the audience chamber where those whom she had presented were being served with cups of a strong concoction, a mixture of rum and wine. She had no doubt that she would be summoned by the King before the day ended and that a private audience would be requested for Ah-wen-ga.

Ja-gonh took one sip of his drink and immediately returned his cup to a liveried servant. Under the best of circumstances, he did not care for alcoholic beverages, and the mere smell of this particular libation made him ill. Ah-wen-ga quickly followed his example.

Arlene was sorry that the couple had refused their drinks. She would have found it much simpler and easier to handle them had they been even slightly under the influence of liquor. But she smiled sweetly at Ah-wen-ga and said, "Congratulations, my dear, you scored a triumph!"

Ah-wen-ga was pleased but not overwhelmed. "Do you think so?"

"I know it," Arlene said forcefully. "I've been well acquainted with His Majesty for a long time, and I can tell when someone arouses his total interest."

Ah-wen-ga smiled calmly. "That is good," she said. "Then it should be that much easier for me to gain his attention when I plead for peace between the French and English possessions in the New World."

"Of course," Arlene said glibly.

Roger and Patience exchanged a quick, private glance. They knew that arousing the King's interest in peace in the colonies would be a very delicate matter, not necessarily accomplished as easily as Ah-wen-ga apparently envisioned.

A dozen other newcomers were formally presented, and then, as Arlene had anticipated, Louis withdrew to an adjoining private suite. Within moments, a chamberlain approached and informed her that His Majesty wanted a word with her.

When she entered the living room of the suite, she sank low in a curtsy, bobbing so that her head almost touched the floor.

"Please get up, Arlene," Louis said irritably. "No one else is here now, and there's no need for such pomposity."

She immediately stood and smiled at the most powerful man in France, who sat in a tapestried chair, glaring at her.

"You look well, I must concede," he said grudgingly. "Your stay in the New World seemed to be good for you."

"It was better in every way than I anticipated, Louis," she replied.

"Yes, I was told you lost no time establishing a liaison

with our intelligence officer there, and I can't say I blame you. He's both good-looking and endowed with considerable acumen.''

She concealed her satisfaction, relieved that Louis approved of her affair with de Bienville. The monarch had been known to be jealous of former mistresses even after they had lost his interest.

"You also surprised me this morning,'' he said. "I take it you found the Indian beauty in the New World.''

"Indeed I did, Louis,'' she replied earnestly, "and I instantly thought of you.''

"Your loyalty is quite touching.''

"Furthermore, she's worthy of you.''

"I heard you call her princess,'' he said. "Was that for my sake or for the benefit of the court?''

"I was speaking only the truth,'' she replied in a quiet tone. "It so happens that her father is the leader of an Indian nation known as the Seneca.''

"I am not particularly impressed.''

"You should be,'' she said. "They're known throughout the New World as the bravest and most ferocious of fighting men. They have never been defeated in a battle within the memory of anyone living, and if I understand correctly they have defeated your regiments and those of your great-grandfather in more battles than you would care to have recounted for you.''

Her words seemed to have an effect. "I'm not denying anything you say, Arlene,'' he told her. "I must say that her rank does offer certain conveniences. Does she speak French, or must I address her in English? I was more astonished than I can tell you when that young blood of a half-naked white savage spoke to me in English.''

"Ah-wen-ga speaks English, it's true,'' Arlene said, "but she is also capable of conversing easily and at length in French.''

His expression became quizzical. "Oh?''

"I've spent several months teaching her our language myself,'' she said, "along with various of our customs.''

264

He brightened and tried in vain to suppress a grin. "Aha! You're telling me she's a protégée of yours?"

"In a manner of speaking, I daresay she is."

"Does she happen to share any of your proclivities and your talents for them?" he persisted.

Arlene folded her hands demurely and stared down at them. "I think you'll be in a far better position than I to answer that question for yourself, Louis," she answered.

Her subtlety was not lost on him, and he leaned forward eagerly. "Do I take it that she's prepared for a private audience with me?"

"If she remains unprepared," Arlene said, choosing her words with care, "that is her fault. I have devoted my full time and attention for many months making her ready for just such an audience."

Louis XV rubbed his hands together. "It strikes me," he said, "you've earned a considerable reward."

Her reward, she thought, would be far greater than he believed possible. When the assassins' knives spilled his blood and brought the Bourbon dynasty to an abrupt close, she, as a member of the de Guise family, would immediately assume the rank of a princess of royal blood.

"Since you've been devoting yourself with such single-minded zeal to this project," he said, "I would guess that you have a time and place in mind for a rendezvous?"

"Indeed I do. I suggest your hunting lodge on the far side of the grounds of Versailles, and I suggest that the hour be set in the early afternoon. I happen to know that the young lady has no particular plans for today, so there's no need to wait indefinitely."

Louis smiled broadly. "I must say you're thorough. Suppose we arrange the rendezvous for two o'clock this afternoon."

Arlene concealed her wild surge of elation. "This afternoon at two," she said. "Ah-wen-ga will be there."

"I assume," he said, "that you will bring her to me yourself."

"Oh, no, Louis," she replied, simulating horror. "I'll

be watched too closely by too many people at the court who are expecting just that very thing to happen. It would be far better if someone else, someone trustworthy, such as Major Henri de Bienville escorts her.''

"That would be just as well," he said, and was lost in thought for a moment. Then he frowned. "Why the hunting lodge? It's really located a rather considerable distance from the palace."

"That's exactly why I selected it," she said. "The lodge is located a sufficient distance from here, and it's necessary to go through some rather deep stretches of woods in order to reach it, as you know, so that almost no one—certainly none of your present mistresses—will have any idea that you're meeting her there. If you exercise ordinary caution when you leave the palace, you can reach the lodge undetected, and if you have no servants on hand, so much the better."

He considered her suggestion for a time and then he smiled approvingly. "You seem to have thought of everything."

"I've had a great deal of time to think of little else, Louis," she replied.

He studied her, his eyes becoming searching. "Why are you doing all this for me?" he demanded. "I've known ladies in your position who've been so annoyed with me that they've absented themselves permanently from my court, and I'm told that when I go into Paris on occasion they actually leave the city until I've gone."

"The difference, I suppose," she said, "is that I bear you no grudge. On the contrary, I wish you only happiness for however long you may stay on this earth." And that, she told herself, was to be only a matter of hours.

He was duly impressed by her seeming zeal. "You won't regret this," he assured her.

"I don't intend to," she said. "My only goal is to make this occasion memorable in every sense of the word."

"I shall do my part," he said. "The hunting lodge it shall be, and I shall go there alone, arriving in time to greet the young Indian lady promptly at two."

Arlene rose and swiftly curtsied again before she swept out of the suite. As she approached the audience chamber where a large number of nobles and other courtiers still lingered, she deliberately slowed her pace to a casual saunter. She felt someone looking at her from across the chamber, and she felt certain that it was Cousin Charles. A swift glance confirmed her guess.

She maneuvered closer to him as she crossed the room, moving in such a way that she did not appear obvious. He left the group with whom he was conversing and contrived to meet her halfway.

"He's going alone to the hunting lodge at two this afternoon," she said in an urgent undertone. "I'll see to it that Ah-wen-ga is there. Henri will escort her."

Aside from the tightening of the muscles in his jaw, he did not visibly react in the least. "Very well," he said, "I'll take care of Harkness and his wife. What of the young Indian warrior?"

"Leave him to me," Arlene said and put her hand on the Duc de Guise's arm. "Good luck, Cousin Charles," she said. "If all goes as it should, we'll be riding high by the time the sun goes down today."

"You may depend on it," he replied. "This is the opportunity I've been waiting for for years, and I don't intend to fail now!"

Roger was surprised when a good-looking, handsomely attired young Frenchman, wearing a sapphire and diamond ring worth a king's ransom, approached him and Patience and bowed deeply. "Your pardon, Mistress Harkness, and I crave your indulgence as well, Captain Harkness," he said. "I am the Comte de Flandre."

They concealed their surprise, wondering why a nobleman of the rank of the count should seek them out.

"I was surprised when you were presented to His Majesty this morning," the comte said, "and I felt certain that I had heard previously of both of you. You are the daughter of General Jeffrey Wilson, are you not, madame?"

"Indeed I am," Patience replied.

"Ah," he replied, lying glibly as he relied on the detailed information Arlene had supplied. "Then I have indeed been told of you, and your husband as well, I believe, when I recently visited at your parents' home."

"You've visited Fort Springfield?" Roger asked in surprise.

The French nobleman smiled. "Indeed, sir," he said. "I was sent on a special mission to the New World by His Majesty, and I visited many English colonies for protracted periods of time. I am interested in establishing trade missions with the English in the New World. I think that both our countries can benefit vastly by an increase in trade."

That was Roger's opinion, to be sure, and was a view his father-in-law had long espoused. "Apparently, we think in identical terms on the subject, milord," he replied.

"Perhaps we can find a place where we can discuss this subject at greater length and arrive at some conclusions that will benefit both your colonies and ours," the Frenchman said. Roger was delighted, and Patience beamed.

"My rank entitles me to a fairly nice apartment in the palace," the Comte de Flandre said. "I suggest we go there. It leaves something to be desired in the way of comfort, but at least we'll have privacy."

Roger and Patience heartily agreed and accompanied him. Neither realized, of course, that he was party to a scheme designed to keep them occupied during the critical hours to come.

Dinner, served at noon in the great mirror-lined hall, was, relatively speaking, the least important meal of the day because the King habitually ate in private and never visited the hall at that hour. Consequently, persons who ate there observed no special mealtime and wandered in and out whenever convenient.

Ja-gonh waited in vain for Ah-wen-ga and was about to go to her room in search of her when de Bienville materialized beside him.

"Have you seen Ah-wen-ga?" Ja-gonh wanted to know.

The major lied convincingly. "No, and I haven't seen Arlene either. I daresay they're doing a woman's errand of some kind." He spoke very casually, knowing full well that Arlene was in Ah-wen-ga's room, helping her to primp prior to her rendezvous with Louis XV, and telling her that she was about to enjoy the opportunity of a lifetime.

Ja-gonh hesitated as he weighed the information. The major caught hold of his arm. "Hold on," he said. "We'll have a bite together, and they'll probably appear before we're finished."

Ja-gonh saw no reason to question the Frenchman's word, and so he readily accompanied him. They walked to their regular places, and the first thing the young Seneca noticed was a sealed square of violet parchment on a plate at his place. On it was written his name, and below, in large printed letters in English, was the single word, *private*. He picked it up, saw that it was sealed with a violet blob of wax, and noted at once that it was heavily perfumed.

De Bienville pretended to consult the servant on the various dishes available for dinner.

Ja-gonh broke open the seal, unfolded the parchment, and saw a printed note that bore the signature, *Arlene*. It read:

Show this message to no one. Please come to my quarters at a quarter to two this afternoon on a matter of great urgency. I will be waiting for you there.

Ja-gonh folded the parchment and shoved it into a deep pocket in his buckskins. He had no idea why Arlene regarded it as urgent that he consult with her, nor what business she might have in mind. But he was true to his trust. She had asked him to mention her request to no one, and so he said nothing.

De Bienville put on an air of being too polite to inquire regarding the message, but was in fact already thoroughly familiar with its contents.

He and Ja-gonh chatted in a desultory way as they were served a half-dozen rich courses of heavily seasoned food. Ja-gonh had little appetite for the strange, rich fare, and as usual, the plates held far too much to eat.

He had never found it particularly easy to talk with de Bienville, but for a reason he couldn't quite fathom, they seemed to be getting along somewhat better than usual. It occurred to him that perhaps the major was going out of his way to be friendly today.

Shortly after one-thirty, de Bienville excused himself from the table, indicating that he would return shortly. Ja-gonh continued to nibble. He had found that he was subsisting principally on beef. At his request, it was served to him without sauces. He was homesick for the corn, squash, and beans that were staples of the Seneca fare; the beans and squash served at Versailles in no way resembled those in the dishes his mother cooked, and corn was totally unknown in Europe. He had no appetite for the wine that the courtiers drank so greedily with every course. It was astonishing, he thought, how many ladies and gentlemen of the court were less than sober by the time they finished a meal. It was clear that they had nothing better to do than drink and eat. He had been assured by de Bienville that all expenses for their meals at Versailles came out of the Crown purse, and he marveled at the profligacy of the French court. At least as many people were living at the palace as lived in the main town of the Seneca. But even feeding a crowd of this size seemed to make no appreciable dent in the royal budget. European monarchs, he reflected, were far wealthier than sachems of the Seneca.

As a matter of fact, the differences between rulers here and in the New World was vast. A sachem led his people because he had gained their total respect in all things, and they followed him willingly because they were aware of his strength and wisdom and courage. Here, a man inherited

270

his place, regardless of his abilities, and he ruled whether or not fit to reign. It was a very odd system.

Suddenly realizing that his mind was wandering and that he had lost all consciousness of time, he looked at the ornamental clock that stood on a nearby mantelpiece and realized it was almost time for his appointment with Arlene. He must leave, even though the major might be annoyed when he returned and found his companion missing.

Ja-gonh rose and made his way out of the hall, then walked quickly through the maze of corridors to the small apartment of Arlene and Ah-wen-ga, who shared a sitting room with separate bedchambers.

He had no way of knowing, to be sure, that de Bienville actually had preceded him to the suite a quarter of an hour earlier and had left before he came.

As Arlene had planned so carefully, she was alone in the suite when Ja-gonh arrived. She stood, took his hand, and held it far longer than necessary as she pressed it with seeming gratitude. "Thank you for coming here," she said. "I can never thank you enough."

"Is something amiss?" he asked in English.

She shook her head. "No, no, that isn't the problem."

"I was afraid," he said, "that it concerned Ah-wen-ga."

"No, she doesn't enter into the picture at all."

He breathed more easily. "That's all right, then," he said. "Do you happen to know where she is?"

Arlene contrived successfully to look surprised. "Why yes, she was with me in the dining hall."

"I looked for you there, but I didn't see either of you," he replied.

"Oh, dear. We were dining with a de Guise relative of mine at his request, and both of us waved to you across the hall and we were sure that you saw us. Apparently you didn't."

"I'm afraid I missed you," he said. "But as long as Ah-wen-ga is safe and well, nothing else matters."

Ah-wen-ga, Arlene reflected, soon would be as dead as

would Louis XV. Ja-gonh had seen her for the last time in
this world.

"May I know your problem, then?" he asked politely as
he produced the sheet of parchment which she had sent
him, and held it out to her.

She quickly took it from him with much relief; she
would have no need now to ask for its return, and before
he changed his mind, she threw it into the sitting room
grate, where a small fire was burning. The heavy paper
soon caught and was consumed. So much for that evidence, she thought.

Arlene smiled at him. "I don't mean to sound mysteri-
ous," she said, "but let us suppose that I had a sudden
and rather unexpected change for the better in my status
here. Suppose I became a great lady—"

"You are already a great lady," Ja-gonh interrupted.

"Thank you," she told him with a smile, "but I mean a
great lady according to the standards of Versailles. If that
should happen, I would be entitled to my own escort of
infantry or cavalry, and I wondered—that is, I was hoping—
that I might be able to persuade you to accept the post of
head of my bodyguard."

He wanted to reply as diplomatically as he could. "I'm
flattered by your offer," he said, "but I'm afraid it cannot
be. My place is with my own people."

"I knew you'd say that," Arlene replied, "and I'm not
suggesting that you leave the Seneca permanently. I was
thinking in terms of your taking such a post for approximately a year."

He remained dubious. She waved him to a divan,
poured him a liberal glass of brandywine, and then sank
onto the cushion beside him, close enough so their shoulders and thighs brushed. "A number of factors must be
considered, and I wish you'd listen before you give me
your definite reply," she said.

He could imagine nothing that would impel him to delay
his return to the New World once he and Ah-wen-ga
completed their strange mission here. But politeness

272

demanded that he listen, though under no circumstances did he intend to touch the brandywine.

Arlene saw the distaste flicker in his face as he glanced at the potent liquor, so she took hold of the glass herself, inhaled the aroma, and then sipped. "This is truly a delicious brandywine," she said. "I know you're not overly fond of alcoholic beverages, but I really urge you to try this."

He felt he had to oblige her and took a small sip. To his surprise, he felt no burning sensation in his mouth or throat. The liquor warmed his insides, but in no way made him uncomfortable as it slid down. It was as she said, a rather exceptional beverage.

She smiled up at him, flirting with him blatantly, and linked her arm through his. "In return for your services," she said, "I'd be willing to pay a very large sum of money. Much more, in fact, than you could earn in any other way. At the end of a year, you'd have enough money to return to the land of the Seneca with as many luxuries as you might crave."

Ja-gonh concealed a smile. He could think of no luxuries of the so-called civilized world that would make his life or Ah-wen-ga's more enjoyable in the years ahead. But he refrained from expressing his thoughts.

Carelessly, as though by accident, Arlene dropped a hand onto Ja-gonh's thigh. It remained for some moments, motionless, as though she wasn't even conscious of what she was doing. Then her fingers began to apply a gentle pressure, and her hand slid higher. "Most of all," she said softly, raising her face to his, "you and I would have a whole year together."

He was completely disconcerted by her brazen advances. Nothing in his experience had taught him how to deal with her, and he felt as though he was foundering in quicksand.

"You forget," he muttered, trying without success to forget the hand that continued to creep slowly up his thigh, "that I am going to marry Ah-wen-ga when we return to the land of the Seneca."

"I forget nothing," Arlene murmured. "I have no intention of coming between you and Ah-wen-ga or interfering with your marriage to her. But I am adult enough to know that when I want a man and he wants me, we are obliged to do something about it. If we make love together and we tell no one of what we're doing, we harm no others or ourselves. Ah-wen-ga will not be hurt because Ah-wen-ga will be none the wiser. You and I will be satisfied, and in time we'll rid ourselves of this great desire. I believe that a man and a woman should never fight their basic natures."

Suddenly she pressed close to him, and he was intensely aware of the powerful exotic scent she wore, of the proximity to his face of her scarlet lips, of the supple warmth of her body as she pressed against him.

Reacting instinctively, he swept her into his arms and bent his face toward hers. Arlene's lips parted for his kiss.

Her self-confidence seemed to have been fully justified. She was capable of gaining the full attention of any man whenever she wanted him. This Indian was no different from all her conquests, and she gave herself up to the sheer pleasure of the physical reactions that she was relishing.

All Ja-gonh felt was an overwhelming desire for this attractive woman, who was making herself available to him. He loved Ah-wen-ga, but his mind refused to function properly and his body took command and dictated what he would do next.

Arlene wriggled ecstatically, and one hand crept inside his open buckskin shirt to gently massage his chest.

That was when she made her error, although she never realized it, either then or later. A Seneca woman was trained to be docile in the early stages of lovemaking; only after she and her partner became thoroughly aroused was it permissible for her to seek her own pleasure in her own way. Until then, she was expected to be circumspect and demure.

Ja-gonh was startled that the young Frenchwoman was continuing to make advances. That was not right; her actions were contrary to all that he'd been taught about the relations of a man and a woman. Ah-wen-ga never would be guilty of such gross misconduct.

Ah-wen-ga! The mere thought brought her image to mind so forcibly that he could see her clearly, as though she were standing before him. At once his desire for Arlene deserted him. He found her too brazen, too eager, too anxious to please, like an Indian woman captured in battle who hoped to win her freedom by giving more than full measure to the man who took her.

Gently but firmly, Ja-gonh disengaged himself and moved away.

Arlene, thoroughly aroused, needed several moments before the realization dawned on her that the white Indian was putting her aside, that he suddenly wanted no more to do with her. She stared in stunned disbelief.

"If we go too far," Ja-gonh told her, "we will suffer regrets. You're far too lovely, and a man quickly loses his reason in your presence."

His compliment did much to assuage her humiliation and frustration. She forced a sultry smile. "I'm willing to risk suffering regrets if you are," she told him.

Ja-gonh stood and put a greater distance between them. "I have too much respect for you to take such a risk," he said.

Arlene's mind was whirling. Never—save when the King himself had grown tired of her—had any man rejected her charms. Even worse, it was imperative, she knew, to keep Ja-gonh busy while Ah-wen-ga was escorted to the hunting lodge.

It soon became all too plain to her that the young Seneca meant what he said. He obviously had no intention of becoming intimate with her. She consoled herself with the idea that in a very short time Ah-wen-ga would be dead and Ja-gonh would be free of his presumed obligations to her. Then, while grieving for her, he would be far more vulnerable than at present, and Arlene was confident of her ability to enmesh him in a romance under those conditions. In the meantime, she thought, he had no idea where

Ah-wen-ga had gone and, even more important, had no way of following her. De Bienville had left with her at least a half hour earlier, and by now he undoubtedly had delivered her to Louis. So, the drama would be played out to the end, and Ja-gonh could do nothing to halt the scheme concocted by Charles de Guise and Arlene.

Ja-gonh conceded thankfully that Arlene was accepting his rejection of her with the best of good grace. Almost in spite of himself, he admired her for her strength and her resourcefulness, and as he bowed to her and took his leave, he reflected that if she had not been so treacherous, and if he had not been promised to Ah-wen-ga, he might have been able to develop a deep interest in this woman.

Henri de Bienville offered Ah-wen-ga his arm as he led her down the corridor from her apartment. "Just where are we going?" she asked.

He replied quietly. "His Majesty has requested that you and he meet in another place. I will take you there."

"Oh!" she said and slowed her pace, troubled by the revelation. "The way my meeting with him was planned, Ja-gonh was to accompany me in order to explain to King Louis the feeling of the Iroquois and the need for an alliance between the French and the English."

"I'm well aware of that need, and you can be sure that your original plans will be fulfilled," de Bienville replied soothingly. "But the wishes of a ruling monarch cannot be denied, and he expressed the desire to see only you, so naturally he must be obeyed. I'm sure he'll be most agreeable when you explain to him that Ja-gonh also wishes to confer with him."

His answer mollified Ah-wen-ga, at least to an extent. She cast a sideways glance at him and he appeared sincere, but her instinct warned her that more was at stake here than met the eye. Perhaps what Henri was telling her was true, and she need have no cause for concern. On the other hand, it was possible, certainly, that he was taking advantage of her inexperience and that she might find herself in serious difficulty. After all, just why had Arlene insisted that she dress and use cosmetics with such great care; why had she fussed over her at much greater length than usual?

Aware that she could not refuse to accompany de Bienville without creating an embarrassing scene, Ah-wen-ga nevertheless resolved that she would take no chances. Her mind functioned swiftly and coolly in the emergency, and she decided quickly what she had to do. At least a half-dozen layers of pink silk net covered her skirt, and the removal of one of them would in no way effect the appearance of her costume. So, while clinging to the major's arm, she used her long fingernails of the other hand to dig into the top layer of net overskirt and tear out a small portion, perhaps a half-inch in diameter. This she dropped to the carpet, at a point where the corridor merged with several others.

She was putting into effect a plan that she could hope would bring help. By leaving a trail of net, she could insure that Ja-gonh would be able to follow her—if only he felt that she was in any danger when he learned what she was doing this afternoon.

De Bienville, who had no idea that she had dropped the snippet of silk net, led her to a staircase, then went toward the rear of the palace. He was deliberately avoiding the public room where they would be seen.

Ah-wen-ga, realizing that she was being taken to parts of the palace that she had never before visited, was now thoroughly suspicious.

When they emerged into the open, a de Guise retainer with which she had become familiar in Gascony awaited them with two horses. One was equipped with a sidesaddle; de Bienville helped her mount and then vaulted into his own saddle. He smiled at her. "We're going," he said, "to visit the King in a place that he's chosen that is away from the court. He dislikes having his every move seen by a thousand eyes."

Increasingly convinced now that her instinct for danger was accurate, she tore another bit of net from her skirt and dropped it.

The major led her onto a path that extended through a

grove of poplar trees. Again, she dropped a bit of the fragile cloth.

To her surprise, she found they were riding through deep woods as thick and as lush as the wilderness of North America. Here she saw plane trees and cedar, hickory and maple and oak. Although the autumn was well advanced, many of the colorful leaves still clung to the branches.

At intervals of every one hundred to two hundred yards, Ah-wen-ga dropped another piece of pink net. The trail she was leaving would be simple for Ja-gonh to follow, she knew, because their path seemed to be the only one through the woods. Now and again, she heard a rustling sound and realized wild animals were lurking in the thick underbrush.

"Is there game in this forest?" she inquired.

De Bienville chuckled. "Yes," he said, "deer and several kinds of fowl, and I believe wild boar as well. The woods are kept stocked by a gamekeeper, so that King Louis, like his grandfather, can go hunting when the mood strikes him. He doesn't have to leave home in order to do it."

Ah-wen-ga marveled at the power of the French monarchy. The very idea of stocking a private forest with game for an individual's amusement was too much for her to grasp. The Seneca, like all other tribes, depended for their livelihood on the animals of the forest, and she could not conceive of any man having his own private preserve created for him.

The trees thinned, and Ah-wen-ga caught a glimpse of a building ahead. To her surprise, it was a rustic lodge of logs that resembled the cabins of the English and French settlers in North America, though far sturdier and better constructed. Smoke curled from a chimney, indicating that someone was inside.

"This is our destination," her escort said. "King Louis awaits you."

She tore off a larger chunk of net from her skirt and dropped it to the ground as the major helped her from her saddle.

"Where can I go to check on my appearance before I meet him?" she demanded.

He took this as a good sign, and was heartened by her apparent willingness to play the role assigned to her so many months earlier. "I'm afraid there's no mirror," he said, "but you look fine."

She knew she would have to resort to subterfuge in order to be alone for a few moments. "Leave me to my own devices," she commanded, and turning her back to him, took a small pot of lip rouge from a reticule she carried and began to dab her lips.

De Bienville was sufficiently accustomed to feminine moods that he withdrew without further discussion. The instant that Ah-wen-ga was alone, she took her knife from her garter and carefully cut away the rest of the now-jagged overskirt of net. As she had anticipated, it was impossible for anyone looking at her to see that she had removed a portion of the costume. Not knowing what to do with the remains of the overskirt, she quickly stuffed it into the lower branches of an evergreen near the front entrance to the lodge. There she examined it, then pulled a bit of the material out so that it showed. Ja-gonh would see it, and would realize that she had gone into the lodge.

Satisfied with her handiwork, she called to de Bienville. He reappeared at once from the side of the building, where he had assured himself that Louis was indeed alone. The King had dismissed all his servants, as he had told Arlene that he would do, and no sentries or members of his personal staff were on hand to guard him. Fortune was truly playing into the hands of Charles de Guise.

To the amazement of Ah-wen-ga, de Bienville remounted his horse and took hers in rein. She stared at him in open-mouthed surprise. He smiled at her reassuringly.

"I was instructed," he told her, "to deliver you to the lodge and then to take myself elsewhere. You are to meet His Majesty alone." Giving her no chance to protest, he promptly rode off into the deep woods, and she was by herself. A sense of panic assailed her, but she managed to conquer it.

Ah-wen-ga knew now what she should have realized from the beginning. Arlene and Henri had not abandoned their original plan to make her the mistress of King Louis, but had pretended to accept the approach that she and Ja-gonh had suggested. She could not question that King Louis fully intended to seduce her once they were alone.

Two choices awaited her. First, she could flee; but she rejected the prospect of making her way through the woods and returning to the palace dressed as she was and wearing such flimsy, high-heeled sandals. In any event, she was afraid the effort would avail her nothing. Arlene would simply conspire again, and another rendezvous would be arranged.

The second alternative was dangerous but appealed to her far more. She would meet with Louis, as arranged, and would confront him with the truth. Certainly the Great Sachem always listened to the complaints and explanations of Iroquois before he passed judgment, and so did her father in his capacity of sachem of the Seneca. Louis, ruler of a nation larger, richer, and more powerful than even the entire Iroquois League, would be almost certain to be fair-minded. He would listen to what she had to tell him and then act accordingly. She had an opportunity, perhaps, to make him her friend, and through that friendship Ja-gonh would be able to win his support for the overall peace in the New World that they had envisioned.

Taking a deep breath, Ah-wen-ga turned, squared her shoulders, and walked to the front door, where she raised the brass knocker.

The sounds seemed to echo through the lodge and match the hammering of her heart.

She heard footsteps inside, and then was surprised when Louis himself opened the door. He was informally attired in silk breeches, an informal, open-necked silk shirt, and boots.

She realized that he had been expecting her, and he studied her quickly with practiced, appreciative eyes.

Ah-wen-ga's training had concentrated on just this moment. Keeping her face turned toward his and smiling limpidly, she sank to the floor in a deep, graceful curtsy.

Louis immediately offered her a hand. "There's no need for such formality, my dear," he said. "We're completely by ourselves here. I've seen to it that we will not be disturbed."

Ah-wen-ga knew beyond all doubt that he intended to seduce her, but her smile did not waver and nothing in her manner revealed the consternation she felt.

As she recognized at once, her peril was great. The King of France was no ordinary man and could not be treated as other men were treated. If she tried to protect herself by drawing her knife, she could be condemned to death, or, at the very least, imprisoned for many years.

Her one hope was to procrastinate and hope that somehow the monarch would lose interest in her. Viewing the situation realistically, she knew she was counting on a slender hope. Since she had no choice, she told herself to play the game as best she could and rely on that hope.

"You are very kind to satisfy my curiosity by meeting me here," King Louis said.

"Not at all, Your Majesty," she replied. "I'm flattered that you issued me the invitation."

Her response was only what he had anticipated, and he smiled. "Such formality is not necessary in private," he said. "I grant you permission to call me by my Christian name."

She knew that, according to his lights, he was granting her a great favor, so she reacted accordingly. "You're most generous, Louis," she murmured.

He led her into a very large drawing room and poured wine into two waiting glasses. "You, I gather, have an unusual Indian name," he said.

"I am called Ah-wen-ga," she replied simply.

"What does it mean?"

She found it difficult to translate from the Seneca tongue into French. "I can best explain it by saying that my name means that I am a steady shot," she replied.

He could not conceal his astonishment. "You're joking, surely!" he exclaimed.

Ah-wen-ga shook her head. "I don't suppose you have any bows and arrows on hand in this place?"

He smiled broadly. "As it happens, I do," he said. "My great-grandfather's favorite sport was deer hunting with bow and arrow, and I've been persuaded to follow the pastime myself although I've never been very much interested in it. Let me find you the weapons." He began to rummage in a large closet that opened off the sitting room.

She was relieved, because the activity was impersonal and temporarily, at least, took his mind off his purpose.

"Ah, here we are," he said at last and brought out an unstrung bow and a quiver of arrows.

The bow was considerably smaller than that used by the Seneca for either hunting or war, but Ah-wen-ga came alive at the sight of the familiar weapon.

Louis was astonished by the transformation in her. One moment she looked passively seductive and the next instant she was alert, surprisingly active, and agile.

She strung the bow expertly, tested it, and remembering her manners, asked, "May I?"

Not knowing what to expect, Louis assented.

She drew an arrow from the quiver and walked to the nearest set of French windows, which she proceeded to open. Notching an arrow into the bow, she gazed out across a neatly trimmed flower bed. Her gaze was concentrated on the woods that stood about fifty yards from the house, and at last she found what she was seeking. On a branch ten feet above the ground, a single, reddish-gold leaf was clinging stubbornly. She measured the distance carefully and felt confident she could hit her target.

Her confidence was not misplaced. She had fought hard and effectively beside Sun-ai-yee, her father, when a Huron force had surprised the main town of the Seneca during the absence of the warriors on a military expedition. With her invaluable help, the Huron had been repulsed, and Renno himself had praised her when he had returned home.

"With your permission," she said, "I shall dislodge the gold leaf from its resting place."

Following her pointing finger, Louis could not resist smiling. Everyone, it seemed, was guilty of boasting in his presence in order to impress him, and this Indian was no exception. Well, he thought wryly, she was sufficiently lovely that in her case he was willing to be generous, and after she shot the arrow he would listen to her inevitable excuses as to why she had missed the target. "You're sure it isn't too difficult?" he asked considerately.

Ah-wen-ga shook her head and notched the arrow into her bow. Again, her whole manner changed. In spite of her great femininity, she stood like a man with her feet planted apart, the muscles in her arms and back straining as she drew back the bow and sighted the target by staring down the length of the arrow.

Louis was impressed. If she was no archer, she certainly was a splendid play-actress.

The arrow made a sound that was part hiss, part whine as it sped through the air. Suddenly the leaf vanished and the arrow disappeared with it into the forest.

King Louis stared at the spot where the target had been, unable to believe the evidence before his eyes. Never had he seen such marksmanship with a bow. Never had he realized that anyone could use the primitive weapon with such skill.

Ah-wen-ga was quietly pleased, but reverted instantly to her Seneca ways; her face became expressionless. Under no circumstances would she gloat or otherwise indicate that she had succeeded brilliantly. "Is there some other target you would like me to hit?"

The monarch shook his head, unable to overcome his astonishment. This remarkable young woman was much deeper than met the eye. He had been thinking of her only as a mistress, but it appeared she was capable of being a great deal more.

At last he was able to speak. "I think it would be impossible to improve on your remarkable exhibition," he said, his wonder reflected in his voice. "Sit down with me, drink your wine, and tell me how you happened to acquire such an unusual talent."

Ah-wen-ga accompanied him to a divan and lowered herself demurely to a seat at arm's length from him. "I see nothing miraculous in what I have done," she said. "Any woman of the Seneca could duplicate my feat. The warriors, who practice constantly and often go hunting, are far superior to us, of course."

Louis, staring at her, wondered if he was dreaming. His erotic desire for her was somnolent for the moment, and he wanted to hear more about the people who took such feats of extraordinary skill for granted.

Ja-gonh breathed more easily after he had left Arlene's suite. He had suffered a narrow escape and was relieved that he had not further complicated his existence. Puzzled by his inability to locate Ah-wen-ga, he needed time to try to figure out her whereabouts. That was not easy in a place as extensive as the palace of the French King.

When he came to the end of the corridor, he caught sight of a bit of pink net on the dark carpet, and he bent down to pick it up.

As he held it in his hand, examining it carefully, he realized at once that it was part of the skirt that Ah-wen-ga had been wearing when presented to King Louis that morning. It looked as though the bit of fabric, ripped from the skirt, had fallen to the floor.

Taking no chances, he walked more slowly, and ultimately his patience was rewarded when he caught a glimpse of another bit of silk net. It was not accidental that these scraps from Ah-wen-ga's skirt were lying on the floor, he decided: she was deliberately signaling to him, telling him her whereabouts and asking him to follow a trail left for him. He had no doubt that this was the case. The leaving of a trail when in danger was a standard Seneca procedure, and he felt positive that Ah-wen-ga was following the custom of their people.

He dismissed everything else from his mind, and concentrated his full attention on the trail. Occasionally he glanced at his surroundings, and ultimately he noted that having left the palace, he was headed toward the thick woods behind the formal gardens.

Plunging into the forest, he felt a deep wave of nostalgia for the wilderness that was so far away. The smell of earth and rotting vegetation was like rare perfume in his nostrils, and he breathed deeply, happily. At last he felt at home, now he was in his element.

Unthinkingly, he broke into a rapid trot and, still following the trail left by the bits of cloth, had no difficulty in making his way down the path through the woods. For whatever reason, Ah-wen-ga had gone—or had been taken—to some destination outside the palace.

With all of his senses alert, Ja-gonh moved silently and stealthily when it occurred to him that he was not alone. Other men were abroad here and, as nearly as he could tell, had not yet become aware of his presence; very well, he would not disclose himself.

He heard voices to his left and paused to investigate. What he saw surprised him. Three burly guards, all of them carrying muskets, were speaking in low tones as they made their way slowly in the same direction that he was traveling. They were wearing the green uniforms of the Duc de Guise, uniforms with which he had become so familiar at the castle in Gascony. Why these same troops—or others, very much like them—should be abroad in the forest of Versailles was too confusing a riddle for him to solve.

He returned to the path and continued to follow the trail that Ah-wen-ga had left. Covering ground swiftly, Ja-gonh caught a glimpse of daylight ahead and realized that the woods were thinning. Then he halted, his eyes narrowing when he recognized Captain de Sanson, who carried a loaded, cocked pistol in one hand while leading a file of troops who were spreading out. Apparently they were in the process of surrounding a building that stood in a clearing beyond the edge of the woods. All were armed and, like Captain de Sanson, were grimly intent on their business.

As Ja-gonh watched, any doubts that lingered in his mind

were quickly dispelled. The "household troops" of the Duc de Guise very definitely were surrounding the building. Suddenly, he saw the remains of Ah-wen-ga's overskirt peeping out from the branches of the evergreen near the entrance to the lodge. This, he knew, was where the trail ended.

He knew, too, that for reasons he could not fathom, Ah-wen-ga, inside the lodge, was endangered by the maneuvers of these retainers of the Duc de Guise. He moved boldly into the open and pounded on the door.

A startled Louis XV, annoyed by being interrupted in his rendezvous, came to the door and was furious when he saw the white Indian on the threshold.

Looking over the monarch's shoulder, Ja-gonh caught a glimpse of Ah-wen-ga sitting on a divan in a large room. Relieved beyond measure that he had found her, his one thought was for her safety. He brushed past Louis as he hurried to her. The outraged King closed the door and followed, intending to give the intruder a piece of his mind.

Ah-wen-ga, seeing Ja-gonh, jumped to her feet. She was almost overcome with joy that he had found her trail and had followed it, but at the same time she was afraid that he now would be in serious trouble with King Louis, who so obviously resented this intrusion.

For the monarch's benefit, Ja-gonh spoke in English. "You may be in grave difficulties here," he said. "Did you know that troops of the Duc de Guise have surrounded this building?"

Color drained from Louis's face. "You're joking!" he gasped.

"I do not joke about serious matters," Ja-gonh replied tartly. "Ja-gonh, son of Renno, speaks the truth to Louis of France. I know the troops of de Guise when I see them, and I know their commander. They are armed with muskets, and they are at this very moment in the process of encircling us."

Too late, Louis realized that he had fallen into a vicious trap set for him by ruthless, ambitious foes. Using Ah-wen-ga as bait, they had tempted him into coming alone to the hunting lodge. Now they could dispose of him as they wished.

Louis sank into the divan. "I'm doomed," he said. "If you two are acting in concert with de Guise, I surrender to you without a fight."

Ja-gonh and Ah-wen-ga exchanged a startled glance. "I don't know what you mean," Ah-wen-ga said in French, and then repeated the words to Ja-gonh in the Seneca language.

Perhaps she too was a dupe, Louis conjectured. He was too frightened to determine any connection that Ja-gonh might have with his enemies. In short, halting sentences, he explained that the Duc de Guise apparently had isolated him and undoubtedly was planning to murder him and seize the throne himself. Ah-wen-ga gasped, then hastily repeated to Ja-gonh what the monarch had told her.

Ja-gonh strode to the nearest window and, concealing himself behind the thick drapes, peered out. "It is as I have said," he declared. "Many men have gathered, and all carry muskets." He turned to Louis and demanded sternly, "Are you sure these men are traitors who seek your life?"

"Unfortunately, I am very certain," Louis replied in a broken voice. "I dismissed the musketeers who would ordinarily stand guard over me, and I'm to blame for the situation in which I find myself. Now I'll pay the supreme penalty for my folly."

Ja-gonh smiled grimly. "It is never wise," he said, "to surrender before one gives battle. One can always find ample time to surrender only when no alternative remains."

"What alternative is there?" Louis demanded miserably.

Ja-gonh picked up the bow and the quiver of arrows that Ah-wen-ga had used and handed them to her. "You know what to do," he told her in the language of the Seneca. "Go to the windows that face toward the south. I will attend to the windows that face the north." As he headed across the room, he removed his own bow from his shoulder and reached for an arrow.

Louis gaped first at the girl, then at the young warrior. His situation was impossible, hopeless, and he began to laugh hysterically. He, who commanded the largest army of any ruler in Europe, who had a navy of hundreds of powerful ships, was forced to depend on a savage Indian and a girl of the same breed for his very life.

Ja-gonh paid no attention to the King but pushed open a pair of French windows and looked out carefully.

"Take no risks," he called to Ah-wen-ga in the Seneca tongue. "Our foes' muskets are not accurate, but it is likely that de Guise's men have learned to compensate for their inaccuracies."

"I understand," she replied calmly.

"Shoot only to kill. Shoot only when you have a clear target. Many attackers are out there, but only two of us are here to defend Louis, who pities himself so much that he has rendered himself useless."

"I will do as you direct," Ah-wen-ga said. She was in her element at last. The seductive poses and flirtatious tricks were forgotten as she faced this moment of supreme crisis. This was the essence of Seneca living, the purpose for which all Seneca were trained from earliest childhood. She understood what had to be done, and she rejoiced in her ability to do it well.

Still concealed behind the drapes, Ja-gonh notched an arrow into his bow, took careful aim, and let fly with it.

A high-pitched scream was followed by a shocked silence as the arrow struck its target and one of the de Guise retainers crumpled, dead before his body struck the ground.

Now it was Ah-wen-ga's turn. Taking care not to be seen by the men lurking outside, she drew a bead on one dark, square-shouldered figure, and her arrow sang its hymn of death as it sped toward its target. It, too, struck home and a second of de Guise's men died.

The attackers had assumed they could accomplish their mission easily and quickly, inasmuch as they were assaulting a helpless King and an equally helpless young woman. Now they were discovering how badly they had erred.

Before they had a chance to react, Ja-gonh had drawn another arrow from his quiver and once more let fly. Again, he struck his target squarely, and another of the de Guise troops was felled.

Ah-wen-ga took longer to fit an arrow into her bow and sight a target, but she made up in meticulous attention to detail what she lacked in speed. She, too, enjoyed another success.

Captain de Sanson, watching the unexpected developments from a vantage point in the forest, was so astonished that he stood motionless until the Duc de Guise galvanized him into action.

"For God's sake, Captain, do something before your troops are all killed!" Charles de Guise demanded in a grating voice.

Captain de Sanson was jarred into reality and ordered his men to take cover. As they broke ranks, Ja-gonh's bow and a fresh arrow unerringly sought and found yet another victim.

What made the situation so eerie was the silence in the hunting lodge. The defenders made no sound, and they managed to stay out of sight of the troops, who began to think that perhaps some supernatural force was at work protecting Louis from his enemies.

The King, watching the spectacle from the center of the sitting room, stared hard at Ja-gonh and at the briskly competent young Seneca woman who had taken up her battle position opposite the young warrior. The realization gradually dawned that perhaps his situation was not as hopeless as he had feared.

"I have a pair of dueling pistols and a considerable quantity of spare ammunition in the bedchamber," the King said. "Shall I fetch it?"

Ah-wen-ga, speaking softly, translated his words into the Seneca language.

Ja-gonh took care to reply again in English, which he knew the monarch understood. "By all means, get the weapons," he said. "We've no way of telling when your help may be needed, but don't walk out of this room. You could be seen from the woods outside and you'd be a prime target the instant you're recognized."

Louis was bewildered. "If I don't walk," he said, "how can I get the weapons and ammunition?"

It seemed to Ja-gonh that although Louis XV was a powerful ruler, he was lacking in common sense. "Crawl!" he directed.

Dropping to all fours, His Christian Majesty crawled from the sitting room into the adjoining chamber. The seduction of the Indian woman was far from his mind now. All that mattered was survival.

Ah-wen-ga measured another target and fired again.

Ja-gonh heard the singing of her arrow and without turning, demanded, "Well?"

"I missed," she said in a crestfallen voice.

"That happens to anyone, even the greatest of Seneca warriors," he replied. "Dismiss it from your mind. Do not for a moment think in terms of possible failure. You will succeed because you must."

"I will succeed," she repeated, "because I must."

"Count the enemy as best you can," he said, "and let me know what you find." He immediately began his own count.

It was very quiet in the room as Louis crawled back to the sitting room, his dueling pistols in his belt, his pockets bulging with spare ammunition.

"There are at least thirty, I think," Ah-wen-ga said.

Ja-gonh reverted to English. "Add it to my count, that makes a total of more than seventy. We can hold them off for a time, but if they decide to make a concerted rush, we shall not be able to survive."

Louis had recovered his wits, and his mind was functioning again, even to the point of his communicating in English so that Ja-gonh could understand him. "I think it unlikely that they'll rush the lodge," he said, "because they would have to use their firearms in order to neutralize your arrows. We're isolated here, it's true, and it appears that help is very far away. But that isn't really the case. We're only two miles from Versailles, and over one thousand of my musketeers are stationed there. My personal staff knows that I'm here at the lodge, and if heavy and continuous gunfire is heard, a troop of mounted musketeers is certain to be here within minutes."

"Do you have any method of communicating with your subjects in the palace?"

"I come to this place only when I want to be totally undisturbed," Louis said.

Ja-gonh understood clearly that Louis had arranged for a rendezvous with Ah-wen-ga and that she had been inveigled or tricked into meeting him here. But this was not the time to think of such matters—when their lives were at stake.

"Ah-wen-ga, do you have any thoughts?"

"The de Guise troops know me from my stay in Gascony," she said, "and I know their captain is very much attracted to me. Perhaps if I were to try to reach the palace, they would allow me to pass."

Louis was very firm. "I refuse to permit it," he said. "Men who are intent on killing their monarch are not going to draw the line at murdering a young woman, no matter how innocent she might be. They'd take a shot at you the minute you stepped outside."

His words gave Ja-gonh an idea, but before he could explore the thought, another of the de Guise retainers presented a clear target and he fired another arrow. Again his aim was unerring. "What were they planning, do you know? Do you have any idea how they were intending to kill you?"

"I assume," Louis replied, "that they had intended to sneak up on the lodge and to burst in. In that way, they could have killed the girl and me with a very few shots, and they would have had time to disperse quickly before the musketeers could assemble and make their way here from the palace. Your unexpected arrival put a crimp in their plans."

Ja-gonh fell silent for a time. "You can thank Ah-wenga of the Seneca," he said, "for leaving a trail that led me here. Who brought you to this place, Ah-wen-ga?"

"Henri de Bienville," she said.

The white line around the King's mouth grew tighter.

"That means that he was a member of this conspiracy, and so is Lady Arlene. Both are traitors," Ja-gonh mused.

"If I survive this day," Louis said softly, "may the Lord have mercy on their souls."

"How long will your staff remain absent from this lodge?" Ja-gonh asked.

Louis's laugh in response was hopeless. "No help will be coming from them," he said, "because no alarm will be given. When I am engaged in a private rendezvous with a lady, all in my employ are instructed not to disturb me under any circumstances. I would say it would be tomorrow noon at the very earliest before they would begin to suspect something amiss."

Though Louis had intended to seduce Ah-wen-ga, the manitous, watching over her, had saved her from such a fate, Ja-gonh thought.

Oddly, the realization encouraged him. The manitous had not intervened on her behalf only to see her and Ja-gonh lose their lives in a battle with the troops of the Duc de Guise.

A basic tenet of Ghonka's was that the tactics of any military situation should be dictated by the circumstances and conditions found at the time of combat. Renno, too, believed in this theory and had practiced it. Now it was Ja-gonh's turn, and his mind revolved rapidly.

At last, a scheme took shape in his mind. Risks were involved in it—serious risks—but unless he took an initiative, the chances were that he and the others would be overwhelmed. It seemed better to be daring and take a chance than to acknowledge certain defeat.

"Louis of the French," he asked solemnly, "are you quick on your feet? Can you move rapidly?"

Unaccustomed to being addressed so bluntly, the King would have taken umbrage had his dilemma not been so grave. "I've never had any particular reason to be swift on my feet," he said, "but I daresay I'm fairly agile. What do you have in mind?"

"We have seen and killed several of the troops who are intent on murdering you," Ja-gonh said, "but we have not yet set eyes on their commander."

"You think that Captain de Sanson is directly involved?" Ah-wen-ga asked in surprise.

"I have learned enough about the armies of the Old World," Ja-gonh replied, "to know that the troops never take action on their own. Always an officer guides them. Not only is the captain undoubtedly concealed in the forest, but I assume the Duc de Guise is there as well."

"That's a shrewd observation," Louis said. "Charles de Guise will claim my throne the instant that my heart stops beating. I'm sure he is waiting nearby to assure himself that his men will be successful."

"That fits my thinking," Ja-gonh said. "I propose a daring and unorthodox move. I propose that Louis of the French unlock the front door of this house, open it, and stand in the frame for several seconds. His presence will electrify the enemy. Their commander will instruct them to fire at him. He will make no move until he sees the troops start to raise their muskets, then he will shut the door as rapidly as he can, and will throw himself to the floor. If their fire is accurate, the bullets will pass over his head when they penetrate the door."

Ah-wen-ga was puzzled. "Why should Louis take this great risk with his life?"

A gleam of hard humor appeared in Ja-gonh's pale eyes. "It is my wish," he said, "to flush out the leaders of this conspiracy. You and I will station ourselves in hiding at the windows on either side of the door. When the troops first see and recognize Louis, they will call out this information. It is my hope that the captain and the Duc de Guise, also, will come to see for themselves that it is truly Louis who stands exposed before them. That is when we act. I claim the Duc de Guise as my target, and I demand this right as a senior warrior of the Seneca. But you will be active also, Ah-wen-ga. You will put an arrow into the heart of Captain de Sanson."

Ah-wen-ga reflected momentarily that because the captain had been her ardent admirer, she would find it extremely difficult to kill him in cold blood. Then she reminded herself that though he knew of her presence in the lodge, he was in no way deterred. Instead, he planned to kill her. She hardened herself for the ordeal to come.

"With their leaders dispatched to the land of their ancestors," Ja-gonh said, "the troops will have no one to guide them. Then after we have sent a few more arrows into their midst and have killed or wounded several of them, they will rapidly lose their appetite for battle. They will retreat. Then they will realize the enormity of the crime they have committed. They have raised their hands against the Great Sachem of the French, and they are traitors to their homeland. They will be concerned only with their safety, and they will flee from this place and from the palace. We will then be free to summon help as best we can or to go ourselves to the palace in safety."

Louis XV was deeply impressed by this reasoning. Though the man was a savage, he understood human nature, and it was impossible to find fault with his plan.

"Does Louis of France have the courage to play his part in this plan?" Ja-gonh demanded bluntly.

The King laughed ruefully. "If I don't have the courage," he said, "at least I am sufficiently lacking in good sense that I approve heartily of the scheme. You may count on my complete cooperation."

Ja-gonh grinned at him, and the courtiers would have been horrified had they seen him grasp the monarch's shoulder and shake him affectionately.

"We will win a victory as complete as it is totally unexpected," Ja-gonh assured him. Then he began to speak solemnly in his own tongue.

Louis looked at him, glanced at Ah-wen-ga, and was about to question her, but she shook her head.

The monarch assumed that he was praying, and in a sense, he was right. Ja-gonh was asking the manitous for their help in the coming, critical stage of the battle.

He crawled across the living room so he would not be seen from the forest through the window, and Ah-wen-ga followed his example. He concealed himself behind the drapes at the window on one side of the door, and Ah-wen-ga did the same at the window on the other side. They took their time selecting arrows and fitting them into their bows, and when Ah-wen-ga was ready she motioned to Ja-gonh.

"We are ready, Louis of France," Jagonh called softly. "You may begin at any time."

Louis drew a pistol and, holding it in his right hand, opened the front door with his left. Pale but erect, looking more like a monarch than he did wearing his robes of office, he faced the forest.

In the background Ja-gonh, with his keen eyesight, was able to make out dark, scurrying shapes. Suddenly Ah-wen-ga's voice broke in. "There's Captain de Sanson and there's an older man with him."

"Now, Louis!" Ja-gonh called urgently, "close the door!"

The monarch obediently slammed the door and dropped to the floor.

Almost simultaneously a volley of shots rang out from the edge of the forest. Just as Ja-gonh had anticipated, the King had proved to be too tempting a target, and the Duc de Guise had ordered the shots fired because he was, by this time, willing to take the risk that the volley might be heard at Versailles.

Ja-gonh did not hesitate. Aiming his arrow, he pulled his bow taut and released the shaft. It flew straight for Charles de Guise and was a perfectly aimed shot, landing directly between his eyes and felling him instantly. He bled surprisingly little as he died.

Captain de Sanson watched in horror as his superior dropped to the ground.

Ah-wen-ga knew that now she had to do her part; no excuse for evasion nor for failure was possible. She took aim, and when she released her arrow, a cold, clammy sensation enveloped her. She unconsciously held her breath and did not release it until she saw the officer fall to the ground, his life ended. For reasons she could not understand and did not want to analyze, she felt like weeping.

"Now," Ja-gonh called softly, "kill as many troops as you can." He shot arrow after arrow with astonishing rapidity and deadly accuracy.

Ah-wen-ga knew she was no match for him but was determined to contribute what she could. She brought down two more of the de Guise retainers.

The survivors drew back into the woods and disappeared from sight. Ja-gonh breathed a trifle more easily. "We'll wait for a time before we venture into the open."

It was strange, the young Seneca thought, that he felt no satisfaction at having outwitted the enemy. Actually, he shouldn't have cared which faction won the battle, but he was instinctively on the side of the constituted authority. Aware of the problems his father had encountered in the past with occasional rebellious Iroquois, he had an intuitive dislike for traitors.

To the astonishment of all three, who were peering out from behind the blinds, Major Henri de Bienville appeared out of the woods and walked slowly toward the lodge, his sword gripped in his right hand.

Ja-gonh instantly fitted another arrow into his bow, but Louis touched him on the shoulder. "Wait!" he whispered.

Dr. Bienville halted about fifty feet from the house and searched the windows in vain for some sign of life. "Your Majesty! Do you hear me?" he called out.

"I hear you, Major," Louis replied from his place of concealment.

Henri de Bienville was taking a great risk in pursuing his bluff, but he knew he had no alternative. "I call on Your Majesty to surrender," he shouted. "The lodge is surrounded by the forces of Charles de Guise, and I call upon you to give up your throne to him."

Louis laughed. "Charles de Guise is dead," he said. "As dead as you soon shall be." He raised his pistol, took careful aim, and squeezed the trigger.

Henri de Bienville staggered backward, his hands grasping his chest, a look of utter bewilderment on his face. Perhaps he could find some shred of satisfaction in the knowledge, in dying, that he had been shot by the King himself.

A long silence followed, as the sound of the shot echoed and subsided.

"Louis uses a pistol well," Ja-gonh observed mildly. "It is good that you killed yet another leader of the traitors."

Ah-wen-ga was disturbed. She had come to know Henri de Bienville well in the months since her abduction, and though he had been her captor, she felt a twinge of regret.

"I think," Ja-gonh said, "that the soldiers of de Guise have run away. We shall soon find out." Hastening to the door, he opened it and walked slowly into the open space.

No one fired at him and no sign of life came from the woods.

He walked toward the line of trees and dropped to one knee near the body of Charles de Guise. His knife flashed in his hand.

"What in God's name is he doing?" Louis XV demanded, reverting to French.

Ah-wen-ga smiled. "Ja-gonh killed Charles de Guise in fair combat," she said, "and he is claiming the spoils of battle as his right."

"The spoils?" the monarch asked faintly.

"Ja-gonh," she said, "is taking the scalp of de Guise, and he will wear it in his belt for all time."

The King averted his gaze as Ja-gonh stood and returned to the lodge, the scalp dangling from his belt.

As he entered the building, the sound of pounding horses' hooves filled the air, and suddenly several score of mounted King's Musketeers poured into the open and surrounded the lodge. All were armed with their sabers and pistols; their commander, a colonel, looked very concerned.

Louis XV chuckled. "It will give me great pleasure," he said, "to inform my musketeers that they have arrived too late. We won the battle without them!"

Lady Arlene, stunned by the defeat of Charles de Guise, as well as by his death, and Henri's, had started to flee for her own life. On second thought, she recognized that she had no place to go, no place to hide. Perhaps, she speculated wildly, she would not be connected with the plot on the King. That hope seemed to be nurtured by a message summoning her to his private apartment.

She changed with almost unseemly haste into a form-fitting black gown, patched her makeup, and hurried to the King's quarters. Everything appeared normal as she arrived, and the officer of musketeers on sentinel duty saluted as he admitted her; clearly he had orders to send her in immediately.

Louis was taking his ease in a comfortable chair, wearing an open-necked shirt and a pair of house slippers that he preferred to the toe-pinching shoes that fashion dictated. He smiled broadly, sipped his wine, and scrutinized her carefully as she curtsied.

"Well, Arlene," he said. "You do preserve your beauty. I must say you're every bit as lovely today as in the days when we knew each other more intimately."

Her hope flared higher, and she answered demurely, "You're being too kind."

"Kind?" he inquired. "Not at all. I'm stating facts. And while on the subject of facts, I'm slightly surprised to find that you were involved in a serious conspiracy against my life."

Panic welled up within her. "I was not a party to conspiracy!" she protested vehemently. "I'm sure I can explain to your complete satisfaction—"

"No explanation will be necessary," he interrupted. "I've already learned the whole truth from other sources, including Ah-wen-ga."

Had Ah-wen-ga become Louis's mistress and told him the whole story of her abduction and training, Arlene wondered, now regretting that she had not protected herself by inventing some plausible story and insisting that Ah-wen-ga repeat it to the monarch.

"The question now is what to do with you," Louis said pleasantly. "De Guise, your cousin, is dead, and so is de

Bienville. I would order you executed, but truly that would cause me pain."

Arlene finally realized that he did indeed know the full story of the conspiracy; anything she might have told Ah-wen-ga to repeat to him would have been irrelevant.

"I have pondered this problem and have happily found a splendid solution," Louis told her. "It is one that not only satisfies my sense of justice, but enables you to employ your considerable talents to their best possible use"

She sensed that he was only toying with her, amusing himself at her expense, but she was too frightened to try to respond.

"France and the Ottoman Empire," he continued, "have been gradually moving toward an alliance. That pact is now all but sealed. The Sultan sent me a magnificent diamond-hilted dagger, and it is so dazzling that I cannot possibly compete with him by sending him diamonds or emeralds in return. Consequently, I will send him a priceless pearl."

He smiled broadly. "*You* will be my gift to the Sultan. I command that you now be removed to the port of Brest, where you will be taken on board a French warship for immediate transport to Constantinople."

Arlene gaped, certain that he was joking, but a chill crept slowly up her spine as she realized that he was in earnest.

"You—you are sending me to join the harem of the Sultan of the Ottoman Empire?" she asked incredulously.

Louis rubbed his hands together. "An admirable solution, as I'm sure you'll agree. Your natural proclivities are such that you will soon become a favorite of the Sultan. You're very quick-witted as well, so you'll have no trouble in learning to speak Turkish, and I'm sure you'll find ways to get along beautifully with others in the harem."

She clenched her fists and, sputtering, started to protest.

The King snapped his fingers, and two burly musketeers hurried in from the adjoining chamber. They caught hold of Arlene's arms and began to drag her from the suite.

"Be sure you give my best regards to the Sultan," Louis called in an amiable voice, "and do remember that you're representing France at his court."

His dry chuckle followed her down the corridor as she was carted off to a punishment unlike any that she had imagined possible.

By command of Louis XV, all members of his court were ordered to attend a formal audience to be held in the Hall of Mirrors at sundown.

The smokeless tapers, a proud invention of the French, burned in the huge chandeliers and were reflected in the mirrors that lined every wall in the vast chamber. The ladies and gentlemen of the court, aware that this would be a special occasion, wore their finest. The men pinned their various decorations to their tunics, and the officers of the army and navy appeared in full-dress uniforms. Louis appeared at one end of the hall, his gold crown, a heritage from Henri IV, on his head, and his slender frame encased in a robe of ermine. As the men bowed low and the women curtsied, he made his way slowly to the dais at the far end and mounted his throne. When he had seated himself, a deep hush settled over the assemblage.

"Many stories have come to our attention concerning our recent brush with death," the monarch proclaimed. "Let us still those rumors by saying that the conspiracy against us has been crushed, and those who participated in it have received their just deserts. Some have lost their lives, and others have received chastisement of a different sort.

"We must stress that we owe our life and our well-being to two remarkable young people, neither of whom is our subject. Will Ja-gonh, the son of Renno, and Ah-wen-ga, the daughter of Sun-ai-yee, please step forward and approach the throne."

The white Indian, attired in his buckskins, and Ah-wen-ga, radiant in a gown of white silk, marched arm in arm down the length of the red carpet. It was apparent from their expressions that both were surprised and had not anticipated taking part in the ceremonies.

"France is permanently in your debt," Louis told them when they had mounted the dais and stood before him. "You saved my life, giving no thought to your own safety. Your unselfishness and your courage will be remembered in this country for all time."

The members of the court broke into wild applause.

"If you were French," Louis continued, "I would make you members of my nobility, but that would be superfluous because you already are nobles in your own land. If physical possessions had meaning to you, I would reward you with gifts of land, but I don't wish to insult you by impugning your motives when you came to my aid with nothing but my welfare in mind. Therefore, I have determined to give you special gifts that will serve as reminders of me and of the nation that will always hold both of you in high esteem."

He signaled to a chamberlain who approached, carrying a velvet pillow on which rested two gold chains.

King Louis looped the chains around the necks of Ah-wen-ga and Ja-gonh, and members of the court gasped. Each chain supported a French fleur-de-lis, made entirely of diamonds. As the gems picked up the candlelight, their brilliance dazzled the assemblage.

Ja-gonh, answering for both, proudly elected to speak in his own language, which Ah-wen-ga translated phrase by phrase into French. "We rejoice in the friendship of Louis and of his people. On behalf of the Seneca and of the Iroquois League, I must express the hope that we never again meet on the field of battle as enemies, but that we will join hands with each other and with the colonists from England to create a permanent peace in the New World."

As Roger Harkness remarked later in the carriage that, surrounded by an armed escort, took them all to a French warship at the port of Brest, from where they would sail to the New World, "I never expected to see the day when you'd put the diplomats of France and England to shame, Ja-gonh."

"Yes," Patience Harkness added. "You didn't speak very long, but your words had quite an impact. I don't see how it would be possible in our lifetimes for France to make war on the Iroquois or the English colonies again."

Ja-gonh looked down at the fleur-de-lis on his chest. "I hope you're right," he said solemnly, "but when we reach home I shall urge my father to remain vigilant. I have learned much about Europe and its rulers, and I think it is wise to take no chances. They mean well but they have short memories."

The voyage homeward in the man-of-war was uneventful, and the vessel—the first French fighting ship ever to visit Massachusetts Bay peacefully—put into Boston Harbor. A huge crowd gathered, and after Roger and Patience came ashore, they were treated to the spectacle of seeing two Seneca wearing magnificent diamond French fleurs-de-lis come down the gangplank.

Roger paid a courtesy visit to the governor of Massachusetts Bay and brought him up to date on developments in France. The two young couples then made their way to Fort Springfield, where General and Mrs. Wilson were delighted to see their daughter and son-in-law again. The young couple planned to stay for several days while Patience enjoyed the reunion and Roger prepared reports and made ready for the trip to Virginia.

But the Seneca couple did not linger in spite of the overwhelming hospitality offered to them. They were eager to return home after so long an absence. Their eagerness was sharpened when they learned of Renno's desperate illness and of El-i-chi's marriage to Deborah.

Refusing the loan of horses, Ja-gonh and Ah-wen-ga set out on foot through the wilderness. This was their natural element, and they made excellent time as they moved ever closer to the land of the Seneca. At last, late one morning, the sound of sentries' drums told them that they had truly come home. The sentinels were passing along word that Ja-gonh and Ah-wen-ga were arriving.

Ordinarily, they would have gone all the way to the main town of the Seneca to be greeted by their parents—but Renno and Betsy, Sun-ai-yee and Talking Quail, were too impatient for the reunion, and they hurried out through the forest to meet them.

Renno saw them first from a considerable distance. Studying them carefully, he noted that his son's heavy tan had faded somewhat, but that otherwise he looked fit. He observed, too, that Ah-wen-ga appeared radiantly happy and none the worse for her grueling experience.

What puzzled the Great Sachem were the glittering objects that both wore on gold chains around their necks.

A few minutes later, they were finally reunited. Only Talking Quail forgot her dignity as the wife of a Seneca sachem and had to brush tears from her eyes. All four parents embraced Ah-wen-ga; Ja-gonh solemnly bowed to his mother and Talking Quail, then exchanged salutes with his father and Sun-ai-yee.

"I have fulfilled my mission," Ja-gonh announced solemnly. "I have obtained vengeance for the murder of my grandfather and for the abduction of Ah-wen-ga. The Huron half-breed who was responsible for both crimes is dead, by my hand. The French officer who assisted in the abduction of Ah-wen-ga has also gone to the land of his ancestors, and the woman who worked with them has received a terrible and cruel punishment from the King of France."

Renno promptly offered thanks to the manitous for their help in enabling his son to keep his vow. Then, his curiosity overcoming him, he asked about the meaning of the diamond fleurs-de-lis. Ah-wen-ga answered, her eyes dancing. "They were gifts to us from our good friend, Louis, King of the French."

The older people looked astonished, and Renno said to the young couple, "It appears that you have quite a story to tell."

"That is so," Ja-gonh replied. "But I will say now that all is well."

Sun-ai-yee still was trying to digest his daughter's remark. "Is it possible that the King of France is truly your friend and has made you these gifts?"

"He is our friend," Ja-gonh said, "but Europeans place a different value on friendship than do the Seneca. I am sure that France will not make war on the Iroquois or the English colonists this year or even next year. Beyond that time, I will not venture to speculate. I urge Renno, the Great Sachem, and Sun-ai-yee, sachem of the Seneca, to see that the warriors of our nation keep their tomahawks sharp."

Looking at the grim smiles of the two sachems, Ah-wen-ga realized that the time when the wilderness would find permanent peace had not yet arrived. Too much hatred and suspicion had been aroused, too many ambitions still flared for the English and Iroquois on one side, the French and their Indian allies on the other, to lay down their arms. She and Ja-gonh had saved the life of King Louis and he had been properly grateful—but the Seneca must expect to take to the warpath again.

That, however, lay in the future. In the immediate present, something vital and primary stirred her to speak directly and forcefully to the assembled parents. "Ah-wen-ga and Ja-gonh," she said, "have waited long enough to become man and wife. They wish to be married as soon as the arrangements can be made."

Talking Quail was ecstatic, and Betsy smiled broadly at her future daughter-in-law's impetuosity.

Ja-gonh's first feeling was one of embarrassment, but he quickly decided that Ah-wen-ga was right. "It is true," he declared, "that we have waited long enough."

The fathers exchanged glances, and when both smiled warmly, the young couple knew the issue was happily settled.

Before the small group emerged from the forest, two other figures suddenly materialized before them. Goo-ga-ro-no had come to greet her brother and Ah-wen-ga, and she was accompanied by No-da-vo, her husband.

Ja-gonh and Ah-wen-ga knew immediately that they were married. Goo-ga-ro-no no longer allowed her hair to fall loose after the manner of maidens, but arranged it in a tight braid that encircled her head. In addition, she stood a pace behind her husband, as befitted a wife. She was obviously pleased by her brother's happiness, as well as that of her friend Ah-wen-ga.

Ja-gonh noted that No-da-vo had smeared fresh paint on his face and torso in honor of the occasion, and as he raised his arm in greeting to his brother-in-law and returned his welcoming gaze, he felt a great sense of pleasure and relief come over him. He saw in No-da-vo's face the signs of respect that the young warrior felt for him as the noble son of the Great Sachem.

Renno and Sun-ai-yee were old men, Ja-gonh mused, and though he hated to think about it, the burden of leading the Seneca and the entire Iroquois League would soon pass to the younger generation. As the son of Renno and the grandson of Ghonka, Ja-gonh would be required to play a leading role in guiding his people. Only now that he had returned to the land of the Seneca did he fully realize how much his people needed him, how much they would rely on him in the years ahead. He would need help in fulfilling his role, and he sensed that in No-da-vo he would find a worthy lieutenant, one who was strong, loyal, and courageous.

As the party started on the short journey through the wilderness to the main town of the Seneca, the fingers of Ah-wen-ga and Ja-gonh touched, and a moment later they had clasped hands.

Renno chose to ignore this unprecedented display of affection, and Sun-ai-yee was blind to it, too. After all that the young couple had undergone, they were entitled for now to do as they pleased—and perhaps even to create new customs for themselves and for generations of Seneca to come.

★ WAGONS WEST ★

A series of unforgettable books that trace the lives of a dauntless band of pioneering men, women, and children as they brave the hazards of an untamed land in their trek across America. This legendary caravan of people forge a new link in the wilderness. They are Americans from the North and the South, alongside immigrants, Blacks, and Indians, who wage fierce daily battles for survival on this uncompromising journey—each to their private destinies as they fulfill their greatest dreams.

☐	24408	**INDEPENDENCE!**	$3.95
☐	24651	**NEBRASKA!**	$3.95
☐	24229	**WYOMING!**	$3.95
☐	24088	**OREGON!**	$3.95
☐	24848	**TEXAS!**	$3.95
☐	24655	**CALIFORNIA!**	$3.95
☐	24694	**COLORADO!**	$3.95
☐	20174	**NEVADA!**	$3.50
☐	25010	**WASHINGTON!**	$3.95
☐	22925	**MONTANA!**	$3.95
☐	23572	**DAKOTA!**	$3.95
☐	23921	**UTAH!**	$3.95
☐	24256	**IDAHO!**	$3.95

<u>Prices and availability subject to change without notice.</u>

Buy them at your local bookstore or use this handy coupon:

Bantam Books, Inc., Dept. LE, 414 East Golf Road, Des Plaines, III. 60016

Please send me the books I have checked above. I am enclosing $_____ (please add $1.25 to cover postage and handling). Send check or money order—no cash or C.O.D.'s please.

Mr/Mrs/Miss _____

Address _____

City _____ State/Zip _____

LE—1/85

Please allow four to six weeks for delivery. This offer expires 7/85.

SPECIAL
MONEY SAVING
OFFER

Now you can have an up-to-date listing of Bantam's hundreds of titles plus take advantage of our unique and exciting bonus book offer. A special offer which gives you the opportunity to purchase a Bantam book for only 50¢. Here's how!

By ordering any five books at the regular price per order, you can also choose any other single book listed (up to a $4.95 value) for just 50¢. Some restrictions do apply, but for further details why not send for Bantam's listing of titles today!

Just send us your name and address plus 50¢ to defray the postage and handling costs.

FURIOUS ADVENTURE AND FIERY PASSION FROM THE PRODUCERS OF WAGONS WEST

A TEST OF COURAGE. Ja-gonh, son of Renno, the valiant Iroquois Sachem, has sworn an oath of blood: There will be no escape for the murderer of Ghonka, his beloved grandfather. Boldly, he rides to avenge the cruel death. But as Ja-gonh seeks to destroy the evil-doer, the killer wickedly schemes to steal his love, a passionate Seneca beauty. Ja-gonh must strike back swiftly, charged by his unbridled fury.

A CHALLENGE OF DESTINY. As Renno lies fighting for his life, Ja-gonh sweeps to the rescue of his untamed love, to challenge his destiny, and to fulfill the legacy of the proud Seneca. He must triumph over strife and treachery with the same unconquerable spirit that forged the mighty Iroquois nation.

25039

0

76783 00395

N 0-553-25039-6>>395